After graduating from Oxford, Juliette Mead pursued a career in finance, working in Dallas, New York and London for various investment banks. She left finance to work as a headhunter in the City and now lives in Wiltshire with her husband and four young children, where she writes full time.

For my mother, and for my daughters

Sentimental Journey

Juliette Mead

POCKET
BOOKS

LONDON · SYDNEY · NEW YORK · TOKYO · SINGAPORE · TORONTO

First published in Great Britain by Simon & Schuster, 1997
First published by Pocket Books, 1998
An imprint of Simon & Schuster Ltd
A Viacom Company

'Sentimental Journey' by Bud Green, Les Brown and Ben Homer Copyright 1944 Morley
Music Co. Copyright renewed 1972 Morley Music Co. Used by permission

'Ac-cent-tchu-ate The Positive' by Johnny Mercer and Harold Arlen Copyright 1944
Harwin Music Co. Copyright renewed 1972 Harwin Music Co. Used by permission

'I'll Be Seeing You' Lyric by Irvin Kahal/Music by Sammy Fain. Lyric reproduction by
kind permission of Redwood Music Ltd. in respect of Irvin Kahal's interest only

'Waiting For The Train To Come In' by Sunny Skylar and Martin Block. Lyric
reproduction by kind permission of MCA Music Ltd.

Simon & Schuster Ltd
West Garden Place
Kendal Street
London
W2 2AQ

SIMON & SCHUSTER AUSTRALIA
SYDNEY

A CIP catalogue record for this book is available from the British Library.

1 3 5 7 9 10 8 6 4 2

ISBN 0-671-85578-6

Printed and bound in Great Britain by Caledonian International Book Manufacturing,
Glasgow

Author's Note:
The location and activities of the 37 Squadron are a matter of record, as is the existence of
the US Mission in Cairo, but all individual events and characters are entirely fictional. For
the purposes of the story I have allowed the song 'Sentimental Journey' to have been
written a year before it actually was.

Acknowledgments

One year ago I set out to write this book from a position of complete ignorance about the Second World War in North Africa, the RAF, and photojournalism. Many people shared their memories with me, gave me the benefit of their experience, corrected some horrible misunderstandings and generally pointed me in the right direction. I would like to thank the following in particular: Douglas Radcliffe of the Bomber Command Association, Frank Sullivan of the 37 Squadron Association, Wing Commander Pat Hancock, OBE DFC, Ian Debenham DFC AE, Nancy and Charles D'Arcy Irvine, Mike Maw, Maddalena Miele, Clive Quick, Butch Stuttard, Ed Gorman, Tom Stoddart, Robert Ogburn of the US Embassy in Cairo, and most of all, my mother, Eleanor Mead. Any inaccuracies and all implausibilities that remain in the novel are wholly of my making.

I read a great many books; the following not only helped enormously in my research but continue to stand out in my memory: *Cairo in the War 1939 – 1945* by Artemis Cooper, *Wellington Wings* by F. R. Chappell, *The Desert Air War* by Richard Townshend Bickers, *No Moon Tonight* by Don Charlwood, *Anyone Here Been Raped and Speaks English?* by Edward Behr and the outstanding *Love Thy Neighbour: A Story of War* by Peter Maas.

I am immensely grateful to my friends Tina Jenkins and Janos Nyiri for their judgement, hard work and invaluable advice. Also to Anette Falkner, Christine Mead, Rebecca Green, Amanda Lay, Marian McCarthy of Simon & Schuster and my husband Guy for their endless encouragement and practical support, and my father Tom Mead who has been nobly correcting my spelling, among other things, for the past thirty years.

Last but never least, I am ever more indebted to my editor Jo Frank and my agent Carole Blake for their enthusiasm, confidence and professionalism.

It would be a terrible omission not to acknowledge the record of all those who flew in the Desert Air Force. No book can pay sufficient tribute to their contribution.

"The tragedy of life is that we only understand it backwards, but we have to live it forwards."
Søren Kierkegaard

PROLOGUE

I am going to tell you a love story. A true one. Before I begin, I want you to know a couple of things. For starters, neither boy nor girl is love's young dream, certainly not the girl, seeing as she's me, and not the boy either, who happens to be the man I love and is about to celebrate his fortieth birthday. For a second thing, however much I want the story to be neat, and fit into a tidy box, it doesn't involve two people, but five – or even six or seven, depending on how you look at it. That in itself is no break from convention. All good romantic stories involve people beyond the magic inner couple. Third, the story revolves around war, but it is not my intention to address the horrors of war or whether any war can ever be 'good'. Whatever the physical, emotional and moral suffering caused by war, men and women carry on wanting to fall in love, or out of it, wanting babies and wanting to raise them. Finally, I have to warn you straight up that I don't know how it will end, because I am starting this story from the middle. Does that sound too confusing? I hope not. You see, it's about people falling in love with each other, and people falling in love with their children, and people falling in love with their parents. It didn't really fall into place until I was thirty-one, and pregnant. That's when it began.

About three weeks before my due date, I took the tube to visit a seamstress in Hangar Lane, who had been slowly expanding my mother's waistlines over the last fifteen years. I rang the bell. A short, plump woman of indeterminate age opened the door. My mother had told me that Mrs Shokaralou was a Cypriot who had lived in England most of her life and raised four children single-handedly after the sudden death of her husband. She patted my heavily pregnant stomach, and gave me a cup of sweet tea while we talked about the clothes I wanted. When I struggled heavily to my feet, ready to leave, she took my hands in hers and asked me whether I knew if I was having a boy or a girl. I said I would be perfectly happy with either, so long as the baby was healthy. She smiled at me and, leaning close, said conspiratorially, "Ask God to give you a little girl. Every woman needs at least one strong, healthy son. I have three. But we have a saying in my country: from the moment of birth the journey of a son is one that must take him ever further away from his mother; that of a daughter will bring her ever closer."

I thought about this all the long journey home.

CHAPTER ONE

I hate birthdays. I haven't been able to stomach a birthday since my twenty-third. Ever since I left home and bought my own flat, I have woken up on my birthday (and quite a lot of other days) and done what my friend Rebecca and I call 'the ten-foot, five-foot' test. You start off as far away from the mirror as the wall of your bedroom or bathroom (whichever has the cruellest light) will allow. Then you approach slowly, perhaps a step at a time, until you can see the wrinkles. On the morning of my thirty-first, I was still pretty good at ten foot, OK at five foot, but at twelve inches I was looking at someone I didn't know, and she was not a pretty sight. I was about to go back to bed in disgust when I thought, Hey, who ever gets to look at you that close up and without makeup anyway? No one, unless it's your dentist (in which case you have bigger things to worry about than crow's feet) or someone who is kissing you, and any decent kisser

5

should have their eyes closed from around that point anyway or they'll be focusing on the blur at the end of your nose. I wasn't particularly perturbed about doing the test – it wasn't the first time I'd done it after all. I knew I had to wait at least three minutes for an accurate reading, so I put the little stick on the bathroom shelf and killed time standing inches away from the mirror, staring at the passage of time.

With a puddle of moisturizer in the palm of my hand, I checked off my features one by one. Hair – definitely Mother's: dead straight, fine as a cobweb, and of an indeterminate shade between dark blonde and light brown. My mother always called it 'dirty blonde' and before I hit eighteen shoved me in the direction of a good highlights technician. Forehead – broad and high, with a pale green vein visible at each temple. My father says he could always tell when either Ma or I was about to explode in a tantrum because one vein would begin to throb a signal for him to retreat to his study. Eyes – probably Daddy's, but really nobody's. All my childhood, my mother used to thank God that both her children had inherited their father's eyes and not hers but, in fact, neither I nor Charlie have either parent's eyes. Mine are OK, a decent size and green, and the whites are still white and not showing yellowish blotches or red spider tracks – not yet. My nose doesn't deserve any comment at all. My mouth belongs to both my parents, one lip each: a thin top one and a full bottom one. Bang up to the mirror, I could see a fine tracery of lines everywhere, but leaning back, I could only detect one heavy line across my forehead, and two creases either side of my nose, and for yet another year, I offered a silent thank- you to my mother, who at seventy-three still has remarkably good skin. Just as I felt a tiny frisson of smugness, it occurred to me that perhaps passing the ten-foot, five-foot test says more about deterio- rating eyesight than it does about a good complex- ion. At least I know what to expect: I have my mother as the blueprint for what to look out for in the years to come. I tried to remember when I had noticed my mother's neck slackening, when her eyelids had first begun to droop, but I couldn't. My mother was over forty when she had me, and I never thought of her as 'old' until I was well into my twen- ties. Until then she had been perpetually middle- aged, that vague state of 'past it, and quite probably really never *at* it' to which every child condemns their maternal parent.

My towel fell to the floor, and as I bent to pick it up I saw them. My mother's feet. There it was – old age splayed out before my eyes. I remembered as a child watching my mother padding around the house barefoot, and wondering why she had such peculiar feet. As far back as I can remember, they seemed oddly flattened out, spatchcocked, the shape of bricks, with funny little toes that curled under, so different from my own girlish, high-arched and elegant ones. Looking down at mine, I was mesmer- ized. It was as if a wicked fairy had stolen my own familiar feet in the middle of the night and swapped them for a middle-aged woman's – and I had no excuse of pregnancy to explain away these collapsing insteps. There's an awful lot you can do to your hair, your lips, even your wrinkles to cheat the years, but I have never heard of a foot lift.

Until I was twelve, I called my mother Mummy. Then it occurred to me that it would sound stupid saying Mummy when I was eighteen or twenty, and by then it would be too late to change. I knew I would never, *ever* be able to call her by her first name, so from my thirteenth birthday I started calling her Mother and Ma. She noticed the change, and asked me about it, and I talked through my reasoning with her. She thought it was funny, and told me I worried too much about things. As a child I was always worrying about something. My father said I had an old head on young shoulders (a worrying thought in itself) and my mother used to say, "Don't borrow trouble," but I still can't help it. Despite all the heredity, I am not the same as them. For example, my father says that the best thing about my mother is that she has never said a cruel word about a single person in forty years. I find this unfathomable, and sometimes I suspect that she must *think* them, even if she doesn't blurt them out. Most of the time I have to resign myself to the fact that she probably never even thinks them. Both my parents are gentle people. I used to think that they represented a marriage of innocence and wisdom – my mother the former, my father the latter. The older

I got, the more I realized that they are both innocents and both wise. They share an optimistic attitude to life, and they always give people the benefit of the doubt. I just don't understand why I didn't inherit this trait along with the throbbing vein.

I still borrow trouble. Sometimes, when I was lying in bed next to David, I would imagine that we were married. Then I would imagine that *were* we married, and lying in bed, I would be imagining what it would be like *not* to be married, and we'd be only an inch or two apart, so that if I could will it strongly enough, the fine hairs on my skin would lift up and connect with his hairs, and if we *were* married, and I didn't want to be, that connection would make me tremble with the awful realization that I was so close to a man I didn't want to be with. This is definitely borrowing trouble. Thinking of that made me smile at myself and start putting on the slap, dragging out the minutes well beyond necessary, and that's when Charlie's face appeared in the mirror over my shoulder. He was grinning, and at the same time trying to hum, "Some day my prince will come, some day . . ." I snatched the little wand off the shelf and held it clenched in my fist.

"Fuck off, Charlie. Can't a girl have a moment's privacy?"

"Not if the girl has only one bathroom."

Much as I loved my brother, when he was staying he always pissed me off. He reached over me for his razor and started to shave, leaning into my shoulder and elbowing me out of the way. "Come on, Elle, play fair – I've got an interview in half an hour."

I stepped back and leant against the wall, watching him watching me in the reflection. "You know what, Elle? You look more like Mum every year." He wiped his foamy face on one of my towels. "Happy birthday, by the way." The doorbell rang. "Get that, could you? I'm expecting a courier."

I let him get away with murder, really I did. I stomped to the door, my towel still clutched under my armpits, one eye mascara'd and one not. It wasn't the courier, it was David, and suddenly I remembered the stick in my hand. I suppose that was when I started to grow up.

David and I had known each other for two years. I first met him on an assignment for the *Sunday Times*. I had been commissioned to write a feature on Britain's top twenty self-made men, and David had been persuaded somehow to do the accompanying portrait photographs, which was a bit of a coup for the paper. I knew him by name, of course – David Turcan ('Turk' to his mates) was one of the big names in photojournalism, but he was generally perceived as being above celebrity or portrait commissions. David's niche was the theatres of war and disaster. Even if you couldn't pick him out in a crowd, you would be bound to recognize at least one of his photographs. Maybe the Kurdish soldier with a drip in his arm and a rifle pointed casually at the camera. Or the one of the old woman cradling her grandson, one shoe on and one off, after the Armenian earthquake. Or the devastated bar in

Saigon. That was one of his earliest.

The *Sunday Times* must have paid him a fortune, or blackmailed him. By the time I got round to asking him why he had agreed to do it, we were already in bed. He said he had wanted the chance to meet me. This was complete crap. David Turcan could never have heard my name, let alone wanted to meet me. He is American – originally from South Carolina, not that you'd know it. He left the States when he was eighteen and although he's lived in London and Paris off and on for the past twenty-some years, you can still detect a slight drawl in his voice, when he's very tired, or seriously pissed off. I was and am a freelance hack, and I write easy-on-the-eye features for anyone I can sell them to. I have never been caught in the crossfire, and there's no way that anything except the fickle finger of Fate brought us together.

In 1990 we spent four days together, travelling round the country, interviewing and snapping Britain's great and good – or, at least, Britain's lucky and rich. I was initially intimidated by David, and then grateful to him. He is a real professional and, better than that, he's a good driver. I hate driving. I had had to hire a car and spent the first day crashing the gears and swearing at every other motorist. My ideal driving conditions would be an automatic Land Rover in an uninhabited desert. That first evening we stopped at a pub somewhere near Newcastle for the night (the *Sunday Times* being generous with fees but not with expenses) and David called Hertz and got his name on the insurance.

To be honest, I might have slept with him for that courteous gesture alone, but it wasn't until the third night that we ended up in bed, and by that time we were at a smart hotel in a little village called Castle Beauchamp in Wiltshire. I had been interviewing Gary Boyd, a man who lived in a manor house some ten miles away. He had been a complete bastard, arrogant, tetchy, threatening to sue the paper, and me personally, if we were anything other than complimentary about his manifold successes. He had been a foreman in a business in the Black Country that made hospital beds and had set up his own company, undercutting his old boss, and secured a massive contract to supply NHS hospitals. He had also moved into property, with several of the nastiest out-of-town retail warehouse developments to his credit. He had drip-fed large amounts of money into the Tory party coffers, until he was coincidentally rewarded with a knighthood. A friend of mine who works for Conservative Central Office told me an anecdote about Sir Gary Boyd that I swore on my mother's grave not to include in the feature. The campaign director had called Boyd directly to discuss a new anti-Labour advertising slot, and had explained that they were short of a bob or two. Sir Gary, never one to beat about the bush, had retorted that if they were down on their knees and begging then he supposed he could 'spunk up another hundred grand or two'. A cheque arrived by the next post. Such charm.

David shot only one film, in about ten minutes

flat, and assured Boyd he had everything he needed. "I'm counting on you to lose me twenty years and twenty pounds – understand, mate? Is the little lady your girlfriend then? Nice work if you can get it!" David had winked back at him and I seethed at his collusion.

As we left Hartstreet House, looking for yet another pub or motorway hotel, David suggested we stayed somewhere better to compensate for the humiliation of the assignment. He drove into a country-house hotel in Castle Beauchamp and said he'd put the rooms through his expenses, and if the *Sunday Times* didn't cough up, he was willing to bear the damage – he said he had something to celebrate. In the bar, I told him about the spunking up. He told me that the photographs would show Boyd for the arse he was, featuring prominently his fat little beringed fingers.

Over dinner, he told me how he had started his career towards the end of the Vietnam war in 1972, when he was eighteen and had been temporarily kicked out of Princeton University. He ordered a bottle of champagne, and said that that week represented his having spent precisely half his life in war zones. I didn't know him well enough to suggest that this was hardly an obvious cause for celebration. I calculated roughly that this made him eight years older than me – thirty-six against my twenty-eight. He looked a bit older than that, but I guess the experiences he'd gone through had aged him in more ways than one. He made me feel inexperienced, and shy. I've never been slow to talk, but when someone that intimidating shows such an interest in you, it rather pulls the rug from under your feet.

Over a nightcap, David mentioned he had been divorced for eleven years. I wanted to ask him whether he'd been destroyed by this – I mean, my God, to divorce at the age of twenty-five . . . My God! To be *married* at twenty-five! Instead, I told him that I had just broken off a two-year relationship with a fund manager. It wasn't really an equal trade: a failed early marriage versus the end of a half-hearted affair with a complete prat in braces, but it was all I had to offer. When David asked why, I had no good reason, and wondered myself; I didn't even know why I'd been with Peter in the first place, but I didn't want to admit that. He asked me if my parents had been sad or pleased when the affair ended, and I remember thinking this an unusual question. It was odd for a total stranger to realize how much I cared about what my parents thought. I was conscious of him jiggling the coins in his pocket. The nervousness of the gesture contradicted the weary look in his grey eyes, his slow, lazy smile. It struck me then that I was completely crazy to feel so drawn to this stranger, and I felt a rush of pure erotic possession. I had to steel myself to speak, rather than reach out and touch him. I said that they had been relieved and deeply concerned. By this I meant that my father had been relieved and my mother concerned.

The *Sunday Times* paid for two bedrooms. We only got as far as the first door. We spent a lot of that night talking. People talk in the dark like it doesn't count. The world seems to open up with the night sky, and everything in you spills out over the edges. If you can't see their face, somehow you think they won't remember what you said, so they won't be able to hold it against you. Darkness gives *carte blanche*, a get-out-of-jail-free card, a guaranteed escape from reality. Now I'm not sure: far from a white card, I think by talking in the dark you hand people a yellow card for future use.

The day after, we had bookings with two more people. We got back to London at half past ten, and David stayed at my flat in Notting Hill. After that night, I didn't see him for three months. It wasn't that he didn't call – he did, often, but he was always abroad, or about to go, or shattered having just come back. A couple of the times when he came home I was out of town; the third time, he was only in London for one night, and I perversely said I was busy. I was schizophrenic in my feelings about him, I desperately didn't want him to see it as a casual fling, and was equally determined to play it cool. The fourth time he was back in town I was genuinely busy: it was my parents' fortieth wedding anniversary, and I toyed with the idea of taking David with me to the Savoy for dinner, but decided against it. I didn't want to get my mother's hopes up. The next time, four months after we'd first met,

David came to my flat and stayed for three weeks. It was the oddest time. He slept nearly all day for the first three days and we made love ferociously most of the nights. He didn't talk much, and I had come to see him as a magical, blisteringly sexual but categorically temporary interlude in my normal life. If someone had asked me then if I was in love with David, I would probably have said that I supposed I was – at least, I believed that I was in love with him. This is what I would have told the inquisitive stranger at a drinks party. And the truth? The truth was that I could hardly speak for love of him. I was wiped out with love for David Geldhart.

When you ask married girlfriends about their pre-marital affairs, they almost always say, "Oh, well, we fell in love," and immediately qualify it by saying, "Well, we *thought* we were in love at that stage but we were so young." I'm not at all sure about this as a concept. I have nursed a lot of friends, male and female, through happy and unhappy romances, when they have claimed to be 'hopelessly in love' and I have not doubted them for a moment. I have seen my friend Rebecca in love five times, each absolutely genuine, the most recent object of her affections being her husband Michael. And when I talk to her about his predecessors, she says, "Oh, come on, Elena! OK, I *thought* I was in love, but it wasn't *real* love, not like I feel for Michael." Rubbish. Perhaps once you are married, you are obliged to renounce all previous loves. Renunciation ought to be in the marriage vows, because the married women I know treat it like a vow: "I never *really* loved X – not really. I *thought* I was in love with Y, but I was just so young. It took Z to teach me what love really meant. I was just playing at it until then." Of course I can't speak for Becca; I can only tell my own story. Which is that I know I have been in love three times. Once, for several years, with Nick; once briefly with the prat Peter; and once with David. I am still a little in love with Nick, although I haven't seen him for six years. I can't for the life of me understand what I ever saw in Peter, but I am honest enough to admit that I *did* love him, once.

I fell in love with David right from the start, madly, and that made it hard for me, because I am always nervous about losing control, and that was perhaps why I was so evasive in our new relationship. Not that David's work made it easy. During the first months when he called, his messages on the machine were terse, no more than "Hey. It's me. How're you doing? I'm in Moscow . . . Vilnius . . . Jerusalem . . . I'll see you when I'm back." Sometimes I was in the room when he called and I didn't even pick up the phone, for fear he'd be just as terse if he got me on the end of the line.

I used to watch the news compulsively, but after meeting David, I stopped. It wasn't that I was frightened for his safety. I never let myself think like that. I just couldn't bear coming face to face with my selfishness in watching scenes of death and destruction and wondering, Where's David? Is he in a bar? Is he with a woman? Is he telling somebody else about his divorce / his life / his work / his inability to commit?

During David's sporadic stays in England, we pretty much lived at my flat. A couple of times we met at his, a wonderful place converted from an artist's studio, back up against Chelsea football ground. He didn't spend much time there, but he would go and work there, and sleep the odd night there if I was away or entertaining. For several days after an assignment, he avoided social functions. We got along fine. We didn't push each other, we respected space, we were both working. There were times when our expressions of intimacy were at best coded, if not downright dishonest. Sometimes David called from the studio, and said: "D'you want to have dinner? Are you free?"

I would reply, "Well, I'm kind of tied up tonight – I've got a drinks party and a dinner with an old friend. What about tomorrow?"

He'd say, "I'm flying to Tel Aviv at eight."

I'd say, "Oh. OK," in what I hoped was an understanding yet sufficiently wistful tone of voice to tempt him to say, "Can I come round *after* dinner?" but he wouldn't.

He'd say, "Fair enough – look after yourself. I'll call when I'm back."

I'd say, "You take care too," and hang up and cry, and kick myself for not saying, "Darling – *darling* – please come now – I don't care about the party or dinner –" If there were plenty of those phone calls, there were also some good times, even whole weeks, and I honestly felt OK about it. I think.

It is hard for me now to describe how I felt then. I can't say that I was utterly fulfilled and blissfully happy, but I had my life in order. I was working well, in that I had enough offers to pick and choose and turn work down, which must be the pinnacle for any freelancer. Most of all, I loved David. I found him extremely attractive, and wildly exciting, and I got a vicarious kick bathing in the reflected glory of 'the Turk'. My friends were agog with curiosity about him, and I was always evasive, partly because I wanted to keep him for myself and retain his mystique, and partly because I didn't really know what to say about him. I told them I was happy to have a relationship that didn't take me over; I considered myself blessed for finding a man who didn't expect to own me. OK; it might have been nicer if he had *wanted* to own me, just a little, but . . . It was a convenient relationship. When he was in town, we were happy. When he wasn't, I had my own life and my independence, and I didn't allow myself to dwell on what would be, or what might be. It suited us both. If it ain't broke, don't fix it – that was my maxim at the time.

I remember one night in 1991 when there was a fifty-fifty chance that David would come back. I had invited Rebecca and her husband Michael round for supper. I had even cooked.

It was not one of my more memorable attempts.

The problem was that David didn't show up, and the veal was (a) bloody expensive, (b) politically incorrect, and (c) dried out to the level of stiff cardboard. Rebecca peered over my shoulder at the congealing wine sauce. "Sometimes I think I despise men . . ." she observed, "and sometimes I know I do."

"What has Michael done now?" I prompted obediently. He was in the living room, looking through my CDs and complaining audibly about my wretched musical taste. I opened the oven and shut it again quickly. I had a vague memory from science O level that at high heat, charcoal simply disintegrates; perhaps the veal would too, and I could forget it had ever existed. I took a bowl of sour cream and some taramasalata out of the fridge and scattered crisps around them with gay abandon. Rebecca dipped one long finger into the cream and sucked it thoughtfully.

"Only the usual. Gross insensitivity and selfishness masquerading as struggling new man, hard-done-by bread-winner crap." She used one red-painted talon to pick the cream from under another. "*And* the sex thing."

On cue, Michael joined us in the kitchen. "Are we going to eat tonight, Elena, or was the invitation for breakfast?" he asked, sticking *his* finger into the tarama. "And *what* sex thing?"

"I just don't understand why men think that having a semi-rigid cock bumping up against your buttocks in the middle of the night can be considered foreplay, that's all," Rebecca explained sweetly. "I mean, I'm intelligent, I've got a perfectly respectable Oxford degree, even if it *is* in geography, but strangely, nobody ever explained that one to me. One of those things Mother should have told me. I bet yours told *you*, Elle – you have no idea how lucky you are to have that kind of a mother." She sucked her finger suggestively, for Michael's benefit. "Last night, just for starters, Elle, we got home well after midnight. Michael had been banging on about how tired he was, how much he hated going out in the middle of the week, how he fantasized about just watching *The Bill* and going straight to sleep, so we went to bed, lights out, no nooky, and fifteen minutes later this *thing* bumps up against my bottom. It's like something from a schlock horror film. How the hell am I meant to react?" She scooped another fingerful of cream into her mouth.

"I would have thought it was perfectly obvious," Michael grunted.

"Do you two need me here, or shall I just go out and leave you to it?"

"I just wanted to know what you thought about the sex thing, that's all."

"No, you didn't. You just wanted to humiliate me." Michael wagged his finger at his wife.

"I have a theory," she continued, "that all marriages divide into two camps. There are the husbands who go in for the bum-bumping lark, and then complain that their wives are sexless, frigid old bags, or there are the ones whose wives are always moaning that they don't get enough sex and their husbands can't keep up with their insatiable demands. Surely it's more humiliating for a man to be considered under-sexed than over-sexed, don't you think, Elle?"

I put the sauce pot in the sink to develop of its own accord. "I don't know anything about husbands and wives, Bec. *I* think you just love bitching about Michael."

"And isn't he a sweetie for giving me so many opportunities to do it?"

I ordered an Indian for three; it was then nine thirty and I had given up on David. I opened another bottle of wine while we waited for dinner to be delivered, and as soon as it was, I told them to start.

"What about David?" Michael said, his mouth full of prawn puri.

"Screw David."

"Do you, much?"

"Is it any business of yours how often she does?"

"Idle curiosity." Michael opened yet another bottle of wine. "And given that you want Elena to participate in *our* sex life – or the miserable activities that pass for one – I feel entitled to participate in hers. So, Elena, even if Rebecca isn't interested in your love life, I am. Tell us all."

"There's nothing you don't know. He's American. He's a photographer."

"Oh, a *photographer*. Only Turk Turcan. Only the most famous photographer this side of the planet. We all *know* he's a photographer, Elle, we're just not convinced you've actually met him. *We* haven't. He never shows up; his boxers aren't in the laundry basket. I checked."

"I met him last year on an assignment. That profile on Britain's new millionaires? He did the pictures. He's almost always abroad."

"Good-looking?"

"In a way."

"How old?"

"He's about thirty-six or -seven, I guess."

"You don't know?"

"OK, he's thirty-seven."

"Single?"

"Divorced."

"And you have slept with him? Is marriage on the cards? Are you still sleeping with him?"

"Yes, no, and I don't know."

"Still the same old clam-lipped, poker-faced girl we all know and love, aren't you, darling?" Michael patted my hand.

"There just isn't that much to say about him," I'd insisted stubbornly, rather than admitting I just didn't know that much about him.

"Well, my love, time's moving on, you know. You're what – twenty-nine?"

"You know perfectly well how old I am, Bec. I'm the same age as you –"

"Ah! The magic twenty-three!" Michael interjected. "Anyway, age is irrelevant. Elena's never had a problem *getting* men, she's just had a problem sticking with one, and if she needs time to think about it –"

"Could you just fuck off, Michael? I don't spend

any of my time worrying about men. I'm not agoniz-
ing about David. I'm not interested in settling down.
I'm very involved in work at the moment. I'm doing
a major feature actually –"

"Big fee?"

"Oh, sure, record-breaking; probably about ten
quid, if I'm lucky –"

I heard the front door open and close.

David always had an effect on people when he
walked into a room, not least because he was tall,
broad and very dark. He made Bec turn all fluttery,
and Michael became bluff and laddish. The rest of
the evening was not a success. David was dog-tired,
and in no mood for chit-chat. He struggled to be
polite, but went to bed early. When I was standing
on the doorstep as Michael and Bec got into their
car, Bec ran back up the steps and hugged me tight.
"Elle, I want to know *all* about you and him. Every
little thing."

I wonder if men discuss their relationships with
their friends the way women do. Call me sexist, but
I don't think so. But perhaps – and this is an
appalling thought – while we think they are
discussing the England squad, or the next Test match
against the West Indies, they are actually talking
about their lack of emotional and physical fulfilment
to the guy in the next door office. I remember thinking I was OK, because David wasn't in one place
long enough to have real friends, and the wire-service
photographers, senior network correspondents and
special assignment types that formed the itinerant

international press corps surely couldn't count as normal people. David would never use the term 'best friend' but, if pushed, he would probably nominate Steve Heffner, a *Newsweek* staff reporter he had known most of his life. I've met Heff often, and he's an original, but no one in their right mind would call him normal.

That dinner took place a year before it all started, a couple of days before my thirtieth birthday. We were about to begin another project – the first we'd done together since the *Sunday Times* assignment. This one was at my instigation. I had met a publisher at a friend's book launch a few months before and started talking about the RAF and flying, in which I have been interested since history lessons at school and the divine Mrs Heavens, who used to talk about the 'poor, darling Abyssinians' firing bows and arrows at the Italian planes overhead. I suggested it might be interesting to do a series of interviews with old RAF heroes before they all pegged out – some waffle about investigating the *real* nature of heroism and comradeship, anecdotal yet visionary, I think I said. I was on a roll, having had three glasses of wine too many, and you could have knocked me down with a feather when the editor called me the next day and asked me to lunch, and the lunch turned into a commission. Graham – my editor, who is similarly addicted to Second World War nostalgia – said a book would be perfectly timed for the seventy-fifth anniversary of the founding of the RAF. He wanted the interviews accompanied by a series of current portrait photographs and old wartime snaps. I mentioned that I vaguely knew David Turcan, and Graham started dribbling into his pumpkin soup with excitement. I never seriously believed that David would go for it, but he said he'd welcome a break. He had spent most of the year in Israeli-occupied territory around Gaza, and was prepared to lend his name and genius to the project if they'd get me a better advance. I told him all I really wanted was a competent driver, which wiped the smirk off his face.

So there we were, on the morning of my thirty-first birthday, with Charlie monopolizing the bathroom, me in a towel and half made-up, and David on the doorstep with his satchel and three cameras slung over his shoulder. I didn't even know he was due back; I wasn't even sure where he'd been. After two years, I didn't really know anything about David Turcan at all.

Then I blurted it out. "David, you've forgotten my birthday, and I'm pregnant." And I held out the little wand with the thin blue line across it like a child extending a hurt finger.

CHAPTER TWO

After Charlie had left, David and I went to bed. He laid his hand gingerly on my stomach. "Are you really pregnant?"

"No, I can't be. I held the damn thing for so long, and my hand was so sweaty, it probably messed up the result. Well, yes, I think I probably am. I thought last night I should buy the test, just to be on the safe side; I honestly didn't even think about it – I just did it moments before you walked in the door. I guess I might be. They're meant to be pretty accurate, but not if you mess around with them like I did." David said nothing, and I carried on blathering. "I suppose I should do another one, to make sure. I don't know what to say, David. I certainly didn't plan this. I don't know what to think about it. There's no point in making any decisions until we know one way or another." I felt oh-so grown-up, so mature and self-sufficient, lying there aged just thirty-one and possibly pregnant in my pretty brass bed, with the sunlight streaming patchily through the dirty windows. I didn't have the faintest idea what I was talking about, it was all far too unreal, but I couldn't let David turn his tired eyes towards me and say, "You realize I can't make any commitment?" so I carried on talking. "When I get up I'll go out and get another test and do it again tomorrow. There are a million explanations, you know. This could have just been a dud." There was that awful silence, but David had his eyes shut.

"I hope not," he said calmly.

"You hope I'm not pregnant?"

"No. I hope it's not a dud."

I chewed my lip, watching him lying against the pillows. There were dark purple shadows like bruises across his eyelids, and I yearned to touch them.

"Would you want to get married, if you were?"

"No, of course not. Let's talk about something else," I said very hurriedly. David wasn't exactly proposing, it was just a casual question, and he didn't repeat it. He started telling me about some correspondent he'd met in Mogadishu, but fell asleep almost immediately, mid-sentence, as happened so often on his return from a job. David could sleep like nobody else; he was a devoted sleeper. I think he liked being in a state where he didn't have to react to anything or anyone. When the phone rang, I snatched it to stop it waking him.

"Elle?" It was Rebecca. "Just calling to wish you happy birthday, sweetheart. Just wanted to make sure that you weren't too depressed by the onslaught of the years."

"It would be understandable if I was."

"Well, not for a total *babe* like me, but for you, yes." Becca laughed, but she didn't sound very cheerful. "Got anything fun planned, or shall I bring round a bottle of plonk and your birthday present?"

"Depends what it is."

"A Zimmer frame with a red ribbon on it. We could just hang out all day, paint our toenails, do girls' stuff, like the good old days."

"David's here. He's just come back from Somalia."

"Oh." I heard Becca's disappointment. "Well, that's great. Two always make the best party." There was a little hiccup in her voice.

"Are you OK, Bec?"

"Fine. It's just that I never imagined that, in the prime of my life, my major decisions would be whether the kids can get by with their shoes for another term, and whether I can be shagged to go to M&S to buy Michael new boxer shorts. How could we have been reduced to this, Elle?"

I didn't bother to point out that I never spent time thinking about children's shoes or boxer shorts, nor did I dwell on the sudden realization that children's shoes might be set to play a big role in my future thoughts. I assumed Bec was using the collective feminine 'we', and thought it better to tease her than let her wallow.

"You love it, Bec. You always said you wanted to be some rich man's spoilt wife, and that's exactly what you are. Just call Harrods and get them to send round thirty pairs of Calvin's." I eyed David nervously to check that he was still asleep. On the few occasions when he had sat in on Rebecca's and my bitching about the female condition, he seemed to find it monumentally tiresome.

"Good idea. Well, hon. Say hi to David for me. Happy birthday. We'll celebrate another day."

"You sound like something out of a magazine." David's head was resting on his arms, flung up behind him. He had one eye open.

"What kind of a magazine?"

"Not one written for thirty-one-year-olds." He stroked my back to prevent me taking offence. I rolled onto my tummy to see his expression better. There were deep hollows below his eyes and he looked drained, but he was smiling with the quizzical twist in his lips that I had first fallen in love with. David's lazy smile would melt stone.

"What would you like to do today?"

"Guess."

"I hate guessing. I like to be sure of things as absolute fact, and I've never relied on instincts without having them tested."

I wondered if he was getting at the pregnancy thing, but didn't want to raise the subject, even to myself. "That's crap. You're always saying that good photography is ninety per cent instinct and ten per cent technical skill."

"Wrong, darling. I'm always saying that good photography is ninety per cent *luck* and ten per cent technical skill. Maybe I say that because I am a technically inept photographer. If a lucky one."

"That's not what Graham says. I mean, he agrees, naturally, that technically you're crap," David thumped me on the backside at this point, "but he says that even if one of your pictures is flawed – say the focus is wonky – it's still magic."

"The focus is wonky?" David stared at me, incredulous. "Kindly remind me how he's ever seen a frame of mine where the focus is *wonky*."

I ignored him. Discussing photography was the closest David and I ever came to talking about his work, and I didn't get that many chances. David had been doing the job for long enough, and with enough acclaim, not to need me or Graham to give him any tips. The picture editors only saw the good shots, so although David prided himself on having a better good-to-shit ratio than most, this wasn't what Graham saw.

"*He* says you have pure instinct. He says your pictures tell you something that you don't expect to learn – that people look at a photograph with a certain expectation, and yours soar beyond that. He says they create a dialogue."

"Well, I'm mightily grateful to him, but if I hadn't learnt enough about narrative in photography by now, I would have hung up my hat a long time ago." He kissed me then, pulling me over to lie across his chest. "You haven't answered my question. What would you like to do today, honeychild?"

I rolled off him and stretched languorously, then

trailed a finger slowly across his chest. "I'd like you to make me eggs Benedict. Then I'd like you to take me to Portobello Market with an IOU for anything my little eyes spot as a birthday present. *Then* I'd like to have a late lunch at Kensington Place. Then perhaps an afternoon in bed," his eyes were widening at each demand, "*then* you could buy me a new dress from somewhere seriously expensive, then we could have champagne at Joe's, then we could drop in on my parents to show off my presents, then we could go for dinner – how about L'Interlude de Chavrot?"

"Now you *are* talking like a magazine. And if you've got that sort of an appetite, you must be pregnant, in which case you shouldn't be drinking. Just how big is this advance from Graham, and what's my share of the royalties?"

"That depends on whether or not you can sort out your wonky camera work," I answered smugly.

In fact, David's fee was substantially larger than mine, thanks to the superior negotiating skills of his agent, and the level of demand for his work. He growled and pulled me again into his arms. I felt extraordinarily happy to be there.

"I'll make you a bacon sandwich – provided you've got bacon somewhere in your festering fridge. I'll have to spend an hour or so at the studio and caption some film, and you can go to that junk shop on the corner and pick yourself out anything you want under thirty quid, or whatever's in my wallet. Then let's head out of town and have dinner somewhere in the country."

"What are we going to do when we get there?"

"Nothing. Sleep. Make love."

"D'you think we should talk?"

"Tell you what, sweetheart, you talk and I'll listen."

"I'd like it the other way around. Can we talk about Somalia?"

The second those soft grey eyes closed I could have cut out my tongue. "Forget it. We won't talk about it. Ever."

He sat up and shook me a little, almost roughly. "Elena, just give me a break here. You're an intelligent lady, even when you work hard at being a dumbass. I'll say it real simple. I do not want to talk about my work. It is not part of *this* world," and here he shook me again, "at all. I'd like to keep them separate. If I ever feel inclined, I promise you that you'll be the first to know. Do you understand that?" His eyes were fixed on mine, but I couldn't read anything in them.

"Yes," I lied. I didn't understand anything except that he wanted me to drop the subject. I had long known David for a chameleon: he was one person with me, and another when he was on assignment. Perhaps it was the quality of detachment that let him slip so easily from one context into another. This was not necessarily a good omen for fatherhood, not that that was a thought on which I wanted to dwell.

"Couldn't we ever just talk about normal things? The weather? Or poetry?" He sighed, and lay back in the bed, his eyes still on my face, but with a gentler expression. "I'll tell you what we *can* talk about: we can talk about your book. I'm ready to start, providing you've done your stuff. I'm all yours, so to speak."

"And for how long are you intending to be all mine?" Even this was a dangerous question where David was concerned; he could so easily switch off again. I waited for him to shift his focus. On me; away from me; on me; away from me again.

"A month, six weeks? Two months? Whatever it takes. Depending on what blows up. Literally. I'm your chauffeur, don't forget."

"Don't *you* forget it, buddy, because there are plenty of good snappers around and plenty of good drivers. Now, where's that sandwich, or are all your promises worthless?"

David pulled back the sheet, gave me a considering look and pinched my waist. "Comin' up, ma'am. I wonder if pregnancy will make you less of a slave driver. If you *are* pregnant, that is."

The pillow caught him smack on the head as he left the bedroom.

David bought me a pair of earrings that cost him seventy quid. He was a generous man, and would quite easily have spent ten times that if he'd had the money, which he didn't. He spent money flamboyantly and carelessly, as much as he'd earned and as soon as he'd earned it, and he didn't give a damn when it ran out. His hour in the studio turned out to be three, and as I was keen to take him up on his offer of dinner out of London, I decided to visit my parents while he was preoccupied with his captions. What I absolutely refused to do was wander around London thinking about what I was going to do with a baby in tow. I had another test in the bottom of my handbag, and it could stay there for the time being, out of sight if not quite out of mind.

I found my father alone in their flat near Sloane Square. He opened the door and flung his arms wide. "My dearest girl! My dearest daughter!"

"Your *only* daughter, you mean."

"Elena, I have warned you before about pedantry. It's a nasty trait you picked up from that history teacher of yours – what was her name? The one with the orange hair?"

"Mrs Heavens."

"That's right. Charming woman."

"You thought all my teachers were charming."

"No; only the ladies. I rather took against that English master who wore those black sweaters and rode a motorcycle."

"Mr Fletcher? He was my first crush."

"He had no business enticing young girls in his charge, and certainly not at my expense. Now, darling, how about a drink, as it's your natal day? I took the precaution of putting a bottle in the fridge, although perhaps we should wait for your mother: she's just popped out to the shops. She'll be furious to find you've arrived before her return. She said you'd never be out of bed before midday, and wouldn't be here before early evening."

"I like to surprise her sometimes – keeps her on her toes."

"I'm glad you did. It's a treat for me to have you all to myself. When your dear mother's here, I rarely get a word in edgewise."

It was a Stewart family joke that my mother never stopped talking, but we are all devoted to the sound of our own voices. We had a glass of champagne, and started talking about Charlie, whom my father viewed with a mixture of pride and consternation. Pride, because Charlie had so far sailed effortlessly from one achievement to another – from school captain of cricket, to a scholarship at Worcester College, Oxford, to a double first, and twenty different job offers – and consternation, because at the age of twenty-nine, he still hadn't decided what to do with his life, and continued to flit from one degree to the next in the hope of accidentally lighting on his chosen field. He had recently completed an MBA, and was now toying with the idea of a career in investment banking. I passed on this new development to my father, but he remained sceptical. "Oh I don't doubt for a moment that Charles will be offered a job, but whether he'll take it. He's been offered so many before which haven't tempted him. No, I daresay your mother and I will be bankrolling him for a good many years to come."

"Just cut him off, Dad, then there's more for me."

"My dear girl, each time your mother steps outside the front door with her purse your potential inheritance is decimated. I do hope you're not counting on a trust fund."

"I told Charlie he couldn't use my flat any more unless he was prepared to contribute."

"Very sensible. But whereas you and I are ironwilled in our resolve, your mother is putty in his hands. She dotes on the boy. Your *mother* –"

She stepped into the drawing room, her arms full of carrier bags and an expression of outrage on her face. She was somewhere in her early seventies, and looked twenty years younger.

"Elena! What are you doing here?" she said accusingly. "Where's David? You're not meant to be here. Ben, you shouldn't have started enjoying yourselves until I got back."

"Aren't you going to wish her a happy birthday, my dear?" My father reprimanded her gently, and Mother flew across the room and hugged me fiercely.

"Happy, happy birthday, baby girl. Now, Ben, pour me a glass of whatever's in that bottle while I give Elena her presents. Darling, you'll probably want to put them straight back in the bags and take them back to the shop, so I've left all the receipts and price tags on – but there's one *gorgeous* blouse I'm convinced you'll like, even if I did pick it out." My mother stooped over the carrier bags, flinging tissue paper and articles of clothing over her shoulder. "Don't say I left it on the counter? Sometimes I really do think I must be going senile, darling, what do you think? – and I'm not asking *you*, Ben, before you butt in with one of your sarcastic remarks, I know exactly what you'd say and thank you very much I don't want to hear it . . ." I caught my father's eye over her lowered head. He rolled his eyes heavenwards and made a circle in the air with one index finger.

"Ma—"

"Is this it? No – that looks horrid, I can't think who I bought that for, possibly for Lynn's daughter. You see, darling, I bought a green blouse – sale or return – because you never wear green and I've told you a hundred times that it's positively the best colour on you, because of your eyes, Daddy's eyes I mean, although his have gone that murky, puréed pea colour in his dotage, and yours are still apple green; I'd get Daddy to wear it too if he wasn't such a stuffy old fool. Honestly, I mean everyone back home wears green, and pink too – my God, I saw your Uncle Matthew wearing *lilac* last time we were over, and Americans are at least as macho as Englishmen, not that *that's* saying much—"

I couldn't verify the exact shade of my father's eyes, as they were closed long-sufferingly, but he was smiling. "Ma," I tried again, "please come and sit down and have a glass of champagne." She emerged triumphant from the debris of her shopping, with a blouse still on its hanger, and held it against me. She smiled with satisfaction. "I knew it."

"It's lovely, Ma, I'll wear it every day," I would do nothing of the kind, "but please come and sit down. I have to leave soon."

"I see. So you only came over to talk to your father and now that I'm here you have to rush off?"

"Mother, are you *sure* you're not Jewish?"

"Not as far as I know, darling, but I could be – I'm an awful old mongrel, bits of Hungarian and Czech and Slovak and one hundred per cent American." This was true. My grandparents had emigrated to the States before my mother was born, and although she had spent over fifty years abroad, she clung fiercely to her roots and not least to her accent.

"One hundred per cent crazy is all I know," my father muttered.

"What did you say, Ben? Just because your hearing's going doesn't mean mine is. Elena, you cannot imagine what a trial he is to me in his old age. But enough of us, sweetheart. Tell us about *you* – we're all agog – and where's that gorgeous man of yours?"

"Working." I saw my mother's lips purse for a fraction of a second. "Just for an hour or so," I added hastily, and she beamed again. "You know we're just about to start this book together – I have a prospective list of about eighty men and a few women, almost all RAF. We'll probably be able to include about fifty in all. David got back from Somalia this morning, so I thought I'd let him have a day or two off and then we'd get stuck in. I wish *you* two would be in the book."

"But, my darling, we have no right to be in it!" my father said. "I've told you so often that I passed a very unillustrious war in the colonies. Are you going to include both Allied and Axis heroes? That might be more sensitive."

"I suggested that to the publisher, but he wasn't keen. It's RAF, rather than all pilots."

"What a shame. One would wish to avoid the taint of jingoism at all costs, I imagine." My father often used this rather deflected angle for giving advice, but I have always heard his message loud and clear.

"Ma? Did you know anyone you think would be interesting?"

She motioned to my father to refill our glasses, and it occurred to me that I had never seen her pour herself a drink if a man was in the room. Despite having had an unusual career for a woman of her generation, she had no truck with the feminist movement so far as it released men from their gentlemanly duties. It also occurred to me that perhaps I shouldn't be drinking, but I buried that unwelcome thought.

"Well, sweetheart, I'd have to rack my poor addled old brain. When I was in Cairo with Arthur McClure I knew hundreds of officers – Americans, of course, but British, Australian and Canadian – and a divinely handsome Free French captain I danced with who proposed six or seven times in one evening."

"Dirty dog! Trust a frog –"

"Shush, Ben – I'm trying to think. Anyway, he was by no means my only prospect; at one time I must have had a proposal every night – not that it meant so much then, darling; we single girls were in very short supply, so were the married ones in fact – and you know – the War, well, people felt entitled to be a little more *impetuous* than they might have been in peace time. I could see if I can find any letters for you – I have boxes of stuff in the store room I could let you look through, but heaven knows what's in them. I might have kept an old dance programme or something. You could look through—"

"And *then* you could consign it all to the garbage bin, as I told your mother to do twenty years ago—"

"Shut up, Ben, you old fool, I was obviously right to keep it if it helps Elena – I'm sure I can think of a few names for you to look up, darling, except they're probably all dead. The RAF had the best uniform of all, of course; the dress blues." She closed her eyes with a beatific smile. "Most of them you know, or you've heard me talk about over the years. Billy Russell perhaps. I don't know that I'd call him a hero, exactly, but he was certainly a great womanizer. George – he flew Halifaxes, or was it Lancasters? – had a lot of close calls. I met him at the Berkeley. Millie bumped into him recently and said he was as bald as a cue ball, and had shrunk six inches . . . I don't even know that I'd want David photographing those poor men – they used to be so dashing and glamorous that it would be rather sad to see them now. I'd prefer to remember them as they were. Those were the days when men were *men*, believe me. Archie Campbell – no one ever made me laugh as much as he did, until I met your father, of course, but that was years later. He's probably long dead, dear Archie. Daddy never stops finding names in the obituaries – that's the only reason he buys the papers these days . . ."

"I buy them for the cricket," my father said in the background, but my mother carried on talking.

"Now what I want to know about is David. Are you still together? I mean, *seeing* each other – or are you just working together? You never bring him over." My mother mostly approved of David, not least because he was tall, good-looking and American but she objected to his lack of what she called a 'sensible job'.

"Oh, we're still *seeing* each other. It's a bit difficult, Mummy," the old word still slipped out from time to time, "you know, he's rather independent. A bit . . . I don't know. Contained. I'll bring him over to dinner next week, if you like. At least this book project pins him to my side for a while:" I intended this as a joke.

"Now, Elena, the last thing you should do is start getting possessive. All men hate feeling trapped."

"Too darn right they do," added the background voice, and I smiled. "Thanks, Mother; I'll bear that in mind."

"I'm not telling you how to run your life, darling."

"No, I know you'd *never* do that."

My mother and I never stopped arguing about

the subtle difference between well-intended advice and interference. These disputes only concerned my romantic life: in every other area my mother insisted she trusted my judgement, which added insult to injury. From about twenty-five, when I had finally brought joy to her heart by breaking up with Nick, I stopped giving her blow-by-blow accounts of my dealings with the men in my life, and this had averted much, if not all, of the flak. When I broke things off with Peter, of whom she had rather approved as a son-in-law if not a husband, she had restricted her comment to, "Well, darling, I can't say I'm not a little sad, but you're the only one who knows what's in your heart." By the time David arrived on the scene, she barely interfered at all, except when impulse overcame caution. Anyway, despite being a fellow American, David was not the sort of man my mother found easy to deal with; at the time, I thought she was even a little frightened of him. To be honest, there were times when he frightened me a little, too.

"You may be a mature young woman *now* –"

"Now? You mean I wasn't two years ago?"

I raised my eyebrows in the style I had copied from my father and heard him chuckle. "There are still some things I can teach you, Miss Smartypants. All I'm saying is that if you want him, you'll have to accept him the way he is. If you don't like that, fine, dump him, and wash your hands of it. But if you *do* like him, well, just enjoy yourself, and stop borrowing trouble. You've still got your looks, not a bad figure, in fact a pretty cute one –"

"Oh, Mother! *Please!*"

"And you've got a man – OK, he hasn't married you but there may be an even better one down the road."

"Thanks, Ma. I'll bear that in mind, OK?" Not for the first time, I felt that I was listening to the soundtrack of *Fiddler on the Roof*. "Now: how are *you*? You look great." I wondered if I'd look that good at her age. "Are you still on the diet?"

CHAPTER THREE

David and I stayed at a small hotel somewhere in Berkshire. Although it was only mid-April, and the evening was cool and foggy, we had drinks on the riverside terrace before dinner. We had come to a tacit agreement not to talk about a baby until we knew for certain one way or another, but when we went to bed, and I pressed myself against David, he asked, "Is it safe?" and I giggled rather hysterically. I mean, if I *was* pregnant, there couldn't be a better example of shutting the stable door after the horse has bolted. "I meant, is it safe for the baby?"

"If there is one."

"If there is one."

"I have no idea. I guess so." By the time this short exchange was completed, I was no longer in the mood for making love. David sensed this, and drew me into his shoulder. We went to sleep without talking about anything significant at all.

I woke around dawn, and slipped carefully out of bed so as not to wake him. I stood looking out at the river. It was chilly, and I slipped David's robe over my shoulders before I opened the window, willing it not to creak. The damp air hit my flushed cheeks. I had taken the test out of my handbag, but that morning there was little doubt in my mind as to the result. The problem was what to do about it. I was ninety-nine per cent certain that David would support any decision I made. He took his responsibilities seriously – professional ones, at least – but we had never had the need to test our personal responsibilities. Undecided as to what I felt about being pregnant, I was convinced that I had to offer David a way out. Whatever I did, I faced losing him. The sensible thing was to let him play as big or small a part as he chose, and carry on my life as planned. Except that I didn't have a plan.

It seems to me that I stood there, motionless, for an hour or so and watched the dawn arrive, but it can't have been more than five minutes before my bladder drove me to the bathroom. I forced myself to read the instructions carefully, although I had no need to.

The most accurate reading will be taken with the first morning urine. Hold the wand at an angle of 45°, and insert into the urine stream at the point of steady mid flow . . .

This is much easier said than done. I did my best,

46

and popped the wand into the tooth mug, and splashed cold water on my face. I didn't need to wait for three to five minutes – after thirty seconds the blue line was discernible, as I had known it would be. I had a glass of water, and looked at myself in the mirror. I looked exactly the same, so-so pretty, a little peaky and ragged around the edges – certainly not the face of warm, wise motherhood. I leant right up against the mirror and breathed a fog onto it. "You poor little bastard, to have a mother like me," I whispered, and wiped the misty patch away with a finger. I sat down on the loo and trembled.

Despite all the gentle talks with Mother, and the biology lessons at school, and the even more painfully vague 'personal relationship' talks; despite the fact that friends of mine had been pregnant and seemed to have survived it, even enjoyed it, that friends of mine had been pregnant, and I had held their hands after abortions, that I had myself twice wrongly suspected pregnancy when I was with Nick; despite the fact that I had two infant godchildren of my own, that I was a mature woman of thirty-one, with my own flat, and a mortgage, and a relatively reliable income; despite the fact that *I knew everything there was to know about being a woman*, I was shocked to my bones, and I shook from my bones out – marrow, muscles, tendons, flesh – everything began to shake uncontrollably. This couldn't have happened to *me*. It was lousy timing, and it didn't suit me at all. I opened David's robe and looked down, half dreading the sight of milk spurting from my breasts, but nothing had changed. I pressed my fists into my belly, and felt the first surge of amazement and wonder, that a baby was there with me now, my baby. I also felt a rush of utterly numbing fear – for myself, for the baby, that my relationship with David was far too young and tender a plant to survive the strain of having a child, let alone raising one.

I heard a noise, saw David climb out of bed through the half-open door, and pulled the robe around me protectively. I stared at him as he appeared at the bathroom door. He looked at me without saying a word, then walked to the basin and filled a glass with water. His eyes flicked to the wand standing in the beaker. I don't think I was even breathing. He sat on the edge of the bath, facing me on the edge of the loo, and gazed at me.

I heard a voice inside my head scolding, "It shouldn't happen like this; you should be in a pink négligée; you should be frail, and weak, and he should turn to you and say, 'Are you alright, my darling, heart of my heart?' and you would say, 'There's something I have to tell you' and turn away blushing, and swoon, and he should catch you in his arms, concern spreading across his face, and you would laugh quietly, and say, 'We're going to have a little addition to our family,' in a soft but clipped voice, like Celia Johnson's, and he would gaze at you in wonder, and cradle you to his chest, and say – in David Niven's voice, or Trevor Howard's for preference – 'Oh my darling, oh my dear love, what joy you bring me – but are you sure you are alright, light of my life?' and you would touch your hand to his cheek, and smile bravely, and he would carry you to the bed . . .''

Now this is not what happened, that morning when I was thirty-one years and one day old, and probably about seven weeks pregnant. What happened was that I was sitting on the loo, and David was sitting opposite me on the edge of the bath, leaning forward. He held out his hands, palms upturned, in a gesture of inquiry and impatience, and said gruffly, "So you *are* pregnant?"

I nodded glumly.

"Right," he said, "at least we know what we're talking about," and sat there on the edge of the bath. I stared down at the carpet, and to this day I can remember the pattern of the grey and blue swirls, and the powdery smell of that bathroom, and David's blank face as he looked at me. I saw the questioning look in his eyes, and answered it quietly, "It doesn't need to concern you at all."

And David rubbed his hand over his eyes, and said in a rather clipped, Cary Grantish voice, "No, I suppose it needn't," and I saw all the intimacy, warmth and life drain out of his eyes like the water from a basin when you pull the plug. "How do you feel?"

"Fine," I replied. "Let's talk about something else."

We had a rather silent breakfast. I wanted to know how he really felt before I committed myself, and for all my much vaunted intuition I hadn't the faintest idea of what was going on in his head. Without asking him I gave it my best guess. As we pulled apart croissants, I sensed that he was worried about commitment. He had once told me that he never expected a relationship to last more than six weeks. He swore this wasn't the way he wanted things to be, it was just how it panned out. I had told him laughingly that he'd just met the wrong sort of girls, and he had told me that he'd met many of the right sort of girls, who had been too sensible to have anything to do with him. He used to quote Philip Larkin, adding that he wished his Mum and Dad had had the *chance* to fuck him up, rather than die in a car crash when he was twelve.

*   *   *

David had been fucked up by Mitch Hallam, his godfather, if anyone, and then unwittingly. David didn't meet Mitch before his parents' funeral. The little boy and the two bodies had been brought back from New York to Charleston for the ceremony, and Mitch tipped up at the church. I have seen a photograph of David at that age – a dark, curly-headed boy who even in the frozen snapshot looks as if he's about to erupt into a punch or a kick, an angry, obstreperous face, infuriated at having to stand still for the camera. Mitch was a war photographer, an old friend of both David's parents. David's mother was a beautiful woman with a perfectly heart-shaped face, a minor stage actress who might have become a major one had she not died at

the age of thirty-one. David always believed that
Mitch had been his mother's onetime lover but all he
knows for certain was that Mitch remained the best
friend of both his parents. David's father was a
photographer, and it was Mitch who introduced him
to his wife. Mitch was a classic: I look at the photograph, and see a golden, leonine man, somewhere in
his thirties, with a great mane of hair, standing laughing behind the dark and angry little boy. While
David was at boarding school he didn't see much of
him. Mitch would turn up unannounced two or
three times a year, *en route* to or from somewhere,
and take David out for the afternoon, then disappear back to whichever hell-hole he'd come from.

He spent most of his school vacations with his
father's parents. When he was eighteen, he was
kicked out of Princeton University for failing to
turn up for an exam, and pitched up with a ruck-
sack on Mitch's doorstep in Washington DC. It was
1972. Mitch was heading back to Vietnam for the
Washington Post, and David pleaded to go with him.
Mitch refused. David swore. Mitch swore back.
David damned him to hell and said if Mitch would
take him as his assistant, he would do as he was told
and stay out of trouble. Mitch said he could come for
four weeks and he'd teach him a little about photography, on condition that David returned to
Princeton next semester to resit his exams. David
promised faithfully. Mitch took him to Saigon, but
refused to let David accompany him outside the city.
One day, they were having a beer in a bar while

Mitch told stories about David's parents. He told David that his mother had once danced naked on a bar table in Greenwich Village, and that his father had sat nearby, bursting with pride, and taking pictures. These pictures have not survived. He told David that his parents had been rare, wonderful people, and that he should always be proud of them. Then he sent David to the jeep for some extra film. While he was running the errand, a bomb exploded in the bar. Mitch must have been killed instantly. David was told later that it had been placed in a knapsack close to their table. He watched the bar burn for a time, then took Mitch's third camera out of the jeep, loaded it, and started taking photographs. When they found Mitch's body, his coins and keys had melted into a lump of motley-coloured metal. It was this lump that David carried still, and jingled in his pocket whenever he felt uncomfortable.

David never returned to Princeton. He went back to the *Post*, with fifteen rolls of film that Mitch had taken, and two he had taken himself. The next week, Mitch's photographs of Vietnam were spread across the front pages of the papers along with a couple of studies that David had made of Mitch, and David's snaps of the bar where Mitch had died. The *Post* asked David if he would go out to Nicaragua, where an earthquake had left ten thousand dead and David agreed. While he was there, his grandmother died, and his grandfather, his last surviving relative, followed eight weeks later.

David has never been sentimental. In his studio

he had one photograph of his parents, whom he claims barely to remember. They look impossibly wild, beautiful and too young to have a child, and I am not sure how much they spared from their own love affair for David. He has a few photographs of Mitch. He carries that lump of metal with him at all times. He still occasionally uses one of Mitch's Leicas. He has no memento by which to remember his grandparents, although he says that it was their legacy that allowed him to buy the studio in Chelsea, which he has never sold. I think sentiment prevents him from doing so. I understand all this, but I have never understood how he was able to take those photographs while his godfather was burning to death.

David told me this story only once. There are many questions I would like to ask, but I am too frightened – that I might hear things I don't want to hear, that he won't be prepared to tell me anything, that in the telling he might betray himself as callous, which I couldn't stand. Most of all I am too frightened that if I know the secrets of David's heart and soul I will be too scared of him to stay with him. Sometimes he has nightmares, and the sheets are wet with sweat. He is surprised on waking, and doesn't remember them. I have often thought that lovers should be allowed to watch the footage of each other's dreams before they make any commitment. Surely that would let you know if your prospective partner is too mundane or too crazed for serious consideration. A film based on David's dreams would not make easy viewing, but I would still like to see it.

David and I had great secrets between us, as we sat at breakfast. I wanted to let him know that I expected nothing from him; I couldn't stand the risk of forcing him to do the decent thing.

"David." I looked around the dining room, but there was only one other couple on the far side of the room, arguing about where they would have lunch. "David, I just want to tell you that I have decided to have the baby and I don't expect anything from you."

"I see."

I had intended this as a positive comment, to remove from him a responsibility that I knew he hadn't chosen, but he sounded more angry than relieved. "It really isn't anything to do with you. It's just that I'm thirty-one, and I don't expect I shall ever marry, and I know for certain, suddenly, that I *do* want to have a baby. This baby."

"Good. I want you to have it, too."

"You do?"

"Yes."

"Why?"

"Elena, you've just told me that it really isn't anything to do with me. Allow me, at least, to express some support of your choice. If you want to have a baby, then I'm happy for you that you are having one. Besides, I like babies, other people's anyway, and I guess I'd be pretty fond of my own." He looked at me steadily. "You don't seem very happy about it, I have to say."

"Well, I am."

"Fine. Then so am I."

We were both very flat. I felt let down, yet I couldn't say why David's reaction had disappointed me. He is always level-headed, calm and considered. I could hardly expect him to be whooping for joy when I wasn't myself. I don't think we felt all that differently, but we just weren't together, and somehow a physical separation seemed called for. We packed our bags, returned to London and agreed to spend a couple of days apart. I was glad to find a note at the flat from Charlie saying he had gone away for the weekend, possibly longer.

I moped around, thought about sorting out some cupboards, did the washing up, tidied up the guest room halfheartedly, then washed my hair for want of anything better to do. I phoned two wing commanders (retd) and a squadron leader, and booked them in for the following week. I arranged to meet Michael and Bec for dinner Saturday night, made an appointment to see my GP in the morning, and went back to bed with three magazines, a bowl of cornflakes and a pot of tea, wishing with all my heart that I had the nerve to phone my mother and ask her to come and look after me.

My GP was perfunctory about the whole business, and I grumbled that he was acting as if he had a pregnant woman in his office every day. He looked at me over the top of his glasses and said that he generally had four or five pregnant women in his office every day. "It is a far from uncommon occurrence, Miss Stewart." I must have imagined his emphasis on the 'Miss', because he had no interest in my marital state, and little more in my physical one; I was back on the street within fifteen minutes. So far I had told two people my glad tidings, and had bombed with both. Not an encouraging start.

On Saturday night I went to the agreed restaurant, but found only Michael there. Their nanny had walked out in high dudgeon at 7 p.m., and Bec had literally drawn the short straw for staying at home. She didn't miss much. Michael was tired and crabby, and I was subdued, particularly after he greeted me by saying, "Hello, sweets. You look awful."

"Thanks. You don't look that hot yourself," I replied, and studied the menu. Towards the end of a rather lethargic dinner, we started talking about their nanny and how awful it was going to be trying to find a new one, especially since they were in the middle of redecorating the kitchen. "Your lives are full of au pairs and kitchens, aren't they, Michael? It must be nice to have everything so straightforward. Bec can't leave that house alone. She's always revamping the kitchen, or stencilling the loo or something –"

"You don't have a very high opinion of her, do you?"

My fork stopped midway to my mouth in surprise. "Of Bec? I have a *very* high opinion of her."

"No, you don't. You think she fritters her time

away, and fills her head with nonsensical ideas rather than grown-up things like nobility and honour and right and wrong."

"I do not!" I was taken aback by Michael's accusation. "I think she's highly intelligent, and perfectly entitled to spend her time as she pleases. She also happens to be very busy looking after *your* two children, and I don't think she needs my blessing on what she does with the little free time she has . . ." I trailed off, because in my heart I had to admit that I *did* slightly patronize Rebecca for being so domestically preoccupied. "We may not always share the same interests, but that doesn't mean I don't respect her."

"You're protesting too much, Elle. Don't be smug about how pure and high-minded your life is. It's only because you have the time, not having to deal with domestic trivialities like us poor marrieds."

I felt as if he'd slapped me in the face. "That's total crap," I growled. "Marriage doesn't have to be banal."

"If I may be so bold, Elle, you haven't the faintest idea what marriage is about. When you get married, Elle – *if* you get married –"

"Fuck you, Michael. What the hell has got into you?" I was feeling far too raw to deal with a friend turning on me out of the blue.

"I'm sorry, Elle. Sure, you'll get married, if you want to, and then you might begin to understand what I'm saying. This is the bottom line. You get married to somebody you love, or have fallen in love with. Over the years, you may be lucky enough to have children, make a home, build a life, and a pattern and routine will emerge that makes some sense of it all for you. Often, somewhere along that path, the conversations about school fees, or the bathroom curtains, or the new au pair become the *primary* ones in your relationship, rather than the secondary ones."

"Oh, spare me, Michael, for God's sake! You don't get an automatic guarantee of satisfaction when you get married. It's not like buying a dishwasher." I knew I sounded like a sixty-year-old bespectacled cow spouting banalities at a marriage-guidance session.

"You are romantic. Or maybe you're just smart. You and the Turk have cleverly insulated yourselves from all this. No nappies, no baby-sitters, no uphol-stery and wall-to-wall carpeting for you two, just war and passion, hmm?"

"Stop being so cynical. And stop bloody calling him the Turk, for God's sake."

Michael covered his face with his hands for a second, then smiled at me.

"Far from being cynical, I savour your return to the pure romantic tradition. I think you're very clever."

"You don't know what you're talking about."

"All I'm saying is: keep your relationship with David exactly as it is. Don't clutter it up with any external, secondary issues."

"Like children?"

"Oh, God, I mean they're great, really. They give

your whole life meaning, but don't think they don't take it away, too." He patted his lips in an irritatingly punctilious manner.

"Thanks for sharing that profound and timely observation. As it happens, I'm pregnant."

Michael dropped his napkin into his unfinished meal.

I walked home down Ladbroke Grove feeling wretched for Becca, and for Michael, and wretched for David and, most of all, for myself. I was no longer certain that I wanted to have the baby. As I let myself into the flat, muttering, "Sod it, sod it sod it," the phone was ringing.

"Elena, it's me."

"What a surprise, Bec."

"Michael just called me on the mobile."

"I bet he did."

"He told me you're pregnant?"

"Yep."

"Oh, God, Elle, how absolutely bloody. You poor, poor thing. How utterly *ghastly*."

My poor little baby couldn't find one person to welcome its arrival in the world. Three strikes and you're out, kid.

CHAPTER FOUR

I had arranged lunch with my parents the Sunday before David and I were due to start work, and I spent the morning tidying up and staring into the fridge, thinking about cooking a traditional lunch, before deciding we'd go to a pub. I had not spoken to David since Friday afternoon. My mother arrived with a poppyseed strudel from her favourite patisserie and an anthology of war poetry, my father with a bottle of wine.

"Darling, when did you last get your hair done? Your roots are showing."

"That's what roots do, Ma." I replied. I wasn't bothered by her criticism. On the contrary, it was a comfort to me that some things in my life were constant. "I'm going tomorrow."

"That's good, darling. Isn't Charlie here?"

"He's away for the weekend."

"Did he get the job?"

"He's trying to get them to fly him to Paris to

wine and dine him, which is bound to put him off. You know Charlie, he never wants what he can get. He's in search of the Holy Grail."

"Nothing holy about Charlie." There was a note of pride in my father's voice. I told them about the interview I had booked for the following day, and we talked about how best to approach it.

"Just be yourself, Elena. You'll find a way to bring them out."

"But the whole thing was so grim . . . How can I even imagine what they went through? Conditions were awful. Life was fragile. D'you think they were all really motivated by the cause of freedom?"

"It wasn't like that, Elena." My mother's eyes danced. "I can't speak for what it was like in Europe, or in London during the Blitz, but what I remember about Cairo was that we had enormous fun." I raised my eyebrows in disbelief. "I mean it. We worked hard, and we grieved each time someone we knew was lost, but we had *fun* – there was something special in the air. In many ways, those were the best days of my life – apart from being married to your father and having you two, of course."

"But, Mother, you were sitting in an office in the embassy in Cairo, aged what? Twenty-four? Being wined and dined and going to three parties every night. I don't see how your experience had anything in common with the lives of these men. Didn't you ever dance with a man or date someone and then find out he was dead a week later?"

My mother's expression changed. "Of course. Of

course people died. But we couldn't afford to dwell on that. You had to put it behind you. The only way you could survive was to live for the moment, and make the most of whatever life gave you. There was a real sense of joy – and of honour – a special spirit about those days, wasn't there, Ben?"

My father held up his hands. "Leave me out of this, my dear. I was more concerned with tax collection in the Northern Territories at the time . . ."

"You have to understand something, Elena," my mother continued, and there was a hint of fervour in her voice. "Young people then weren't any different from the way they are now. Millie and I were just the same as you and Becca at that age. We were trying to build careers, we were falling in love, we were dancing. The place was full of attractive young men with an air about them. . . When they came to Cairo on leave, we didn't talk about active duty – I was much too frightened to hear about it, and the last thing they wanted to do was relive those moments they were struggling to forget. Besides, they weren't *allowed* to say much. Careless talk . . . The only difference between the way we were, and how you are now was that we weren't so – well, so *serious* about life."

"I don't understand how you can say that."

My father wagged his finger at me, and said, "I do hope you're not about to contradict your mother, my dear. That was something I learnt to avoid many years ago, and if I hadn't learnt that lesson –"

"Do be quiet, Ben," my mother interrupted. I saw

the flash of my father's schoolboy grin as his eyebrows lifted above the frame of his glasses. He wagged his finger again at me, this time mutely.

I continued stubbornly, "How could you be 'less serious' about life when people's lives all over the world were being risked minute by minute, when you had the Holocaust, and the atom bomb, when the world was such a bloody awful place –"

"It wasn't an awful place,' my mother insisted. "Yes, we knew the Jews were being persecuted, but not about the camps. There was a man in our office in Cairo whose job was arranging passage to the States for Jews fleeing Europe. He was allowed to negotiate with the Germans. It was all hush-hush, but yes, we *knew*. We didn't talk of it as the Holocaust, but we all knew. When the atom bomb came, no one thought about it the way you do now, we thought of it as another, bigger bomb. Think about it, Elena. When David comes home from the Gulf, or Somalia, do you talk about war atrocities? When he's out of a war zone, do you spend your time dragging him back to it, or do you get on with the concerns of your own life, with the day-to-day stuff of where you're going to eat, and what the latest gossip is, and whether or not you'll get that plum promotion, and how you're going to pay the mortgage?"

I bridled at this, in part because I did try to drag David back to the war, but also because I resented the implication that he had any part to play in my mortgage. "We never talk about mortgages," I said stupidly, "and don't tell me that was the main topic of conversation in Cairo either."

"Of course not!" She laughed. "Most of the men there – the unmarried ones, at least – didn't have houses or mortgages. They didn't even have civilian careers. Many were barely into their twenties – their whole adult life was the war. And they didn't want to talk about it. Much. Also, there were ideals at stake. How do you think these boys shot total strangers, or bombed cities, without hanging on to some kind of ideal?"

"I just don't know, Ma. That's what worries me."

"Well, stop worrying. Believe me, when you meet these men you'll understand how they did it."

We went to the Windsor Castle for lunch, and I started moaning about what Michael had said to me about marriage and families. My father said that Michael was an idiot, and my mother said that he must be going through a mid-life crisis, and that children were life's greatest blessing, and if he didn't realize that, then he didn't deserve to have them, or Becca either. My mother was always fond of Becca. I couldn't stop the tears pouring down my cheeks.

"Oh, darling, I know it's awful, when you and Rebecca are so close. What a stupid fool that boy is, to upset you so . . . Don't give it another thought. If the time comes when you and David begin to think . . . There, there, darling, everything's fine now . . ." As my mother came out with those familiar words of comfort, the sound of her voice, gentle and supremely reassuring, flooded across me.

I saw various heads at the bar turn to watch us, as I wiped my nose on my sleeve just like a child and sobbed in a broken whisper, "It's not that, Mummy. It's not Michael – it's me . . . I'm pregnant." For less than a moment, my mother and father stared at me blankly, and then my mother's eyes filled with tears, and she took me into her arms, and murmured, "What wonderful, *wonderful* news! Oh, my darling girl, what happy news!" and over her shoulder, I saw my father silently wipe his own eye, as if he had a bit of dust in it.

When my parents went home my mother gave me strict instructions about changing my GP, eating properly and getting enough sleep. My father said that he wanted to shake David by the hand, and told me to bring him round so that he could do it. Neither of them asked if we intended to get married.

After I had been to the hairdresser's the next morning, I changed into a skirt for our appointment with Wing Commander Rodney Babington. Something in his voice on the phone had told me that jeans wouldn't be appropriate. I had agreed to collect David and go on to the Babingtons' in Putney together. When I got to the studio, David held me by the shoulders and took a good look before kissing me. "You look different," he said, and I told him it was just my hair. David's eyes were veiled; I wondered if he hoped I would tell him that I wasn't pregnant after all. He looked different, too, but perhaps it was more that the weariness I was accustomed to and the determination in his jaw were more than ever pronounced. There *was* something new, though, an outward gentleness that I hadn't seen before and didn't altogether trust.

The Wing Commander met us at the door of his house and ushered us into his garden. Moments later his wife appeared with a tray of coffee and biscuits. I dithered about whether to call him WingCo, Rodney or Mr Babington, and settled on the full Monty.

"Wing Commander Babington, it's so very good of you to let us come and see you." He inclined his head. He was a wiry man, with the alert blue eyes of a bird and the straight-backed posture of a long-term military man. He was about my height, no more than five foot five or six, but his carriage gave the impression that he was a good few inches taller.

"Well, my dear, I'm flattered to be asked. Can't see what you want with the likes of me. Always happy to oblige, but wouldn't want to waste your time. Not at all sure that the old brain's up to it – not what it was, you know." He spoke in a clipped short-hand, and I wondered if he would relax. He would be no use to me or David if he didn't. He eyed David nervously, and I asked loadedly, "David, don't you need to check the stuff in the car?" He looked at me blankly, and rose to his feet. "Would you object, sir, if I take a stroll round your garden? Until you're ready for the photographs. I see you have a datura over there, which I'd like a closer look at." I gawped. I had never heard David profess an interest in so much as a pot plant before, but Babington welcomed the question.

"Of course, old boy! Make yourself at home – several more round the corner, behind the house."

I looked at my notes. "You flew Kittyhawks, is that right?" I prompted.

"It is."

"You'll have to excuse me if I'm not very good on the technicalities of planes. I've tried to learn, but you'll correct me if I'm wrong?" He bobbed his head. "So Kittyhawks are fighter planes?"

"Fighter bombers, or dive bombers might be more accurate. We carried two 250-pounders and a five hundred."

"I see." I groaned inwardly and wished I'd studied the plane specifications. 'So you were always a fighter pilot?"

"No. I trained as a bomber pilot, having taken a short-service commission with the RAF back in '38." He was sitting on the edge of his deck-chair, listening intently and offering little. I'd hoped for a garrulous old type, at least for my first session.

"What made you change? Wouldn't it have been easier to stay with bombers?"

He laughed as if I had said something asinine, which I suppose I had. "Had I stayed with bombers, young lady, I would almost certainly have gone for a burton my first tour. I was damn lucky to convert to Tomahawks. Always flew Yankee planes, now I come to think of it. That photographer is a Yank, isn't he? Good chaps, the ones I knew at least. All good chaps."

"Could you tell me about the aircraft? Just explain the differences between them." At last I had stumbled on the right button to fire Babington's engine.

"The Tommy was a decent kite, barring a landing peculiarity." He leant forward clicking his tongue against his teeth as he thought. "If you didn't keep your wits about you, she'd do a twirly on landing, which could bust the undercarriage and tail. Very tricky it was – a chap would get short shrift if he busted a crate on landing. Now the Kitty, mind you, wasn't a piece of cake either. You needed a strong right arm to control her in some manoeuvres. If you went into a dive, a Kitty could really let rip and was inclined to roll to the right, and you'd trim out with the left hand PDQ, as you couldn't take your hand off the throttle," the Wing Commander re-enacted the physical manoeuvres required from a deck-chair in his Putney garden, "but then, pulling out of the dive, the Kitty would roll violently to the *left*," he braced a leg against the garden table, "which had to be corrected by trimming out half-way through the dive, and holding the stick central by bracing the right arm against the right leg and the cockpit side."

"Would you mind if I turned on my tape recorder?" I asked numbly. I had expected to tease out a terse and reluctant biography, and his sudden flood had caught me unprepared. If I tried to take this down in shorthand there was no way I was going to make head or tail of my notes.

"By all means, so long as I don't have to handle the machine. Can't be doing with gadgets." He took a sip of coffee, and stared into the distance of his garden. "The Kitty could be a bugger all round, if you'll excuse my French. You had to fly very smoothly to have any chance of aim, or she'd fish-tail just as you were getting ready to squirt an enemy aircraft. Now when you got into medium to heavy bombers, like your Wimpey, design was all important. You could have driven a Halifax down the high street, she was that steady."

"Did you like your squadron?" I know, this was a pathetic question. It sounded like I was asking him if he'd enjoyed his breakfast.

"It was a decent squadron – decent record. Jolly types, most of them. We had a couple of Yanks who'd had the balls to join up before Pearl Harbor, and some Aussies, Aborigines, we called them, just to put their backs up. Mainly sergeant pilots – non-commissioned blokes. Their lives were made wretched by having to call the officers 'sir' – they'd spit it out through clenched teeth."

"Was there ever a time when you thought you wouldn't make it?"

His blue eyes twinkled at me wickedly. "Make it? You mean, did I ever think I was heading for the chop? Didn't have time to worry about that sort of business. There was a time in the desert when I led a small sortie of six planes up to Mersa Matruh – know the place? Where Cleopatra had her bath. We dropped a load of incendiaries, turned tail and up for a quick flip back over the Qattara depression. All very neat and jolly. The CO was tickled pink. Slapped me on the back and said, 'Boys, let's do it again, but this time in the opposite direction!' so like mugs we set off the next night." He paused for effect and winked at me. "That time the Jerries, being no fools, were waiting for us. Shakey do there for a minute, but we all got home safe and sound. I had another scare once with an Italian fighter – a Macchi 202. The Eyeties may not have been great soldiers, but my God they were good flyers, and had some great fighter pilots. We were in a dogfight, both the Macchi and my kite went into an inverted spin – almost impossible to pull out, and bloody to handle as all the controls are reversed. The Eyetie saluted me as he spun past. I was sure I'd bought it then. I'm sure he did. Bloody impressive chap, despite being on the wrong side. Not his fault, that."

He stopped again, but only for breath. "I went back to Tangmere shortly after. Met a gorgeous nurse in King's Lynn, not that you're interested in *that*, of course."

"Oh, yes, I am."

"Not in mixed company." He winked again. "Nearly lost my commission."

"Because of the nurse?"

He had a huge laugh for such a small frame. "Lord, no. For a spot of shooting up."

My eyes must have been wide. "Shooting up?" I repeated.

"Very low-level flying. We all did it. You'd come

in very low over the officer's mess, or a training field, buzz them up, just as a prank." At this point on my tape he chuckles and makes a strangled whining noise, and then the soft thudding of the engines pulling out. "A great laugh to see the top brass hit the deck."

"What did they do to you – instead of the court-martial?"

"The punishment depended on the type of commanding officer. I had a good sort. Tore a strip off me, then stood me a drink at the pub. The worse punishment was being suspended from flying, as your mates would have to take over your duties, and you'd be putting them at risk. That was against the spirit of the whole thing."

"Was there much difference between being a fighter pilot and a bomber pilot?" I asked this question because I had scheduled an interview with a bomber pilot the following day, and I wanted to give him the impression that I was a little better informed than I had been for Wing Commander Babington.

"Good God, yes. At least in the early years. Bombers were far more likely to get the chop."

"What made a man a bomber pilot rather than a fighter?"

"Oh, it took a different character altogether. Bomber boys had long flights – six, seven hours, maybe more. They had to be prepared to drone on hour after hour at slow speeds. They had an awesome responsibility, not just for their crew but for hitting the target. It was very dispiriting for them to miss. We sometimes escorted heavy bombers, acting as top cover, but most of our sorties were short – ninety minutes tops. If you made a complete balls-up as a fighter pilot, you might get some flak from your mates or the CO, but you didn't have other chaps depending on you the way bombers did. Fighter pilots had the freedom of the skies, and it wasn't a cliché then. You were up there on your lonesome ownsome." I was aware that David had rejoined us, and was listening intently. He worked on his lonesome ownsome too.

The Wing Commander didn't appear to notice him. "We could communicate by radio, but we stayed off the line to listen out for the leader. If you were in formation, you played follow my leader, and kept your eyes glued to the tail tip in front of you. Bloody tricky not to get too close, yet not to break formation. Sometimes you couldn't see a blind thing. Imagine emerging through cloud into brilliant sunshine and finding a posse of enemy fighters waiting for you – whup! Back into the clouds, then jinking into formation again soon as you could see your arse for your elbow. Sometimes we'd just stooge around, idly flapping about wondering what the hell we were doing there. But they were good days. For most of us. Some chaps couldn't take it, cracked under the strain."

"In what way?"

"What the RAF in their wisdom called LMF – 'lacking moral fibre'. A nonsense. I never met a man who lacked moral fibre in that war. If you want to talk to a bomber, I have an old friend from Oxford days, Theodore Hamilton. Flew Wimps – Wellingtons – in the desert. He'd be the right type to fill you in, and spin a yarn or two. Lives in France, now. I'll fish out an address if you want to look him up."

Some time later, Mrs Babington came into the garden and invited us to stay for lunch. I looked at my watch in horror. We had been talking for over two hours but the Babingtons would take no refusal, and as the Wing Commander insisted that he'd feel far happier having his picture taken after a few glasses of wine, we stayed. During the meal, I chatted with Mrs Babington, a sweet lady who had been a nurse during the war and had tales of her own to tell, but I kept one ear on David's conversation with her husband, cursing the fact that manners forbade me to leave the tape recorder running while we were eating. The Wing Commander was asking David about photography, and David was explaining his job carefully. Rodney Babington clearly thought that David was some sort of a tabloid snapper by profession, and David had not, as far as I'd managed to hear, told him of his own combat experiences. David tended to be pretty covert about his intentions with his subjects, but he was relaxed with Babington.

"All photographers hope to receive something from the person in front of the lens while they stand behind it, some transfer of feeling. You want to be faithful to your subject, and yet use what is in you. It's a shared experience that comes out, however fleeting the moment may be."

"I'd be much obliged if you would have a word with Claire." Rodney nodded at his wife across the table. "She always takes our snaps and manages to get her finger in over the top of the picture."

"It's a very common mistake," David said kindly, smiling at his flushed hostess. "One I made myself for years."

"I still don't understand why you want my ugly mug in your book, or what experience we share."

"That's one reason why I like to listen to Elena's interviews before I take photographs," David explained, reprimanding me for having tried to shoo him away earlier. "It's a question of knowing what you're looking for, and how to look at it, rather than how to photograph it."

"And you think you know what you're looking for in me?" Rodney asked gruffly.

"Yes, I believe I do," David said simply.

"And what's that?" I could see that the Wing Commander was apprehensive, and held my breath. David was capable of both deep charm, and icy detachment.

"I want people to see your courage, and that you belittle it."

"Good Lord – I wasn't particularly courageous! There were men back there who had ten times the balls that I had, who aren't here to tell the tale." From the colour high on his cheeks, however, I knew that David's comment had pleased him.

"Then I shall look for them, too, in your face. A

photograph rarely tells the story of only *one* person, not in my experience."

"You're not a common or garden photographer, are you, young man?"

"Oh, all too common, I'm afraid."

"David is really more of a combat photographer," I interjected, and carried on, avoiding David's frown. "I'm sure you've seen his photographs from the Falklands, and the Gulf, and the Lebanon . . ."

Rodney Babington didn't seem surprised, and luckily for David he changed the conversation.

"The Gulf War – now *that* was interesting stuff. All that talk about precision bombing. Not like my day. My word, planes today are so technologically equipped they can be flown by a computer, I suppose. One man can do more damage in a minute than five of our squadrons could have done in a year. And the cost of damage if you prang a plane – bending a Spitfire was bad enough, but if you look at the sophistication of what's flown now . . ." His cloudy blue eyes took on a dreamy, faraway look again. "We'd be flying in tight formation, and then dive individually to bomb dispersed targets – transport and supply lines, airfields, bridges – well nigh impossible to hit, and you'd just cross your fingers and hope to hell it frightened the enemy as much as it frightened you." He took another swallow of wine. "But at least we had a relatively clean war – and most of all in the desert. That was one of the few theatres of war in all time, to my knowledge, where there was no real action against civilians. That's the bloodiest part of any war, isn't it?" David nodded. "We didn't have any of that, particularly as fighters." He put his arms up in the stance of a pugilist. "It was pilot-to-pilot stuff: Catch me if you can, but if you can't, I'll kill you, no hard feelings either way, and the best of British luck to you!" He spoke with a cheerful brutality. "We had a lot of respect for each other – fighter pilots had a natural empathy and understanding, which wasn't quite the same for the bomber boys. When we did shoot one down, I always tried to fly low, and see that the pilot had got out safely. Of course, it was important to destroy the enemy aircraft but it wasn't done to strafe the crew. Not the done thing at all. I have never forgotten, early on in the desert, when we learnt that the great pilot Italo Balbo had been shot down by his own anti-aircraft guns over Tobruk. Collishaw sent a Blenheim over the enemy lines to drop a wreath at his funeral. I think that our lads were just as upset as the Eyeties about the loss of such a man."

He swirled the wine around in his glass, lost in memory. "The chivalry wasn't all on our side, you realize. One of our officers was taken POW by a German pilot. The poor lad told the Jerry that his wife had just arrived in Cairo and was waiting there to meet him and the German managed to drop a message so that the lady wouldn't be distraught thinking her husband dead. Decent, that."

While David and the Wing Commander discussed the best setting for the photo session, Claire Babington offered to show me round their garden. It is one thing to sit in on an interview, and quite another to gatecrash the delicate balance of a photo shoot; I trusted David and left him to it.

As I bent down to sniff an early rosebud, Mrs Babington touched my arm hesitantly and said, "You've done him a power of good, you know. He's not always so – cheerful. I'm grateful to you."

I told her that it was I who should be grateful, and that her husband had opened my eyes to many things. I meant this sincerely.

"He *was* a brave man, you know, in his way. He still is." She kept her eyes averted and began to dead-head a shrub further along the path, snapping off the stems between practised fingers.

"I bet you have a tale or two of your own to tell. I'd love to hear them." She looked startled by my comment, and shook her head nervously. "Were you and the Wing Commander married when the war started?"

"Oh, no. We met in hospital, after the war. He told you he had been wounded?"

"No, he didn't."

"I shouldn't have mentioned it."

By this time, I was longing to strap her into a chair and hear all about her life, but it was difficult to find a way through her reticence. I continued to coax her. "Your husband seems to have mainly good memories. He seems very positive."

"Yes, he is. He never lost the will to survive, not Rodney."

"It must have been very hard for you, as a nurse."

"For me? No, not at all, not compared . . ." She knelt down by the flowerbed, and began to paw the earth away from a weed, before teasing out the roots. I watched her in silence.

"I'm sure that it was a decent war, just as he says. Rodney knows far better than I do. But some of those poor boys lost so much."

"Do you remember them?"

She shook her head sadly. "Not all. We cared for so many of them, you see. I can't remember those poor boys' names, but I still see their faces. They all lost – something." She sat back on her heels, hands lying loosely in her lap. "Sometimes I have wondered if those who died weren't the lucky ones. I had girl-friends who used to pray for nothing except their man's return. It was a dreadful bargain to make. Sometimes those men came back in a way that the women didn't want them. Some had lost their families, limbs, even their faces. And worse." She brushed some dirt off her skirt. 'Ah, well, I'm glad they're remembered by people of your generation, even if it's only because of a seventy-five-year anniversary."

She stood up smoothly, her back as straight as her husband's, her voice just as clear and precise. "All those boys lost something. They always do. And none of them had any – what do you call it? Counselling. Not like today. Nowadays, you get counselled and compensated for all manner of things. But they didn't get compensated for what they lost."

I stood facing her, wondering what was worse than losing your face. I hardly dared to ask, but I did.

"They lost their faith."

"In God?"

Claire Babington considered my question as she examined a leaf in her hand. "In everything. They simply lost track of themselves. They didn't know who they were, or why they were alive, and they didn't care any longer. Would you like to see the greenhouse?"

As I admired the cucumbers, she turned to face me and said a strange thing, which I have never forgotten: "You must always remember to remove the male flower. If you allow the male to blossom, the female will become embittered."

When we said our farewells, Rodney Babington gave me a little slip of paper with an address in France for Wing Commander Theodore Hamilton, DFC, DSO. "Don't know if he's still there, my dear; don't even know if the old fellow's still alive, but he'll have some interesting tales to tell if he is."

I promised to write to him, but I already had a surplus of names to chase, and I doubted this was one I would pursue. I didn't want to get bogged down in the desert.

Cairo

On graduation Theodore Hamilton had volunteered for Bomber Command. At the outbreak of war, he had joined the Oxford University Air Squadron, and thus been able to skip the elemen-

tary pilot training course, and qualify quickly as a Wellington bomber pilot. He had flown two missions with his crew from England before being sent out to the North African front in February 1941. Egypt seemed far from home, and far from the war as he knew it. He was undecided as to whether or not this was a good thing. It was not that he hungered for war, but he longed to fly again, and had not enjoyed the past two months of inactivity. They had taken off from Hampstead Norris for the ten-hour flight to Gibraltar, spent three days in Gib waiting for clearance, before another ten-hour flight to Malta. Not one but two of the Wellingtons assigned to his crew had been destroyed on the ground there, and they had twiddled their thumbs beneath horrendous bombing raids, waiting for the lucky third to arrive. Theodore had no expectations of life in the desert; all he knew was that anything had to be better than being planeless in Malta, and that it was high time he was back in the air. He and his crew had arrived in Egypt the week before, and were waiting assignment to a squadron in the Almaza transit camp.

The complexity of Cairo assaulted all his senses. He could distinguish the smell of horse-hair, the reek of manure, sweat and kerosene amongst the rich waft of roasting coffee. Visually it was both a ragged place and a beautiful one. When he strolled through the quiet streets of Zamalek, he gazed on lush gardens, potent with the scent of eucalyptus, overflowing with jacaranda and bougainvillaea, and admired colonial-style verandas necklaced with trailing roses. As he approached the centre, riding in a gharrie drawn by a horse with a frilly contraption to keep the flies out of its eyes, Cairo changed colour, from greens and tropical reds to a maze of swirling browns and greys, brightened only by a flash of puce or flame on a donkey's harness. The noise reached cacophonic proportions – the cymbals of a liquorice sherbet street-seller clashing with the street cries of the dragomen and scarab merchants, and the eager shouts of 'Effendi! Effendi!' from the children who raced beside the trap with arms extended.

Theodore instructed the driver to take him to Shepheard's Hotel, a Cairo landmark second only to the Pyramids. The terrace overlooking Ibrahim Pasha Street was dense with tables, and at each table four or five wicker chairs were pulled tight around. There were uniforms everywhere, officers on leave, officers celebrating, officers back from 'the blue', officers commiserating, officers drinking themselves into a stupor. Shepheard's was off limits to NCOs. Although the hotel's clientele was overwhelmingly male, that evening a few women were dotted around the terrace, some possibly Egyptian, some European, some of unknown origin, and three British girls of Queen Alexandra's Nursing Corps, on leave from the hospital at Abbassia.

Around each woman the men stood three deep, ordering drinks, suggesting dinner, offering romance, and proposing marriage.

Unlike the women, each man could be easily identified by his dress and speech – there, an officer of the South African Air Force, on the far side two Canadians, at the back a Free French soldier, and everywhere the buccaneers of the 7th Armoured Division, and the officers of the 11th Hussars, Englishmen whose voices spanned from the banks of the Tyne to the playing fields of Eton. Not only did their uniforms proclaim their nationality, but also their rank and function: the Fleet Air Arm pilot, the gold insignia on the sleeve of a naval officer, the red-banded hat of a brigadier, and tables of consorting tarbooshes.

Theodore was immediately hailed by Lawrence Hayworth, a fellow pilot in transit at Almaza. Hayworth, known familiarly as Rita, just as a man called Lynn was invariably called Vera, was from New Zealand and flew Kittyhawk fighters. He took every opportunity to goad Theodore on the shortcomings of bomber pilots, or bus drivers, as he called them, as compared to fighters. Theodore had known him for less than a week, yet Hayworth had told him three times the joke about the bomber pilot who was so stupid that he didn't know the difference between arson and incest, and kept setting fire to his sister. The first time, Theo had laughed, enjoying the immediate camaraderie; the second time he'd smiled a little tightly, and thought the man an ass; the third time he'd turned his back. Nonetheless, he was glad to see a familiar face. That evening at Shepheard's, the talk was of the desert and of the pestilential flies. There was also much joking about the brothels of the Berka, Cairo's red-light district. No officer would deign, or admit to deign, to visit a brothel; it was universally accepted that brothels and their residents were for the benefit of non-commissioned men, or 'other ranks'. As respectable women were few and far between, and generally spoken for in Egypt, many an officer would have been tempted to trade his commission for an hour or two's consolation from one of the unrespectable working women of Darling Street, but this was not an option. Theodore was amazed by all the creature comforts offered in Cairo: having left London in the grip of air raids and rationing, it was a shock to find the cellars of Shepheard's comfortably stocked with French champagne, good wines and a seemingly endless supply of gin.

Hayworth introduced Theodore to his friends. "Lads, this is Flying Officer Hamilton; flies Wimpeys, he's a sprog." Theodore took no offence at this description — he was certainly an inexperienced newcomer when it came to desert flying. He nodded at his companions. Apart from Rita, he was introduced to a Canadian navigator called Richard Flecker, another British officer called Henry – Theodore didn't catch his last name – and a South African wing commander from the 43rd called 'Drongie'. This was a nickname as inappropriate as Rita; 'drongie' was Afrikaans for drunkard, and WingCo Broek was teetotal.

Drongie began to tell the tale of one of his squadron pilots who had brought down three Italian Macchi fighters and been awarded the DFC, although he was still missing, and had most probably been shot down.

Hayworth downed his beer in a long swallow, and wiped his mouth with the back of his hand. "What matters is staying in one bloody piece, not honour and medals and all that cock."

"If I'm going to face the chop, I'd rather have a gong than not." Theodore noted the thoughtful look in the South African's eyes. "Might bring some comfort to the wife and kiddies." Later Theodore learnt that Drongie already had the DFC and, more importantly, a wife and three young children at home on his farm on the Cape. As Wing Commander, it fell to him to write the letter to the family when one of his men was killed or missing, presumed dead or captured. Every time he wrote, and he had written eighteen such letters, he found the paper marked with his own tears. Theodore thought often of gallantry awards, and often of death. Just short of his twenty-third birthday, he was too young to think of the latter with fear or sadness. Both death and glory made something related to excitement buzz in his veins – an anticipation, a profound curiosity.

After an hour, Hayworth suggested a move to the rooftop restaurant of the Continental Hotel. Henry and Richard Flecker were game, but Theodore remained at Shepheard's with Drongie for a final drink, and then returned to the camp to find that his crew had been posted to the 37th. The squadron were set to move the following morning from their base at Shallufa up the Blue, to an advanced landing ground in the desert. Before he slept, he wondered if he would ever lay eyes on Hayworth, Flecker, Henry and Drongie again. He picked up the prayer book that he had been awarded at school, and read: "O that I had wings like a dove: for then would I flee away and be at rest. Lo, then would I wander far off and lodge in the wilderness."

Pilot Officer Hamilton's arrival at the 37th Squadron in the early spring of '41 coincided with the desert war's most intense eighteen months. There was little time to adapt to conditions, or to the night flying that gave the 37th its motto: "Wise without eyes". In some ways Theodore was grateful for a baptism by fire. He took to heart the Arab saying, "To the man who knows it, the desert is a fortress; to him that does not, a grave," and learnt fast. Three weeks in the desert turned the young man's face brick red, the skin on his nose and lips cracked, and his dark gold hair was streaked white by the sun. He rapidly adopted the single most versatile piece of desert equipment – the Arab headdress. He used it as a tented sunshade, a tea strainer, a blanket, a towel, a wind-break. After three months, Theodore was no longer a sprog but a 'gen' man, a desert dweller, an experienced operational pilot, accustomed to 115 degrees of heat, used to washing his shirts in petrol, because water was in such short supply, to the smell of disinfectant rising from the latrines, and to the horrendous desert wind, the Khamseen, which blew so hot and hard that he couldn't see his hand in front of his face. 'Khamseen' was Arabic for fifty – the number of days that the wind was said to blow. Apart from the damage the wind and sand did to the men's faces and other body parts – certain medical officers became expert at circumcision – the Khamseen could convert a plane into a brick, by depositing eighty pounds of sand aboard.

This was the time of the first battle of Alamein, afterwards known as the Flap, a time when the powers at HQ in Cairo were sufficiently concerned about the rapidly approaching enemy line to order the incineration of all secret files at the various headquarters. Theodore, stationed with the 37th at landing ground 09, was only belatedly aware of Ash Wednesday, when the smoke rose above the houses of Cairo and the streets were littered with the charred confetti of confidential documents. The talk in the officers' mess was solely of the shortage of water relative to the availability of whisky, and the bravery of one of their pilots, who had had the simultaneous good luck and misfortune to detect eight hummocks of sand during a night bombing op. Suspecting they were too uniform to be natural sand dunes, he had bombed and hit two of them: the ammunition stored below had exploded. The blast blew out part of the Wellington's fuselage and tail unit and wrecked the instrument panel. The skipper had ordered his crew to bale out, but he himself fell through the lower hatch while assisting his front gunner and was killed instantly. The men in the mess were subdued that night, but drank a toast to their friend. The squadron flew every night for five days, and the men were grateful for the constant activity; it was better to be frantically killing the enemy than killing time. The 37th leap-frogged across the desert like a chess knight from landing ground to landing ground, from 09 to 224 (Cairo West), which they reached in July 1942.

From LG 224 Theodore was able to snatch two days' leave in Cairo. When he stepped onto the terrace at Shepheard's, he now knew many faces. He went inside to the Long Bar to join friends from a sister squadron, the 70th. Among the throng, he was delighted to spot Rodney Babington, with whom he had shared a staircase at Balliol. They had not been particular cronies at the university, but they clutched each other like brothers. Theodore towered a clear foot above his wiry friend.

"Rodney! I had no idea you were out here! What brings you here? Or is it just the good weather?"

"Good God – Hamilton, is that really you, old boy? You look like a wog! They wouldn't know you down at the King's Head. I fancied a shufti at the Pyramids. What's your excuse? Keeping well?"

They were barely able to exchange squadrons and landing grounds before they were swept back into the crowd and out to the terrace. It was fifteen months since Theodore had arrived fresh-faced from Malta. He was almost unrecognizable, his lips a pale streak in a light mahogany face, his hair bleached near white by the desert sun, and blue eyes aged by twenty years. Though Theodore had changed, the conversation at Shepheard's had not: it was still of brothels.

One of the intelligence officers from LG 09 raised his voice above the din. "You know Mary's, Hamilton? The knocking shop?"

"In Alex? of course," Theodore replied, with a broad grin that split his face. "No personal experience, you understand."

"Well, you've lost your chance now, old chap. It was hit in a raid. Lot of our lads there at the time, army types. The story goes that few of the boys were badly injured, but sixty were sent to the local hospital to be checked over. There's this British nurse, see, walking through the wards and enquiring as to where each had been during the raid, and they all reply, 'At Mary's.' Poor cow goes to the ward matron and says, 'Whoever Mary is, she certainly knows how to throw a party!' It's the honest truth – heard it from the CO."

Theodore and his companions laughed loud before one asked, "Say one of the lads had bought it. Would it go down as 'killed in action' or 'on active service'?"

Theodore speculated, his arms crossed leisurely above his head, chair tipped back.. "That would depend on the conduct of the man in question, whether he was cowering under the bed or nobly shielding the lady of his choice . . . And whether his mission had been satisfactorily completed." The listening airmen guffawed.

"Knowing the brown jobs, it wouldn't have been . . ."

"That matron's the bloody cow who gave me an enema – just for giving her some lip. Who's for another round, lads?"

They waited thirstily for the overworked suffragis and repeated the sour but oddly comforting joke that the only thing that could slow Rommel's relentless advance would be reaching Shepheard's.

As they swapped tales of direct hits and near

misses, Theodore's eyes roamed the bar. He was as bored of mess-room banter as he was of being alone. Across the terrace, he caught sight of a young woman in civilian dress, her golden hair held back off her face by a black bandanna. She was holding court at a table surrounded by officers. Theodore couldn't hear her voice, but she had the men around her in the palm of her hand. Each time she stopped speaking, there would be a gale of laughter from her escorts. She had the extravagant gestures of an actress, her arms moving constantly, expressive hands acting out her anecdotes, green eyes flashing and opening wide as she reached the climax of her story.

Theo leant towards Rodney Babington and gestured towards the blonde woman. "Know who she is?" he asked quietly.

Rodney's eyes followed his friend's across the hotel terrace. "No such luck," he replied, his bright eyes twinkling appreciatively. "I spotted her yesterday in fact, at the Sporting, but couldn't fight through the crowds to get close enough to introduce myself. Pretty little thing, isn't she? Wouldn't disgrace a gent's arm."

As Theodore stared at the woman, she paused, her red-lipsticked mouth half open in speech, and her eyes met his. She wasn't pretty; she had a face that could make a man simply forget all about the war. She half smiled, as if in partial recognition, then turned her attention back to her avid attendants. Theodore considered the option of sending a drink to her table, but lacked both the energy and the confidence. Something about her told him she was out of his league. He cursed himself for a coward and allowed Rodney to entice him to the Continental for the performance of Hekmet Fahmy, one of Cairo's most celebrated ghaziya, or belly dancers.

Hekmet was particularly popular amongst the Allied officers, not only for her dancing skills but for the linguistic coincidence that rendered the Arabic pronunciation of her name – with only the slightest shift in stress – as Hekmet Fuck Me. Her greatest rival in Cairo was the equally undulating dancer Tahia Carioca, who performed at Madame Badia's, and was familiarly known as Gippy Tummy. This enabled those lucky beneficiaries of what a gentleman would call her off-stage performances, to report back late from leave, and give their commanding officers the permissible, and honest, excuse: "I'm sorry, sir, I was in bed with Gippy Tummy." Theodore admired the mesmeric rhythms of the dance, the way Hekmet camel-walked across the stage, fluidly transferring her weight from the ball of one foot to the toes of the other, shivering her shoulders and rotating her hips. He was transfixed by the shimmying, elastic movements of her body as it erupted into a flat spin accompanied by the table drum and lute, and the unearthly banshee wail of the zhagareet. Although his eyes were held by Hekmet's lyrical dips and sways, his *thoughts were of the woman he had seen on the terrace at Shepheard's.*

The next day, Theodore went to the Gezira Sporting Club. He stayed at the swimming-pool terrace all day until sundown, but the woman was not there. In the evening, he returned to his squadron, and flew that night, bombing the enemy landing ground at Derna.

CHAPTER FIVE

The evening after we had met the Babingtons, David came back to the flat with me. There were four messages on my answerphone, an apologetic one from Becca, and three from my mother, each longer than the last. The first was to tell me that she had sent her sister in the States to buy some Materna vitamin pills – essential for the health of American expectant mothers. The second was to ask whether I had considered having the baby in the States; surely safer than in England. I saw David's mouth twitch involuntarily as he heard that. The third was to say that it was six o'clock in the evening, why wasn't I home yet; was I all right; did I realize that this was the most vulnerable stage in pregnancy, and that I ought to be at home with my feet up, wouldn't it be wiser to postpone this book business for a few months at least, and would I phone her the second I got home?

I labelled my Rodney Babington cassettes before

I called my mother.

"Is David with you, at least?"

"Uh-huh."

"I want to talk to him."

I held out the phone to David. "She wants to talk to you." He backed off, with his hands up. "She hasn't got a shotgun, and she doesn't bite. Not hard." He took it gingerly.

"Hey. How are you doing?" He smiled while he was listening to her. "I couldn't agree more. . . Yes, I surely will . . . I'm sure she is . . . Delighted, just delighted . . . Really. . . No, not exactly expected, but no less welcome for that . . . I couldn't care less, it's really the same to me. . ." He gave a great belly laugh. David is fond of my mother; she amuses him a great deal, but they keep a level of mutual respect between them. "Never out of my sight? I'll certainly try. Perhaps I'll use some kind of electronic tagging . . . Yes, I can promise you that. She is, I agree." I found this conversation almost unbearable. The last time that David and I had talked about the pregnancy, the conversation had been stilted and grim, and here he was schmoozing away with my mother as if he was already the father of four and she was advising him on nursery schools. "Gabriella? No, I have no objections, but Elena and I . . . Exactly . . . She is, isn't she? No, not exactly difficult, but . . . It could be that, I reckon. I'll bear it in mind." He chuckled. "I surely will. Give my regards back to him. You take care too."

He replaced the phone, and looked at me carefully.

"Well?" I demanded.

"She just wanted to congratulate me, and –"

"And?"

"And she's worried about you, naturally, that you're eating properly, and –"

"And?"

He shrugged. "She asked me whether I minded if we had a boy or a girl. I said not at all."

"And?"

"And if we had a girl, would we consider calling her Gabriella?"

"Gabriella?" I glared at him, as my mother wasn't there.

"And then she told me that if you were acting strangely, or irrationally, or getting bolshie, or bursting into tears, not to pay any attention because it was perfectly normal and just down to the hormones."

"Oh, for God's sake!" I stormed, threw my coat onto the floor, and jumped up and down in fury.

David grinned. "If you could only see yourself. You look about four years old." And he crossed the room and hugged me, and I relaxed into his arms, and realized how much I had ached for his touch over the past three days.

In bed that night, David asked me what I thought about my mother's suggestion of delaying the book project for a while, but I refused. Point one, the project couldn't be delayed, if publication was to coincide with the seventy-fifth anniversary of the founding of the RAF. Point two, what the hell was the good in sitting around my flat doing nothing but get bigger and bigger till I popped? Point three, interviewing old men wasn't exactly an arduous occupation. Point four, my work was none of my mother's business. Point five, I didn't want to have all that time on my hands doing nothing except wondering about the baby. Point six, I had to earn a living, particularly now that I would be supporting two (I made this particular point in something of a rush – the last thing I wanted was to have a financial conversation about maintenance payments and what David was prepared to do or not do, but it had been nibbling away at the back of my mind ever since I had done the first test). I quickly ran through seven to ten, but faltered at eleven.

"What's the matter, Elle? Run out of fingers?"

"Piss off."

"I have only one word to say to you," he said firmly.

"What's that?"

"Hormones."

I hit him with the pillow while warning him that retaliation was *verboten* now that I was pregnant. "Do you really not mind whether it's a boy or a girl?"

"Of course I don't. I'm having trouble believing that you're going to have a baby at all." I registered the 'you're', rather than 'we're', but didn't comment. He was right, biologically, whatever the implications. We both looked at my stomach. It was flat, and disgustingly white. I wished I had a tan – a brown tummy would somehow have seemed less vulnerable, less naked, maybe even less pregnant. David's finger traced ever increasing circles on it.

"Can you believe there's a living, breathing human being in there?" I said, staring at it in disbelief.

"There isn't. I mean, it's living, all right, but it isn't breathing. Embryos and foetuses don't breathe, not until birth."

I smiled at him. "Since when have you been an authority on foetal development?"

"Since I bought a book on pregnancy on Friday night," he answered smugly. "And read it over the weekend, twice, while you were gadding about with your friends. Any objections?"

I had none. David reading up on pregnancy touched me more than anything else he had said or done.

"So what d'you think about Gabriella?"

"I'd like it a whole hell of a lot better if we'd thought of it ourselves," I grumbled. "I can't possibly begin to think about names, and my mother can. What do you think?"

"I like it. I like all girls' names."

"Even Enid? Gertie?"

"Sure, if you want."

"What if it's a boy? I'd like something heroic."

"Horatio?" David mused. "Agrippa? Hercules? Arthur? Martin Luther?"

I just stopped myself trying 'Hercules Turcan'

out loud. The first name wasn't going to be half as difficult as the last one. "What about David?"

"Nope. I don't want the poor little sod looking to me as a heroic role model."

"I wasn't thinking of you, I was thinking of David as in David and Goliath."

"Smartass."

"Just watch it, buddy, don't forget that you're addressing the mother of your child."

"I don't think I'll ever forget that, as long as I live." He spoke lightly, but there was a sad undercurrent in his voice and a shadow in his eyes. "If it's a girl, I hope she has your best qualities," he went on and I nestled deeper against his shoulder, settling myself for a main course of flattery, after such a tantalizing appetizer.

"Oh? Which ones in particular?"

"I hope she has your looks. As to character, intelligence, practicality, emotional depth, reasoning abilities, integrity, manual skills and moral fibre, then I hope she takes after her father."

I raised my head, and gave him a dirty look.

"And I fervently pray she has my sense of humour," David concluded.

Looking back, it seems strange to me that I felt so happy then. If I were rewriting my story, I think I would be tempted to change my feelings for the sake of credibility. Who would believe that, newly pregnant, and in a fundamentally unstable relationship with a man who made the Scarlet Pimpernel look like a stay-at-home accountant, I could have felt so contented? But I know that I *was* happy, not only because of the baby, with whom I was having a bit of a love–hate knock-about, but because I was wholly enchanted by its father.

When I called Becca back she sounded preoccupied. "Oh, hi, Elle. Hang on a minute, can you?" I waited for an age. "Elle? Sorry about that. Camilla was crying. How are you? Look, I'm sorry about being so bloody the other night, about your being pregnant. I didn't wait to hear how you felt about it before shooting my mouth off."

"That's all right."

"So how *do* you feel about it?"

"Funnily enough, I feel good."

"Honestly?"

"Yes. Honestly, I feel great about it."

"Well, terrific. You even *sound* happy. I'm glad for you. Hooray. Savour it while you can. Just wait till the kid starts to crawl, and then you'll feel differently. Wait till you're trying to winkle Rice Krispies out of the crevices in your precious coir matting and see how good you feel. Have you ever tried to get a jam sandwich out of your car ashtray or, worse, out of the *seatbelt* casing? It took me an hour this afternoon."

"I don't have coir matting, let alone a car."

"Oh, yeah, I forgot. Well, believe me, you soon will have, or you'll go stark staring crazy. Mind you, I've got two cars, and it hasn't stopped me going crazy."

"Oh, Becca," I whispered, "I wish you'd be a little

more encouraging. Until you get pregnant, everyone else is all smug, and you feel left out in the cold, and then as soon as you join the club, you're hit with a flood of depression."

"Sorry. I'm sure you'll love it. I'm just pissed off."

"Do you want me to come round?"

"Nope. I'm in bed, watching a video of *Gone with the Wind*, and that's all I feel up to at the minute."

"Is Michael with you?"

"Michael? Watching *Gone with the Wind*?" she asked sarcastically. "He's at the office. Listen. I'm sorry, I'm just not in the mood. I *wish* you'd got pregnant three years ago. I wish it had been when I was pregnant with Jasper and thrilled about it, and we could have swanned around the baby department at Peter Jones and got fat together. We're out of step at the moment, aren't we, sweets? I guess you and David are feeling all lovey-dovey and cosy, tucked up in bed with a book of baby names. Well, I'm glad for you, I really am. Hooray. I'll say it again. Hooray for you. Now I've just got to the bit where Rhett dumps Scarlett on the road to Tara so, if you don't mind, I'm going to pour myself another gin and watch it. No offence."

"I'll call you tomorrow, OK?"

"Fine. Oh, and Elle?"

"Yes?"

"Don't go rushing off all bright-eyed and bushy-tailed to buy the pram and crib and clobber. You can have mine, OK? I won't need them again. If you're going to go through with the whole shebang, you might as well save your pennies."

Just as I said I am tempted to rewrite my feelings in those early weeks of pregnancy, for the sake of credibility, and with the benefit of hindsight, so I would like to edit what I felt about my conversation with Rebecca. But because I am honest – as my beloved father so often says, "I am nothing if not honest" – I will put it down straight, as it happened, and as I felt at the time. When I hung up the phone I was spitting blood, and I hated Bec. I couldn't stop feeling that if I were in her shoes, I would have rejoiced for her, and shut up about my own problems. I stomped back into my bedroom and threw myself onto the bed, saying, "Becca is such a bloody bitch," burst into tears and let David comfort me, and reassure me that I had been horribly wronged. When I repeated our conversation, supposedly verbatim, I exaggerated Becca's sourness, while David stroked my hair. Maybe hormones do warp the brain.

Most friendships rely on a harmony of timing, a happy coincidence of shared experience. Nothing relieves the fear of isolation as much as meeting someone who feels exactly the way you do at exactly the same time. Even if you know in your heart that they couldn't have had the experience quite as *profoundly* as you did, it provides enormous comfort to have one's own emotions, convictions and conclusions reinforced. Maybe that's why women bond so frantically at antenatal classes. Rodney Babington had talked with devotion over lunch about each and every man he had been stationed with, barring one commanding officer, whom he had described as a cold-blooded shit. Then I thought that I would never be part of David – he and I had no common experience. However many games we played and however well we got on, I was outside his real life. But there he was, stroking my hair, and making all the right soothing noises.

"David? What was it like when you and Felicity divorced?"

He ran one hand through his tousled hair, his other arm pulling me closer into his side. "We were very young. We weren't married for two years in all, and I was away most of it. We had no belongings, no roots, we never considered having children."

"Nor did we," I whispered, and he kissed the top of my head.

"Elena, it was completely different. Flick and I married for crazy reasons, and split up for sensible ones. It didn't mean anything to either of us." ·

"I don't believe you. You're not the type to get married without it meaning something, are you?"

"Aw, I was a pimply-faced kid back then. You didn't know me. And you wouldn't have wanted to." I didn't agree there. I was fascinated by the idea of what David would have been like in his early twenties. "Flicky and I met in New York in 1977, I was twenty-three, she was twenty-one. I remember the day we met only because it was the day Jimmy Carter was sworn in as President, and I should have been in DC. She was English, studying Comp. Lit. at Columbia. She was pretty, and wild about books, which I found kind of appealing. I loved her voice," he squeezed me, "but I've always been a sucker for an English accent. She mistakenly thought I had a glamorous job." I blushed guiltily, but the room was too dark for David to see, and he continued, "For my part, she was something bright and innocent, and I was pretty sick with loneliness. By then, I'd done time in Vietnam, Nicaragua, been in Chile, South Africa, all kind of shit. Why she thought that glamorous rather than plain crazy I don't know, and I sure didn't ask. We had fun for a while. We married ten weeks after we met. I had a sublet on a place on the Lower East Side and Flicky stayed there and carried on studying."

"What did you do about money?" I was curious about every detail of their life together.

David scratched his head. "I think her parents paid her an allowance, but we never talked about money. I paid the rent, I guess she paid the bills when they came in. I only met her folks that once, at the registry office. The four of us had lunch after, with Heffner and his girlfriend, who'd been our witnesses." This was news to me. Heff had never mentioned her when we'd met. "A few days after we married, I went to Pakistan, when Bhutto was arrested, and a few other places. I came home and I couldn't recognize my flat. I'd just forgotten it. I could barely recognize Flicky." He began to rub my back. "The next year I was everywhere but home –

I'd be plenty surprised if we spent a week a month together. Most of the first half of '79 I was trying to get into Kabul. When I got back, Flicky said she'd had it, and wanted to split up, and I just felt goddamn tired and relieved not to have to think about her any more. I signed a shitload of papers, and went back to Pakistan as the Soviet troops arrived in Kabul. I tell you the truth, Elle. I remember less about being married than I remember about trying to sort out my transport at each place."

David's voice was quiet in the dark room; he had rarely spoken at any length about his past, and I didn't want him to stop. I hoped that the baby was listening to its father's even voice, and would be soothed by it. "And then?"

"And then?" he repeated. "I didn't see Flick again. We swapped postcards a bit. She was involved with someone when I came back from Nicaragua the second time. She left the flat, and moved in with him – I think he was a professor, something to do with history of art. She'd met him at the Guggenheim, I remember her telling me that, and I remember she was crying, which was a shame, because she was a nice kid and I had no problem with her going with him. You don't want to hear all this crap."

"I do, I really do. How did you feel about him?"

"I was glad for them. Some time later she sent me a card saying they'd got married, asking if I'd send her one of my photographs, one she'd always liked real well, as a wedding present. I also sent him one I'd taken of her. Last time I heard from her was right before I met you. She was still in New York, lecturing at Columbia, and she had three kids. End of story." His hands drew a line below the episode.

I felt as I had when my father used to sit on the chair next to my bed, telling me tales of darkest Africa, lion hunts and witches, and I used every trick in the book to make him carry on, thinking myself clever for conning him into a new story. The only difference was that my father liked telling them, and David didn't. "What happened then? After she left?"

"Darling, I can hardly remember. Nineteen seventy-nine . . . Must have been Gdansk, Afghanistan." I felt him stretching against me. "Just work. You know the score. You don't want to hear this shit, and I don't want to talk about it . . ."

I wasn't at all sure that *I* did, but his voice was so deep, so soothing, and I was so close to sleep, I didn't want him to stop talking. "Please, David . . ."

"You tell me about being a schoolgirl and what you wore to play hockey."

"Don't be such a pervert. You're about to be a father. What about the Gulf War?"

"The Gulf was all right. For correspondents, it was OK. What else? Shit, I haven't kept a list. Ask the agency if you want a record."

"David . . ."

He groaned. "Azerbaijan. Pakistan. Kabul again. Havana. Beijing. Fucking Disneyworld. Then I met you."

This was David's litany. And I crept in under the wire, somewhere between Tiananmen Square and

Nelson Mandela. What a lullaby for a baby. As I drifted into sleep, the names that echoed in David's even voice blended with the words that Rodney Babington had used. They were all foreign to me, all rich with vague associations, each name prodding my mind with the message: "Don't forget me! You should know what happened . . . Don't lie there in your comfy little bed and forget about *me* and the people to whom my name means everything – life, death and the whole shebang . . ." David's photographs and Rodney Babington's memories were images I both wanted to look at and was too scared to see. I felt like a little kid watching a horror film through my fingers, from the safety of my mother's lap. The words carried me into sleep, but they carried me and my baby into dreams of a world and a life in which we had no apparent place.

For the next few weeks David and I had a busy schedule of interviews across England. After the first three days, I rearranged all the 9 a.m. appointments to later in the day, as I spent the first two hours of each morning with my head in the loo. I had started reading the newspapers again, now that David was with me, and after my first chuck on waking, I would get the paper and a glass of water, and retire to the bathroom floor to read the news, leaning my head against the bowl. If I stayed on the floor for an hour or so I was fine, but if I stood up to attempt to get dressed before nine thirty, I was seized with waves of nausea. David was in turn perplexed, bored, sympathetic and amused. He looked up morning sickness in the directory of his pregnancy book, and assured me it would only last another few weeks – there it was in black and white. His confidence did not help me much. We would leave for an interview with me looking like I'd been on the razzle all night, my hair limp and my face ghostly, and David the glamour photographer. He never wore black leather, or a camouflage jacket; I would have left him instantly if he had. By mid-morning, I would feel normal but the transformation from being non-pregnant to pregnant is as shocking as transformations get, and there is no return down that particular path. Not that I had fully accepted that I was going to have a baby. As far as I was concerned, I might have been developing an ulcer.

We saw all sorts of people. We met an elderly working milkman who had been a tail gunner, and went to Wormwood Scrubs to interview a convicted armed robber, now in his eighties, who had flown in the Battle of Britain, and to Glasgow to meet a navigator who had covered a convoy through Bomb Alley *en route* to Malta. We met men whose frail dignity made me weep. We met a handful of women, servicewomen and widows of servicemen who, without exception, considered themselves unworthy to be included in the book, always passing credit to those who had been in active combat.

Time and again I thought my heart would break, meeting these people at the end of their lives, but this didn't bother David. He was far quicker to identify with them; his charm was dazzling. While I skirted around an interviewee, wary of over-intimacy, David buried himself in them. When we finished, I was immersed and David had extracted himself intact. I watched his films develop as keenly as I replayed the recordings of my interviews. I knew that the success of the book lay in the words and voices of the interviewees, and in the way that David captured their faces, and there were times when I felt I had no real part to play. I was nothing but a technician. David grew angry when I said this: he had little tolerance for what he considered unprofessionalism.

The dreaded day came, when I was only a little over twelve weeks pregnant, when I couldn't do up my jeans. David and I were getting ready to go to Chelsea to have dinner with my parents and I was in a bad mood. I hadn't handled that day's interview well: I had been distracted and found the subject, a stiff staff officer, deeply unsympathetic. I lay on my back on our bed, with a piece of string threaded through the eye of the zipper of my jeans, holding my breath as I tried to tug it up.

"Could you just quit that, Elena? Think what you're doing to the baby."

"Could you just stuff it? It's not your body that's swelling like the Goodyear blimp. It doesn't even belong to me any more. I'd like to see how you felt if one day you were wearing your jeans and the next you couldn't get them up over your ankles."

"I'd feel goddamn proud, and I'd wear a dress."

This made me smile for the first time that day. "I'd like to see you in a dress."

"I bet you would."

"Can I take a picture when you do? Just for your mates, Turk?"

"Sure you can, provided you can point and shoot."

I peeled off my jeans and threw them into the cupboard. They'd probably rot there for the next twenty years, until the day I could shake them under my daughter's nose, and wail, "Look what you did to me! I used to be able to wear these!" My *daughter*? I was going to have a boy, I told myself. A boy I intended to call Hercules, and both he and his father could lump it. I put on the shirt my mother had given me for my birthday, which I hadn't worn yet, and a kind of sack, and waved adieu to my waistline.

The first thing my mother did was compliment me on my blouse. "Darling, that's lovely – it brings out your eyes so well." She had already bought a dozen outfits for the baby, which she showed me before we sat down to dinner. We had left my father and David in the drawing room, and when we returned, they were deep in conversation, David listening intently.

"The thing about babies is that one so desperately wants to spare them all the troubles and grief that one has gone through," my father was saying.

My mother laughed. "What, pray, do you know about babies, Ben? Did you ever even change a diaper?"

"Never, my love, but I admired your skill at doing so countless times." He raised his head towards me. "A little-known fact, Elena. Your sainted mother was one of the best diaper changers in the Northern Territories . . . She had a nose for it. Within three minutes she could smell a dirty diaper and summon someone else to change it."

David threw up his hands. "Sounds smart to me!"

"Don't listen to Ben, David. You're a new man – it'll be second nature to you. I think you young couples today are lucky to be able to do so much with your babies. In our day, David, fathers weren't even allowed into the maternity ward, and now you can be in at the start."

"Dear heart, I think fathers have always been in at the start," my father corrected mildly.

"Don't talk dirty, Ben, you know what I mean. These days, couples can have water births and take videos and play whale music and do whatever they feel like, although I certainly hope you're not considering anything like *that*, Elena, it's far too risky."

"Taking videos?"

"No, all that water birth, no intervention, natural labour stuff. I've been reading up about it." Everybody had been reading up except me. I was still in the 'the less I know, the better' camp. "My God, I would have given ten years of my life for the drugs that you young mothers have now, and what are you doing? Refusing them, and saying you want to give birth in a country field with music playing and some sort of scented oil burning, and not a doctor in sight, just your *birth* partner." My mother nearly choked on the words.

"Mother, are you about to say for the hundredth time that you don't know what the younger generation is coming to?"

"No, baby girl, I'm about to remind you for the hundredth time not to teach your mother to suck eggs, and to tell you and David to go into the kitchen, where dinner is waiting for you."

David took my arm to help me off the sofa, which wasn't necessary but I appreciated the gesture. In the doorway of the drawing room, I turned back to say something to Dad, and saw my parents kissing. I felt a stab of pain, and although I thought immediately it might be the baby, I knew the real cause. I was jealous of them.

Since I had first discovered I was pregnant, I had spent a lot of time thinking about my mother. I had a fixed image of her: plump, ebullient, irrepressible, warm-hearted, meddling, always knowing best, always loving, ever youthful – somehow younger than me. Throughout my teens I had repeated the time-honoured cries of the adolescent daughter, "You *don't* know what I'm going through! It's different for me! I live in a different world. You have no idea – this is *my* life," and as I saw my father kiss my mother firmly on the mouth, I thought that I could hear my own daughter saying the same things to me, and I saw myself shake my head, as my mother still shakes hers, and say, "But, darling, I *do* understand.

I was young once. I *do* know what you're going through, and I just want to spare you some heartache . . ." And I saw my as yet tiny daughter stamp a foot, her face – but what face? I couldn't imagine a face – suffused with passion, saying, "No, you *don't* understand. I don't even *want* you to understand . . ." And I wondered if I was going to be any good as a mother – if there was anything I would be able to teach my daughter at all. *Daughter?* I corrected myself: I'm going to have a son. And what the hell would I ever drag up to teach *him*?

In that split second in the doorway while my parents kissed and David pulled on my arm, I had another vision of my mother. I do not know if this was something I had once seen, or something I dreamt, or something I imagined. I have a recurring image of her standing in a shower cabinet, unaware of me, then a little girl, watching from the doorway. In my mind, I hear the water running, and I need to ask her something, and find the door unlocked. She's standing in the shower, the heat of the water steaming up the sides, and her eyes are closed. Her palms and forearms are braced flat against the glass walls, and the water cascades off her body. Her face is tipped right up so that the water will hit her full on, and she is smiling. I see her then as fearsomely beautiful, detached from me and separate from everything in my world. She is not my mother. This is the one and only image I have of her as a woman, neither wife nor mother, just a woman enjoying the sensation of hot water hitting her face. She seems suffused with that sensation of sensory joy. I have never spoken to her of this.

David also saw my parents' kiss. He pulled me away into the kitchen, and there he kissed me. When my mother arrived in the kitchen – my father walks rather slowly, and often now with the aid of a cane – she had a slight blush on her cheeks, and I have never loved her so much.

My girlish, seventy-something mother. I felt sorry for everyone who hadn't met her, and I wondered if I knew her at all.

CHAPTER SIX

We were two-thirds of the way through our interviews when David started getting antsy. Over six weeks we had seen thirty-seven people, most of whom I was keen to include in the book. Graham didn't want more than fifty in the final version, and we were going to have to be rigorous in our selection. I found it impossible to exclude anyone: they had all risked their lives and played a part and had a story worth telling. David was more ruthless: he had more experience than I in selection and rejection. When we went home at night, we'd replay the cassettes together, and I'd sit down at the computer and tap away at my notes. If the day's interview had been middling, I pleaded for inclusion while David demanded the axe. There was always a stream of messages on my answerphone from Ma, but also from editors and the agency suggesting assignments. As the weeks passed, the suggestions became more and more insistent.

David refused to have an answerphone of his own: he said if anyone really wanted him, they'd find a way of getting in touch. He was right there: they bombarded my machine with messages. Although he swore he wasn't going to take up any offers until the RAF interviews were done, he was showing every symptom of advanced passport withdrawal.

One night he came clean. "Why don't we go away for a bit? Change of air – time to reflect on what we've got. What d'you think? Tempted, darlin'?"

I was at the desk, struggling to decipher my notes. "Hmm? Sounds great, but I can't go away – I've got my first antenatal class tomorrow, remember? I'm meant to go every Thursday for eight weeks and you're meant to come to one of them, I put it in the diary, let's see – yup, Fathers' Night, you'll love that, won't you, Turk?"

"We could go for a long weekend."

"I sort of want to finish everything up, then relax. I don't want stuff hanging over my head."

"I thought you had some interviewees abroad. Why don't we go see one? Busman's holiday." In the corner of my eye I could see him almost twitching with impatience.

"They're all in the Costa Brava or something – not much of a holiday for us, even if the excuse was a working trip. There *is* that Welsh navigator. Is St David's sufficiently exotic for you?"

I wasn't paying much attention. I was preoccupied with writing up a guy who had been a key figure in the emergence of Fighter Command and radar defences, and was confused by my scribblings. I switched on the tape again, wearing the headsets, as Mozart was blasting through the flat. David had added a lot of Mozart and a little Springsteen to my music collection. I was aware of him leaning over my shoulder and rifling through my desk drawers. I am very possessive of my desk. It was my Dad's for thirty years and he'd carted it all over the world with him. It's one of the few things that have been around me all my life, along with a little brooch of a winged horse that Ma gave me yonks ago, and a weird painting of a dog from God knows where. None are valuable, not even particularly nice, but they are my tap-roots, and I won't let anyone mess with them. I took a hand off the keyboard long enough to swat him away, but not before he'd picked up a couple of folders, and retreated to the sofa. I carried on typing for an hour or so.

By the time I'd stopped work, David was leafing through an atlas with an open bottle of wine next to him. David drank a *lot*. I don't mean he was an alcoholic, but he could drink a lot, like two bottles of wine and a few bourbons, and not show any sign of it. When I poured myself a glass, David looked at me as if I had poured a tumbler of neat diesel fuel.

"What are you going to do with that?"

"Well," I drawled, "I *had* planned to lean out of the window and tip it over the head of some innocent passer-by while singing the Hallelujah Chorus buck naked, but if you think that would be bizarre, I guess I'll just have to drink it."

"You're not meant to drink."

"Who says?"

"The book."

"Ah. The Good Book. The same bloody book that says I should have an afternoon nap every day, and massage my perineum with olive oil while I think of summer meadows? Great stuff. I'll have you know that my perineum is just dandy, and my mother says she drank *and* smoked throughout her pregnancies because her doctor told her red wine was good for thinning the blood, and cigarettes would settle her blood pressure."

"It stunts the growth. You're living proof of it."

"Frankly, when I think about trying to get an eight-pound cannonball out of me – which I try to do as little as possible – growth restriction seems an appealing idea." David was stony-faced. "Come on, one little glass isn't going to hurt."

"One glass. Don't make a habit of it."

I saw four yellow Post-it notes in the atlas.

"OK. Here's the choice. We've got a guy who lives near Lisbon."

"I can't stand Portuguese food, apart from the shellfish, which The Book says I am not allowed to eat, and you *know* how conscientious I am about my diet," I countered smugly.

"We've got a guy in Hong Kong."

"Terrific! Let's call Graham this minute and ask him how he feels about first-class tickets and a week at the Peninsula Hotel." I picked up the telephone.

"Fine. There's the intelligence guy in Tangiers."

"Nah. Bec and I did Morocco five years ago. What made him retire to Tangiers, anyway? He's either a drug addict, a weirdo or gay. Probably all three."

"You are either very conservative, very narrow minded, or very hormonal. Probably all three. Not to mention being a shit journalist if you aren't itching to find out why he's there."

"The only part of me that's itching is my stomach."

"Come over here and I'll scratch it for you." David took out three of the markers, and rubbed my tummy when I lifted my T-shirt. "I like this. You remind me of a dog I had when I was a kid. OK, Fido, so it's France."

"You never told me about a dog. Where in France? Not the Côte d'Azur – I told you I'm not going anywhere where I have to wear a bathing suit. Paris, maybe." I peered over his shoulder, and he stabbed a page in the middle of nowhere.

"There. Sainte Cécile. Lot-et-Garonne."

I looked more closely. "That's not my mother's Free French pilot, is it? I didn't think she'd found an address. I'd like to meet *him* – he could have been my father. God, just think! I might have been French, and called Béatrice or Cécile, and been incredibly elegant and *soignée*."

"You *are* incredibly elegant and *soignée*. For another week or so at least." David pulled a file from the floor, and extracted a slip of blue paper. "But it's not the French guy. It's Wing Commander Theodore Hamilton, DSO, DFC. Babington's buddy."

"I'd forgotten about him. What was he – a bomber pilot? I don't know, though, we've done bomber pilots. We might have already seen someone from his squadron. Does it say which he flew with? Wasn't he Desert Air Force? You're always going on about not retracing our steps." I reached for the wine, but David took it from me and drained the bottle into his glass. "I don't see the bloody point of going to France and not bloody being allowed to have a glass of wine," I grumbled. "I bloody bet pregnant French women are allowed to drink."

"Not if they act like dogs they're not."

The next day I drove all the way to Islington for my first antenatal class. I'd intended to go to classes in Notting Hill Gate, but my mother had been so concerned that I went to 'the best' that she had called Bec, and bullied her into giving me the low-down on Miriam Hilton, an obstetric physiotherapist who was a legend among the pelvic-floor brigade. Bec agreed that she was the best person to go to, but said it didn't matter much anyway: as soon as I'd had the baby my stomach would relocate somewhere around my knees, I'd lose sight of my tits, and life, as I knew it, would be over. I went to the first class like a lamb to the slaughter.

Miriam took the classes in an annexe of her house

in Canonbury Square. My eleven classmates were all far more pregnant than I was and when I sat on a cushion on the floor I felt like a fraud. The other women eyed me suspiciously, and I smiled nervously, assured them that I *was* pregnant and was just trying to get ahead of the game. This went down like a lead balloon; they seemed part of a sorority into which I hadn't yet been inducted. Miriam herself was tall, wiry and had a no-nonsense, military air that reminded me of my housemistress at school. She was the only person who had a chair; the rest of us sat in a circle on the floor, like storytime at a kindergarten.

"Right, ladies. Now, I would like you to go around the room and introduce yourselves in turn. Please state your name, your age, your occupation if you work, previous children, if any, your expected delivery date, where you live, what type of birth plan you have, and your greatest fear about pregnancy and labour." She balanced a notebook on her lap, pencil poised.

This was clearly a Test, and one I felt sure to fail. 'Previous children' sounded uncomfortably like prior convictions. I tried desperately to think of something clever and profound to say about my birth plan, but I didn't have a birth plan. And I was not prepared to tell *anyone* my greatest fear about pregnancy and labour. We went round the circle, starting with a blonde woman in a tailored black maternity suit.

"My name is Susannah Parker. I'm thirty-two,

this is my first pregnancy, and I am a fund manager with Fidelity, specializing in European equities and special situations. I manage three different funds for a broad range of institutional clients. My husband Mark is also a fund manager, but invests in the UK only." My eyes must have been out on stalks and I wanted to lean across the circle and say, "Hey, you must know my old boyfriend Peter Bagshawe, he works at Fidelity," but this wasn't the time or the place to name-drop fund managers, and I had no idea if Peter still worked there. If he did, I had the feeling that he was probably a close friend of this woman's, and the less said the better. "My EDD is the eighth of July, so I have seven weeks to go, provided I deliver on schedule which I fully intend to. Peter and I currently live in Holland Park, although we have just made an offer on a house across the square," she smiled at Miriam, "so we may be neighbours." Good luck to you, Miriam, I thought meanly. With neighbours like that, let's hope you don't have a dog that craps on the pavement. Susannah continued, "I'm having the baby at St. Thomas's, under Mr Ferguson," Lucky old Mr Ferguson, "and will be having an epidural. My concerns about the labour are that I cannot spare more than two weeks away at this time of year so I dread late delivery or any other complications."

She turned a tight smile around the circle, as a small dark woman began breathlessly, "Hi, every-one. My name is Lucy. I'm twenty-eight, and this is my second baby, but my little girl Maisie is seven now, so I thought I needed a refresher course. They say you never forget labour, but it went clean out of my head – probably all that gas and air!" She giggled impulsively, as if she was still gulping the stuff. "We – Maisie, Bill and I – live in Islington, too. I work at a book shop, but only part time because of Maisie. When I had her, I wanted a drug-free birth, but I lost it, I was out of my head, and sucking Entonox for all I was worth. I don't know what'll happen this time – I guess we'll know around the eighteenth of July! I'm hoping for a boy. Most of all, I'm just hoping he's OK. The only thing that really scares me is there being something wrong with the baby. That's it." She shrugged rather self-consciously, and proffered the baton to another blonde sitting next to her. Then it would be my turn. Drug-free birth. If I absolutely *had* to do birth, I wanted a pain-free, consciousness-free birth.

"My name is Imogen Gargiulio. I'm a GP," there was an audible intake of breath around the room, "so you might think I should know everything about having babies but I probably know less than anyone else here." Not me, sister, I thought. "I'm thirty-eight, so I'm what we call an elderly prima gravida. I hope to keep an open mind about a birth plan. I'm not against drugs and pain relief, *per se*, but I would like to attempt to have the baby naturally, if only for my self respect. My EDD is the thirtieth of June so I only hope I can complete the course in time." She dipped her head, and spoke to the carpet. "My worries? Well, I'm worried about lots of things –

placenta praevia, post-partum psychosis, pre-eclampsia, cord prolapse –"

"What the hell is that?" the woman on my left said loudly.

"We'll come to that in class six," Miriam said soothingly. "Don't worry about it. Could you just tell the class where you live, Imogen, and your partner's name, perhaps?"

"In Hackney. My husband is called Mario."

It was my turn.

"Uh . . . hello. I'm Elena Stewart. I'm thirty-one. I live in Notting Hill Gate." I saw the fund manager, whose name I had already forgotten, lift up her head, and wondered if I would get an invitation to coffee one morning, but she must have had second thoughts as she looked away again pretty quickly. "This is my first baby, and I can't remember what day it's meant to be born," I stammered apologetically. "I'm a bit more than three months pregnant, so I know it's due around early November. I'm a journalist, and I don't have a birth plan, beyond having it at St Mary's. I don't quite know what my worries are – sometimes I have so many, sometimes I forget I'm even pregnant."

"Wait a couple of months, dearie, and you won't be able to forget it!" said a large woman at the far end of the circle with a laugh.

"I suppose not. I think I'm frightened about labour itself. I'm quite nervous it will hurt too much. That's it, really."

"Partner's name?" Miriam was taking notes, eyes

on her folder.

"David."

And so it went on, round the room, such different women, such different fears.

"—I'm frightened of having to have a Caesarean section. I just don't want my stomach cut open. I'd rather die in labour."

"—I'm mostly annoyed that Ian doesn't want to attend the birth."

"—I'm terrified of stillbirth."

"—I'm not worried about being pregnant, or giving birth, but I'm damn worried about how I'm going to cope *after* the birth."

"—I'm just worried about midwives putting the pressure on me to breast-feed – I think it's disgusting. Everyone says just try it, but I know I'll puke if I have to do that."

"—I'm frightened of not getting to hospital in time. Last time I just about delivered Mickey on the steps. What if I don't make it and I'm alone at home?"

Some women shared doubts and concerns and started chatting among themselves. There was a mini debate about the new 'walking' epidural. One woman said that anything was better than pethidine, which had made her vomit over her husband's head last time round. The single most common fear was that there would be something wrong with the baby. This hadn't crossed my mind before, and as I listened I felt like a complete idiot for not thinking this one through for myself. What *had* David and I discussed about this baby? Nothing. We had not once asked ourselves what we would do and how we would feel if we had a Down's syndrome baby, or if there were other problems. I hadn't had any tests, and I didn't want to. I had assumed that the baby would somehow get born, would be fine, and that we would live happily ever after in our own peculiar way. What I hadn't told the class was that I was frightened that I wouldn't be able to do it, that David might not be around when the baby was three or four or five – months or years – and that, most of all, I was just frightened that I didn't have what it took to be a mother. I didn't tell them because I did not want to think about it yet.

Miriam raised a hand, and the chatter died.

"Ladies, we will cover all your questions and concerns over the next eight weeks – fingers and legs crossed that you all make it through eight weeks, that is." I didn't think this broke any records as good jokes go, but my peers enjoyed it. "Those of you with closer due dates may need to join one of my more advanced classes for the last few sessions. Today, I want to start with issues of pregnancy, and some exercises that you need to do today, tomorrow and every day for the rest of your lives. We will start with the pelvic floor. I'm sure that most of you have already been exercising your pelvic floor, but I will teach you a simple, five-minute routine which I want to become as instinctive as brushing your teeth. You need to do it far more frequently, of course, or far worse things than your teeth might drop out."

By the time the class ended I hated every woman in the room, the over-informed GP, the smug fund manager, the earth mothers . . . The only one I warmed to was a feisty twenty-year-old with a punk haircut and no partner, who was studying environmental engineering at University College, and who told me during the coffee break that her mother, Lady Caldwell, was paying for her to attend the classes, and dropping her off and picking her up to make sure that she did. The idea of bringing David into this group, with their spouses and 'functional equivalents', filled me with horror. David was a supremely dysfunctional equivalent. Despite all that, I adored Miriam Hilton. I could have sat at her feet for hour after hour with my head on her knee. When class was dismissed, I hung around for a private word, but as most of the rest of the group were doing the same, there was a wait. When it was my turn, I asked my most pressing question. "I'm wondering if you really think I should be in this class? Do you think I should leave it till later?"

She glanced at her notes. "Elena. EDD early November. Well, as I said on the phone, I think in some ways it *is* a little early for you. There's a trade-off between doing these classes early on, and setting your mind at rest and getting on with exercises that might help you relax and strengthen muscles, and doing the classes in the final months so that everything is fresh in your mind and you're not stale by your delivery date. It's entirely up to you."

"I feel a bit out of synch with this class." I hung my head.

"Why do you think that is?" she asked gently.

"I don't think I've come to terms with the fact that I'm really, truly going to have a baby. It doesn't seem quite real."

"I see." Miriam considered me for a moment, then gave me a quick squeeze around the shoulders. "Listen. It's high time you did come to terms with it. Maybe the class will help you do that, but maybe it will rush you into things which you need to take at your own pace. The most important thing about pregnancy and labour and motherhood is doing what comes naturally and feels right for *you*. The only thing you *must* do is think about it. Start the exercises I taught you today," she glanced again at her notes, "have a talk with David, and if you want to join a later class, call me and I'll reschedule you." I wished it was as easy to reschedule the baby. The rest of the class had drifted into the hall and the street outside, some chatting, some clambering and squeezing into cars, gunning accelerators to get away as fast as they could. Through the annexe window I could see the punk student climbing into a Jag with a sulky look on her face.

"Tell me just one thing, Elena. Are you happy that you're pregnant?"

"Yes." I said fervently. "But I just don't know what it's going to mean."

"That's a perfectly healthy reaction. It only means that you're going to be a mother, and you'll find your own way of being one, and your babe will adapt to that, because you are the only mother it's ever going to have. Why don't you think it over for the next few days and give me a call before the next class if you want to rearrange?"

I nodded gratefully. Why was it that I couldn't think clearly or take decisions about anything on my own? I prayed it was hormonal, and drove home in a dither.

David was waiting for me when I got back, and I filled him in on the class. "Frankly, it was pretty disgusting. I just don't consider myself pregnant. I've changed my mind, and decided not to have the baby after all. I don't mean I want an abortion or anything, but I'm not going to have it in November. Maybe in a year or two I'll be ready. Not now, OK? Honestly. It just wouldn't suit me, not November. It's a bad month to have a baby – inconvenient, too bloody cold . . . We can wait, don't you think?"

David pulled me onto his lap. "I can't wait."

"Well, *you* have it, then. Do you know what Miriam said? Just before we were leaving, she said not to be surprised if we went backwards and forwards between looking forward to the birth and dreading it. She said one woman had been fully dilated, and in transition – d'you know what transition is, David? Bet you don't."

"Yes, I do, darlin'. It's the final stage of labour, the stage between contractions and delivery."

"So The Good Book says."

"So The Good Book says."

".Well, this woman, in transition, tubed up and wired to every goddamn machine in the hospital, suddenly heaved herself off the bed, and said, 'Actually, I don't think I'll have the baby today, thank you very much. If it's all the same to you, I just want to go home. I'll have the baby next week, or maybe Friday, I need to check my diary,' and her husband was trying to hold her down, and she told him to go fuck himself, and the midwives were dashing around, and the doctor was saying, 'Now, now, Mrs Williams, your baby will be along any minute,' and she shoved them aside, and started waddling down the corridor, trailing monitors and drips and IVs and the lot, and she nearly had the baby in the hall. What if I do that?"

"So what if you do?"

"Won't you mind?"

"Darlin', I won't mind anything so long as you and the baby are OK."

"Good. I might just be in transition already. I'm thinking about postponing the classes. I spoke to Miriam about it. Most of the other women are at least six months pregnant. I don't belong there."

"Good."

"Why good?"

"Because I think we should go to France, maybe for three or four weeks. *You* could take three or four weeks. There's time. You need a holiday." At his careful emphasis, I felt a cold trickle of suspicion run down my spine.

"David, have you taken a job?"

"I wouldn't say that."

"Yes or no. Have you accepted an assignment?"

'No. But I'm *thinking* about a short one, maybe just ten days. I thought I could leave you in France, you could sit out in the sun, sleep a lot, read novels . . . Maybe your mother would go with you."

"Where are you going?"

"Sarajevo, maybe. What d'you think? A week together, Elle? Then I'd go off and be back with you a week later – ten days at a stretch. It'd do you good, some time to yourself, in a pleasant village, a country inn." He was jiggling the stuff in his pocket, turning the coins and his lucky lump over and over in his fingers.

"You've already said yes, haven't you?"

"No, not yes. I said probably. It's for *Life*."

"And do you have any village in mind to dump me in?"

"Well, sure, darling. We talked about it last night. Sainte Cécile. We'll do the pilot together, then you chill out."

"Where?" I was tempted, not that I wanted David to know that yet.

"Sainte Cécile. The RAF book. Theodore Hamilton. DSO, DFC. Bomber pilot. And no, we aren't seeing anyone else from his squadron. The 37th, if you're interested."

"We don't even know if he still lives there. If he's even still alive."

"Yes, we do. He does and he is. I called him. It

took me about three minutes to get his number. Efficient, these French guys."

I don't know what made me angrier – that he'd agreed to go to Bosnia, or that he'd planned the French jaunt without asking me. I felt heat surge through me. "David, are you crazy? You just called him out of the blue? Without talking to me first? I can't believe you did that. What the hell did you say to him? I hadn't even agreed to interview him. How –"

"How dare I? I'll tell you how, Elle. I picked up the phone and called him. We both need to get out of London. You're tired, I'm stale. He's a good candidate, I spoke to him, and he's real *good*. He's articulate, he's different, he's interesting. He also happens to live in France, and I want to get you away."

"You should have checked with me."

David stared straight through me. "You mean, take the pictures and keep your trap shut? I wasn't aware that I had abnegated the right to all independent action. I thought you might appreciate me taking the initiative, when your mind was on other things."

I pointed a finger at him. "Are you implying that just because I'm pregnant I am no longer competent to do this book or set up interviews as and when I decide to?" I was trembling, still cross, but mainly because the row was going further than it should have, and I didn't know how to get out of it.

David looked at me coolly and took his time

before answering. His eyes had that half-closed, lazy look that made me as nervous as a cat. "Tell you what, Elle, how about this for an idea? I'll go call this Hamilton guy back now, and tell him that I fucked up big time, and we won't be troubling him after all. We'll forget about his DSO and DFC, and the fact that he was a member of the Late Arrivals Club, an' all he had to say about the desert air war." He picked up a newspaper from the floor and read for a minute while I chewed my nail. Then he continued casually, "By the way, he thinks he was *lucky* to be there. He told me he has – what was it? – a crater in his heart when he thinks about those days . . . But let's quit, forget about him bailing out with his crew. OK? I'm bored to death with the whole business, and I'm bored with sitting on my ass. I'm going to get on with some work. You go make yourself a nice cup of something hot and *sweet*, tuck up in bed and I'll call the guy and blow him off."

Most of the time, David's accent was stranded somewhere in the middle of the Atlantic, and his vocabulary eclectic. He was as likely to say 'bloody' as any Englishman I knew, but could say 'mother-fucker' the way no Englishman ever has. When he was angry, his voice took on a dangerously silken drawl that caressed the ear, but rippled with a sultry menace. As well as scaring me, it aroused me badly. I knew that David was going to Bosnia whatever I said, and backed down sharpish.

"I'm sorry, I'm sorry. He sounds like a good guy

– I should interview him. And it resolves my decision about the antenatal classes. It's a good idea. I just wish . . ."

"What d'you wish, honeychild?" The silkiness was still there, and he was now tossing the lump from one hand to the other, distractedly.

I wanted to say, I just wish you wouldn't go to Bosnia, and would stay with me for a couple of months. Doing nothing. "I just wish there was a nice hotel there," I finished lamely.

"You're in luck. There's an auberge in the village, run by some friends of Hamilton's. I wrote their name someplace. I thought I'd give them a call, if you agreed, that is, and you don't think I'm being . . . presumptuous."

"No, call them, and book whatever you like. I guess we're free. I guess it depends on your schedule. When you're going to Bosnia – I mean *if* you go to Bosnia. When you're back, we should set up the last UK interviews. Would that be all right?"

He shrugged. "It's your call." He took me into his arms again, and some of my fears dissolved. "Elle? I have to go to the studio tonight for an hour or so. I'll come back, OK?" When he said that, my fears came back, too.

"Sure. The old bad penny."

David left while I was in the bath, without saying goodbye. But David never says goodbye, not on the phone, not leaving a party, never. The word doesn't exist. I've known men who say goodbye all the time, without leaving, but if David were to leave me, he certainly wouldn't say anything like goodbye. I don't think he'd say anything at all.

I swear I could feel the bones around the small of my back expanding as I lay there up to my chin in steaming water. When I got out, I thought about having another glass of wine to spite him, but I had a headache. Instead I called my parents. My mother picked up the phone on the second ring.

"Pumpkin! How was the class?"

"How do you know I had a class today?"

"You think I don't care about you? You think I don't worry about my grandchild? I put it in my diary the minute you told me you'd signed up. I would have called you hours ago, but Daddy told me not to pry."

"It was fine, Ma. Sort of. Actually, it was yuck. Maybe there are women who can do childbirth, and women who can't. What if I can't *do* it?"

"Darling child, babies come out one way or another. They can't stay in. That's life."

"But what about me, Ma? What's it going to do to me?"

"Darling, hush a second, I need to check that your father isn't on the extension."

"Daddy knows where babies come from! He can deal with it."

"Well, of course he *knows*, but that doesn't mean he wants to hear the gory details from his little girl . . . Men aren't always as strong as we'd like to think."

"Nor women. I've postponed the classes for a bit. It's better to do them later on, and David's busting to get away. We have to see some old geezer in France, so we thought we'd make a holiday of it."

"Just what you need. A bit of fun, a bit of sun, a bit of romance . . ."

"Oh, Ma," I snivelled.

"What is it, darling?"

"Nothing. I'm going to be a lousy mother."

"You couldn't be. Now, you listen to me. There are great things ahead of you – the greatest lesson of your life. Having you and Charlie, the joy of seeing you two, is certainly the greatest experience of mine and your father's." She paused. "This isn't about David, is it?"

"No . . . Not entirely, anyway. But he's going out to Bosnia."

"He is?" I could hear her thinking it through. "Let him do whatever it is that he has to do, Elena, and make the best of it. He's a fine, decent man. You're far too inclined to go borrowing trouble. Feel lucky, darling, feel *happy*. These things sort themselves out."

"What are you up to in the next couple of weeks, Ma?"

"I've been roped into hosting the Commonwealth Society dinner the week after next. I don't know what to do. You know I can't cook – I'll have to get a caterer, and mess the food up so it looks like I made it. You know these English women, they always take such pride in their lousy cooking. What should I serve? Curry? Maybe I could bully the Bombay Brasserie into doing a take-out . . . You and David *will* come, won't you, darling?"

"If we're not in France, Ma."

"Where are you going?"

"Some village called Sainte Cécile. In Lot-et-Garonne."

"Sounds like the boonies."

"It is. I've got to go – kiss Daddy for me?"

"I can't. If I do, he'll know you called, and he'll bawl me out for not putting him on the phone. Now, call and tell us when you're away, how long for, and leave us a phone number where we can reach you. I don't want my baby disappearing, OK? Either of them."

"Ma?"

"Yes, darling?"

"Did you like being a mother?"

"Did I like it? Darling, I *loved* it, still do. It's what life's all about."

"Weren't you worried?"

"About what?"

"What would happen to you, whether you'd like us, whether you'd be any good, whether you'd ever be fanciable again?"

I heard my mother's rich laugh pealing down the phone line.

"Darling, I was forty-two when I had you. A ripe old age, and I didn't know *anything* about babies. I was lucky to be so pig ignorant – I assumed everything would be fine, and it was. Like falling off a barrel. It will be for you, too. Don't go looking for heartache. You know what I've always said – when you're happy, there's trouble sitting on the end of your bed, and when you're blue, there's happiness waiting there." She began to sing a song which used to drive me up the wall, but this time I rather liked it.

> You've got to ac-*cent*-tchu-*ate the positive*,
> Ee-*lim-in*-ate *the negative*,
> Latch on to the affirmative
> Don't mess with Mister In-between.
> Spread joy up to the maximum
> Bring gloom down to the minimum –
> Have joy – or pandemonium
> Don't mess with Mister In-between!

"It worked for me, baby girl, and it'll work for you too. Sleep tight."

I had a strange dream that night. I dreamt that I was at home in my flat and I cut my finger off. I walked calmly into the flat next door, which was a hospital, holding my finger. A doctor told me that he could either save my finger, or save the baby, but I would have to choose one or the other. I told him to save my finger. He looked down at my hand and said, "But you're not even married." Until that point, I hadn't realized which finger I had severed, and I looked down with curiosity. I had cut off the ring finger on my left hand. I waved my right hand around wildly, flashing a ring: "Yes, I am, yes, I am! I'm wearing it on the other hand." He looked at me very gravely and said, "That's just not good enough. I'm afraid I can't help you."

Cairo

Theodore didn't meet her again at Shepheard's, nor at the Gezira Club, but at a nightclub in Cairo called the Kit Kat. Six months had passed since he had first caught sight of her on the terrace, and it was now January 1943. He had spent Christmas at Landing Ground 140, Baheira No. 1, near Gambut in Libya. The Desert Army, and its supportive air defence, was advancing steadily west. Christmas had been a frustrating time, with little action due to bad weather, but the men had put up a tree of sorts in the mess, decorated it with discarded light bulbs painted red and figures cut from tin cans, and sprinkled it with soap flakes which Theodore would have preferred to keep to wash his dress uniform. Food had been plentiful: a lorry had delivered pork, turkey and all the trimmings, plus some good Chianti pinched from occupied Italian bases, to the pilots' mess. The only thing they didn't have was pure water. Water was transported to the advanced landing grounds in petrol tanks, and was so treated that the petrol was almost masked by the flavour of ammonia.

Yet it was the most beautiful Christmas Theodore could remember. Standing alone for a smoke outside the mess beneath an endless sky, a tear ran down his cheek – not from joy or sorrow but from intense experience. He returned for the revelries that were essential for the morale of the crews, air and ground. Theodore, now Flight Lieutenant Hamilton, had joined in the singing of carols, and even given a rendition of 'Good King Wenceslas' with the Wing Commander. The WingCo had fallen into a stupor during the last chorus, and Theodore had had to support him, and sing twice as loudly. He and several pilots put the WingCo to bed in his tent, by which time their commanding officer was half snoring, and half singing 'O Little Town of Bethlehem . . .' Theodore left the tent when the junior pilots opted to dress their unconscious CO as Father Christmas. It was what one might call a drunken occasion.

In the new year, after some eighteen months' active service in the desert, he was posted for three months' ground service to the Officer Training Unit at Ismailia. He had four days' leave before taking up his new assignment, which he had been reluctant to accept as it meant leaving the 37th, albeit temporarily. His sole consolation in returning to Cairo was the hope of seeing again the woman who had figured for six months in his troubled dreams. He went first to Ismailia, for lunch at the club and a swim, then on to

Cairo. First stop, as ever, Shepheard's Hotel.
Theodore was delighted to see Drongie Broek
sitting near the front of the terrace. He had last
seen him on his first arrival in Cairo, and had
often wondered what had happened to the grave
South African, whether his wife was now a
widow and his children orphans. It didn't do to
think too much of what had or hadn't happened
to any of those fellows – not the ones he could do
nothing about. It was better to concentrate his
efforts and energies on his crew.

Drongie had survived, but his eyes had
acquired the thousand-yard stare of men who had
been too long at the front. Theo found this look
far more unsettling than the nervous tics that so
many men developed in the desert, the hands that
automatically twitched to disperse real or imagined flies, the uncontrollable fluttering of eyelids.
The 'stare' was the worst: it was like looking into
an ocean, as blank and vacant and deep as you
can ever imagine.

"Hamilton – Flight Lieutenant, I should say.
I wondered if you'd tip up again. The boys and I
are about to go off to some sort of a knees-up on
one of those house boats. Fancy joining us?"

"Doesn't sound like your sort of a scene,
Drongie."

"No? I'm rather past scenes of any sort now,
old man. But it'll certainly do the young lads
good. Some of them are fresh out of the training
units – might as well have some fun before we

head up the Blue." Drongie's voice was as expressionless as his eyes, and Theodore wondered if it wasn't time for him to take a break in an operational training unit himself. He agreed to go along with the party to the Kit Kat club, which was on a boat moored on the bank of the river Nile.

When they arrived it was only nine o'clock, but the club was overflowing, and officers from all services and many nations spilled outside into the cool evening air. The doors were open, and Theodore could hear the band clearly.

Goin' to take a sentimental journey
Goin' to put my heart at ease
Goin' to take a sentimental journey
To renew old memories . . .

Never knew my heart could be so 'yearny'
Why did I decide to roam?
Goin' to take a sentimental journey
Sentimental journey home . . .

He saw her from the doorway. She was sitting on a stool at the bar, and she wore a red flower tucked into her hair above one ear. Two men, one an American pilot, one in civilian dress, stood propping up the bar on either side of her, but her head and shoulders were visible above them. She was laughing, red lips parted. She wore a black dress and her eyes were narrowed against the wreaths of smoke that rose around her. While Theodore watched, she raised a hand to her lips and inhaled on a cigarette, turning her head towards him to shield her eyes from the smoke. Theodore registered the long line of her neck, the acute ridge of a cheekbone, the slant of her green eyes, the upwards sweep of her hair, the shape of that red flower set against the gold, all this before she saw him, and he felt the rabbit punch of exhilaration and fear that struck him moments before he flew. Stronger than that. As her eyes met his, she gazed at him for a moment, slowly turned back to the bar, put out her cigarette, and inclined her head briefly towards the ear of the man in civilian dress, who turned to look curiously at Theodore. She slipped off the bar stool and made her way through the crush towards him, hips swaying, on high-heeled, strappy shoes that he hadn't seen since leaving England. It seemed to take her ten – fifteen – long minutes to cross the room; every time she stopped to greet someone, Theodore kicked himself for having imagined she was heading his way, but after a word and a smile or a laugh, she continued her steady if circuitous path. She came to a halt inches before him. She was smaller than he had imagined, her head coming only half-way up his chest, but she raised her face and met his eyes boldly. He could smell her perfume quite suddenly, something sweet with a sharp undertone.

"Hello there." She spoke first. Her voice was

soft and warm, and distinctly American. "We meet again."

"No," he replied slowly. Above all, he wanted to avoid sounding like a tongue-tied schoolboy, and floundered wildly. "You're mistaken. I'd never have forgotten meeting you."

"Maybe we weren't formally introduced, but I'm certain I recognize you."

Theodore took her hand in his. "I can't tell you how happy I am to make your acquaintance. Would you like to move on somewhere else?"

She laughed. "You've only just arrived!"

"I've seen everything I want to see," he replied earnestly.

"Well." She paused, looking at him with her head cocked on one side, a hand on one hip.

"Please."

"I guess that would be fine, but . . ." She looked over her shoulder.

"Your friends? The pilot?"

"He's a boy from back home. The other one's my boss . . ." The man in civilian dress was still watching them.

Theodore spoke urgently, in a low voice. "Please. Please let me buy you a drink somewhere quiet. Dinner. Anything. I don't want to meet your friends. I don't want to know anything about you. I don't even want to know your name. I don't want to do all the social niceties and chit-chat. Not until we're alone. Please say yes. Then I want you to tell me everything about you, where you grew up, what your mother's name is, what you're doing in Cairo, how long you're here for, who was your favourite teacher at school, the name of your perfume, who gave you that flower . . ." He half raised a hand, fearful that if he touched her she might dissolve like a mirage. "We could go back to Shepheard's."

"You think that's a good place to be alone?" she asked, amusement making her voice ripple.

"I won't be able to see anyone else."

Again she looked at him quizzically, and Theodore feared she'd heard his heart pounding. Then she handed him a little ticket. "OK, effendi. Would you get my coat for me, and I'll meet you just outside – I need a quick word with the boss."

Theodore couldn't take his eyes off her as she wove and swayed back towards the bar. She looked once over her shoulder and smiled at him reassuringly, and he handed the ticket to a suffragi, his eyes riveted on her. He wanted to see how she parted from the two men at the bar. Suddenly it was supremely important to him that she didn't kiss them goodbye, that they didn't touch her at all. He dreaded witnessing the civilian touch her waist or her cheek, seeing his hand lingering a fraction too long on her arm, or making some other proprietary gesture as they said goodbye. He could barely breathe. Whether he lived or died in this war, he could at last know that he had really been alive for at least one evening of his life. Neither man laid a hand on *her, although Theodore imagined that her boss's mouth tightened in a sudden frown.*

When she rejoined him, he held out a red coat to her. "No one but a goddamn Yank would wear a coat like this in Cairo," he murmured in wonder.

The day after his return to Ismailia, Theodore sat down to write to her. Not with his crew, or his fellow officers, or his family at home had he been able to find his own voice, but when he addressed her, his heart flowed from his pen.

Flt./Lt. T. R. Hamilton
37th Squadron
Officer Training Unit, Ismailia
DAF

12 January 1943

Dear G.D.Y.,

Not the most romantic form of address, I admit, but I was torn between my darling, my dearest, dear heart, sweetheart, my own girl . . . Each time I wrote one down, I was obliged to tear up the paper, realizing that I had neither the right nor the sheer nerves to use such possessive if tender forms until you granted your permission – your blessing, I hope. The floor of my room is littered with rejected titles. Be kind enough to select the one of your choice, scribble it on an airgraph, and send it post haste. I will haunt the mail rack until it arrives.

A mere twenty-four hours have passed since I left you at Shepheard's, and those twenty-four hours seem to have lasted longer than all the months I have been in this Godforsaken country. You said when we parted, if I remember correctly, "No looking back." Well, my lovely young lady, I cannot describe to you how clamorously and eternally hope beats in my breast. We must have no secrets and no deceits between us, so I will make my very first confession: I did sneak a quick shufti back for a last look at you, golden girl. I greatly regretted not obeying your instruction, as I could barely glimpse you through the crowd – it seemed that half the personnel of a US Army Air Corps squadron swarmed around 'our' table while my seat was yet warm. Lucky devils. I'm sure that your eyes sparkled as merrily for them as for me, and yet I nurse the fond hope that perhaps their light was a little less bright? Ah! How one clings to that little word – hope!

I arrived back at the officers' bar to find a typical Sunday lunch-time session in progress – the party lasted from 1.30 until somewhere around 7.30 that evening, as the Italian POW barmen were persuaded to keep open in exchange for cigarettes. Up until yesterday I was not renowned for 'heavy sessions', but my sorrows at leaving Cairo had to be drowned one way or another, and the water here is as filthy as it is in the desert. Come supper, some of us decided to go to the mess without changing from our shorts to our longs. Plenty of black looks for that – apparently such conduct may be overlooked when up the Blue, but not here at Ish. Dinner – not something that would tempt you away from the Continental and the P'tit Coin de France – just the regular flat bread and bully beef and veg stew, washed down with ample supplies of grapefruit juice and vermouth, a sickening combination, and literally so after ample quantities have been consumed and chased down with brandy.

Back to the bar, where one of the chaps was reading aloud from John Oxenham's book Desert Patrol – "For every man there openeth a High way and a Low, and every man decideth which Way his soul shall go." All utter nonsense. My apologies as much to you as to Oxenham if I misquote, but my thoughts are a little scattered, and my memory of recent hours a little cloudier than those of thirty-six and forty-eight hours past ... When we meet again – if we meet again – I shall bring you a copy of the book; its tales of perfect heroism, pure idealism, noble souls dicing with the deadly Hun's 'V-shutters' have had the mess in fits of laughter for a week or so. To Oxenham's mind, all pilots are instinctively 'death or glory, blood or sand types'. We poor *frightened souls, clutching our brandies and trying to soothe our inner trembling as well as our stomachs, find this a fit subject for scorn. We are united in feeling that the only book about an airman's life that isn't pure flannel is* Winged Victory *by V. M. Yeates. It changes hands at £5 a copy in the mess.*

Whilst I write with cynicism, I find myself in a strange paralysis of will, for although I am most assuredly not a 'death or glory' type, I confess that I had little taste for this training assignment. My heart tells me that if I'm to be here at all, I should be flying, and I should be with my crew and with the squadron, and not drumming my heels teaching the sprog types here, however great the need. We owe our best efforts not to some noble cause but to those who believe in us, and believe we can do the job that we have been asked to, and I find the frustration of being removed from them well nigh intolerable. Yet I wrote to you of paralysis of will – yes, because since meeting you, my thoughts have switched from returning to the squadron to how the devil I can prolong my tour here and manage to get another two days in Cairo, for the sake of seeing you again, however briefly. The realization that the latter is the stronger and more persistent thought fills me with shame and delight.

Dear lady, you do not yet know me well enough to know that I am not a sentimental type, that these feelings surprise me as much as they probably surprise you. But for all their unmanly emotion, and whether they are justified or not, feelings they are, and genuine ones to boot. How can I feel so strongly about someone whom I have known so briefly – an evening's talk, a morning's walk, a luncheon, a swim, a felucca ride before dinner, and then adieu? Can I believe in love at first sight? Hell, no – and yes. I have already warned you that I am not a 'gen' man when it comes to matters of the heart. I mentioned a sweet girl, the sister of my good friend Peter, whom I took out a few times at Oxford, and I omitted to mention Jeannie the barmaid at the Golden Cross in the Cornmarket, for whom I also felt a degree of attraction, but these vague and faint recollections of boyish passion offer me no assistance now. I have no experience to hand, and my head has filled with scraps of verse – all useless. I can only hold onto my heart with both hands to still its dreadful beating – does the drumming of it disturb you in Zamalek? I will hold it still until you can send me word that you would allow me escort you to dinner once again. When I know that, neither heaven nor hell will stop me getting a twenty-four or forty-eight hour pass. And if your answer is no, that there are too many Tommys and Johnnies and Hanks and the like with better claims to your time than mine then, for pity's sake, dear lady, send word saying so, that I may release my heart and get the dratted drumming out of my own ears.

You told me so little about yourself, and yet the thought and sight of you won't leave my mind. I will never see a woman without thinking that she should wear flowers in her hair, and I'll never see one doing so without thinking how ill it becomes her. Nothing can dislodge the portrait of you that hangs in my mind – your golden hair, your bewitching eyes, your smile, breaking through even when you were trying your hardest to be grave. There are seconds when the image is dispersed, but only by a mosquito. If you are curious about the marks on this paper, X marks the spot where yet another has pranged. How's that for romance? That my only distraction from thoughts of you are the mosquitoes, who are conducting a large-scale war all of their own. I prefer Jerry any day. I am applying our own air-defence systems to the wretched things – as 'top cover' I sit here, on the edge of my bed, with my pyjamas buttoned to the throat, a towel over my head, my trousers tucked into my jack-boots, a handkerchief around my neck, silk flying gloves on my hands, a blanket over my knees, and still the blighters keep getting me. One good reason for returning up the blue, where the mossies are less bothersome.

I tell you this with two hopes (that frightening word again!). The first, that this ludicrous image of me (so far from the borrowed glamour and glory of the dress blues) might provoke one of your delicious bursts of laughter, and the second a poor attempt to distinguish this letter from the piles of those epistles of lovelorn suitors fortunate enough to have spent an hour or two in your company. What in heaven's name do you do with them all? If I didn't know that your Uncle Sam offers creature comforts that make every other legation sweat with envy, I would get some small consolation from the notion that this offering might join the others in the noble act of keeping your fires burning on a cold winter evening, and thus be willingly sacrificed for the truly worthy cause of keeping a golden girl warm . . .

There is a third reason for recounting my battle with the mossie, and as I have said I will always be honest with you, and I fear that this letter may just be my one and only opportunity to prove that, I will make my second confession: I am writing everything that comes into my head in order to avoid signing off. If selecting an opening form of address was dicey, then settling on an appropriate closing is even more hazardous. Common sense (of which I feel little tonight, and every moment since I met you at the Kit Kat) tells me that I must close if I am even to hope (! again!) for a reply.

Therefore, dear golden girl, this comes with my warmest greetings, and my fondest thoughts, and my wildest hopes,

Yours, if you'll have him,

Theodore

She replied with a signal that she would dine with
him whenever he was able to get a pass to Cairo.
Theodore cabled back, and set a rendezvous three
weeks later. During those weeks, he lived for 6
February. She, in turn, tried not to think of the
appointment until she arrived as arranged at the
hotel. The bar of the Metropole was jam packed,
as it was every night. She sat at a small table for
two, watching the door expectantly. His signal
had said that he would meet her there at seven,
and it was after seven thirty. The seat next to her
was not unoccupied for long, as men of all
nationalities laid claim to it. Some were known
to her and others strangers, but she met an
approach from either with the same good-natured
reply: a pretty smile, a pleasant word or two, and
a shake of her head, leaving the impression of
polite regret. One well-oiled compatriot was
particularly persistent, and after five minutes of
relentless patter, the young blonde woman
allowed him to buy her a drink. He lit her cigarette, taking the opportunity to lean across the
table until his face was inches from her own. The
American began to tell her the story of his life,
and she, expert listener that she had become,
inclined her head attentively and did not see the
arrival of the tall English pilot until he stood
immediately behind the American boy. Her eyes
drifted up to meet his blue gaze.

"Excuse me, old chap, I believe you're in my
seat." Theodore Hamilton spoke as if he were

taking his seat at Covent Garden, but his eyes were fixed unblinkingly on the young woman's.

"Now, listen to me, bud. House rules – first come, first served. Besides, the lady invited me to join her, and heck, she's a Yank, all the way from Washington District of Columbia. She's my . . . sister, dammit, so butt out, Tommy."

The pilot raised his eyebrows momentarily, and glanced briefly at his rival for the first time, before returning his gaze to her. "In that case, please accept my apologies. Would you be gracious enough to introduce me to your . . . sister?" Her eyes sparkled in reply.

"Why, sure," the American soldier replied good-humouredly, and leant back across the table. "What did you say your name was, honey? I forget."

The Englishman politely but firmly pulled his chair away from the table, and jerked his head towards the door as he tapped the stripes on his shoulder.

"Goddamn Brits, always pulling rank . . . Don't mean nothing to me," the American grumbled, but rose to his feet obligingly, if a trifle unsteadily. He kissed the woman's hand, and saluted Theodore. "If I hadn't had one beer too many, an' if I weren't posted out of here tomorrow, I'd give you a run for your money, big guy."

"I don't doubt it."

"All yours, Tommy, but don't go leaving American girls in bars again, or you don't

deserve 'em. You take care of her, ya hear me?"
He slapped Theodore on the back.

"I certainly intend to, Captain." Theodore
took his place at the table, and pulled his chair in
close to his companion's. She gazed at him
intently. He did not touch her, but spoke in a
quiet voice close to her ear to combat the hubbub
around them. "If I didn't know you were a lady,
I might accuse you of hanging around bars
picking up strange men."

"And if I didn't know you were a gentleman,
I might accuse you of discourtesy to a lady. I've
been here for forty-five minutes. I was beginning
to get strange looks, let alone strange men, so in
my book he had a legitimate point."

"He simply had an excuse. I'm sorry I was
late. I nearly couldn't get away at all. Good thing
that I have some legal training – I had to fight my
case very hard to have leave for the second time
in a month. I argued compassionate grounds. Put
up an impressive self defence and escaped without
a conviction."

She smiled slowly. "I didn't know you were a
lawyer."

"You don't know much about me at all, do
you, golden girl? Perhaps it's best to leave it that
way."

"Oh, I don't know about that. If I were you,
I would say every impressive thing that comes
into your head to try to correct the image I have
of you."

"And what's that?"

She narrowed her eyes, as if trying to see something on the horizon. "Well, 'big guy', if I look hard enough I can just about see a guy in his pyjamas, buttoned right up to the throat like a good little boy, with a blanket over his head, and gloves on his hands . . ."

"How brutal. I, poor innocent, bared my soul to you, and you can only mock. Did my letter make you laugh at least?"

"It kept me warm," she replied simply.

"Then I will write every day. Twice a day. Would you permit me?"

She nodded slowly, and Theodore felt heat rise to his cheeks. He longed to know what she thought of the tentative sentiments, expressed so nervously in his letter, but he feared asking anything that might break the mood. Had he been able to stand, he would almost have willingly turned his back on her and walked away from her for good, if in return he could have fixed in amber the soft look her eyes held at that moment. He touched her hair, tucked behind her ear, with a hesitant finger, and cleared his throat to speak. Again she shook her head, and raised her hand to halt him, knowing exactly what he was going to say.

"No, Theodore. Remember? We agreed that we'd just let things be, we wouldn't anticipate the future, we'd just be happy with what we have. And if things work out, then well and good, and we'll have all the time in the world to talk."

"And if they don't?"

"Then no regrets, and no tears. Promise me?"

"Anything," Theodore replied, with the full and certain knowledge that if things didn't work out, this was a promise that would go for a burton.

"I'll keep you to that. I like a man of his word."

"I give you my word."

Her eyes sparkled, and she tapped him playfully on the cheek. "Now. Hit me with the facts, Lieutenant. How much time have we got left?"

He shook his head sadly. "You don't want me to break it to you gently?"

"No, I'm woman enough to take it. Don't spare me the details." She closed her eyes, and pursed her lips, as if steeling herself for a blow. Theodore couldn't help himself. He leant across and kissed her mouth, and as he did, her eyes opened wide on to his.

"Two days."

"Two whole days? How did you do it? What on earth did you tell your CO?"

Theodore sat back and slowly took two cigarettes out of a silver case, passing one to her. "It wasn't easy." He sighed. "I've always been fond of the old man, but he left me no choice. I'm afraid I had to shoot him. It was over very quickly. Straight between the eyeballs. Painless. It was for a good cause. You have my assurance that he didn't suffer needlessly." As he lit her cigarette, *her hand cupped his, pulling it towards her, and the small flame lit her face for a instant.*

"That's what you call compassionate, Lieutenant?"

"It was him or me. His life or . . . my life." He looked at her with yearning. "To tell the truth, this is compassionate leave. I told him that my fiancée had come to Cairo to ditch me."

Her eyes opened wide with genuine horror, and then narrowed. "And what'll you tell him if you ever really need to use that excuse?"

"Oh, that'll be easy. That time I'll blow my own brains out."

When she frowned, he regretted his flippancy and touched her cheek. "You wouldn't believe how many fiancées have ditched how many airmen in the past few months. They almost always get jilted when they're stationed within an easy drive of Cairo. Strange, that. Perhaps it's the promise of consolation."

"You mean the brothels?"

Theodore was surprised that she said this. She was an inseparable mixture of worldliness and innocence, and he didn't know which aroused him more forcefully. He admired her lack of coyness even as it embarrassed him. "So I imagine."

"I spent this morning typing a report about brothels, that's why I asked. The Allied forces aren't quite in accord about whether they should operate Army-sanctioned brothels on health

grounds, or keep well out of it on moral grounds."

"What do you think?"

She studied the red tip of her cigarette, deep in thought. "From what I've read, I'm in favour of Army-approved . . . services. I don't see why the boys should risk gonorrhoea, and I don't see why their folks back home should ever have to know about it. Not that my opinion was asked. I was typing it up for my boss, Mac, and he went all shy about my even reading it. He'd spelt gonorrhoea wrong, too. I had to correct it." She put out her cigarette. "Which reminds me. Mac's having a party tonight. Asked if we'd drop in."

Theodore's heart sank. The last thing he wanted to do was share her with anyone, least of all with a bunch of Yank diplomats. She helped herself to a cigarette from his case, and he fumbled with his lighter. "I told him no. I said we were booked tonight, but we might meet up with him tomorrow evening if you weren't otherwise engaged."

"You are an angel," he murmured. "A golden angel."

"You're the one with the wings, Theodore. Do you want to go dancing?"

As they left the bar, one of his hands cupped protectively under her elbow, several pairs of eyes, both male and female, gazed after them enviously, although none of the spectators would have been able to put their finger on exactly what it was about the couple that they so envied.

CHAPTER SEVEN

F ive days later David and I landed at
Toulouse airport, hired a car, and drove to
the village of Sainte Cécile. It was a charming place. Throughout the flight from London I had
envisaged a British-infested, Dordogne-cum-Henley-
on-Thames village, but I was mistaken. Sainte Cécile
was idyllic in its ordinariness – a small village on a
hill, with an unremarkable market square and oblig-
atory bar, a nondescript church, the little hotel-
restaurant and not much else. David pulled up in
front of the Auberge Lion d'Or and carried our bags
into the foyer. A small dark-haired woman with the
black eyes of a bird looked up from the desk, and
bustled out, skirts swinging, to greet us and show us
to our room.

I flung myself on the small double bed. "Heaven
and *bliss*. Why can't I be Mademoiselle, David?"

He had introduced me as Madame Turcan and
kicked me in the shin when I had objected. "We

don't know how these people feel. You're beginning to look pregnant, they're sure to be Catholic, most of all I don't want to end up with two single beds rather than a *lit matrimonial*."

"Fair enough." David was used to making snap decisions, and his instincts were pretty good. I closed my eyes as the faint scent of lavender wafted from the bed linen. "David, have I ever told you what a star you are?"

"Not that I recollect."

"Well, you are. It's perfect here. I can't tell you how glad I am that we came."

"You didn't give that impression when I suggested it."

"Well, I was wrong, and I'm sorry." I began to hum, 'You've got to ac-cent-tchu-ate the positive', promising myself that this time I was just going to trust in everything working out, and make the most of our time together, however short. The mattress sagged under David's weight as he lay down next to me, and I felt a series of soft kisses on my eyelids, and purred with contentment. Since I had become pregnant David's manner towards me had changed. With mild suspicion, I revelled in his new gentleness and solicitude. Various people had warned me that it was dismaying how quickly the conception of a baby changed a woman's view of the world, and the world's view of the woman; from my experience with Becca, I had assumed this was for the bad. But right then, I felt the whole world was a bright new thing, and that it belonged to me. When we heard a discreet tap at the door, both David and I shot up off the bed as if we'd been caught *in flagrante*. A young girl, the spitting image of her mother, sidled nervously into the room carrying a tray laden with a bottle of champagne, glasses, water and a pot of tea with lemon.

"Est-ce que j'oublie quelque-chose?" she asked me in a shy voice, unable to look at David.

"Non – c'est tout à fait parfait, mais ça suffit." Lovely how my O level French floods back to me in times of need. I flung my arms around David. "All this, and champagne too!"

"You get the tea, sweetheart. The booze is for me."

David and I spent an hour or so in bed, making love while chatting idly about baby names. We had narrowed the choice dramatically – down to fifty. After a shower, we strolled to the bar in the main square, and sat at a little iron table near the fountain to while away the time before dinner. I was as sleepy and smug as an old cat in front of the fire, with David holding my hand loosely in his, and in the most companionable of silences. It made me jump when a man appeared at David's shoulder, inclined his head, and spoke to us in perfect English.

"Excuse me, forgive the intrusion. I couldn't help but wonder if you are the writer and photographer of the RAF book – Elena and David? Is that possible?" We both nodded, gazing up into the steel blue eyes of an immensely tall, grey-haired man in a Panama. "I'm Theodore Hamilton. We're scheduled to meet tomorrow, but I happened to see you, and as it's still early in the season for tourists, I took a chance."

David stood up and pumped his hand. "Good to meet you. We've just arrived, and checked in at the hotel you recommended." They were almost exactly the same height, except that the pilot had a slight stoop. David was a lot chunkier.

Theodore Hamilton smiled warmly at David, still holding his hand. "Not so very selective a recommendation, I'm afraid. The Lion d'Or is the only place to put up in Sainte Cécile, but the Guillots are a good couple, warm and welcoming, and he's a tolerable chef. You should have told me you'd be arriving tonight. I would have entertained you myself."

I stood up, and held out my hand across the table, sweeping my hair – which I wished I'd brushed – off my face. "Hello, I'm Elena Stewart."

The old man turned his head to look at me, and the smile melted on his face, but reappeared as· he took my hand in his. His touch was cool. "I'm so sorry." His eyes travelled down me and back up to my face, but it was a strange examination: there was nothing of the leer in it, just a careful look. I wondered if he could have spotted my pregnancy beneath my loosely tied dress. A man of his generation might not approve of working women, and even less of pregnant working ones. The word 'bastard' flashed through my mind, but as my smile tightened, his relaxed. He was a handsome old man, with a craggy, sun-tanned face and broad shoulders, dressed in a classically haphazard English expat style – cream trousers, a striped shirt that might as well have had a Jermyn Street label on the outside, sleeves rolled up, a handkerchief in his breast pocket, and a cream linen jacket hooked over a finger. And, of course, the Panama. I would have put money on it being from Lock's. As he smiled at me, a thousand creases fanned out from the corners of his eyes and across the top of his cheekbones. He was going to make David a lovely model.

"Won't you join us?" I asked. "We were just talking about the book." I was wincing that he had caught us unawares. He'd never take the book seriously if he thought David and I were 'involved' and I was determined to do my best to knock that idea straight on the head before we began the interview proper. I took a deep breath and let rip. "I was just explaining to David Turcan the objectives of this particular interview. The North African front is one of the theatres that gets so little space in accounts of the war, and has a special character of its own. That is one of the reasons why we chose you – apart, of course, from your impressive war record." I cleared my throat and met David's eyes.

He was leaning far back in his chair, arms folded across his chest, and looked as if he were enjoying himself. "*Do* go on, Ms Stewart. I'm gripped," he prompted, earnestly.

"Why don't I order drinks first, and we can get acquainted a little before we talk shop"' Theodore

Hamilton said mildly, making me feel clumsy. He signalled to the waiter, who came at once and took his order. "I'm more than happy to help you in any way that I can, and flattered that you've come so far to see me, yet I can't but feel that far too much has already been written about that war. There's no new material to uncover, or wisdom to be found."

We did not talk about the war. Wing Commander Hamilton talked at length about the region, and suggested various trips we should make if our schedule allowed it – the *bastides*, or walled towns of Monflanquin and Monpazier in particular. He spoke about Monségur, and Simon de Montfort, and the Crusades, and volunteered to act as our tour guide if we could spare the time for a sortie. He gave us names of nearby restaurants to patronize, and some to avoid, and after an hour or so, stood up and bade us a gracious farewell.

"Wing Commander Hamilton?" I asked.

"Theodore, please. I haven't been a wing commander for a very long time."

"How are we to find your house?"

"Ask anyone, they all know it. It's officially called Le Bosc, but the people here will insist on calling it the House of the Englishman, however much I protest that I should have attained honorary French citizenship by now. Have a pleasant evening, and come over to us in the morning."

"What time would suit you? We don't want to disturb you."

He laughed, a deep, warm laugh, and said, "I have

long been in the habit of rising with the lark. Old men don't need sleep. Come when you like. If you have no response from the house, I will be in the *pigeonnier*. I'm painting at the moment. Don't hesitate to disturb me."

As he walked away from the bar, we watched him greet people, a wave of an arm, a solicitous incline of his head to this or that woman, a pat on the head for a small child. When we tried to pay the bill, we were firmly told that Monsieur 'Amilton had already taken care of it. David and I returned to the hotel, two streets away, had a delicious dinner and collapsed into bed.

As I was on the edge of sleep, David said, "You know what? That's what I hope my father would have been like. That's the kind of man I wish he'd been."

When morning came, I felt a surge of well-being, and not the faintest touch of nausea, which I put down to having had three or four glasses of wine the night before. I had expected David to come with me to Theodore Hamilton's, but he declined. He had time to do a separate shoot, and no worries about getting acquainted with the pilot. I set off on foot to find Theodore's house. It was on the outskirts of the village, but less than two miles from the hotel, and as soon as I turned the bend, it was obvious which house belonged to an Englishman. It was the only one along a stretch of road that showed the hand of a dedicated gardener – roses climbing up the front of the house, honeysuckle on the point of bud, spring bulbs fading in beds and urns around the steps to the raised terrace.

The front door was open. I was expecting a formidable housekeeper, grey hair twisted into a tight bun, a large bosom and a stark black dress with a white frilled apron round her waist, but when I called out, "Hello?" and banged on the door, a pretty young blonde in cut-off jeans came out of a room, and greeted me in broken English. "You are Elena, no? For the book? Theodore tells me to say he's in the *pigeonnier*. *C'est là-bas* – down there," and she pointed across an orchard of plum trees. The *pigeonnier* was a tiny two-storey, stone building, which looked ideal for a holiday rental. I presumed that was why he was painting it.

"Theodore?" I poked my head inside. "It's Elena Stewart." He was standing in front of an easel. The whole rear wall of the building had been removed and replaced with glass, so that the sunlight flooded into the studio. He wiped his brush on his shirt, and came towards me, running his hand through his hair before checking to see if there was paint still on it. When we stepped outside, I saw flecks of blue and yellow in his nearly white hair.

"Welcome! Was the hotel all right? How was your dinner?" As we walked towards the house, he cupped his hand under my elbow, exactly the way my father does.

"Delicious. It's a lovely place."

"I'm glad you like it. They're a grand couple –

good friends of mine. Now, shall we sit on the terrace, or will that be too hot for you? Would you prefer to be inside?"

"The terrace would be lovely. I haven't seen the sun this year."

"That's one of the benefits of an expat life. Giselle, *citron pressé, s'il te plaît.*"

"Is that your daughter?"

Theodore laughed. I was to grow accustomed to his frequent laughter. "No, Giselle's my housekeeper, and a fine one. She gives me no end of trouble. I do have a daughter, but she in Paris. She's around your age, perhaps a little older."

We settled on a terrace covered with vines, which provided dappled shelter from the sun.

"You don't mind a tape recorder?" I asked automatically, my hand already deep in my bag.

"Yes, I'm afraid that I do, rather. Perhaps when I know you better it won't bother me, but I don't like those machines. I would prefer to talk without one."

"Fine. It's entirely up to you. I won't take up your whole morning – I'm sure you'll be keen to get back to your painting. It looked awfully good."

Theodore was looking at me carefully, and he said, "Hmm? I'm sorry . . . Do carry on." His blue eyes had an intense gaze that unnerved me a little.

"I'd like to start by asking how you come to be in France," I began. "I've interviewed forty or more ex-RAF types, all retired in England, so I'm curious what brings you here. Were you stationed here?"

"No, my squadron –"

"The 37th," I interjected, just to show him I'd done my homework.

"That's right," he continued evenly. "The 37th was never posted to France." OK, so I hadn't done my homework all *that* thoroughly but it wasn't as if David had given me much time. "We were in Italy from Christmas 1943 until the end of the war, briefly in Palestine and back to Shallufa before the squadron was disbanded."

"Shallufa?"

"Egypt. The 37th was essentially a DAF – desert air force – squadron: Egypt, Libya, Tunisia, then Italy. We considered the desert home."

"So how did you come to France?"

"My wife's family come from this area. We decided to move here when I retired."

"Will I get the chance to meet her?" I asked. So often the wives revealed more than the men themselves. "I'd love to talk to her, too."

"I'm afraid that isn't possible. My wife died ten years ago."

"I'm so sorry. How sad."

"It was, but ten years is a long time. One comes to terms with death. There is no other option."

"I suppose not. You decided to stay here?"

"Yes. Sainte Cécile had become home. Few of my English family and friends survive, and those who do welcome the opportunity to visit me here."

"I bet they do. Have you kept in touch with many of your old squadron cronies?"

"Oh, a few here and there. You realize, squadrons are fluid things. Chaps are transferred in and out and, of course, many didn't survive the war." He spoke matter-of-factly, which disappointed me. I would have liked a good emotional quote about the loss of brothers-in-arms. He was going to be a harder nut to crack than Babington so I dropped any idea of the neat biog. I might get one or two experiences out of him. I cleared my throat, and sat with pencil poised. "Perhaps you could tell me about getting your DSO and DFC?"

"If you insist." He laughed again. "Not a tale that brings great honour on my head, believe me. I received both of them for being a bloody fool."

"Would you tell me how?"

"Do I have a choice?"

"Sure, so long as you don't mind seeing a grown woman weep."

"That I could not stand. When I was a junior officer, a newcomer to the desert, we received intelligence that ten Heinkels, big German planes, y'know, would be landing at Benini aerodrome, just west of Benghazi, transporting fuel. Rommel was in retreat, and short of petrol. We had the good luck to find six of the Heinkels already on the runway, and the rest queuing to land. We bombed in five sticks, started a couple of fires, and I went in low to give Bob, my gunner, a go at the aircraft on the deck. He loved having a crack at things. It was rare on those operations to have such visible results. The next night we went back – I was with a new crew that night, my own boys were off duty – and although the weather was bloody, we again managed to shoot up the target. I got the DFC for those two ops."

"It sounds pretty good to me. Where does the bloody fool come into it?"

"I should have been flogged for risking the kite and crew. It was a damned stupid way to treat a Wimp, going in below five hundred feet and pretending to be a fighter. RAF reasoning was always a bit dicey – one day you'd be grounded for low-level flying, and the next you'd be festooned with ribbons for the same prank. There was no justice in it, really. If anything, the whole crew should have been recognized. I scared the daylights out of the new boys, and we were lucky to run into only light flak – the Germans were ill prepared that night. My ground crew gave me a bollocking when we got the plane back, just to teach me a lesson. If anyone deserved the DFC, it was the intelligence boys."

"How common was the DFC?"

"I'm not honestly sure. Far more common than the equivalent awarded to non-officers. You mustn't think that there was anything unusual in what I did. I simply manned the controls. The gunners were the talented chaps. I was relieved simply to hit the target – we rarely had that satisfaction bombing at night."

I hadn't seen enough of him to decide how sincere his modesty was. For all I know he might have been genuinely heroic and genuinely modest. On the other hand, perhaps he was telling the truth and he'd just been a show-off. I doodled a question mark beside my notes. "And the DSO?"

"Ah. There are two versions to that story too. Which one would you like to hear?"

"Both. Then I can make my own mind up."

"Sensible girl. The official version is that we were flying night ops from the base at Kairouan. This must have been – oh, towards the end of '43 . The North African campaign was long over, and the bombardment of Italy had begun. D'you know Tunisia at all?"

"I'm afraid not."

"The locals called Kairouan the Holy City, probably still do. The word is actually a corruption of caravan. It was a dreadful place then, surrounded by stinking water pools – we called it the Holy Smell. It was a bloody period in the memory of most men stationed there. Our Wimpeys were used intensively against ports, airfields, communication centres from Palermo and right up through the Italian mainland. We had few stand downs –"

"What do you mean?"

"Oh, times when we couldn't fly for one reason or another. It might be tactical, or weather-related, or simply that the war came to a lull. Wars aren't constant, you know – there are great bursts of activity, and then stretches of tedium."

"But you had no stand downs in Kairouan?"

"Few. We were as mean as mad dogs by the time winter came. One night, we were badly hit returning over the coast. The starboard engine bought it, and although we jettisoned all we could, I realized that I couldn't make it home and couldn't land safely – the country was broken up by a mass of wadis. I ordered the crew to bale out, and discovered that my front gunner had been hit by shrapnel. He wasn't too bad, but he wasn't too good either. The navigator gave him a shot of morphine and patched him up as well as he could, but there's not a lot you can do in the air, not when the deck's coming at you that fast. I saw the others off, and helped Sam out through the lower hatch. We can't have been more than eight hundred feet above ground. I landed all right – luck of the devil, nothing more than a sprained wrist – and saw Sam not far away. As I made my way towards him, the kite went up in flames a couple of miles off. That was the end of T for Tommy – one of them. We kicked our heels for a while to see if the rest of the crew would turn up, had a smoke, you know, but when they didn't, we set off and made it back to base by the evening of the next day. That's when they gave me the DSO."

"And the other version?"

"The true one. I cursed myself for a bloody idiot when we got hit. I knew the fighter was on us – if I'd had my wits about me, we wouldn't have been hit badly. Even so, I should have been able to get the plane home, or to better ground. Planes were precious – in some ways, more so than their crews. One could say I was awarded the DSO for ditching my kite and falling out of it."

"Was Sam hurt?"

"His shoulder was a mess and he'd lost a lot of

blood. That didn't help his landing technique. He didn't thank me for making him bale out."

"How did he make it back to the base?"

"We found water supplies at the kite, so I could wash him a bit and give him a drink. I left my kit, all but my revolver, with the wreckage and hauled Sam on my back. That was my only significant achievement. He fought me like the blazes, and I nearly dislocated his remaining shoulder doing it. My guardian angel was working overtime that night."

"Sounds like Sam's was, too. Was he OK?"

"For a while. His angel saved his life that night but went off duty nine months later. I did him no great service. He should have been invalided out, but he volunteered for another tour. The blessing was that the rest of the crew made it back, and all in one piece. We were all members of the Late Arrivals Club, and wore the badge on our flying suits – a winged silver boot. The club motto was 'It's never too late to come back.' Again, I was the only one to get the DSO, which was damned stupid. I did nothing the others hadn't done. After that, I realized that the best service I could do my crew was perfect my jinking."

"What's that?"

"Evasive flying, a type of corkscrewing manoeuvre to avoid enemy fighters or ground gunners setting their sights on you. That was my only skill – I became so good at it that my navigator regularly threw up. He had a infamously fragile stomach, however, so I won't take credit even for that."

I scribbled out the question mark I had drawn a few pages earlier.

"I have the distinct impression that you don't take credit for anything."

"Do you?"

"Yes. You're apologizing for every distinction you've won, and it's quite obvious that you deserved them."

"I meant, do *you* take credit for your achievements?"

I laughed. "Oh, Lord, I don't have any achievements! It's not as if I spent five years risking my neck night and day for the cause of freedom!"

"Is that how people have described the war?"

I looked at him for a moment before replying. I understood this to be a question that mattered to him, and answered carefully. "No, to be honest, no one that I've talked to has said that. I suppose it's just an impression I've had from watching old movies."

"I'm glad to hear it. Freedom is not all it's cracked up to be. People had many different reasons for their conduct in that war, and you should remember that for many of them it wasn't entirely voluntary."

"But it was in your case?"

"I volunteered for the RAF at the outbreak of war. I had already done about eighty hours flying in the university air squadron so I didn't have to do elementary training, and that speeded up the process. I didn't make any choices after that. They were made for me. I certainly didn't set out to defend freedom. I was motivated by the spirit of adventure, and the fear of boredom engendered by studying law."

"You're a lawyer?"

"Retired. Excuse me for a moment."

I looked over my shoulder and saw Giselle signalling him from the kitchen door. I watched him loping towards her. After a moment's discussion he came back. "Shall we break for a spot of lunch? Giselle gives me the devil of a time if I eat late – she says it throws all her plans out and that it's bad for my health not to keep to a strict schedule. I've always been at the mercy of the women in my life – my wife, my daughter, now Giselle."

Giselle laid a small stone table for two at one end of the terrace and set a tomato tart, dripping with pale green olive oil and fresh basil, before us. I was ravenous.

"Tell me your best and worse memories of the Desert War?" I prompted, wiping oil off my chin, and resolutely pushing away the glass of wine that Theodore had poured.

"Not until you answer my question, I won't."

"I'm sorry?"

"I asked you if you ever took credit for your achievements, and as I recall, you jinked rather athletically."

I laughed. "I wasn't being evasive. I simply don't have any achievements."

"Nonsense, everyone has achievements, and failures. You're writing a book, you seem very accomplished. You must have family – a husband, children perhaps?"

"No, neither. And most of the stuff I write is reporting other people's words anyway."

"You're too modest. Perhaps you pride yourself on your modesty?"

He was teasing me, and although I rather liked it, I was busting to say what I really felt. Ever since starting the project, I'd been increasingly envious of his generation. My friends and I had no means of testing our honour and value codes the way they had, and the more I listened to their tales, the greater my frustration. It all came pouring out in a flood. The poor old man must have been stunned.

"Believe me, I'm perfectly vain when I have reason to be. I simply don't think that people of my generation have anything to shout about. What do we do with our lives? If we're 'good', we pay our taxes and turn up at the polling station, but most of my friends can't be bothered to vote. The ones who get paid a lot vote Tory and defend it saying that real democracy relies on people voting selfishly. The ones who get paid badly vote Labour or LibDem, because it won't make any difference to them, anyway, and it lets them feel like revolutionaries. Sometimes we shove a cheque in the post to Save the Children. We very properly disapprove of racial and sexual discrimination. We get married, or we don't – it doesn't make much difference. We have children, and if we carry on working, then we agonize about whether the nanny loves them as much as we do – or, worse, whether they love her more than they love us. If we stay at home with the kids, we feel trapped, and hit the sherry bottle mid-afternoon. If we work, we hit the gin later. We fall in love worrying that it won't last. We don't fall in love, and feel we're missing out on the Big Thing in life."

"Men and women have always felt that –" Theodore interjected, but I didn't even let him finish. I was on a roll, if one can roll on a soapbox.

"It's not the same at all. We don't go to church except at Christmas and perhaps at Easter, yet bitch about the decline of Christian and family values and blame it on the telly. We worry about not doing anything worthwhile with our lives, and just carry on doing the same old, same old. We care *deeply* about Bosnia, but we don't know *quite* where it is. When yet another feature appears about famine in Africa, we find our eyes slipping to the TV schedule. A tube strike or the minor infidelities of a junior cabinet minister are the most important things to discuss in world events. Do you think that all of that is stuff to take credit for?"

"Are you telling me that *that* is what I risked my life for? For the protection and freedom of such an entirely degenerate generation?"

I giggled at Theodore's feigned outrage. "I'm sorry, but it's time someone had the guts to tell you the truth."

"How fascinating. Tell me, what else do your generation do with our hard-won peace and liberty?"

"We try not to smoke, and bemoan the fact that we've given up. We deeply disapprove of alcohol dependence."

"What utterly unsympathetic types you are. Is that why you're not drinking?"

I think I blushed. "No – not exactly. I don't disapprove of drinking."

"Then give yourself a pat on the back for that at least, and drink up!" He nudged my glass towards me.

"Uhh, I won't actually, thanks very much."

"Would you prefer red?" He stood up, waiting for my reply.

"No. Thanks, but I can't think straight if I drink at lunch-time. Don't let me stop you, though."

"You must accept one thing, Elena. If you and your generation have so little opportunity to do great and noble things then equally you are free of the temptation – or opportunity – to do bad and ignoble ones."

"Oh, far from it! We constantly do bad things. Just the other week a friend and I were in a bar and I paid the bill with a ten-quid note. The guy must have thought I'd given him a twenty – he gave me thirteen back."

"And you kept it?'

I raised my chin in the air. "I left him a three-quid tip. See what I mean?"

"Heinous," Theodore agreed, grinning at me.

I mopped up the oil on my plate with a bit of bread, and reflected, "OK, OK. So we don't have to deal with big stuff, bombing Dresden, or things like that. But maybe it would be better if we did. Have to live at the extreme. You know, have joy or pandemonium."

"Good Lord, where on earth did you pick that phrase up? It sounds oddly familiar."

"Just some old song my mother sings. Anyway, the point is, I'd like to live life on the front line, just for a bit, just to see if I could hack it, see if I passed the test. Find out if I was really a sheep or a goat."

"I'm afraid there's no doubt at all about that, young lady," he shook his head sadly, "not in that young waiter's mind. He may be on the streets as we speak . . ."

"You don't really think it was that great a sin, do you?"

I wanted his approval, and he gave it with a warm smile. "No, not that bad at all. At most, a minor misdemeanour. Not a court-martialling offence."

"You see, we can't even *sin* wholeheartedly. If I was in your shoes, at least I would know that my noble acts made up for my mean ones. I mean, if you've saved someone's life, then you're entitled to get away with murder."

"I can't agree with you there."

"I bet you never did anything awful anyway."

"We all have things we regret, memories that make us shrink with horror from our own reflection. If you insist on cynicism – and I would suggest that you are rather putting this on – apply it to all equally, of all generations. Challenges are all around us, if perhaps those emotions may have been . . . heightened during the war. It was said to me once that if you waltz with joy, misery is the next partner on your dance card."

It amused me that his view was so similar to my mother's; but they were products of an era. "My mother says something very like that."

"Does she, indeed? Well, I hope you listen to her." He smoothed his still thick hair absent-mindedly, then resumed his teasing. "Tell me, Elena, do you apply such harsh verdicts to all your friends?"

"Oh, God, no. David – David Turcan, the photographer, you met him last night – he leads quite a different life. He's going on to Bosnia in a few days. I wouldn't ever put David in the same camp as me."

"But you, at least, do know where Bosnia is?"

I shrugged noncommittally. "Vaguely."

"My dear girl, you are far too hard on yourself. We never made that mistake."

I had one sip of wine. I had to get back to the interview before I launched into another treatise on myself. "Will you now tell me your best and worst memories?"

"All right. They may surprise you. The desert. Worst memories almost certainly of insects. Mossies, scorpions, the flies probably the worst. I vividly remember one afternoon at Abu Sueir when I was ravenous – we were on short commons at the time. I was in my tent. I wrapped my coat around a tin of jam, scraped out the flies, spread a biscuit, keeping my hand over it, and tried to slip the biscuit from my coat to my mouth. The flies swarmed on to the biscuit and into my mouth, and flapped around inside . . . I still wake up fifty years later feeling those wings fluttering around my mouth, with that fearful buzzing inside my head. I remember Bob saying to me, 'Of all the bastard places in the world, this is the greatest bastard.'" Theodore smiled.

"Not such a bad memory, if you can still smile at it."

"I'm smiling remembering Bob, not the flies. Bob was perhaps one of my best memories – although there are many that jockey for that position."

"Would you tell me about them?"

"My dear, I would be delighted, if you have the time to spare." He had a wistful look, but it might have just been the milkiness of age.

"I have two or three weeks and no other plans, except to harass you as much as you'll let me."

Theodore rubbed his hands together. "Excellent news. In that case, would you excuse me for an hour or so? I have some business I must attend to. My son-in-law is buying a house nearby, and I volunteered to help with the arrangements. I will be back by six o'clock at the very latest."

"Of course. May I come back tomorrow? Or the day after?"

"No, no, you must stay and enjoy yourself. Be decadent, be guiltless for at least an afternoon! I intended to suggest that you and your photographer – David, isn't it? – join me tonight for drinks and dinner. I hope you will be less conscientious then, and have a glass of wine or two. I could leave a message for David and collect him on my way home, as I'll pass the hotel. In the meantime, you have a swim. There's a pool just past the *pigeonnier*."

It sounded tremendously tempting, but I hadn't presumed to pack a cossie in my handbag when I came to interview him. Theodore astutely anticipated my problem. "If you go into the *pigeonnier*, you'll find a vast assortment of bathing attire. I'm sure you'll find something to suit you, if not perhaps the latest Paris fashions. Please be my guest."

CHAPTER EIGHT

I didn't make it as far as the *pigeonnier*. I wandered down to the pool to whet my appetite enough to face trying on swimsuits. It was lovely – rather Roman, with a mosaic floor and terrace, and it struck me that Theodore must have been a pretty successful lawyer to afford a retirement home like this one. I stretched out on one of the loungers dotted around the flower-filled terrace, and closed my eyes for a minute, just to soak up the sun.

I heard water splashing, and sat up to see David pulling himself out of the pool. "Wake up, sleeping beauty, it's well after six, and you have a very pink face."

I had been asleep for over three hours. "Oh, my God! Where's Theodore?"

"He went inside to see his housekeeper about dinner and fix some drinks. Decent guy, isn't he?"

"He's lovely. I can't believe I've slept the whole

afternoon – I meant to have a swim."

"It's good for you. Have a swim now." David placed his hands on each side of my lounger and leant over, his body glistening, threateningly sexy.

"Oh, David, I can't. I can't swim in front of him – he'll see I'm pregnant."

"So what? Why, on God's green earth, do you have any reason to be ashamed of it?"

"I'm not. I just don't think it's very . . . professional, that's all."

"Unprofessionally pregnant." His teeth flashed at me, and water from his hair dripped onto my shoulders. "Unprofessionally prudish, more like. My, oh, my. You women don't make life easy for yourselves, do you? You're too damn complicated. Or just nuts. I'm going back in."

Theodore set down a tray of drinks and olives on the table next to me. "Hello, again. Did you get a swim?"

"I'm ashamed to say that I fell asleep as soon as I stretched out."

"But you had a pleasant afternoon, I hope?"

"The best. Did your appointment go all right?"

"My appointment?" He looked momentarily perplexed – the effect of age. "Ah, yes, the house. Perfectly straightforward, thank you. Now, what will you have to drink? Campari, gin, wine of any colour, a kir perhaps? I brought everything I own in the hope of tempting you."

I shaded my eyes and watched David swimming easy lengths, his long brown arms sweeping out of the water in the arc of a swallow's wing. "A kir would be fantastic." Bugger the bastard, I thought. If he's so keen for me not to be a prude and live dangerously, yet thinks he's the only one who's entitled to, then I'm damn well going to have as many goddamn kirs as Theodore is prepared to pour me. "A large one, please."

"That's more like it!" Theodore sat down beside me, and poured us each a kir.

"When you left, you promised to tell me about the best of times."

"And I promised myself to stop talking shop. Your chap swims very well, doesn't he?"

"My *chap*?"

"David – your photographer. I'm sorry, I assumed he worked for you."

I laughed at the very idea. "Would that he did! David doesn't work for anyone. He's a lone wolf. Freelance type. I am, too, come to think of it. We're doing this book together but David doesn't work for me – and don't let him catch you saying that. Or maybe it would be amusing if he did." We watched David's relentless path slicing through the water. "The best of times?" I prompted again. "Look, I promise I won't touch the machine – not even my pencil. I just want to listen, that's all. For me. Forget the book."

"What a nice thing to say to an old man." Theodore looked at me warmly. "The best of times? Playing beach cricket against some lads from 70 Squadron on the coast near Alamein. There were many good times. It's much easier to remember the amusing episodes than to recall the crumpf of flak ripping through the fuselage as we said our prayers." He topped up our glasses. "Some of my fondest memories are of the bomb fitters. They were lads with skill, and our lives depended on them. A good crew could bomb up a kite in under ten minutes. As soon as we'd land from a raid, they'd be out there loading up for the next one in case there was a scramble. I remember one night when we landed around two in the morning, and the ground crew pulled a prank on Bert Pearson. He was a cautious and methodical chap, good traits in a navigator, but one of the most superstitious I ever met."

"Were most airmen superstitious?"

"Certainly, even the most cynical. The gremlins had to be appeased. Some crews even took a ceremonial piss against the plane before take-off. Most of us were twitchy about our routines before the flight, we liked to repeat the same pattern for luck, and everyone had their own talisman. Bert, not to be outdone, had four. I recall a little wooden pig that he'd made at school when he was just a little lad, as well as a spotted handkerchief, and he never flew without his girlfriend's brassière in his breast pocket." Theodore chuckled.

"What was the fourth thing?"

"Oh, Betty! Betty Grable. Bert kept a pin-up of her over the navigator's table. He always took her with him, just in case the kite was blown up on the landing ground, and whenever we got a new plane,

Betty was the first to be introduced. Before take-off he'd kiss her, and on landing he'd kiss her again, dust her off with his spotted handkerchief and unpin her devoutly. It was a tender ritual. That was why he was always the last to leave the plane, which is the point of the story. That night, the fitters had stowed the bombs before Bert emerged, and they persuaded him that he'd had four hang-ups, and had brought his original load back. Bert came into the mess as white as a lily and trembling like a mongrel in a storm. He was convinced he'd got desert fever, gone bomb happy, swore he'd seen them go – counted them off himself, he said, and couldn't believe we'd landed with a full load. He shook me by the hand for a good five minutes in gratitude for a smooth landing, and said it had saved all our lives. The ground crew split their sides laughing; they called him 'Bombs Away Bertie' for the duration."

He paused as David pulled himself out of the pool, biceps taut, and shook his head like a dog. Theodore threw him a towel and gestured towards the drinks tray as he continued. David fixed himself a large gin and tonic, and stretched out on the terrace in the last of the evening sun. I wanted to lie right down beside him.

"The men on the ground were worth their weight in gold. Particularly our ground gunners. I saw one of them out here not long ago – a Scotsman called Gregor Robertson. He was an ACH/GD at Abu Sueir –"

ACDC? I thought. "What's that?"

"Aircrafthand General Duties, the lowest of the rank and file. Gregor volunteered as a ground gunner for an extra sixpence on top of the three shillings a day the RAF paid. He told me that it wasn't the sixpence that persuaded him. He'd taken a long hard look at his chances of promotion, which would peak at Sanitary Corporal. He didn't much fancy meeting the boys back in Oban and admitting that he knew more about shit than anyone else at the camp. We gave the sanitary chaps their own badge – which I will leave to your imagination – and motto, 'Semper in Excretum'."

Theodore roared. He had a wonderfully contagious laugh, a great bark that seemed to take him by surprise, and broadened out into a throaty chuckle. "Gregor came through here last summer with his grandson and looked me up. We chatted about the old days at Abu Sueir, and when the little lad asked his grandfather what he'd been in the war, Gregor winked at me and replied in that burr, 'Very frightened, lad, just very frightened.' We were all that, but the ground gunners had little chance of surviving an enemy air attack, stuck out there on the edge of the airfield, sitting ducks for any fighter pilot or air gunner trying to shut them up. Gregor told me that before the war he'd felt cursed for being such a little bloke; during it, the only thing that kept him alive was that he could get most of his body under the rim of a tin hat. That's a lot to put up with for three and six a day, don't you think?"

"Go on," I pleaded. "What was life like when you

weren't flying?"

"Rations were miserable. The best you could hope for as a forward squadron was bully beef and tack biscuits. With luck you might get fatty bacon, which dissolved into slop in the tins. No leave, no off duty, no bars, no pictures. The Yanks were greatly to be envied for all sorts of reasons, but not least their living conditions. Many an airman developed a taste for the American way of life."

"Did you?"

"I was very attached to Lucky Strike cigarettes for quite some time after the war."

"Were there many Americans flying in the desert at that time?"

Theodore lost interest. He busied himself topping up our glasses before replying in a tired tone, "I believe the USAAF squadrons began to arrive some time in the autumn of '42, but you'd need to check. I can't be of any assistance to you there."

"The book doesn't concern Americans, or only those attached to RAF squadrons."

"So I imagined. Now I insist that we stop talking about the old days – my tongue will run away with me, and I've bored you, not to mention myself, quite enough for one day." He took a long swallow of wine, and murmured, "Whither is fled the visionary gleam? Where is it now, the glory and the dream?'"

I snatched my pencil, having promised to leave it alone. "Where does that come from?"

"Wordsworth," David replied briefly.

"Why is it that you have selected the RAF for

this retrospective, Elena, rather than one of the other services?"

"Entirely off the record, I don't have a rational reason for picking the RAF. It's completely emotional as far as I'm concerned." I tried to recline the deck-chair, and nearly fell through it. "My knowledge of the war is from the movies. I've never liked all those scenes of men rushing around in the dark, in commando balaclavas, slitting Germans' throats from behind, or parachuting in and crawling along the ground on their bellies . . . It just doesn't 'speak' to me, if you know what I mean. You know, the guns, the bayonets, tanks blowing up – it seems awfully close to the action, and raw and bloody, and a little too . . . male." I saw David wince when I said this.

"What's wrong with the Navy?"

"Nothing at all, but I get seasick. And they always seemed to be in submarines, smoking pipes, with heavy white rollneck sweaters, and their caps set at a jaunty angle."

"Fair enough."

"But the RAF – oh, I've *always* wanted an Irvin jacket, and there's that glorious sense of off we go into the wide blue yonder, and the freedom of the skies, and the knights of the air, and the scramble for dispersal, and the bandit business."

He cocked an eyebrow.

"You know, 'Bandits at seven o'clock, on your tail, Twister! Rabbit to Red Section,' the whole shebang. It's just very exciting."

"You don't think you're romanticizing the situation, do you?" Theodore observed, gently.

"I certainly hope so. What on earth is wrong with romance? When did it ever do anyone any harm?"

"Now *that* is a serious question, which merits a considered reply."

Before dinner, Theodore said he'd have a dip in the pool to whet his appetite. I have to admit to feeling curious about viewing him in his trunks – just to see if he really looked his age. My father's age has always been a mysterious thing to me. When I was a little girl, or so he tells me, I used to describe him 'older as God'. I assume that I meant this as a compliment, a measure of his relative significance and authority in my life. When I hit my mid-teens, I began to describe him, and my mother, as 'old' or 'old as the hills', even 'incredibly old'. They were in their mid-fifties. Now I'm not sure about age. My parents seem to have stood still for at least ten years, and I'm the only one who shows the passing of time. I don't see it in Charlie, or David, or Becca, but I feel it daily. When I was in those early months of pregnancy, and thought about my baby, I couldn't escape the reciprocal thought of my impending doom. This time next year my child will be seven months old . . . When I take him, or her, to school, I will be thirty-six. By the time my little baby goes to secondary school, I will be over forty, and then it was an ever accelerating downhill slalom into old age and death.

My baby, in its impatience to reach the age limit

for the most thrilling rides at Thorpe Park, to be old enough for sleep-overs, old enough to travel on the tube alone, old enough to choose its own clothes, old enough to have a boyfriend or a girlfriend, old enough to drive, was to be my tailor-made miniature time bomb. I had no way of arresting my own dreaded decline without arresting his or her desirable progress. OK, so several billion people had faced it before me, but that didn't make it any easier to swallow. I wanted to hear my mother say those salving words, "It will be all right, it will always be all right, you'll *always* be beautiful, you'll always be happy, I'll always be here for you . . ." The only problem was that she wouldn't. How long could it be before it was my job to say those words, not to hear them? And if I was counting my remaining days, then how many did my mother have left? It didn't help matters that she was the last person I could discuss this with. For starters, she was entertaining fifty or so old Gold Coast hands that very night, and for another it didn't seem particularly tactful to moan to her about my own slow, inexorable path to the grave.

"What's making you so blue, sweetheart?"

David's voice startled me out of my daydream. "Decrepitude," I said morosely.

"I'd say he's doing pretty well."

"Not Theodore's. Mine. I'm jealous of Theodore. It must be wonderful to look back on your life from the security of it being nearly over. Theodore and my parents can talk about their past as something of good account and cast in stone."

"Elle. You're barely thirty-one."

"OK, I'm not exactly old, but I'm not young. It makes me want to puke. I'm in limbo."

"You're hormonal."

"I'm not joking, David. I mean it. I'm not going to be prime minister, or a prima ballerina, or a captain of industry, or the inventor of the new miracle drug. If I was twenty-eight I might just be able to, but not now. All those dreams. They're over."

"You never told me you hankered after Number Ten."

"I don't. Never have. But all the other stuff . . . What can I be now? Editor of *The Times*? Dream on. I don't have the ability, *if* that is a requirement, and I don't have a corporate track record. Likelihood of being invited to New York as editor of *Harper's Bazaar*, or *Vogue*, or *The New Yorker*? Zip. All I've got in front of me is a continuing shakey career as a freelancer, renting a stall in Portobello market selling antique bread-boards, or selling my flat and investing the proceeds in a small flower shop in Truro." And – oh, God – *motherhood*, which was sure to put the scuppers on whatever miserable aspirations I still clung to. If David said I could look forward to being a mother, I swore to myself I would kill him.

"Portobello would be OK, but Truro isn't a great commute for me."

"You never take me seriously, David. I mean it. What am I ever going to be? Except older . . ."

I have always believed that everyone has a predestined age that they hit and stick at for the rest of their lives. From there on in, right to the bitter end, they are emotionally and psychologically static. My mother stopped at about my age then, thirty, or thirty-one, some time around when she met my father. Everything she has done or felt since, she does as a thirty-year-old. My darling dad? I can't decide. I think of him as twenty-two, in the prime of youthful manhood, with bright eyes, a boyish grin and a pith helmet, and I see him as forty. Given that he was forty-three or -four when I first laid my myopic infant eyes on him, this is quite ludicrous. Most of the time, when I see that particular glint in his eyes and that grin on his face, he's twenty-two – it doesn't matter a jot that his teeth are no longer his own. It's only when he's had to sit me or Charlie down and talk about balancing our budgets that I think of him as a forty-year-old. Otherwise, he's 'younger than spring-time'. That would amuse him, if I had the nerve to tell him. My mother isn't spring-time: my mother is the full heat of summer, year in, year out.

Now, Theodore was a different kettle of fish. He struck me as a much older man, a man who hit his golden age as a respected lawyer: sixty-five. I bet when he was a young pilot he was always the guy in the mess calling a halt to the romps, reminding people of their duties and being responsible. I could just see it. Wise, rational Wing Commander Theodore Hamilton, DFC, DSO. Sixty at birth.

I looked across at David, still lying on his back on

the terrace, giving me that ambiguous grin. He was the really tricky one – dicey, as Theodore would say. I had no idea what his perfect age was – maybe fifty? Maybe a hundred and ten?

"How old do you feel, David?"

"How old do I *feel*? Ancient. You make me feel ancient."

"No. What's the age that you see when you think about yourself?"

"Nineteen."

"Nineteen?" I nearly fell off my deck-chair a second time.

"I see myself as nineteen, battling with acne scars and premature ejaculation."

"That's crap. I don't believe you've ever been nineteen."

"If you don't want the answer, don't ask the question. What about you, sweetheart? How old are you, really?"

Me? I couldn't think of my perfect age, because all my life I felt I'd been the wrong one – miserable at seventeen because I wasn't *quite* old enough, and wretched at eighteen because life had passed me by. I was counting, nervously, on a second blooming. It's not that you stop developing exactly, but the relationship between you and the rest of the world peaks at one point in your life and that becomes the frame of reference for everything else. That's why old age is so tragic: beneath the wrinkles and the arthritic joints, everything might be so young. Like my mother, and my daddy. People look at them and see 'old folks' and I look at them and I think I can see what they were. Or are.

"I think I'm a precocious six-year-old."

"Sounds about right to me."

That's why I watched Theodore when he reappeared in his swimming trunks. It wasn't that I *fancied* him, but he was a vibrant and powerful man, and a handsome one, in many ways, and I wanted to see what had happened to his body, much as a coroner might. It wasn't at all bad. He was so tall and long-limbed, and he still moved with an easy animal grace, rather like David. His skin hung slightly around his thighs, that loose sagging that I had seen in my own father's long legs, yet beneath the crêpy texture the bones, muscles and sinews showed elegant and taut. He swam well too, not as fiercely as David but with a steady, confident pace. Maybe he had less to prove. I noticed David watching me watching him.

"I think you've got sunstroke. You're sick, somehow," he said quietly.

"If you think I'm ogling him, you're the one that's sick. I find him fascinating, that's all. Or are you jealous?" David didn't reply. "God, David, you were, just for a minute, weren't you? *You felt jealous.*"

"So what?"

I leapt up and kissed him. "So fantastic, that's what. To tell you the truth, I was imagining what it would be like to be a war widow. I think I'd get a perverted kick out of standing bravely in my entrance hall, babe in arms, when the bloke came with the telegram saying that my husband had met a glorious death, shot down by some Macchi pilot over Sidi Barrani. I tell you I can see myself – I'd muster a brave smile and stroke my baby's silken head and thank the officer politely for bringing me the news . . ."

"You're getting obsessive. I told you before, darlin', you're sick." David wore an odd smile.

I wish I had never said this to him – I wish with all my heart that this was something I could erase, delete from the tape, but I did say it and, in a peculiar and mildly sick way, I meant it.

It was a balmy, clear night, with the full quota of stars, moon and a breeze that made the pool water lap gently against the edge. We didn't talk about much at dinner, certainly not about the war. As I remember, we talked about how the region had both suffered and benefited from English residents. Over cheese, David and Theodore started talking about photography, and I drifted into a dream that had something vaguely to do with me and David and the baby living in a house like that . . .

"Elena?" I started as Theodore addressed me. "Elena, are you unable to swim? I would be delighted to teach you while you're here."

"I swim perfectly," I said firmly. "Like a fish."

"Wouldn't you like to swim now? It's the best time of day – the water's at its warmest. I would like you to feel at home here, particularly if you will be here for a few weeks."

In the seconds that it took me to form an excuse, David leapt in. "She just thinks she's too fat," he drawled. "She's shy of anyone seeing her in a swim-suit."

"In that case, David, perhaps this would be an opportune time for me to show you the photographs I spoke of and my new camera." He pushed back his chair and rose to his feet. "We will leave you in soli-tude, my dear. My home is entirely at your disposal. If you prefer, you may even switch off the pool lights, although I cannot imagine you have anything to hide."

Nothing but a baby, no. He was so hospitable, and I was so tempted by the water that I agreed. To be honest, I could think of nothing better than a leisurely private paddle in a floodlit pool. When Theodore and David had gone inside, I ambled down to the *pigeonnier*, and switched on the light. Four or five paintings were stacked around the main room, as well as the work in progress on the easel. They were surprisingly vigorous: I had expected bucolic scenes in pale watercolours, but these were almost violent, full of passion. The little building was composed of the studio, with three doors leading off it. I opened one hesitantly, looking for the shower and feeling like Goldilocks. The first door was a walk-in cupboard, full of canvases and paints, and on the bottom shelf, as Theodore had promised, a huge variety of swimming costumes. Some were so dated as to be trendy, with polka-dot skimpy skirts and ribbed bustiers. I imagined that these had belonged to his wife. Some were teeny bikinis that I hoped belonged to his daughter, or perhaps to Giselle. I didn't like the idea of Theodore having floozies. I stripped off and put on a shapeless black thing that was good enough to swim in, and wandered back to the pool.

I swam slow lengths revelling in the warm water and the night air and the skies above me and the rose garden around, lit by the discreet lights that encircled the pool. When I feared that I'd trapped my host inside for long enough, I climbed out and headed back to the *pigeonnier*. On my first investigation, I hadn't found a bathroom and so opened the second door, which led into a little windowless room. I stepped in and felt for a light. On the shelves opposite the door was a series of photographs. As soon as I entered the room my eyes fell on a framed but tattered photograph propped up on the floor, and shadowed by the shelf above. It was of a young woman wearing a red coat. I stepped closer, registering the prettiness of the woman, and wondered if this was Mrs Hamilton or even Theodore's daughter. I squatted down, shivering. The thick walls of the little enclosed room made it damp and chilly, despite the warmth outside. I pushed my wet hair back off my face, and picked up the photograph. The face was too familiar – it reminded me of Ingrid Bergman in movies I had seen. I peered closely. It wasn't his wife, or his daughter, or Ingrid Bergman.

It was a photograph I had never seen before, but it was a photograph of my mother.

Libya

Flt./Lt. T. R. Hamilton
37th Squadron DAF
Misurata, Gardabia West

2 April 1943

My dearest Anna, my Golden girl,

I have just woken from a short doze to find my nose burnt again, and the heat hitting 120 degrees in the shade. For a moment I thought I had gone to my appointed place . . . After days of heel-kicking, the wind has dropped and it is a relief to be airborne again. We are having wonderful nights, visibility A-plus for miles, and coming home, all the sense of the wide blue yonder. We've been on the move, no more to say, or the censor will give me a sharp rap on the knuckles. I remember days at Ish when I acted as censor officer myself – I spent three hours one morning reading other chaps' mail, then walked into the mess and found twelve letters and two airgraphs from home for yours truly. At any other point I would have been delirious with joy, but that day I remember having to steel myself to plough through them. Needless to say, this wouldn't have been the case had I recognized your own fair hand, but that was before our correspondence had started.

It is hard to find any privacy at all in which to write. Since our arrival here, the lads have been livening things up – not in comparison to your busy social whirl, my darling, but lively for the desert. Much talk of the Yanks, and particularly those of the fairer sex – the recent arrival of a small group of Red Cross nurses from your homeland has sparked off great interest about 'Yankee Girls', which has become part of our squadron slang, as in the question, "Yankee Girl, wilt marry me?" to which the correct response is, "Why certainly!" One of our own chaps went back to England on a course, got tangled up in marriage to a (English) girl there, and when the vicar asked, "Do you take this woman to be," etc., etc., forgot himself completely and replied, "Why certainly!" So don't ever think that your countrymen haven't made significant contributions to this war business. They have, and I have witnessed it. It is my earnest hope that you have not made any such contributions – not of the 'why certainly!' nature, at least.

I have spoken to you of my rear gunner Bob – he's just been commissioned, a happy excuse for a celebration last night, and deep in his cups he tore strips off me telling me that he'd been an NCO for more years than I had days. I can take a great stomachful from that lad and still have room to spare. He's one of those types, Australian, not with educational advantages but with a lion's heart, who will always turn up trumps and make you feel he gets less than his just reward. There are many of his sort on this squadron, and I consider myself blessed to be with them. I'm convinced the crew rely more on Bob's boomerang than my flying to bring us home safe to our beds. There's another chap here who'd amuse you, a Scotsman from somewhere north of Glasgow. He's one of the ground gunners. I was moseying around the airfield and admired one of the guns – a great cannon of a thing. He patted it, proud as new mother, and said, "A gun like that can rip a man apart in a second." "Or a woman," I corrected (you see how rapidly I am converting to your theories) and quick as a flash, he growled, "Aye, lad, a woman can rip a man apart as good as any gun."

I have been busy for so long, dearest, that most mornings I am too tired to do anything except crawl into bed, and promise myself that I will write to you tomorrow. And I do crawl into bed, only to lie awake thinking of you, and wishing and dreaming we were together. I never used to wake in the night with longing, but that has become a familiar experience since I left you. My leaves are now in the lap of the gods – and much as I crane my neck for a shufti, I am too lowly to see over their great knees. Having had the tour at Ish, and the leaves before and after in Cairo with you, I am not in the running for proper leave for another four months or more. With great good luck I may snatch a few days here or there.

My darling, my darling, my darling – my golden girl – how my heart aches at the thought of you, and burns with envy of all the lads who are able to be with you. We speak of the 'Gabardine Swine' in Cairo with great disdain, but I would trade all the supposed honour of my dirty flying suit to be stationed at Air House and able to see you every day, every night... Some of the chaps here are packing up for a quick move out on Saturday, taking leave in Cairo and Alex, lucky devils! I nearly gave a couple of the best sort your address, in order to live vicariously through their descriptions of you. Then I thought better of it. They are fine chaps in this squadron, and I felt horribly shaken when I realized how they might put me in the shade. If you met some of the types I fly with, I wouldn't rate my chances of keeping hold of you – I'd be struggling to make a graceful bow and head for the nearest exit, in all probability.

I'm not sure that I rate my chances with you at all, with or without competition. Our last few days in Cairo were more than I could handle. You say that we must live for the moment, and I agree; that there should be no looking back, and no regrets and no fears between us, and I will try my best to keep to that. We must seize whatever we can have now in both hands, and not worry

*about what is to come. It's the 'not worrying'
that worries me so . . .*

*I know you are right, and I envy your cool
head, and I love it – not as much as I love your
warm heart, but I love it nonetheless, as I love
every inch of you. I sit in the mess before ops
listening to the records the boys bring back – 'Till
Then', 'Sentimental Journey', 'I'll Get By' –
knowing each of the boys is hearing the same
words, certain they were written for his girl, his
love . . . This morning I heard Jo Stafford on the
WingCo's box, singing 'You Belong To Me';
surely the line 'see the Pyramids along the Nile'
was intended for us? Plus a couple of hundred
thousand Desert Rats no doubt. And, on that
thought, I hope that you are not spending too
much of your time with the other services – whilst
I cannot wish loneliness upon you, I hope you
will remain faithful, if not to me then to the
Knights of the Air. That would be some small
comfort. Were I to imagine you in the arms of
some dashing 11th Hussar in his absurd pink
trousers, that would be the final straw for this
poor desert camel. We comfort ourselves with
tales of the Army officer who was so pig stupid
that even his brother officers were able to recognize it. Let that be a lesson to you, dear lady, to
steer clear of the Cherry Pickers and their ilk . . .*

*I survive on the dream of you in my arms on
the roof of the Continental, and the music fills
my head, and from time to time a tear wets my*

eye, as I imagine the half-light flicker across your face, and how the gentle beams of the moon catch your cheek and hold your hair in a fiery halo – not that your face has anything to fear from full noon, dawn, or even the full glare of a search-light.

In your last letter – dated 24 March, and received, thanks to Tommy, three days later – you say you lost your heart to me against your will. Dear lady, if that is so, then I pray that your will remains as weak and biddable as it now is. You say we will have our time – and I have faith in that. Here, we are expected to survive on hope, an uncomplaining acceptance of our fate, and some deep-rooted belief in ourselves, but it is diffi-cult to avoid the occasional sortie into despair. The service calls this 'moaning' and takes a very dim view indeed of the binding bastards who do it. I am sustained by a different trinity – my love of you, the knowledge that you care for me, and my determination to live to see you again. If there is any chance in heaven that that will be before the next four months run their course, then neither God, nor the devil, nor Jerry nor the Group Captain, nor the four of them united will prevent me. (I confess that I find the wrath of the Groupie the most intimidating of the four.)

My darling, I'm having the life pestered out of me to join the boys at the bar – my heart's not in it, you know where my heart lies, but needs must, and I fear that if I delay longer this *letter will deteriorate beyond its current low level. I am very well and, oddly, very happy. I feel a certainty about my life. My golden, golden girl, consider yourself kissed and kissed and kissed again. When we parted, I placed a kiss in your palm for you to keep and hold, until you could redeem it in exchange for all the love there is in this heart of mine – do you still hold it in your hand? You surely hold my heart, and it is the knowledge that my heart resides elsewhere, in the safe and kindly guardianship of your own dear self (doubtless over-burdened by the many hearts you hold in custody – stay vigilant, good guardian!) that allows me to face the present with a composed countenance. There's nothing that that knowledge and a couple of stiff whiskies can't beat!*

We live in deeds, not years; in thoughts, not breaths;
In feelings, not in figures on a dial;
We should count time by heart throbs; he most lives
Who thinks most, feels the noblest, acts the best.

Dear heart, my thoughts are not always the noblest, but they are always of you. I cherish every memory, every moment since we met. Perhaps memory is as strong and pervasive a passion as love itself. We have shared – five days? Those days are my whole life, and you hold them in the palm of your hand.

Yours ever,

Theodore

When she came back to her flat in Zamalek, Anna Kézdy put this letter, with all the others Theodore had sent, under a silk chemise in her top drawer. She had twenty minutes to bathe, and dress before Mac would pick her up for the evening's function. She placed a drink on the edge of the bath and shut her eyes for five minutes. Tears flowed from beneath her closed lids. Without work, she was quite sure that she would have lost her reason; keeping insanely busy was the only thing that helped. Work provided the anaesthetic that let her switch off, and McClure's chaotic management style was a welcome contribution. As he generally left the offices of US Mission after her in the evenings, she made sure she arrived first in the mornings to restore his desk and hers to some sort of order before the mayhem began anew. From eight until one she worked flat out, typing, shorthand, shielding Mac from calls he didn't wish to take, making arrangements for visiting VIPs, soothing the office juniors and Egyptian staff, whose expectations of diplomatic life had not foreseen the frenetic energy which Mac applied equally to the most important and most trivial of affairs.

As the United States had a mission, rather

than a full embassy in Cairo, Mac's official title was Envoy Extra and Minister Plenipotentiary. He was responsible for everything, and he made sure Anna shared the job.

Beneath his surface bedlam, Arthur McClure was a joy to work with – fast, with a tremendous memory for detail, and both the ability and inclination to juggle ten things in the air at once. Idleness depressed him as much as it did her, and between them they outlawed it from their lives. Mac's number two, Harry, had become Anna's great ally in the short year since she had arrived in Cairo. They often lunched together, when they weren't taking turns escorting dignitaries around the streets of Cairo or arranging transport for them in and out of the desert. Anna would return to the office at five, and work until eight. There was rarely time for more than the quickest of changes before the evening activities began, a circuit of drinks' parties, dinners, dancing, floor-shows and clubs, then at last the chance to crawl into bed in the apartment she shared with her colleague, Millie. For the grandest parties, Anna and Millie had to flip a coin to see which of them got to wear 'the dress' – they had only one full-length formal between them, a silver gossamer delight, purchased with pooled resources from Le Salon Vert. Sometimes the girls only managed a few hours' sleep before having to rise and dress for work, but this was the way Anna wanted it to be. If you have to live through a war at all, then surely it was best to get as close to it as possible, work your rear end off, and be too exhausted to think at night.

That week, the Mission was even more hectic than usual, as military VIPs from all over the world were scheduled to meet in Cairo for the Middle East War Council. Anna could have kissed each and every one of them for keeping her hands and thoughts occupied. It was over a month since she had last seen Theodore, and from his letters, it might be another five before they met again. Already she felt as if a year had passed. When she collapsed into bed at night, she wondered if she would ever see him again, and held her head between her hands to press the doubts out of her mind. Her work kept her far better informed of his probable whereabouts and activities than his letters could, and although this brought her closer to him, she wished she did not have to type up reports on RAF casualties and numbers missing in action. She knew that the 37th were moving from Gardabia to Kairouan; she had known it before Theodore had. Theodore wrote three or four times a week, but deliveries were erratic, and when she hadn't heard for a few days, she feared the worst. Her fingers would slow on her notepad as Mac dictated a report to the War Office, citing this or that successful air mission, with only three planes reported missing or shot down. His drawl would come to a halt, and she would look up to see him watching her over his wire spectacles.

"OK, Anna?"

"Fine and dandy, Mac," and she'd read back the last sentence in a steady voice.

When a stack of letters arrived, she wallowed briefly in Theodore's safety and good spirits, but knew that the letters might so easily have outlived him that they brought as much distress as comfort. Less than a week of her twenty-four-year-old life had been spent in Theodore Hamilton's company, but those days had been more vivid than whole years at a time. She had fallen in love, something she had promised herself on the long journey from Washington to Cairo, and many times since, that she would not do. It had happened so smoothly and rapidly that she had been barely aware of it. Back home, Anna Kézdy had only two wishes: to play her part in the war effort, and not to have her heart broken in the process. Her journey to Cairo had been almost accidental, as she had explained to Theodore the day after they met, in the garden of Groppi's in Sharia Adly Pasha. They had lingered over coffee and pastries until dusk fell and the garden sparkled with strings of multi-coloured lights.

"I was so eager to do something for the war – anything. I would have dressed up as a man. My parents didn't want me to leave home, but I knew I had to go see for myself. I applied for jobs with the Army, the Red Cross and the State Department, but I ruled out the Army because it meant staying in the States. I was stunned when the Red Cross offered me a job in the Middle East. I had no training – I couldn't have put a bandage on my own finger if I'd cut it – but they didn't seem to mind. They just wanted volunteers. The State Department offered me a job, too, in the same zone. I was leaning towards the Red Cross – it seemed more front line than a desk job in an embassy."

"Why didn't you take it?"

Anna blushed. "I'm just too ashamed to say . . . OK. In my last interview, we were setting up the training and then they asked me how I felt about rats."

Theodore had smiled at her. "Rats?"

"Rats. I said that when it came to me and rats, I'd expect the Purple Heart just for looking one in the eye and not fainting. They didn't consider that an appropriate reply, and suggested I withdrew my application."

Theodore rocked with laughter. "I can see you tiptoeing through the desert in your high heels, nervously lifting medical boxes in case there was a rat lurking behind them."

Anna tapped him lightly on the cheek. "That's enough. Anyway, that's how I ended up with Mac."

She had arrived in Cairo and reported to Mac in June 1942 and had been sucked into life like a whirlpool. Again and again she reminded herself *of her vow – I must not fall for anyone; I must not get emotionally involved. This, of course, was a defensive strategy. It had been surprisingly easy to enforce. She had met many interesting and attractive men – those who were not were few and far between – but she met them briefly. Other than those Brits with staff jobs, these invariably young men – some younger than she was – came to Cairo on leave or on courses for only days, at most a week at a time. They took her out to dinner, perhaps dancing, and they talked, about their families, their homes, their dogs and their plans for civilian life when the war was won. They laughed and joked and flirted, and spent all their money as if they would never have need of it again. They went up the Blue – into the desert – with broad shoulders and brave hearts and merry smiles. So often they did not come back. There were the men who assured her they would be back, like bad pennies, and would claim a kiss as a reward. There were many harmless kisses. There were those who feared they would not come back, and did, as often as those who trusted wrongly in their immortality. Anna went out with them all, and laughed with them all. She became an accomplished listener. She visited the wounded in hospital, and took down their letters in shorthand, and smiled at the boys' jokes while she retched at the stench of rotting flesh. Tears were shed and quickly wiped away, and life continued.*

She had seen Theodore at Shepheard's shortly after her arrival in Cairo; he had stood out from the throng by virtue of his height and his unblinking blue stare as he looked at her. The first night that she met him, she had no certainty that he would be any different from the others, although Mac had had a sense of foresight about the tall English pilot. Anna had surprised herself by accepting Theo's request that she spend his last day's leave with him. She had enjoyed his company perhaps a little more than that of the others. He liked to listen to her as much as he wanted to talk himself, and some of her carefully wrought defences had come down. But when he left, she was whole in heart. Perhaps it was that he was at Ismailia, both nearby and out of danger, that made her drop her guard. Perhaps it was his letters, or his English accent, or the intimate yet courteous way he had of teasing her, or perhaps it was his dignity, or perhaps, as Theodore claimed, it was no more than his dress blues, the cut of his jib, that set him apart for her.

When Theodore sent her a signal that he would have a few days in Cairo before rejoining his squadron in the Libyan Desert, she knew quite suddenly that something had happened to her. When they were together, she was under a spell. When he left, she felt as if she had mislaid her fortified heart – put it down carelessly on a table for anyone to pick up. From that day on, her prayers were for him, and she entered into ever more elaborate bargains with God. She promised Him that if only Theodore could be spared, she would give up any claim to future blessings in life; in exchange for his survival, she would accept whatever happened to them, good or bad, without recrimination against the heavens. When casualties were highest, when she typed bulletins for Washington listing losses running at twenty per cent – thirty per cent – during periods of intense fighting and air defence, her promises were wild. She negotiated with God to the hilt, offering her health, her chance of having children, her happiness, while knowing that these were not in her gift.

In exchange for Theodore's life, she would take the end of their 'boy meets girl' story with complete stoicism. She was far too smart to allow God the chance to cheat her: she never asked simply for the chance to see him again. Sobbing into her pillow in fear and loneliness, she knew that she was no better than a child pleading for a present – let him be all right, let him be all right, please God let me have him, just this one thing, and I'll never want anything else as long as I live . . .

In the mornings, she painted her face carefully, and wore her brightest smile into the office. She searched for ways to fill her time: she volunteered for extra duty, she made more frequent visits to the hospital at Abbassia; she took an unpaid job teaching Egyptian soldiers English. She danced and drank and laughed and listened harder than ever before. Wherever she went she sought out airmen, in case they might have news of him. She hungered for his letters and wrote to him daily. Anna did not tell Theodore of her pleadings for his life. She told him that they should make the most of whatever time they had; if things worked out for them, well and good, and if they didn't, there should be no tears. So long as they stuck to that simple rule, God would treat them well and every memory would be a happy one.

As April drew to a close, Anna steeled herself to accept that she would not see Theodore for some time. She went into the office on the twenty-sixth with a heavy heart. It was quiet that morning, as the Egyptian staff had the day off to celebrate the festival of Sham el Nessim. Only a few Americans were working, and as Mac was in Ankara, Anna seized the chance to sit at his desk in front of an open window and write to Theodore, even though she had written the day before, and the day before that and the day . . .

When her phone rang she ran to answer it, and her knees buckled as she heard Theo's voice. She had never heard it on the telephone before.

"Anna? It's me."

"Darling. Where are you?"

"Shepheard's. I've just arrived. I'm only here for twenty-four hours. A complete fluke – had to fly the Group Captain down. There's a flap on about target accuracy. We've a meeting at Air

*House now, and a dinner tonight that I'm trying
to escape. I can't talk, darling. When can I see
you? Can you get away this afternoon – tonight?"*

"Of course."

*"Let me see what I can scheme up. I'll get a
message to you somehow. I must see you, Anna."*

"I'll be waiting."

*Theodore arrived in person at four o'clock.
Anna had waited all afternoon. He looked terribly thin, as if he had lost twenty pounds in the
few weeks since she had seen him. He had a cut
that ran from his cheekbone to his forehead, just
skirting his eye, and his face was grey with
fatigue. They walked through the park behind the
US Mission, together but barely speaking, watching Egyptian families picnicking on salt fish and
preserved fruits, children playing and evening
lovers strolling over the grass.*

*"Sham el Nessim." Theodore inhaled deeply.
"Do you know what that means, darling?" Anna
shook her head, and slipped her arm through his.
"The Smelling of the Breeze. The locals say it is
when the air is at its freshest – you can smell
spring coming. Fill your lungs, sweetheart. Think
of things to come. Perhaps by the summer this
wretched business will be over. Can you smell it
on the wind, darling heart?"*

*As they strolled Anna leant into his side, her
hip moving against his thigh. She couldn't smell
anything other than the regular Cairo smells but
she heard the uncharacteristic heaviness in his*

voice. "How long do we have?"

"The rest of the afternoon. Tonight. I leave right after dawn. I was lucky to get out at all. We're stationed with three other squadrons in Gardabia, and working flat out against Palermo.. The Groupie bust himself on the way down – full of gung-ho, last-push talk. I tell you, I'm just too damn tired to care."

"Do you have to have dinner with him tonight?"

"No. I told him I had a spot of gippy tummy – God's own truth. I was as sick as a dog last week." He looked down at her concerned face with a smile. "You're a tonic though, lovely lady. I feel pretty much a hundred per cent for seeing you. A whisky might bring it to a round figure."

Without any discussion, they steered a course through the streets to Shepheard's. When they had been served drinks, Anna touched the gash on his cheek gingerly.

"Fear not, dear heart, it's a graze. Shakey shaving." Anna gave him a steady stare, and Theodore sighed. "We were only dropping bumph. I never saw tracer, but a shot came through the side of the kite and blew up the instrument panel. Slashed my cheek and I caught some pieces in the leg, but no damage done. Better my face than yours. I felt quite a fraud when the medics patched me up." He waved to the suffragi. Although Anna had barely touched her drink, his glass was empty.

"We lost a few last night, Anna. One of them a first-rate pilot, top drawer, and all his crew. It's harder to lose men when the war's going well than when things are sticky. Rommel's barely holding on, most of his fighters are leaving the desert – the gen is better and better. And then a plane goes with five lads barely into long trousers, and you think, Well, what was that for? Why in God's name now? It's not that I don't believe in the Old Boy, but I don't follow His mysterious ways. Not that my opinion is of any import to Him."

"Oh, Theo, I'm so sorry."

"Nothing to worry about, darling. Just the usual post-ops headache, I suppose, which leaves me feeling clapped out completely and more than usually browned off. Self-pity is a disgusting thing, though." He downed his whisky in one swallow. "Drink never touched his lips, as Bert would say, just went down without touching the sides." He barked out a laugh, but with no following chuckle, and signalled to the suffragi. "I'm being an awful cuss, darling. Enough shop, I've said my piece. Now, tell me how you've been keeping yourself busy in the fleshpots of Cairo. What d'you say to donning the glad rags, hmm? Fein el cocktail?"

"Are you sure you feel like going to a party, Theo?"

"On the contrary, I'm quite sure that I don't, but I'm not fit company for you, my lovely. I'd *understand if you want to give me the elbow and seek out livelier companions."*

"Theodore." She spoke very softly and leant as close to him as she could, looking deep into his eyes. They were the colour of pale glass, clear and empty. "What's the matter? What has happened to you?" He looked away, but she raised a hand to his chin and turned his face back towards her. "Don't you try and hide from me."

"I'm tired, Anna. I'm so tired and so deep in the blues I can't think any longer. I am too wretched even to be happy at being with you. I shouldn't have called. I should have just flopped out, stayed in the bar and drunk myself into oblivion. Forgive me, golden girl. Perhaps it's something in the air. I'll sit this one out alone until it passes."

"Tell me about your friends. How's Tommy? How's Bombs Away Bertie?"

"Alive. When I left." He looked up at the early-evening sky. "They'll be flying tonight – Lord knows where they'll be tomorrow. Gone the way of all good men." His hand shook as he reached for his glass.

Anna took a compact from her purse and checked her lipstick. Her hand was shaking as she held it. She clicked it shut and smiled nervously, but Theo wasn't looking at her. "There's a dance at ten at the Mohammed Ali Club. Harry's hosting the dinner before for some press men. It might take your mind off – if you'd like to go . . ."

"What a shindig that'll be! A bunch of goddamn Yanks rattling the sabres, and correspondents pouring champagne down their necks and ogling the pretty girls in their lipstick and silk stockings. Thanks very much, darling, but no. I'll decline."

Anger flashed in Anna's eyes and she stood up to leave, scraping her chair on the terrace. "OK, Theo. If that's the way you want it, then you can go hang. You don't need me. All you need is a bottle of Scotch."

Theodore shrugged. "Chance would be a fine thing. The Gyppos here are so damned idle it's hard enough to get a glass, let alone a bottle. But thanks for the tip, lovely lady." Without looking at her he waved across the bar and shouted angrily.

For a moment, Anna stood undecided then sat down and pulled out two cigarettes, lit them and passed one to Theodore. "OK, friend. You listen to me, and listen good. I'll tell you how we're going to play this. If you want to get stinking drunk that's fine by me, but just you order a bottle or two of whatever poison you choose and I'm damn well going to sit here and get stinking drunk with you. If you want me to go, just say the word."

He reached for her hand and held it tight. When he raised his eyes, they were full of yearning for something that Anna couldn't identify. "Don't go, Anna. I'm so goddamn down-to-my-toes, sick-at-heart lonely. Don't go. Not now. There's a great beast sitting on my chest and ripping my heart with its teeth. I don't want to be alone with him. I haven't the strength – dear God, I haven't the will . . . I'm so pathetically ashamed of it all. Don't leave me alone."

Anna Kézdy took Theodore to his room in the hotel and stayed with him until he had sweated out the blues like a fever. That was the night she finally lost her heart. The Smelling of the Breeze.

CHAPTER NINE

Fate is a tricky old cuss, and one with whom I have more than a nodding acquaintance. The afternoon that David Turcan first telephoned me and told me about the RAF book, he had mentioned the writer's name – Elena Stewart. I at once thought of Anna. I had kept track of her enough to know from mutual acquaintances that she had long ago married an Englishman by the name of Ben Stewart and I had been told that he was a sound type and that she was happy. After that, I had left well alone, but my thoughts had often wandered back to her over forty years, and my ears always pricked up at the name Stewart. Now I acknowledge that it is a common name, but when I saw the young couple at the Méridien in the village, I had not a moment's doubt that this was Anna's daughter. Elena was not the exact image of her mother, but the look in her eye and the stubborn tilt of her chin and that tell-tale vein at her temple were a dead give-away. I was on the point of asking whether she was related to Anna Kézdy, but as I have said, Fate is a character who has earned my deepest respect, and I endeavour not to meddle in his affairs. I walked home that evening with a light step, and the only action I took was to move the photograph of Anna that I kept in the drawing room to the storage room in the *pigeonnier*. I had no intention of upsetting Anna – even less her daughter – but I confess to a poor night's sleep, and a strange excitement when she arrived the following morning.

Elena was a lovely girl, and had something of Anna's intensity, if not, perhaps, Anna's sense of fun. Being a modern young woman, she took herself rather seriously, and seemed eager that I should do likewise. I found her easy to talk to – oh, far worse than that! She flattered my old ego quite horribly and I wallowed in it, like the fool I am. It was when she launched into her outburst about the lack of moral consciousness of the present day lions and lionesses of Britain that I felt a trickle of apprehension down my spine. Until then I had intended only to observe her from a distance, to indulge myself in the game of spotting the mother in the daughter's gestures and patterns of speech. It was a pleasant way of passing a morning. But when Elena spoke from the heart, Anna came to mind far too clearly to mind for me to sit comfortably. There was the unforeseen danger of us – becoming friends. Elena made the occasional reference to her mother, and it couldn't be too long before she said that her mother had been in Cairo – had I perchance met her? My choices were limited. I could either bid the girl farewell and not see her again, or lie to her, or I could consult Anna. The simple knowledge that Anna was alive affected me more than I can express, and I daresay the slim chance of hearing her voice was what persuaded me to reject the first option. The second was clearly fool-hardy: if I appeared in the book, Anna was bound to read it, and heaven only knows what might happen. I made some limp excuse for leaving, and went straight to the PTT in Sainte Cécile to make a private call.

I advanced no further than calling Directory Enquiries in London, and requesting a number for Anna Stewart: they had only one ex-directory listing. When I asked for Ben Stewart, they offered me four different numbers, all of which I copied down and slipped into my breast pocket. I felt my heart thump-ing in my chest and all manner of scenarios presented themselves: that Anna and Ben were no longer together; that Ben had died; that I now held over my heart the means by which I could see her again. I am far too cautious a man these days to act precip-itously, so I did not resolve any of my questions by calling the numbers I had. I lingered over coffee at the Méridien until I could collect the photographer and return home. Sitting idly in the bar, I enjoyed flirting with the scheming and dreaming of seeing Anna Kézdy again, but had no intention of going further.

I was fortunate in that both Elena and David were

lively company over the course of the evening, and that Elena's questioning was sufficiently persistent to prevent me dwelling on other thoughts. It was a delight to have the opportunity to relive those days, however briefly, and in however shadowy a fashion. Old men are made young again when their memories are brought to life, and Elena Stewart had that effect on me. I felt as if a heavy burden had been gently lifted from my shoulders.

I invited David to come inside to see my poor attempts at photography. Since Chantal's death I have had two chief occupations, photography and painting, for neither of which can I profess any skill so it took courage to expose my efforts to a professional. The young man had the powerful frame and lazy, long-limbed elegance of a tiger. He accepted a whisky and paced the room, examining the odd photographs and bibelots that littered the surfaces. He was clearly no less reluctant to see my portfolio than I was to show it. I let him wander at liberty, and he eventually settled. There was a fine tension in him, a mixture of stillness and restlessness, the balance of which I had no wish to upset.

"Elena tells me you're not a portrait photographer, David, that you primarily work in current affairs."

"That's right."

"Is it possible to switch between the two?"

He spread his large hands over his knees. "You get a name for a certain specialty. Mine is wars or disasters of one kind or another. That's what people ask for, and that's where the agency sends me."

"Against your will?"

He laughed. "Never against my will, no. I'm always willing. It's what I am. Once I'd started, it seemed the only thing to do. It becomes your lifestyle. I'm probably pushing the limits right now. It's a young man's job. There aren't many guys my age lugging their kit around a war zone. Flying must be the same."

"In war, almost certainly. They grew younger and younger, as you can understand."

"We're less likely to get killed off and replaced, not that that doesn't happen. Most of the guys just grow up and realize they don't want to do it any more."

"And you haven't grown up?"

"You could say that." He bared his teeth at me. I liked him, almost instantly. For all his toughness, there was a humanity about him. "You could also say I don't know how else to earn a living. I can't do buildings. I like pictures that tell good stories and I'm not gripped by the story that Notre Dame tells." He pronounced 'Notre' to rhyme with voter, and dame as in woman, but he was far more sophisticated than he was prepared to show. An interesting man, David Turcan, neither one thing nor the other.

"You should go to the *bastides* while you're here – I may have mentioned them last night. I'm sure you would find something to inspire you." Although he nodded, I doubted that Monpazier would interest him in the slightest. "How *did* you get into this line of work?"

"Accidental, like most of the men – and women – in the business. Someone I knew was a pro, a guy I admired a lot. I went on a trip with him, carrying his bags, and I guess I caught the bug. I was looking for an adventure, wanted to prove something."

"And did you?"

"Shit, if I had, I would have stopped doing it. No, it's like the first time was a test – *you* know.'

I realized where David's charm lay. His eyes burned with the message that he not only knew how you felt, he felt it himself.

"You go out there, and you haven't a clue what's going on, or what you're meant to do about it. Most of all, you're thinking, What the hell am I *doing* here? All around you there are these guys who look like they've been there for twenty, thirty years. They may look young, but they're older than rocks. They know it all. Nothing's gonna catch them off guard because they've got all the tricks. And all you think is, Am I the only guy here who's scared shitless? That's *gunfire* outside. They don't hear it. They're just pouring you another drink and giving their five cents' worth, and you're trying to take it all in but longing to get the next bus home, and thinking, Boy, oh, boy, did I fuck up here. When push comes to shove, maybe it's not *there*, you know?"

"I do," I replied.

He ruffled his hair, and stretched up his arms over his head without any self-consciousness. "That's when you realize all the knowledge in the world isn't worth squat compared to what you're about to discover. The first time you're sitting in a bar with the press guys, you see it all before you – you see the awards, the Pulitzer, the cover of *Time* with your by-line, and you go wild with *lust* for your own courage and heroism. It's an exhibition. And if you're going to die, then shit – could there be a lovelier death in the world? To prove yourself a man among men? Hell, the *allure* of that . . ."

He was sending himself up expertly, his voice soaring with romantic ardour. Then he gave a big grin, and touched his shoulder. "Then there's that little tap on your shoulder and the sneaky voice that says, 'Hey, buddy, it's not death you've got to fear. What about the other stuff? What about mutilation? What about having your balls blown off?' And that's when you start fingering your passport again. You know?"

"Yes, I know. What stopped you getting on the next plane home?"

"What stopped you?"

"Oh, a great number of things – court-martial, fear of my CO, the fact that there wasn't a plane home . . . Disgrace. Pride."

"Pride's close. But we don't have to be there, like you did. We can all just go home and take up dentistry or something. If we had the guts. I was too proud to go home and I wanted to know if I *had* it." He laughed. "Did I ever! After about two months on assignment, I was just like the other guys – like

I'd been there for twenty years, like there wasn't a corpse I couldn't shoot, and I'd be the first guy to slap the new kid on the back and show him the ropes. Bottom line, it's takes a true lack of imagination to kid yourself you're a dumb animal."

I agreed with him. Some of our best pilots, the bravest, were those who lacked even the imagination of death. And I knew the allure that he spoke of, the allure of the strong life, life *in extremis*. I had been seduced by it myself. It was close to what Elena missed in her own life, and I wondered if she was drawn to this man for that very reason. At the least, he must have provided a catalyst for her doubts. I wanted to test his excuses, and suggested, "You have the satisfaction of being the eyes of the world. You can make it impossible for people to ignore what's happening outside their own homes. That's no small compensation?"

He was far too clever to fall into that trap. "There's a bit of that stuff around, but it doesn't explain much. It doesn't help you pass the test."

David Turcan talked with self-deprecating confidence, a brutal bravado. I understood what he meant by 'the test': who doesn't? There was the smell of it in the mess before ops: you could see every new chap asking himself, 'Hero or coward?' and trying to balance his terror and longing to have his courage, his masculinity, laid on the line once and for all. I remember my own yearning to be subjected to this trial, and my terror of failure. David asked me if I had known men who had 'chickened out'. I didn't like the expression.

"If you drink hard enough, and laugh long enough, and think only of that moment, you can sleep and get up the next day and continue unaffected. You can excise the fear, as if wielding a scalpel. The higher my rank, the more I was conscious of crews that were marked out for disaster. You could smell it on their breath and know they had only a few operations left. It wasn't fear that hung about them, just a weariness with the whole business, a presentiment of doom."

"What did you do?"

"There wasn't much we could do – make sure the CO knew, make them stand down, which was the last thing that sort of crew wanted. Try to break up the crew, to break the curse, which could be as hazardous as letting them fly. There were a few chaps who literally broke down and were relieved of operational duties, or even from the service altogether. Those men with wives and children faced a different form of pressure. The conflict of responsibilities must have been intolerable. We bachelors could focus our responsibility on our crews or the honour of the squadron."

"So you weren't married until after the war?"

"That's right. What about you?"

"No, I'm not married." He made no reference to Elena, and I applauded his discretion. Of course I had known the two were lovers from the moment I saw them together. I had some hope that I might learn more of the Stewarts from David, without arousing Elena's suspicions.

"How do you answer when your colleague asks about your best of times and worst of times?"

"Elena? She wouldn't ask me. I reckon, when she thinks about my work, she probably thinks I'm a crazy loon, and she's probably right. And I don't like to talk about it much. When you get your feet back on solid earth, it's like it never really happened anyway. There's no use in reliving it."

The man's eyes were too shadowed to support this claim of easy detachment and, in any event, he had his pictures to bring vividly to mind whatever it was he claimed to forget. Even without the aid of photographs I had moments of perfect recall, after which I would wake to find myself fighting in my dressing gown. In addition, I found recounting those days life-enhancing. David Turcan was too young to need such comfort. His work provided his validity. I battled on. "Have you worked with Elena often?"

"No. This is only the second time we've done stuff together."

"She seems enthusiastic about her work."

"Yeah, she is."

"And good at it?"

"She's got a real good name in the business. She cares about it, maybe too much, that's why."

"Do you often work with journalists of different nationalities?" I was floundering in my attempts to lead him to talk about Elena, not from any prurient curiosity but because I wanted a fix on her family.

"Sure, you end up working with everyone. It's

an international community and you find all sorts. Elle's nearly a fellow American anyway."

"Oh?' I tried to sound uninterested. "How nearly?"

"Her mother's American, way back. Used to be State Department." Of course I knew this. The confirmation none the less made my hand shake as I reached for my glass. "Her folks – Anna and Ben – live in London. He's British and she grew up in England, so you wouldn't pick it up from her voice."

"No, I would never have guessed."

David very civilly reminded me that I had promised to show him my photographs. I offered him an album, but I wouldn't have objected if he'd set a torch to it. He was courteous in his comments and feigned an interest in the local landmarks I had shot over the past ten years. The gulf between professional and amateur photographers yawned like a hideous maw. I was leaning over his shoulder and chatting about a *fromagier* at the local market when the door banged and Elena stepped into the room. Her hair was dripping and her arms were folded tightly around her.

"Ah, Elena! Did you enjoy your swim?"

"Yes, it was very pleasant."

"You found everything you needed? Towels? Can I offer you a nightcap?"

"I found *everything*, thank you." She gave me an oddly penetrating look. "I have to go back to the hotel. It's late. I hadn't realized how late. David, are you ready to go?"

"Sure, I'll just finish my drink."

"Don't rush." She shook her head, and tiny drops of water flew around her. "I'll walk. I'd rather."

"I'm more than happy to run you back –" I began.

"Thanks, but we've taken up far too much of your time already." Her eyes moved restlessly around the room, and there was that aggressive tilt to her chin. Something had bitten her: she had the air of a little child fighting back tears. As she waited for David to move, Elena touched a photograph of Chantal. "Who's this?" she asked flatly.

"My wife, Chantal."

She looked at it for a moment, and then raised her eyes to mine. "She's pretty."

"Yes, she was a very attractive woman."

Elena held out her hand. "Well, thanks very much for all your time, Theodore. You've been very helpful. And thanks for lunch – and dinner, and the swim."

Even as I took it her hand pulled away from my grasp. She slipped out of the room, and I heard the front door bang.

David stood up at last, his shoulders lifted in a rueful shrug. "I'd better get after her. I guess she wants her beauty sleep or something."

When I went to the front door to lock up I saw Elena still leaning against their car, whispering furiously, while David held her wet head between his hands. I forced myself to close the door. I retired to bed shortly after and fell asleep with a book on my chest, thinking of Anna and dreaming of the desert.

The next morning, a Saturday, I walked into the village at around eight, as was my custom, to buy bread and a few bits and bobs, and to keep abreast of the gossip that fuelled life in Sainte Cécile. As I drew near the Méridien, I spotted Elena sitting on her own. She looked haggard, rather sad, and I nearly turned around and walked away, but something prevented me.

"Good morning. May I join you?"

She tossed her hair. "If you want." It was a relief that she didn't tell me it was a free country. She sipped the coffee without raising her eyes to me.

"Have I done something to offend you?"

"No. I can't talk to people in the morning. I take after my mother." Her expression was far from subtle. So that was it.

"Can I order you another coffee?"

"What I want is a slap-up traditional breakfast. I looked at the menu but there's nothing except 'sandwich' and omelettes. I'd kill for a plate of pancakes and Canadian bacon." She didn't look like a girl with a hearty appetite. Her collar and shoulder bones were a shade too prominent, for my taste at least.

I beckoned Michel, and ordered, "Des œufs plat – trois – et du jambon, du pain, des tomates grillées, un jus d'orange, et encore deux café au lait."

The briefest of smiles flickered on Elena's lips. "You must think I never stop eating." She folded her arms across her chest, and added matter-of-factly,

"It's just that I'm pregnant. I have to eat a lot or I feel sick."

"Congratulations."

"Thanks." It may not be chivalrous to describe her response as grunting but I'm afraid that's what it was. She sat staring at the table, and I pushed a copy of *The Times* that I had been carrying across the table towards her.

"Thanks," she said again, and gazed at the front page vacantly until her breakfast arrived.

I enjoyed watching her eat, while pretending to read the paper. I haven't cared much about food for a long time, not living alone, but Elena ate with admirable gusto. When she had wiped the last bit of bread around her plate, she pushed it away, leant back in her chair and again folded her arms across her chest. She looked heartbreakingly pretty for all her tiredness, and despite her efforts to look severe.

"You should have told me that you knew my mother."

"I agree, I should have. What can I say? When I saw you here two nights ago, I was certain that you were Anna Kézdy's daughter. You look – well, you have something of her about you. Perhaps I should have asked you then. You see, I haven't seen your mother since nineteen forty-five. I had no idea until you mentioned her that she was alive, and by then I'd left it too late." I wished she would look at me, but she was playing with her spoon, paddling it around in the dregs of her coffee. "I should have told you that I recognized you. You're quite right."

"I saw a photograph of her in the *pigeonnier*, when I was changing."

"Yes, I thought that you might have seen it. It's a very good likeness. An unusual photograph; hand-tinted. We were friends, in Cairo. I saw her there intermittently when I was on leave."

"Why do you leave her photograph on the floor of a store room?"

What could I tell her? How could I justify anything to that angry, suspicious young woman, when I had never explained myself to Anna?

"That photograph is normally in my living room. I moved it after I'd met you. I – Lord." I drew a deep breath, wanting to be simple and straightforward and dispel the notion of any mystery about her discovery. "When David first contacted me, it never occurred to me that I would be interviewed by Anna Kézdy's daughter. Then, when I saw you, I went home and moved the photograph."

She tossed her head and her hair fell about her face. She looked so like Anna, I could have been sitting with her ghost.

"I don't understand. Why? Why would you hide it? If you were friends, why didn't you just tell me two nights ago? Why wouldn't *she* have told me?"

"Did you tell her you were coming to see me?" My voice sounded steady in my own ears, yet my knees were shaking under the table waiting for her answer. Anna would never have volunteered my name to Elena.

"Not exactly. I said where we were going." She

scrunched up her hair, holding all that golden mane bunched up in one hand. "I said we were going to Lot-et-Garonne to see a bomber pilot. She knows all about this book – I *asked* her to suggest people. But she never suggested you. Why didn't she say you, if you were friends?"

"Your mother and I lost touch an age ago. Forty-five years or more? Perhaps she doesn't remember me."

"But you kept her *picture* all those years – you remembered her. You must have been close."

I was self-indulgent. Keen to show what a worthy individual I was, and to prove that I had a legitimate claim to Anna's photograph, I told her daughter, "Your mother and I were close. I loved her dearly. I have never forgotten her, nor ceased wondering what happened to her. I wouldn't expect her to have the same memory of me. She was an utterly remarkable woman in every sense."

"Are you telling me that you and my mother were lovers?" Poor little thing. She looked as startled as a child encountering a large dog for the first time. Could I tell that child what had happened between Anna and me? I had no right to speak of Anna, least of all to her daughter, but that Anna had never mentioned my name hurt me, even after all those years. But, as she had often said, there was to be no looking back, no recriminations: we were only to remember the good times.

"No. Simply that I knew your mother and cared for her very much. I daresay there were countless others who felt equally strongly. Your mother was a rare and special lady."

"She still is. My father's pretty remarkable, too. I'm going to call her and ask her about you. Maybe today."

Poor Elena. She had put me on notice that she would not take my story at face value. She seemed determined to catch me out. Perhaps she thought I had never met Anna, that I had picked up the photograph from some crony as a prurient pin-up. I hadn't the faintest idea whether Anna would refute this or deny that we had ever met. Anna was entitled to rewrite history in any way she chose. I stood up to leave. "When you speak to her, would you be kind enough to give her my very best regards?"

"I don't suppose you knew my father too?"

"No, I did not. Was he also in Egypt?"

"No. They met after the war."

"I see. Sadly, I never had the opportunity to meet him."

I attempted to pay for her breakfast, but she would not allow it. I left her the newspaper. As I walked back through the village, I took the list of telephone numbers out of my breast pocket and threw it in the gutter. I was blind to the streets of Sainte Cécile, and its familiar inhabitants. I was back in Cairo.

"O that I had wings like a dove: for then would I flee away and be at rest. Lo, then would I wander far off and lodge in the wilderness."

CHAPTER TEN

"He did know her – in Cairo." I sat at the foot of the bed back in the hotel chewing my thumbnail. David was propped up in bed on one elbow, flipping through *The Times*.

"I told you that last night. I don't understand why you didn't ask him straight off."

"I don't understand why he didn't ask *me* straight off."

"Honey, why would he? Jeez, if I walked into a stranger's house and saw a photo of someone I recognized, I wouldn't give them grief because they hadn't 'fessed up to knowing them the second we met."

"Oh, don't be obtuse, David – just because you love having your little secrets, and keeping people in the dark, and being a bloody *cipher*. Any normal person would just blurt it out – unless they had a reason not to." I'd nibbled my nail half-way across, and considered either ripping it off or trying to preserve it. I ripped it off. "Besides, this is completely different. For starters, he *moved* the photograph. He *hid* it. And it's my *mother*, for God's sake."

"All the more reason for him to keep schtum. Wouldn't you, in his shoes?"

"No, I bloody wouldn't." I had a horrible vision of one day meeting Peter Bagshawe's son: would I tell him I'd spent two years with his dad? Like hell I would.

David reached into his camera bag, which was lying on the floor next to the bed, and pulled out first a pack of cigarettes and then his Leica. He treated that bloody camera like an idol. He held an unlit fag in his mouth as he fiddled with his baby. One of the greatest demonstrations of David's self-discipline was that he chain-smoked when he was on assignments and abstained when he was 'resting'. A couple of days before he left he'd start again, as if he was getting his gear together and brushing off his uniform. It was my sign that I was about to meet the other man: I could never decide which was Jekyll and which was Hyde. He took a couple of photographs of me chewing my nails, ones destined to go straight down the toilet as far as I was concerned.

"He said they were *friends* in Egypt. He saw her on his leaves and said that he'd been very fond of her, as everyone else was."

"So . . ." David drawled, fiddling with dials. "What's the problem?"

"He made it sound like everyone fancied the knickers off her – like every man there knew her."

David chuckled. "I can just hear Wing Commander Theodore Hamilton DFC, DS whatever, saying that: 'Oooh, that Anna Kézdy – she was a right little goer, she was. Everyone wanted a piece of *that* action' . . ."

"Oh, fuck off, of course he didn't say that. He said he loved her 'dearly', that she was 'utterly remarkable in every sense'. What the hell does that mean, *in every sense*? He was so mysterious. As if it had nothing to do with me."

"Has it?"

"Of *course*. She's talked about other men in her life, but only to tease Dad. Why would she be secretive about him? She would have told me, unless there's something to hide. I thought Daddy was the one and only man in her life. I ought to know everything about her."

"But she's not entitled to know everything about you, hmm, Elle? Your mom has lived every second of your life, with you for most of it, but you feel one hundred per cent entitled to have a private life and keep her out of it. For instance, you don't think our relationship is anything to do with her, it's none of her damn business if we get married or live in sin." He snapped another picture of me scowling. "Now you're sweating because you weren't fully informed about a friendship she had twenty years before you were born. I'd call that a tad hypocritical, sweetheart."

"What if he wasn't just a friend, Turcan? What if he was a *boyfriend*?"

"Oh, baby . . . How old did you say you felt? Six? You hit the nail there!"

I stomped into the bathroom and turned on the taps full to drown the sound of his laughter. If David had ever had a mother, and sometimes I thought it more likely he'd been whelped by a she-wolf in a forest, he would have understood how I felt. At times he had the emotional sensitivity of plankton. He leant against the bathroom door grinning evilly. "There's a real easy answer, darlin'."

"And what's that, smartarse?"

"Call her up and ask her."

I tapped my forehead. "Eureka! You're a genius! Now why the fuck didn't *I* think of that?"

David undid my zip for me and dropped his arms to encircle my stomach loosely. "How's the baby?"

"The baby's just fine, sucking the life out of me. Now could you please get out of here and leave me in peace? I need to come up with an answer for when it turns round and asks me how it came about that I spent two years of my life sleeping with Peter Bagshawe."

David grinned. "Plead insanity. Say it was during one of your frequent bouts of mental instability. The poor kid's going to know about them one way or another. I'm going out for a snoop around the village. Are you going to be OK without me? You won't do anything stupid? You'll be OK getting dressed alone? Doing up your shoelaces?"

"Just get out, will you, and leave me in peace. You don't understand anything."

I love being in the bath. There are days when I have as many as three, just to wallow around like a pig in mud. I lie there, letting the water lose its heat, emptying it out a bit and filling it back up till it's steaming around my chin. You can't do this for too long in small B&Bs. You need a serious luxury hotel. I got out and dripped across the bedroom to phone her, and then it hit me. What if Daddy answered the phone? If I asked him about Theodore, and he didn't know anything about him, I would be drawn into some horrible conspiracy of my mother's and I was damned if I was going to lie to him. I decided to call anyway, and sure enough, my father answered on the second ring. I nearly hung up.

"Dad? It's me."

"Hello, darling. Are you in France?"

"Yep. We got here a couple of days ago, safe and sound."

"Good. Your mother's been fretting like an old hen. Doesn't like her chickens out of her sight. How's David?"

"He's fine. Back on the demon weed, though."

"Allow a man some vices, dear heart. Nothing wrong with cigarettes and whisky – it's the wild, wild women a man has to give up. Just so long as you haven't succumbed to temptation yourself."

"No, I'm being a good girl, Daddy, I promise."

"It's a joy to hear your voice. We old folks can't

help but worry, you know. Not I, of course, I always rely on you to act sensibly, but the old lady . . ." I knew my father worried at least as much about us as my mother did. "I passed on your hotel number to Charlie, by the way. He called from Paris to say he'd bumped into a chum of David's who wanted to get in touch. A chap called Steve Heffner. I hope you don't mind."

"No, I'm used to being David's answer service. I know Steve well – almost too well. Has Charlie taken the job?"

"Not exactly. He appeared to be trying to persuade them to fly him off to Tokyo to have a look at the offices there. He's staying at the Meurice – doubtless running up an enormous bill at Flemings' expense – and said to let you know in case he couldn't reach you. Your brother has all the makings of a professional scrounger, which might be the best route open to him. One should always convert one's hobbies into a career whenever possible."

"Oh, Dad, don't be too hard on him. Maybe I'll go to Paris for a couple of days and sort him out."

"It's high time you stopped taking responsibility for other people and looked after yourself, my girl, especially with a baby on the way. That should be your first priority. Now, as you remain your mother's first priority, would you like to speak to her? She badgering some Indian fellow in the kitchen about this knees-up we're having. I feel obliged to rescue him."

"If she can tear herself away."

"Wild horses wouldn't stop her talking to you, let alone one poor Indian. I'll offer him a beer."

I waited for my mother, wishing I knew what I wanted her to say.

"*Darling!* How's the trip?"

"Great."

"How's the hotel? Is it clean?"

I smiled at my mother's knee-jerk notion that the world was a hazardous, if enthralling, place once you left the Land of the Free. "It's lovely. Very romantic."

"And how's the pilot?"

"Funnily enough, he says he knew you."

"Really? How strange. Who is he? Come on, darling," she said impatiently, and I could hear the excitement in her voice, "I'm all agog."

"Theodore Hamilton."

There was quite a long pause. I could hear her breathing. "Theodore Hamilton. You've really met Theodore? I can hardly believe it."

"So you *did* know him?"

"Oh, yes." Her voice was subdued. I wondered if my father was in earshot. "Yes, I knew him all right. When I was in Cairo, he was stationed in the desert, 37th Squadron."

"That's the man."

"How extraordinary that you met him, of all people. I'm not sure I can quite believe it."

"That's why we came to France, Ma. Specifically to see him. I was surprised, because I don't remember you ever mentioning his name."

"Haven't I? I think I rather assumed he was dead. Theodore. I don't know what to say. You never told me who you were going to see. So he's living in France?"

"Well, obviously."

"With his wife?" I don't know if her voice changed or if I imagined a catch in it.

"She's dead."

"Oh. Poor Theodore."

"He's all right." I waited for her to say something, anything, but when she didn't, I continued, "Ma? He has a photograph of you. I saw a picture of you in a red coat."

"*Really?*" I don't know why she kept making me repeat everything I said – I was the one who should have been surprised, who should have been asking the questions. I don't know if her voice warmed up twenty degrees or so when she heard about the photo, or if that was just what I expected to hear.

"Yes, really. I found a photo of you wearing a red coat, d'you remember it? David and I had dinner with him last night and, lo and behold, there was this picture of you." I wasn't going to tell her he'd hidden it away in a cupboard. Not yet, at least. "You looked like Ingrid Bergman. In a red coat."

"People used to say that. I never saw it myself. I remember the coat."

"So, Mother, was there anything between you? Were you just friends or what?"

"Did you ask him?"

"No," I said immediately and I don't know why. "I wanted to ask you first. In case there was anything I should know." Having said this, I was unable to pass on his greeting to her.

"Oh, Elena . . . It was so long ago, I'm not sure . . . We were very good friends. He was – special. Dashing, rather glamorous, and oh, well, terribly touching, I suppose. We were both so young. How strange, after all this time . . . I can't get over the fact that you stumbled across him. I haven't heard of him for years and years."

"So was he your boyfriend?"

"It wasn't quite like that, darling. There were so many young men – so brave, all so sweet. We went out with all of them, Millie and I. I must have told you – we went out with different people every evening. Sometimes we had three dates a night."

"Yes, you have told me. Often." I felt very mean – I mean, I felt like *being* mean. "So Theodore was just one of the crowd? Part of the gang?"

"No. He was different."

"What made him different? I mean, if he *was* special then it's strange you've never mentioned him before, isn't it? You've joked about all sorts of other men."

"It's very hard to explain, darling. I'm a little – well, frankly, I'm a little shocked. Could I call you back? I have to . . . have to . . ."

I let her struggle for a moment. "Sort out the Indian bloke?"

"That's right. I don't want Daddy to confuse him

247

by giving him the wrong instructions. Let me get rid of him and I'll call you back."

"OK. You *will* call back, Ma, won't you? I mean, if I happen to see him again it would be helpful to know the background, you know what I mean?"

She didn't even reply; she put the phone down.

I lay back on the bed, wondering why I felt so miserable. Many years before, when I was at university, my mother had deeply disapproved of a man with whom I was involved; she wanted to know if we were sleeping together, or intending to. She took me out to dinner to discuss it. I tried changing the subject a hundred times to get her to back off and mind her own business, but she had kept asking questions, trying to pin me down to exactly how I felt and what I intended to do. In an unspeakably horrible way, the tables had turned and I had been bloody to her. I had known from her voice that Theodore Hamilton had meant a great deal to her. What I didn't know was why that should knock me for six. Theodore was a decent, intelligent and handsome man, I reasoned. My mother was a warmhearted, vibrant and beautiful woman. They had been young, single, in an exotic city during a war. It was hardly surprising if they had been attracted to each other and become friends at the very least. Quite suddenly, she had become a stranger, and quite suddenly, my vision of her and Daddy being perfect soul-mates began to dissolve. When Charlie and I were little, Dad used to light the papers off Italian ratafia biscuits and our eyes would follow the flimsy torches as they floated up to the ceiling, disintegrating into ashes as they rose. That's exactly how I felt about my parents' perfect union. I wished I'd never come to France.

I lay on the bed waiting for the phone. All sorts of wild ideas flew across my mind, even the possibility that my mother and Theodore had once been married and that this had been hidden from us. I jumped when the phone rang, and snatched it up.

"Elena? It's Theodore Hamilton."

"Oh."

"I was hoping I could tempt you and David on an afternoon's outing. I need to go to Monpazier to visit an ironmonger and I thought you might enjoy the ride and –"

"No, thanks. I need to catch up on some work. I'll just stay put here, but David might want to go. He's out. I'll ask him to call you when I see him."

"Of course. Well, I didn't want to disturb you . . ." He sounded diffident, and I realized how rude I had been – he was, after all, one of my interviewees.

"It's a great idea, but I'm just a little tied up at the moment."

"I quite understand – another time perhaps?"

"Sure. 'Bye then."

"Goodbye."

My hand was resting on the phone when it rang again. "Hello?"

"Darling, it's me."

"You got rid of the Indian, then?" I was sure that it was my father she'd got rid of.

"Yes . . . Elena, I'm sorry I was so peculiar when you called. I haven't heard Theodore Hamilton's name for an age. I haven't thought about him for a long time. When you said you'd met him, my legs turned to jelly. It was like seeing a ghost."

"So he *was* your boyfriend?" There is no appropriate word for one's mother's ex. I could hardly ask if he had been her lover – and main squeeze, partner or significant other were out of the question, even as a joke.

"I was in love with him."

Why hadn't I just asked her that?

"And he with you?"

"I believe so, at the time. Relationships – romances – were a little different then. We had so little time together, we talked in terms of dreams, not plans for the future. We relied heavily on letters. No one knew what the future held. We spent at least half the time we were together scheming how we could meet again. You couldn't see past the next day or the next time . . . But Theodore Hamilton was the first man I ever loved."

I was gripping the phone so hard that my knuckles were luminous. "Why didn't you marry him? If you loved each other so much?"

She sighed heavily. "I don't know how to answer that. For a time, we *did* talk of marriage, and then the situation changed, and it didn't work out as we'd planned. He was posted to Italy, I had to stay in Cairo, the war ended, and we parted . . ."

I crossed a secret first marriage off my list with a

great deal of relief, but I couldn't dispose of all my suspicions so easily. "So you just fell out of love?"

"I suppose so. Even now, it isn't very clear in my mind."

"Come on, Ma, you must remember. Did you break it off or did he? Did you just drift apart? You met someone else? Had a row? What?"

"Darling, it was long ago – I can't analyse these things. I couldn't at the time. They just happen. It was all very sad."

"I thought you said all your memories of the war years were happy ones, that you had such a good time."

"And that's true. All the things I tried to remember were happy. Of course bad things happened, but it's never worth dwelling on them. I remember feeling sad, that's all, and confused, and then I met your father and that was that. I only thought about the good times we'd had."

"So you were on the rebound when you met Daddy?"

Her tone changed from hurt to one of irritation. "No, I wasn't on the 'rebound', as you put it. I met Daddy long after Theodore and I parted. Now, look, I just don't want to talk about this any more."

"You don't want to know how he is – what he's like?" I taunted.

"Of course I'm curious, darling – anyone would be."

"Well, he's old."

"We're all old. Is he handsome?"

"Oh, God, Mother! He's nearly eighty!"

"Does that mean he can't be handsome?" I waited for her to point out that my father was still a handsome man, but she didn't.

"He's all right, for his age," I said grudgingly. "He's perfectly nice – just a quiet old man, pottering around his garden. He does a bit of painting, bit of photography, the regular stuff. Nothing special."

If ghosts had been stirred, they could damn well crawl back into their coffins as far as I was concerned. The ghosts fluttering around us belonged to somebody else – a foreign woman in a red coat who had nothing to do with my mother. That woman might have done anything, broken Theodore's heart, ditched him when he was risking his life for his country, had a string of lovers, but she wasn't my mother.

"You sound angry, darling. Are you angry with me?"

"No. Should I be?"

"I can't see any earthly reason why." She spoke quietly, but with that edge of wounded pride and maternal reprimand that I knew well. I could have listed a whole string of reasons, not the least being that she wasn't telling me everything.

"Are you planning to see him again?' she asked wistfully.

"I doubt it. I've done the interview. I might bump into him."

"If you do, tell him I asked after him, OK? Tell him . . . Ask him if he remembers Sham el Nessim."

"Sham el Nessim? What's that?"

"Nothing important. Just ask him if he celebrates it. He'll understand. If you see him, that is."

I certainly wasn't about to pass on any coded messages if she wasn't prepared to tell me what they meant. "You know, Ma, you could always call him yourself, if you're so keen to walk down Memory Lane. I'll give you his number."

In the pause before she replied, I prayed she wouldn't ask for it.

"No, darling, I don't think I'll call him, not now. If you see him, just give him my love."

This was worse than taking his number. It was such a harmless, careless little phrase, such an easy thing to give. I have said it a hundred times about a hundred people, "If you see him, give him my love." I could have said it about Nick, even about Peter, without it meaning a damn thing, and yet when my mother said it, it sounded reckless.

"And you give *Daddy* mine, OK?"

"Of course I will." And she hung up again without asking me a single thing about how I was . She didn't even mention the baby.

When David returned to the hotel, I passed on Daddy's message about Steve Heffner. Heff is the hardest drinking, drug-taking, party-going loon I have ever met. David said that his behaviour was mild compared to some of their colleagues, but I didn't buy this. Whenever I saw Steve Heffner I felt that I was chained by the ankle to a live bomb, breathlessly counting down to detonation.

"I'll see him in Paris before I fly. I haven't seen him for months."

"I thought I might go with you. I could see Charlie and I feel like seeing some bright lights."

"Bright lights are the last thing you need. We came here to avoid them. I'd feel a lot better thinking of you safe in sleepy Sainte Cécile, having early nights and late mornings."

"You sound like you want to get rid of me."

"Nope. The whole idea was that you'd have a rest in the country and keep your feet up."

"I've changed my mind. Maybe I just want to wave you off for once." In a relationship that consciously steered clear of patterns and habits, David and I had one rule: I never saw him off at the airport.

"Darling, if you want to come to Paris and see Charlie and Heff, that's fine by me. We'll go as soon as you like – I've got to fly out by Thursday night."

"So it's all confirmed?" I didn't need to ask.

"Yeah. I called the agency this morning, when you were having breakfast. By the way," he added hurriedly, "I met Theodore Hamilton in the square just now. Said something about a trip to Monpazier."

"What is he – some kind of jack-in-the-box?" I grumbled. "He keeps popping up every time we step outside. He's haunting me. Maybe he just hangs around the hotel waiting to bump into me accidentally on purpose – like a stalker. Or a Jehovah's Witness."

David shook his head slowly. "I don't understand

you. You were crazy about him at first. Now you think he's the devil incarnate. He's just a lonely old man, Elle. What's your problem with that?"

I tried again to explain how I felt, but my complaints sounded thin and shabby even to my ears.

"Why does it bother you that your mother fell in love? D'you think she was a nun or something? Shit, Elle, it's not like you had a spotless past yourself."

"What do you mean by that?"

"Whoa there, baby, easy now . . . I mean, you can't hack out a part of her past like it never happened. She'd be a different person. If you hadn't been with Peter, you wouldn't be the same person you are now."

"No, I'd have a darn sight more self-respect." I was trying to lighten the conversation, but I was chewing on David's words. It was ironic. He came back from trips, hacked out great chunks of himself, buried them away with his film and pulled them out again when he left. I guess he hacked me out when he was working and hauled me out of cold storage when he came home. Like it never happened. Huh. Sure.

"Don't go blaming your mother and Theodore because they had some kind of a thing forty-some years ago."

"It wasn't a thing. She was in love with him."

"*So what?*"

"You're being de*lib*erately obtuse. It's my *mother*, for God's sake. She's not *meant* to have been in love with anyone, *ever*, except my father. It's just not right. It's sick. It's not . . ."

"What?" He had one eyebrow quirked and that glint in his eye.

"Just sod off, all right? If I want to resent my mother for whatever reason then I'm entitled to do so, without any interference from you."

"You surely think a lot about entitlement, don't you, darling? It's one of your ob—"

"Look. As far as I can see, I'm not entitled to anything any more. I'm not entitled to want to know about my mother because it's her life. I'm not entitled to drink because it's bad for the baby, and I'm not entitled to ask you not to go to Bosnia, because –"

"Because?"

"Because I'm just not, all right? I'm not entitled to worry about you getting a bullet through your back, I'm not entitled to know if you sleep with a different woman every night when you're not with me – oh, shit, I'm not fucking entitled to anything. Fuck all."

I hadn't intended to raise the Bosnia issue, I really hadn't. It just slipped out, as they say. I had never before told David that I didn't want him to take a job, and even if I hadn't stated it quite so baldly, the implication was obvious. I knew that wasn't the way. Whatever panned out between me and David, he wasn't going to change his whole life just because I asked him to and I didn't want to make him feel guilty about leaving me. I had the feeling I was being left behind by everyone.

"You missed a couple, Elle." David lit a cigarette. "You're not entitled to rave like a banshee and you're not entitled to curse like a trooper in front of my unborn child."

"Asshole," I said lovingly. It was the first time he had said "my" not "your". "You're not entitled to smoke in front of *my* unborn child."

"I'll step outside."

"Oh, forget it, smoke all you like. I don't want to fight on my own. It's too exhausting playing both parts."

"I don't want to fight at all." His hand cupped my cheek and I turned my face into his palm.

"You're no fun, that's your problem. You have this mad, bad, dangerous career just to make up for the fact that you have no spirit of adventure. You should have been an accountant." I bit his hand gently. "So if we can't fight, what *can* we do? Other than worship your Leica."

"Tell you what. How about you scrub your mouth out with soap, then pack a bag, and I'll sweet-talk Madame Guillot into holding the room for you next week. I'm going to call Theodore and tell him we're in Paris for a few days. One of us needs to show some manners. Then let's hit the road. You want to fly, drive or catch a train?"

"So I *can* come to Paris?"

He shrugged. "You're entitled, Elle. You're a big girl now – some of the time that is."

"You won't regret it."

"I already do."

"Let's get a train. It's more romantic. Tell you what – let's go on a sleeper, have a three-course dinner in the dining car and make love in the couchette. I'll even wear a flower behind my ear."

"You and Romance, Elle. It'll be the death of you, mark my words. Romance is going to catch up with you and bite you in the ass."

He couldn't have put it better. Romance – and nostalgia, to be honest – tug me with the strength of a St Bernard hound spotting a lamp-post. I once read that Winston Churchill had a disease that made him weep whenever he read, heard or spoke certain trigger words like honour, decency, valour, nobility, courage . . . At that time, I found my throat closing around all these word, and several others. It hasn't got any better since then, so I can't put it down to an oestrogen surge.

David stopped in the doorway and turned back to me. "Hey, Elle, you were wrong about one thing. It's not a different woman every night." He flashed a grin. "Not *every* night."

CHAPTER ELEVEN

My fantasies of wild sex on a sleeper were nipped in the bud when we found out that the journey on the TGV took less than four hours door to door. We did what we could to conjure up French films (or at least English films set in France), and had baguettes and wine on the train. It wasn't the same as being served breakfast by the steward in our first-class cabin, before alighting at the Gare du Nord in great swirls of rising steam, but it worked for me, and I guess we have to pay some kind of price for mobile phones, air-conditioning and contraceptives – not that I set great store on the reliability of the third. We had come to a tacit agreement to avoid all issues likely to upset the apple cart. David was full of the restless energy that fuelled him before assignments, like a racehorse sensing the off.

On arrival, we went first to the Meurice to track down Charlie. We found him next to the indoor pool with a bottle of wine in a cooler.

"Hey, Charlie, interviews taking their toll?"

"Sis! What a surprise! I was going to call you and come down for a breath of country air." He and David slapped each other on the back in that cautious yet intimate way boys have. "Join me for a drink?"

"Sure, but Elena's not drinking."

"Liverish, Elle?"

"Pregnant, Charlie."

Charlie's eyes opened wide. "Now *that* calls for champagne! Stand up, I want to see it. Are you fat yet? Can I feel it kicking? Boy, oh, boy. Uncle Charles – has a ring to it, doesn't it?" He tucked his thumbs behind imaginary braces and puffed out his chest. "A baby. Hot diggety-dog! Congrats, Turk, and *well done*."

"It was masterful, even if I say so myself. It took skill, determination, impeccable precision timing, no small amount of flair . . ."

Charlie was nodding with admiration "And, seeing it's my sister, I daresay some degree of self-lessness and dedication to duty were called for . . ."

"When your time comes, Charles, I'd be most happy to advise."

"Could you two just shut it and someone get me an orange juice if that isn't too much to ask?"

We caught up quickly with Charlie's news. He'd spent ten days tracking down old friends, intermittently meeting bankers and playing hard to get, and was kicking his heels before flying to Hong Kong and Singapore for another bout of corporate seduction. He had the luck of the devil, that boy, always has had. He'd finally come to a sound analysis of his future. "If they give me the job, and I take it, it'll be snout to the grindstone and tail between hind legs for the next twenty years. If they don't give me the job, or I don't take it, then I'm bust as a bum and I might as well make hay while the sun shines. Fill 'em up, David, there's a good chap."

We stayed with him for an hour before crossing town to check into one of David's old haunts in the Marais – a long way from the Meurice but just round the corner from Steve Heffner's apartment. David said he didn't fancy a long trek home after an evening with Heff.

"You've got a surprise in store," Charlie'd said, tapping the side of his nose, "mark my words."

Steve Heffner, five foot five, nearly bald at the age of thirty-three and swamped in a red kimono, threw open the door of his flat and literally leapt into David's arms, wrapping his legs around his waist. "Turk! Turk! Turk!" he chanted. "Way to go, Turk!" David detached himself like a large dog throwing an over-ebullient puppy off its back .

"How's it hanging, Heff?"

Steve didn't reply as he was occupied in kissing me hard on the mouth with both hands under my buttocks. We didn't have to wait long to hear the surprise. Heff was known for many things – insanity, lechery and depravity spring to mind – but reticence was not among them.

"Guys, this is *great*, this is fuckin' A – fuckin *A* – I want y'all to meet the little lady. Mish!" he yelled, and a tiny Asian woman appeared from a door, sporting a matching kimono. "Mish, these are my best friends, my best buddies on the whole fuckin' planet. Turk Turcan and Elena – what's your surname, Elle baby? Shit, who gives a damn? Guys, this is my *wife* Mishi. Now, ain't she just a peach?"

David roared with laughter, and kissed Mishi extravagantly on both cheeks. I followed suit.

"Now I got me some bourbon – got me some Wild Turkey somewhere around this shit-hole." Heff started throwing clothes and cushions around the small room, found a half-full bottle under a sofa, and wiped out four tumblers with his kimono sleeve. He sat down on the sofa, legs apart, tackle on full display, and filled the glasses.

"Three-legged horses, my friends."

"The One That Got Away," David intoned in a reverential voice.

This idiosyncratic toast originated from the first time Heff and David had met. I'd heard the story from Heff – I'd heard it many times, each one more exaggerated than the last. Heff, David and an interpreter had been travelling together somewhere in Afghanistan going to meet a Kurdish leader. In Heff's words, it went something like this:

"These guys were like fuckin' warlords, something out of the Middle Ages, know what I mean?

There's this Welsh land-mine expert with us and he's trying to persuade the big chief to get his people to stop fuckin' off with the barbed wire, y'know? The poor assholes would risk their lives defusing a path through mine-fields, wiring off the no-go areas so the locals would be safe, and then the natives rip the barbed wire out because they want it to keep their fuckin' *livestock*. So the sheep and chickens are safe as houses but the kids are getting blown into bits and pieces. Bright, no? Mr Big Tribal Lord's in a tent, right, when we get there, and he's got his heavies round him, village elders, and he's standing there, big as a house, arms folded across his chest, with a fucking *sabre* hanging off his belt, and we've got an interpreter, so the mine guy starts explaining, real polite, that if he could just get his people to lay off the barbed wire, it would be for the good of their kids, y'know, because they're running short of the fuckin' stuff, as his people keep stealing it. And the big warlord nods his head real slow, and he thinks for a while, and then he says, real smooth, 'I understand your problem. As of today, this must trouble you no longer. Do not be concerned. I know these people. I will send my people to them tonight and they will be killed. They will not trouble you again.' So the Welsh guy starts jumping up and down like he's learnin' the fuckin' Charleston on hot bricks, screaming, 'No, no, leave 'em alone! They can *have* the barbed wire!'"

If he enacts all the parts, as he is inclined to do, arms folded across his own chest, jumping up and down on the table when he becomes the mine expert, the story can take a good ten minutes before he gets to the horse. Heff is a great story-teller. That's what makes him such a good reporter. Moving right along to the horse:

"We don't know what shit's gonna happen to the sheepshaggers in the next valley, y'know? The mine guy's just gibbering there in a heap. Turk says, real formal like, that he's heard tell of a horse – a *horse*, you hear me – that stepped on a mine and got a leg blown off but survived. This horse is moseying around on three legs, happy as Larry. And Turk explains that people in England are weird, they're schizo, and if he takes a photograph of the *horse*, it might do more for the guy's cause than twenty pictures of little kids hoppin' about on one leg, right? And the big man nods again, real serious and knowing, and he says, 'I know this horse. He is many miles distant . . . Over the hill, through the pass, he lives three valleys away, this horse. It will take you two, three days to journey there. My men will take you to this horse.' And Turk, no fuckin' idiot, right, says, 'Forget it. I'm not spending five days for a picture of a fuckin' horse, three legs or not.' Heff pauses and licks his lips in anticipation. 'And the big guy listens, and his big ol' shaggy head nods again, real slow, and he says, 'I understand, this is not a problem. We have *another* horse outside. We can arrange it for you. You prefer front leg or back leg?'"

That's why they always drink to three-legged

horses, and The One That Got Away.

Now, I know Heff very well indeed and I should have smelt a rat, I really should have, but my nose wasn't working properly. He caught me off guard when we arrived in his flat that night. Besides, I had seen the syndrome among David's cronies before – manic war correspondent goes semi-native shacking up with Third-World girl and brings her back to so-called civilization before she dumps him for a regular guy with a steady job and a nice home in Shepperton. It might have shocked Charlie but it didn't raise a flicker of an eyelash from me. I could have written that script with my eyes closed. I took a sip of the rot-gut, to show willing, and sat down next to the veritably peach-like Mishi. She looked about sixteen, huge eyes rimmed with black silk, gleaming hair with the authentic raven's-wing-blue shine, and flat cheeks like antique porcelain.

"Go ahead, Elle, don't hold back, honey, you know you're busting. Ask her why she hooked up with me. Go ahead. Ask her," Heff encouraged, wiping his mouth with the back of his hand.

"Mishi, do you have any idea what you have let yourself in for?" I responded obediently. "Do you have any notion of the bad habits that are engrained in the excuse for a human being that you now have to call your husband?" I said this entirely for Heff's benefit. If I knew Heff, Mishi had no more English than, "Hi, you want to buy me a drink, buddy? I make you feel real good . . ."

"Bad habits?" Heff looked puzzled, and socked David in the shoulder. "What lies you been telling her, farm boy? Bad habits – shit – I got no bad habits. Booze, for sure, recreational drugs, dandy, but *bad habits*? I don't leave the toilet seat up hardly ever, I've near about stopped pickin' my nose, in public leastwise, and I only eat toe wax when I'm goddamn starving."

I hunched my shoulders. "See what I mean, Mishi? You would have been better off going down to the local zoo and marrying a monkey."

"Funny you should say that. That's exactly where I found the asshole," Mishi replied, in a soft voice with a heavy American accent. "Sittin' on the bottom of his cage picking lice out of his pubic hair. He was so fuckin' helpless I had to bring him home, scrub him down and remind him that lurking some- where under all that shit there was a *bona fide* man."

My jaw dropped, and David and Heff laughed till tears poured down their cheeks. When he could control himself, David said, "Elena, it is my great honour to introduce Sarah Beth Franklin, of the Brooklyn Heights Franklins. Known to friend and foe alike as Mishi. Some folks say that's short for Miss Saigon, and some say it's for Mission Impossible. Mishi works for the *Post*. We all go way back."

"Thanks a bunch, friends," I said, with feeling. "That was really nice. Remind me to introduce my foot to your groin next time we meet, Heff."

When Heff could speak without choking, he

explained, "Mish is one half Vietnamese, one half Chinese and one half Yank. Like a fine cocktail. Stirred, but never shaken." He raised his glass to her.

"Three halves. Maths was never your strong point, was it, Heff?" I countered.

Mishi patted me on the knee. "Ignore the children, Elena. Anyone would have made the same mistake, so long as I keep my mouth shut. I only do it from time to time to amuse Heff. His sense of humour got stuck long before adolescence. I really *am* a Miss Saigon girl – my dad was a no-good-shit GI but he was good enough to marry my mom and get her back to the States and knocked up in between tours. I've known Heff and Turk since I was way high." She held her hand about three feet off the floor. She wasn't much bigger than that now.

We had one hell of a party. Heff was a very different character from David, and Mishi seesawed somewhere in between the two men. Whereas David disliked talking about where he had been and what he had seen, Heff couldn't stop himself collaring any stranger who stepped close enough, draping his arm around their shoulders and giving them a blow-by-blow account of his last trip to Kabul. Those who didn't know him saw him as a crazy drunk, but for all the substances Heff consumed, I don't think I ever saw him drunk. Crazy, without a doubt, but not drunk. We ended the evening the only people in a back street bar somewhere in the 4th drinking shots. Well, they were drinking shots, I was drinking gallons of water and inflating like a balloon. When two young English girls came in, probably on their first ever trip abroad without their parents, Heff waved them over to join us, and gazed deep into the eyes of the prettier one. "Hell, honey, if I was a marrying man . . . there's nothing I wouldn't promise you, baby. You want rose gardens? I'll buy you two dozen. You sure are one gorgeous-looking woman." The poor girl was half blushing, half scowling, uncertain if she was being courted or mocked. She glanced from Heff to her friend, who was seriously scowling, knowing full well she was not being courted, and back to Heff again. He took her hand in both of his, nearly drooling over her. "'She walks in beauty, like the moon,'" he crooned.

Next to me Mishi was giggling uncontrollably. "Shit, now we're for it. When Heff starts reciting poetry – or trying – it's that time again. Time to call the cops . . ."

"'Had I the world's embroidered cloths, I'd lay 'em real gentle under your pink tootsies . . .'"

I was watching Heff, feeling sorry for the poor girl and sorrier for Yeats, when I felt David's lips moving softly against my ear. I closed my eyes, leaden-limbed and drowsy at the sound of his voice.

> *"Had I the heavens' embroidered cloths,*
> *Enwrought with golden and silver light,*
> *The blue and the dim and the dark cloths*
> *Of night and light and the half light,*
> *I would spread the cloths under your feet:*

> *But I, being poor, have only my dreams;*
> *I have spread my dreams under your feet;*
> *Tread softly, because you tread on my dreams."*

When I opened my eyes, I saw Mishi watching us with a sad expression on her lovely face. Heff hadn't noticed a thing. He was playing to the gallery.

"Picture it. We're crouching there, up against a wall, we've been squatting there for an hour or so, shit coming from all directions, and then it goes as quiet as the grave, like the whole city just died in one breath, and my heart's as tight as a football, kind of busting out of my ribs I'm so scared, and then this woman with a little baby comes walkin' down the street like she's out for a Sunday stroll, and I stand up, 'cause if I don't stretch my legs I swear to God they're gonna fall straight off like an overcooked chicken's, know what I mean, and then there's this fuckin' shot, and Turk – this guy, yeah? – he shoves me so hard that my face hits the dirt and I smash my front tooth through my lip. I have this brain flash like, How'm I gonna find a dentist in Bei-fuckin-root, and how'm I gonna get the fucker to pay for the crown work? Y'know what I mean, and in that flash a bullet goes *cra*-ack against the wall, ricochets off, and flies straight into Turk's shoulder, and I've got my face in the dirt and blood coming out of my mouth, but I've kind of craned my head round to show him what he's done and give him shit, y'know, and I see the fuckin' strap on his fuckin' camera snap,

269

and Turk drops down slowly on one knee, and I'm thinking he's dead, wiped, y'know, and he's there on one knee, *focusing* the fuckin' camera on the woman with the baby, and she's strolling down the street like she's in a trance . . . Turk's got this scorch on his T-shirt and underneath I can see just pale pink skin, sweet like a baby's. You know where that bullet was headed?"

He raised his hand in imitation of a gun and pressed two fingers against his temple. I turned to look at David.

Heff paused for dramatic tension and then continued. "Right there. That one had my name on it, it was going straight through one ear and out the other. I'm telling you, this guy – *this* guy – he's the one you want to be with when the shit hits the fan. If you want to save your own ass, snuggle it up to Turk's as close as you can, hear what I'm saying? He's . . . *sacred*." Heff leant across the booth and kissed David on the mouth.

The girls looked scared witless and made excuses to leave. Heff sat nodding, saying, "Have a good one, y'hear?" as they made their way to the door. I felt nauseous, and began to tremble. David looked at me, and shook his head very slowly, once, twice, before turning to Heff. His grey eyes had gone dark. David had this strange thing about him – an air of being semi-detached. People never knew whether he was on the verge of sharing a great joke, or about to get up and walk out of the room. He gave no warning signs.

"You're full of shit, Heffner."

"I call it like I see it, buddy. That's my job."

Mishi leant across the table. "Turk, you leave him alone, OK? Sure, he's a fuckhead but he's *my* fuckhead, and I'll deal with it. Elena, Heff has to say these things, he's just going to blow a fuse if it doesn't come out. It doesn't mean anything. It doesn't make any sense. Think about it. You think either David or Steve is stupid enough to stand up and wave when a sniper's around? Like fuck they are. They know how to take care of themselves."

I nodded, but I had seen the photograph of the woman and baby in Beirut. I'd seen the T-shirt, with a kind of a rip and a smoky burn around it. David had told me it was from a cigarette and I hadn't thought twice about it.

"Hey, Turk, you ever tell Elena about the three-legged horse? He tell you that one, Elle? That was the best. I pissed myself, I'm tellin' you. Literally pissed myself. Shit. There's more than one old nag out there that owes its fuckin' *life* to Turk. Three-legged horses, hey, Turk old buddy?"

They touched their glasses together and called for another round. I ordered a cognac from a guy who looked like he'd pay us a fortune if we'd only agree to go home before trashing the bar. David didn't notice me drink it.

"So, Turk, where's the next tour of duty for the lucky Leica?"

David lit his twentieth cigarette of the night and inhaled deeply, dragging the smoke into him so nothing ever came out again. "I'm going to Sarajevo tomorrow."

I saw Heff and Mishi look at each other quickly, then Heff slapped him on the back.

"Let an old friend give you a tip. Don't go there, man. It ain't worth it. Nothing to see, nothing to do, except get royally fucked. You don't want to mess with it, buddy, you don't need it." David was smiling at him, that slow, ironic smile that made my bones hurt. "It ain't your scene, Turk. I was there, end of last year, but it ain't the place to be now. I wouldn't touch it."

"What's the problem, Heff? They run out of booze or something?"

"It's a weird place, y'know? A dug-out pit of fuckin' quicksand. You get in, you can't get out. Shit, man, that's what the job's all about, ain't it? Getting in and getting out.."

I wanted so badly to listen, I was jingling, but I was overcome with weariness. It must have been three in the morning. I slumped against David's shoulder, willing myself to hear what they were saying, drifting in and out of their conversation.

". . . Martin's there. Micky too – remember Micky – red hair, fuckin' whore."

". . . Bottom line, Turk, fuck out of it, you ain't got nothing to prove no more.."

". . . Don't know what I need, no more than you . . ."

". . . You see Kravski's work? He's gone . . ."

". . . In the end, you've just got to be there . . ."

"... Got to take her home ... around four tomorrow ..."

"... Consider it done, my man ..."

I don't remember getting back to the hotel. When I woke up it was lunch-time. We made love, with a kind of sleepy hunger. David's gentleness frightened me. I kept hearing snatches of words in my head and I didn't know if I had heard them or dreamt them. We walked around the corner to a restaurant and ordered lunch. There was so much I wanted to tell him. I wanted to say that I loved him. I wanted to tell him how proud I was, that there wasn't a man on earth who could touch him. I wanted to tell him that for all my bitching and griping, I knew why he was doing this, and I was glad he did it, and I didn't want to be with anyone else. I'd rather be alone. I wanted to ask him not to go, but I didn't have the guts to do that. I sat there feeling sick and sad, and playing with his lighter, and occasionally looking at him and saying, "I'm coming to the airport," and he would smile and answer, "No, you're not." It was a miserable little lunch.

My heart was full of many things, but my brain and my mouth wouldn't function. I know we talked about the two girls in the bar the night before; we talked about Theodore; we even talked about the weather. We talked about babies' names again, with laboured flippancy. I felt hung over. My mouth was chalky and I had to make an effort to chat about why I didn't like Martin and did like Arthur. I was working hard to keep time moving. David told me not to be frightened, and I said I wasn't. He told me he was coming back to the Lion d'Or for me. I can't say what was in my head at all, except that I wanted the lunch to be over and him to be gone, and that I didn't want to go to the airport, but I kept insisting that I did. I know he told me that he'd be fine, that he knew it in his bones or he wouldn't go. I remember saying that was crap, and what made him any different from any of the other morons. He laughed and said he had the book to finish, and he never walked out on a contract. We joked again about the horse. We drank far too much coffee. I wanted to cry. I wanted to be at home. I didn't know what I was doing there, or who I was any more, or how Bosnia fitted into the whole scheme of things. I just knew that he was going to walk away without saying goodbye.

While David was talking and I was flicking his lighter again and again, Mishi and Heff turned up and sat down at the table, and I looked up and said, "Oh, *hi!*" as if I hadn't seen them for a year or two, and had no idea why they were there. David looked at his watch, stood up, put his bag over his shoulder and picked up his cameras. He came round to my side of the table, laid his hands on either side of my face and kissed me as he had never kissed me before. I knew then, for an absolute certainty, that I wasn't going to see him ever again. He left his lighter on the table, and I turned it over and over in one hand, put my head on the white tablecloth and howled like a dog. It wasn't only that he'd gone. It was that we'd had two years and seven weeks of messing around without my ever telling him what I felt, and there was no way I'd get that time back.

Mishi stroked my head. "He's coming back, Elena. He's gonna walk in your door in two weeks' time like he's never even been away. He's real cool-headed, and that's what makes the difference between the guys . . ." her voice trailed away, but I knew what she was going to say. "He'll be back."

"Fuckin' right he will. The Turk. Fuckin' *A*." Heff raised David's glass to him in his absence, and I could have smashed it out of his hand.

"You better be right, Heff, because I swear to God if he doesn't come back I'll kill the stupid bastard myself."

Charlie did his best to help, bless him, when we had dinner that night. He tried to talk about David and the baby, but I just couldn't face it. I told him briefly about Theodore and our mother, which made Charlie laugh.

"It all fits, doesn't it, Elle? It all makes sense. Last time I talked to Dad about women, he told me that the thing that made Mum so special was that he never felt he knew her at all. Not after forty years together. That she always surprised him. He said he never knew how she was going to react or what she was all about. I'll bet Dad has no idea about this old pilot. She's brilliant."

"That's disgusting. She must have told him."

"Why? If I were him, I wouldn't want to know. And if I were her, I wouldn't want to tell. What's the point? I like the idea of wondering about a woman – there being some mystery, doors you can't pass through. You've always had such a beef about honesty, Elle. Everybody needs secrets to hold them together. That's what keeps them young at heart."

"Are you suggesting that our mother and father had a series of secret affairs throughout their married life?"

"Of course I'm not. I just happen to think that the allure survives better when you don't know every tiny tedious detail . . . So does Dad."

"I never knew you talked to Daddy about women."

Charlie sat back with the air of a man of the world. "Who else is he going to talk to? We've talked about different things – how he felt when Mum couldn't get pregnant."

"I didn't know she couldn't get pregnant."

"Christ, Elle, they got married when she was thirty-one – they didn't have us for years. Didn't you ever ask, when she told you about periods and stuff?"

"I just thought they'd planned it that way."

"And you didn't talk about it when you got pregnant?"

"No. We haven't even been alone since I got pregnant."

"Poor Mum." Charlie looked at me sadly. "Poor old Mum. I mean, you're her only daughter . . ."

"I realize that, Charlie. Mother and I happen to be very close, closer than you can ever appreciate. It's just that everything happened at once."

"So instead of talking to her about having a baby, you bollocked her about this geriatric pilot?"

I put my head in my hands. "God, Charlie. I don't know what to think any longer. I have the strongest sensation that everyone on earth except me has all the answers."

"You know what you need to do, big sis? You need to stop asking so many questions."

I slept in Charlie's bed that night, and the next morning began the journey back to Sainte Cécile. That's where I'd told David I would be. It crossed my mind that when he was killed his agency would probably know first, and they wouldn't know where I was. I'd probably hear it from Heff, or read it in the papers.

Cairo

June 1st, 1943
c/o United States Mission

Dearest Theo,

Work hectic again, as everyone is on the move. Cairo seems deadly quiet. I went to a mess do last night for a departing American squadron, and felt so peculiar knowing where they were going when they did not. Of course I don't know where you *are going, and I'm glad that I don't.*

I have taken on some extra classes at the language school. You would laugh if you could see us. Millie and I are there as 'conversational tutors', and every Tuesday we make up a little tea party of four with two young officers of the Egyptian Air Force. We were instructed to talk just as we would with fellow Americans, but the poor boys don't really have enough English for that, and are terribly shy, just stammering and filling our cups with more and more tea until I'm sure it will gush from my ears. Millie and I take it in turns with Ahmed and Naguib, and they repeat, parrot fashion. Whether this does any good or not I can't say, but last night produced a lively conversation, when Ahmed got into the swing of things:

Millie: How are you today, Naguib?

Naguib: How are you today, Naguib?

Millie: No. How are you today, Miss Barclay?

Naguib: How are you today, Miss Barclay?

Millie: I am very well, thank you. And you?

Naguib: I am very well, thank you.

Me: I am drinking tea. I drink tea, you drink tea; Miss Barclay drinks tea. Are you drinking tea, Ahmed?

Ahmed: I drink tea, you drink tea, Miss Barclay drinks tea. Are you drinking tea, Naguib?

Naguib: I drink tea, Miss Kézdy drinks tea, Ahmed drinks tea, are you drinking tea,

Miss Barclay?

Millie (feeling bold): No, I am not drinking tea. I am sitting on a chair. I sit on a chair, you sit on a chair, Miss Kézdy sits on a sofa. Ahmed?

Ahmed (very slowly and with great care): I am not drinking tea. I am shitting on a chair. I shit on a chair, you shit on a chair, Miss Kézdy shits on a shofa. Do you shit on a chair, Naguib?

Naguib: Yes, I shit on a chair . . .

And so it went on. Poor Millie turned purple trying to control herself. The boys are very proud, and it would be horribly cruel to laugh at them. Millie and I had a couple of martinis after to recover. I can't help feeling that we are not doing the best job here . . .

Other than that, Cairo is all the usual titbits of intrigue – who was last seen with whom, which general's wife has packed her bags and returned home in a fury, which VIP was spotted at the Auberge des Pyramides dancing with 'a certain British lady', whether the Minister for Cultural Affairs was really pie-eyed at the mission dinner, all the standard tales of indiscretion and scandal, political and other, that make Cairo tick.

I accompanied Mac to Ankara last week. It has a very different atmosphere. We dined at Baba Karpic's restaurant on caviare and champagne, with a table of Germans on one side and a table of Brits on the other, the Hungarian orchestra alternating between 'God Save the

King' (requested by the Germans) and 'Lili Marlene' (requested by the Brits). I feared a scuffle, but each studiedly ignored the other. Afterwards there was a brawl at the hotel nightclub, between Turks and some American boys who arrived and cut in on their ladies. We were with a British air commodore and assistant air attaché, who decided that although we Yanks were allies, this was one fight they could afford to stay out of. We took cover, the band vamoosed, and we watched tables flying overhead, just like a scene in a Hollywood gangster flick. I worried that our boys would be arrested, but things calmed down and the band was persuaded to return. Frankly, I think the Turkish gals enjoyed the attention of the Americans. The Air Commodore told me a great tale of the Turks and their POWs – in general they're well treated, and allowed to have food and drink sent in from the hotels, but one Brit so offended his Turkish guards that they banned his alcohol ration. He sent word to the hotel to deliver 'fruit salad' every day for breakfast, lunch and dinner, in the form of a large bowl of clear 'fruit juice' with an olive or two floating on top . . .

The days drag without you. I cannot believe that only a month has passed since Sham el Nessim – only a month of being apart with so many to come. We hear good news from the front, but we all wish this was over, not just in North Africa but all over – and then sometimes

I think that if the war ends, you will return to England and I back home, and I find myself wishing that it will never end, if that's the price we will pay . . . How wicked I am.

It's now one in the morning; we are sharing our apartment with two British girls in transit. Millie and I were shocked to find them washing their stockings every night – they have only one pair – so we gave them each silk and nylons in exchange for lipstick. I am learning to barter as well as any Mouski trader. I must sleep – only to curl up and dream of you, wherever you are – with many kisses and hugs, my darling, good-night, goodnight . . .

Later.
Hardly any sleep at all – our guests rose at five to catch their plane, and Millie and I saw them off, and I can't get back to sleep however I try. In this half light, I can't write of silly little things the way I ought. All I can think of is you, Theo dearest, and whether you are in the air or just returned, whether you are safe and sound and when I will see you. My whole heart wants to believe in the rosy picture you painted at Shepheard's, and then the doubts and fears begin and there's nothing but work to get away from them. Yes, you are right, sometimes I do wish that we hadn't met, that I could be free of fear. Only a year ago I was innocently carefree, and now I don't know who I am or what is to come . . . My

mother used to say, "*Always remember that you are a lady*" and I try, but I don't feel like a lady any more, just a heartstruck foolish thing. Does war fan the flames? Would we love each other so much without it? I don't know, and I don't care to. It raises too many questions.

Your last question being marriage. When I arrived in England, en route for Cairo, a GI warned me about the Limeys. He said they all wanted – and all *they* wanted – was to marry an American passport. Now I know how that will make you smile, in your superior British way, so don't take it to heart. What I am trying to say is that yes, I love you, with all my heart, but I have lost my bearings. A year ago, I was a nice girl from New Jersey, dating a boy back home, loving my parents and not wanting to settle down until I had made something of my life. Now everything has turned upside down, and the room is still spinning, and I don't know where things will settle. So far, it is enough for· me to love you and believe that you love me, and the only plans I can manage are how we can meet again, where we will meet again, and the wishing and the praying that God keeps you safe. And I keep trusting that He will, and one day you and I will be together, and the war over, and we will meet at a little sidewalk café, and have all the time in the world to talk of the future. And until then, let's not talk of it – oh, we can dream of it all right, but only dream. Not too *much thinking or talking, please.*

The most important thing is that you keep your spirits up. It breaks my heart to think of you blue, and it worries me. I don't want you to pretend to me, I don't want you to wear a brave face when you feel sad – but when you are sad, I want you to remember that you made a promise to keep yourself, body and soul, well for me. That's a big responsibility, and I will hold you to it, Flight Lieutenant Hamilton, with every breath and bone in my body – every breath and bone in my body being already yours.

Mac's wife arrived the day before yesterday – only for a couple of days, as she has to return home to the children. I booked them a room at Shepheard's, and Mac was as cross as a bear with a sore head the next morning. They were kept up half the night by soldiers racing gharries in the street outside, and he finally resorted to flinging a bar of soap at them to get them to shut up. The soldiers, of course, were used to having far worse things thrown at them, and didn't pay him any heed. Poor Mac – he had been counting on a romantic second honeymoon. It's strange, because I don't remember hearing anything but your voice the night of Sham el Nessim.

My darling, I must go to work. Mac is more chaotic than ever since Elisabeth arrived, and I have no more to say, except that I pray for you and I love you – so very much, with all my heart and strength – and that I am waiting for the simplest word from you. Until then, darling Theodore,

Your own Anna

It was somewhat ironic that the title Desert Air Force became official only as the war in the desert was over, and the assault on Italy began. En route to Kairouan, Theodore arranged two days' leave in Tunis, and signalled to Anna to join him there if she possibly could. He arrived at the hotel, one of several requisitioned as an officers' club, and asked for messages. There were none. Telling himself that it was unlikely that Anna had received his signal, even less likely that she would be able to get away at such short notice and impossible that she would have found transport, he lunched with Paddy Helsham, a pilot from the 70th Squadron, and strolled about the town, admiring the effect of the little white houses and domed mosques sparkling against the sea.

On his return, Paddy introduced him to two pretty girls, one fair, one dark. Paddy regaled them with tales of derring-do in the desert, and the girls responded with brazen admiration and much fluttering of lashes. The afternoon slid into evening and bottles of Chianti, and the foursome proceeded to a small French restaurant. The blonde was tireless in her pursuit of Theodore, *plying him with flattery and resting her head against his shoulder at every opportunity. Theodore wished that another's head nestled against him and that another's eyes gazed longingly into his own. When the girls went to powder their noses, Paddy nudged Theodore and winked. "What do you think, Theo? A lucky strike, no?"*

Theodore smiled wearily. "They're no worse than all the other Suzettes and Leilas and Nadias . . ."

"Cynical old bastard. It's not as if we've been drowning in the fairer sex for the past year, old man. You need to relax a little. Got someone back home, then?"

"No, I can't say that I have."

"So why the long face? Come along, Theo! Drink up! You don't know when you'll get a chance like this again – handed to you on a platter, so to speak."

The girls came back, lips the colour of blood, eyes predatory. The blonde approached the band leader, and a few moments later they struck up. She stood before Theodore, arms outstretched, fingers wriggling in invitation.

"For pity's sake, Hamilton, what's the matter with you, man?" Paddy hissed, and Theodore took her in his arms and danced.

He closed his eyes, but he could feel her bony hips jutting against his thighs, and he could smell her perfume, pungent and heavy. The cheap, hot smell of her nauseated him. He opened his eyes to find her watching him, eyes narrowed.

"You don't like me, do you, airman?"

"That's not true. I don't know you."

"I can tell. You don't like me. You think I am not good enough for you."

"I wouldn't presume to think that," Theodore said sincerely. "You are an attractive young lady. I can't believe you haven't a hundred hearts chalked up on your score. You don't want mine, too, do you?" He smiled down at her.

"You lie, airman. I see what is in your heart." She pressed her body closer to his and rubbed her head against the front of his dress jacket like a kitten. Theodore didn't reply, but his body stiffened, and she looked up slyly. "You think I have danced with Germans?"

Theodore didn't reply. He wanted to go back to the hotel and write to Anna. He wished he hadn't even come to Tunis.

"You're right. I have danced with Germans – and Italians and French and English, even Americans. You believe me?"

"If you say so."

"I will show you. My English is good, no? Listen to me, airman." She danced on tiptoe, her lips fluttering against his ear as he bent his head accommodatingly. "Ti amo. Ich liebe dich. I love you. Je t'adore. I want you, baby." Her voice was soft and rippling with hatred. "It is not so hard, really. All men are the same."

Theodore held her by the forearms and pushed her back from him.

Her eyes flashed. "I know things, airman, you will never know. You think it is easy to be a nice, proper girl in Tunis? You think I should stay home, month after month waiting for the British to come?" Her carmine lips curled. "You think because you are a proper English gentleman you deserve better than me, no?"

"No," Theodore said, his heart full of pity.

"Kiss me. Kiss me, airman."

Theodore held her firmly away from him, and returned to the table. He left Paddy with a girl on each arm, and walked quickly back to the hotel.

Anna was sitting at a table on her own, watching the door. When she saw him, she ran across the room and threw herself into his arms. Immediately she drew back, her nose wrinkling. "Theo, where on earth have you been? You smell of tart's cologne . . ." Her hand plucked a stray golden hair off his dress jacket. "I moved hell and earth to get here tonight. Mac had to pull every string in the book to get my transport, and you –"

"Anna, will you marry me?"

"Marry you?" she hissed at him. "Are you drunk? Is this your 'Yankee Girl, wilt marry me' lark? Just keep it for the officers' mess. I don't find it very funny."

"I have never been more serious in my life. I have never wanted anything more. Will you marry me, dearest?"

She stepped back to allow a group of more than merry Australians to pass through the door. Theodore took her elbow and led her out of the hotel and onto the street. Anna wrestled her arm free and stood feet apart. "I have to get back to Cairo tomorrow. It looks to me like I shouldn't have bothered to come."

"Anna, you don't understand."

"Talk fast, buddy. I'm a quick learner." Her toe tapped on the pavement.

Theodore pushed his fair hair out of his eyes. He was irritated by her jealousy: they had no time for it. "I had dinner with Paddy Helsham and a couple of local girls he'd picked up. It was monumentally tiresome. Let's not waste precious time talking about a hair on my jacket."

Anna looked him up and down through narrowed eyes, and picked another hair off his collar. Then her face broke into a smile. "That reminds me of something. I brought you a present." She felt in her bag and put a small package in his hands. Wrapped in layers of silk, Theodore found a little golden locket, inscribed with his initials. He opened it to see a small blue stone entwined in golden hair.

"Marry me, Anna."

"No. This isn't the way. Not when I don't know what's going to happen tomorrow, when you're about to leave, when I don't know if you'll be dead next week . . ."

"We're not leaving. Not yet. We're posted to Kairouan. Anna, I love you with my whole heart. I won't let anything come between us, certainly not some sad, silly girl, who deserves your pity as well as mine. I didn't believe you'd get here. I couldn't let myself believe it and then be disappointed. Marry me. Please, Anna. If somebody up there would promise me just one whole year of being with you, I would willingly trade my remaining life for that and consider it a good bargain. I have to pinch myself to believe you're here. Perhaps you should slap me, so that I can be certain."

"I won't." She stared at the ground.

"Go on – you know it'll make you feel better."

"Oh, if you insist . . ." Her arm drew back and, as Theodore flinched, flew to his cheek, to trail softly across it to his throat and come to rest on the silk scarf knotted at his neck. "Oh, Theodore . . ."

His hands went to her throat as he pulled her to him and kissed her hungrily. "Anna," he groaned, "promise me you'll be my wife."

"Not now, Theodore, don't talk, no plans, no promises . . ."

They walked along the harbour. They found a café, and a waiter who was happy to let them sit over coffee hour after hour. Theodore was content just to look at her. When he touched her she shivered. When they kissed, her breath filled his body.

As dawn broke, they left and walked along the coast, watching the sun rise over the sea without speaking. When the sky was pale and hazy with the early heat of the morning, Theodore spoke quietly.

"Anna?"

"Yes?"

"Tell me this is real for you?"

"It's real for me. It's a little too real for me, Theo. A little too close to the edge."

"Do you really have to go back today?"

"I have to be in Cairo by six tonight. There's only one plane I can hitch a ride with. Mac checked."

"I'd fly you myself. I'd steal a kite . . . You can't stay tonight?"

"No, I can't. I wish . . ."

"Wishers were ever fools. If we could have more than wishes . . ."

She shook her head suddenly. "We're wasting time." She gripped his arm. "Let's go swimming."

"Now? Here?"

"Let me just go back to the hotel and get some things – freshen up. Then let's go somewhere alone. Anywhere. I don't care. In an hour this town will be crawling with military. Let's get the hell out."

Theodore borrowed a car from Paddy with a vague promise to return it by lunch-time, and they drove along the coast until they came to a rocky beach. Anna was shy in her bathing costume, changing behind a rock while he smoked impatiently, and then slipping into the water. Her shyness made his heart beat all the faster. She shrieked like a child when he caught her feet under water. When he embraced her he experienced a moment of bliss and, in that moment, longed to die. When they returned to the shore and clambered onto the rocks, Anna draped his jacket around her shoulders, and felt the pockets for his cigarette case. She pulled out the golden locket. "I don't know why I had this made . . . It's such a silly, sentimental thing."

"Such a lovely thing."

She undid the clasp, and fastened the chain around his neck. "It's meant to keep you safe. Always."

"What can I give you in return, Anna?"

"Nothing. I don't want anything." She shook her head so violently that sprays of sea water flew around them. "I have everything I want."

"You're a funny girl, Anna Kézdy. You give me everything, yet I can't have you."

"You have all of me that matters, Theo."

"Why won't you marry me?"

She took a cigarette, and Theodore cupped his hands around hers to protect the flame from the breeze. "I don't want to be a widow, Theodore. That I can't take. I can love you, and I can miss you, and I can leave you if I have to, and I can see you with another girl, and I can even pick *her hairs off your jacket, but I don't want to be a widow at the age of twenty-five . . . or twenty-six, or however long it takes."*

"I'm not going to die, Anna."

She raised her hand to his mouth as the words left it. "That's a stupid thing to say. Take it back – don't tempt anyone to prove you wrong. What do you know? What makes you so sure you're special?"

"You do. You make me believe in everything. You make me believe that God's in his heaven and all's right with the world."

Anna shook her head nervously.

"I would never have believed a woman like you would fall into my lap. I was damn lucky to be at the Kit Kat when Cupid's random arrow struck your heart, my love. Just like poor old Titania and Bottom. Cynical old brute, Willy, but as Bert would say, he knew a bit when he saw it in a Derby winner's mouth. A year ago I wouldn't have admitted the possibility that a young lad like myself could fall in love, less that it would be some goddamn Yank pulling my heart about like any old piece of sponge rubber. I want to stop fooling myself about being such a high-minded heathen, and drop down on my knees to thank someone, very humbly and sincerely, for letting me worship so magical a creature as you . . ." Theodore dropped to his knees, and held her hands in his.

"I'm no goddess, Theo." Anna was half laugh-

ing and half serious.

"Why should I take your word for it? Why shouldn't I pray to you as well as any other image of perfection? Oh, Anna, darling, I do adore you. I love you fit to bust my heart."

"Theodore, love me as I am. Don't turn me into something I'm not. Sometimes I feel you want me to be too perfect."

"The only thing I want is for you to be somewhat less inundated with suitors than you are. Perhaps if you had a hideous scar across your face, if you had a hump back or no teeth, I might feel a little more secure. I might even prefer you that way. Makes me think that the local chaps have their heads screwed on, having their women covered up from head to toe. When I'm with the squadron, there are times when I can't stop torturing myself, wondering how many dates you have that night, how many men are proposing, and if you're saying, 'No, not now, let's not make plans yet,' to each and every one, in that lovely voice of yours. Sometimes I wonder if you're just doing your war duty, darling, sending the boys off to the front with a glad heart, hmm, my golden girl?" He stroked her bare leg, smiling up at her as she perched, his jacket wrapped around her shoulders, on the rock above him.

She scowled down at him.

"What do you want, Theo? You want me to feel sorry for you, or you want me to join a convent?"

"*Anna, forgive me. I want you to be exactly as you are, with all your American freedom of spirit. I can't ask you to stay home at night, weeping for me and turning down dates –*"

"*Darn right – not with blonde hair trailing down your jacket, you can't.*"

"*Hush. What I can ask you is to remember that I love you with all my being – my life is yours. My heart is yours, and you must do with it as you will, cruel lady . . . I want you to marry me.*"

He pulled her on to his lap, and cradled her in his arms, confident for all his banter that she loved him and him alone.

Theodore was correct in this assumption. Anna flew back to Cairo with an American pilot in a supply plane. The pilot was delighted to have such easy-on-the-eye cargo, and elated to find that she, like he, hailed from New Jersey. He was disconcerted that when he asked her if she had anyone special, she burst into floods of tears, and continued weeping until they landed safely at Payne Field.

For men must work, and women must weep . . .

Flt./Lt. T. R. Hamilton
37th Squadron
DAF

Djedeida, 5 December

My own Darling,

I have spent weeks pacing around the mess,
haunting the mail rack and cursing all and
sundry for receiving letters while you were silent,
not least cursing your own lovely self, even
cursing my poor sister, who had been good
enough to write, and kicking doors and the odd
squadron dog, not to mention the odd squadron
erk (several of whom have a score to settle with
you), and saying to myself, 'I don't really care so
much,' and the rest of the lies, and then this
morning not one, not two, but three, all equally
delightful, and the three combined to make me
high as a kite.

You wrote of hopes and dreams, and then
took yourself to task for being sentimental. Now,
if we haven't earned the right to be sentimental
about such stuff, who has? We've lived on damn
all but short memories and dreams of long ones
for nearly a year now, and with the news so good
and hope beating so strongly, perhaps it's just a
question of hanging on for a few months longer,
and then we can have the fitting end to our boy-
meets-girl story — or girl-meets-boy, as I suspect

you would rather have it. So please, darling Anna, more sentiment, not less of it, and I'll take both the sentiment and the -ality, if you are offering it, and have some to spare. Having reprimanded yourself, you then turned on me and chastized me for saying that you would make a lovely ambassador's wife. I stand, chin on chest and mouth drooping, and take the flak: yes, you are right – I should have said you would make a lovely ambassador, and cut the wife. And perhaps you will, and what pride I would have in you, although a dark cloud passes over my rosy vision when I wonder how Uncle Sam will feel about his representative being burdened with an ex-RAF escort in tow, fit for nothing but carrying her baggage . . . We will face your uncle together when we have to, and in the meantime it brings joy to my heart that you take such pleasure and pride in your work. I know when I talk about the Foreign Office, you pout (and what a beautiful mouth to pout with, if you don't mind my saying) and correct me with 'State Department', but in all honesty, my darling, can you really believe that the American version is more appropriate? Let us compromise and say diplomatic *service, and then you can always be my diplomatic lady, and I your humble diplomatic servant . . .*

You also take me to task for being jealous, and have the effrontery to remind me of a certain lady in Tunis . . . Now. This must be addressed and put to bed – so to speak – once and for all, and no further ado. I doubt very much whether the girl in question can strictly be called a lady, but let us not argue about definitions. You ask whether I found her 'bedworthy' – I haven't the foggiest, and I find it a most indelicate question from a lady such as yourself! You claim you were jealous and, impossible as I find this to imagine, I accept the charge, and in mitigation plead ignorance, inexperience and incompetence in how to hold a dance partner without tell-tale traces of her proximity. I wholeheartedly refute any accusation that I enjoyed it, and do so with a spotless conscience. You, dear lady, must face a tougher series of charges: I challenge you with all-night dancing, wining, dining and fraternization with as broad a collection of no-good characters as ever graced Shepheard's, and your only defence has been, "A girl has to have fun, doesn't she?" Well, perhaps she does, my love, but not too often, and not too much of it, or you'll set the heart of one poor fellow beating frantically with fear far more than Jerry can . . .

All jokes apart, I'm delighted that you are busy and happy – I wouldn't wish the opposite existence on you. To compare your busy social whirl to my own, a few nights ago we went to the cinema in what remains of the local town. A very poor show; I'm blowed if I know how they can call that entertainment. We retired in disgust back to the pilots' mess and found some of the

Australian lads from the 70th in place, so we consoled each other by brewing tea around the fire (to wit one small oil stove). Do I write this to make you feel guilty as you don your party frock? Not in the least! If I can't be with you, I would rather be with these lads than anywhere else on God's earth. My last word on the subject of jealousy: as you recount a date you do not need to tell me when I don't have to be jealous; I only expect you to tell me when I should be . . .

An amusing tale from my sister, whom one day you shall meet and love as dearly as I do: Melanie is with the ATS, holds quite a senior rank now, and went to visit a maiden aunt of ours when in Scotland. My aunt took one look at her khakis, shook her head sadly and said she'd never catch a husband if she couldn't find herself an occupation that allowed her to wear more becoming garments. So much for the home fighting spirit! Poor Mel pointed out that she is already promised, and her boy, a very decent type, is with the Army in France, but this cut no ice with Aunt Ida. A part of me agrees with the old bird – uniform isn't for girls, certainly not bedworthy ones – and how I wish I was with you now to see your feathers ruffle as you read that! Another strange and amusing, if rather black, tale is doing the rounds. One of your compatriots, a gunner with a Liberator squadron, was found wandering around Algiers displaying his stomach. He had gone there on leave and had visited a back-

street tattooist, and instructed the poor native to inscribe the words 'If found, return to Mrs Martha Beerbohm, 97 3rd Street, Littletown PA' or some such address. The Brits who found him were perplexed by this, finding it a brutal if practical means of corpse identification, and gently pointed out that his wife, or mother, might not appreciate the delivery. The Yank grinned, and said it wasn't his wife, mother or any known relative. It was the name and address of a former mathematics teacher who had made his tender years a misery . . . A macabre revenge but then, the war affects people differently.

We are beginning to gear up for Christmas, without knowing where we will spend it, possibly here, but Italy is looking increasingly likely – land of amore, Romeo and his Giulietta, piazzas and campaniles. I was last there in 1936, in the company of my parents who believed I needed a hearty dose of culture and civilization before the varsity. I found it a lovely place, although I can't say I absorbed much of the culture and certainly wasn't civilized – it took meeting a lady from a far newer world to work that miracle. If we move on, I have high hopes of introducing you to the place, 'next time'.

This letter is going to pieces for many reasons. First, my mental faculties are not at their sharpest. One of the Australian boys with us is OTE (operational term expired) as the Groupie feels he's done more than enough for one small

Dominion pilot. The chap in question is the size of Westminster, and deeply resents the expression 'Dominion' – I wouldn't dare to use it in his hearing, but the Groupie delights in it, and has the rank to pull it off. We had a small celebration, which involved a major wetting. Second, the letter is being sabotaged. I started it in the mess, only to be serenaded by an ass singing, 'You'd be so nice to come home to . . . So nice by the fire', in ill-disguised mockery. Every time I looked up with a scowl, he made a suggestion as to what I should write to you, most of them unfit to repeat in decent company, let alone to set down on paper. So I moved next door, to a quiet room. No sooner had I settled myself, alone at last with you, when a poker class began and, cross as a bear, I have now moved to my bunk to attempt to finish this letter.

And as soon as I find peace and quiet, my time has all but run out. I stepped outside for a smoke, into a sunset of red, yellow and blue in the sky and gold on the sand below. A delight to see after days of muddy skies and soaking rain. The air in the mess is like the inside of a steam laundry, and in half an hour we'll set out to dispersal. The Group stress maximum effort, all kites to go, and guarantees our sure return. This is when I feel a certitude in my immediate life. This is one of the times when I can think of you most sanely, when I've nothing to do but wait for the scramble. I have your amulet around my neck, and imagine your lips against my throat, and the scent of your hair fills my head, and now I can write nothing but my darling and I love you and I love you and my darling, and only these things make any sense, and what comes between means nothing at all of any significance to us. Yet if I don't make a move now and stir myself to round up the lads, then abuse will fall on my head from extreme altitude and with deadly accuracy and monotonous regularity, and my chance of leave for next time will look slim indeed.

Kiss yourself for me, sweetheart, and keep yourself warm and safe and sure in the knowledge that my heart and life are yours, for evermore,

Theodore

CHAPTER TWELVE

I was more than surprised when Anna's daughter turned up on my doorstep. I was sure I'd seen the last of her after that breakfast the week before. She looked rather miserable, and it was all I could do not to give her a hug. She still had a bold glint in her eye under those deceptively feathery lashes – just like Anna. Bold enough to make a man hesitate to speak.

"I'm sorry for just tipping up without calling. I got a taxi back late last night and crashed into bed. I'll come back later, if it's not convenient."

The poor little waif stood on the doorstep until I ushered her inside, and she slumped into a chair in the kitchen.

"It's not that I need any more from you. I'm perfectly happy with what I've got. When David comes back – if David comes back . . ."

I poured her a cup of coffee.

"*When* David comes back, which should be next

week, he'll need to do a photo shoot."

"Of course. He's in Paris? He mentioned you were going to be in Paris."

"He's in Sarajevo," she howled, and tears began to spill from her eyes. At a complete loss for words, I took her into my arms and held her as tight as I could. Tears have always rendered me helpless. For a moment she resisted, but then she relaxed against my chest and cried her heart out. When the sobs had subsided, I offered her a handkerchief. "I'm sorry – oh, God, I only came up here to say that I was sorry. About being so silly about you and Ma. I shouldn't have said anything, and now – and now, it doesn't seem to matter any more . . ." The sobs heaved up in her again, and I rather ineffectually patted her shoulder while she sniffed. I thought of the time, all those years ago, when I had watched Anna cry, both powerless and responsible. Elena suddenly pulled herself up straight, and I released her, feeling the grief in her slender frame.

"I might as well tell you." She had two black smudges running down her cheeks, from where she had rubbed her eyes. It was oddly touching. "David is my – David and I live together. I didn't want you to know. I thought it might look unprofessional if you knew that that's why we were working together. It doesn't mean the book isn't being taken seriously, you understand." I nodded. I couldn't have cared less about the book. "He just had to make a connection out of Paris, and I . . . I wanted to go too."

"Naturally."

"Anyway, he's in Bosnia," she was now speaking in a tightly controlled voice, "and he'll be back next week. I only wanted to drop by and say that I was sorry if I was rude to you. It was stupid of me. I can't explain it better than that. I spoke to my mother, and she said that she remembered you very well, and that I should . . . give you her love."

I wanted to gaze at the photograph of Anna, which I had restored to the drawing room. I had waited a long time to hear from her, and to hear the words – simply that she sent me her love – from this young thing with Anna's hair and Anna's eyes was almost more than I could bear. I had thought there was nothing I could not bear. What a stupid old fool.

"Tell me about your mother, Elena. Is she well?"

"She's very well. She looks great. She and my father live in London. She told me that you and she had been close in Cairo, had known each other well. She asked me to give you her love, and to ask you if you remembered something . . . Shammer Neeseem?"

I shut my eyes for a moment, willing the image of Anna to appear. "Sham el Nessim," I corrected. "The Egyptian spring festival. They celebrate each Monday after Coptic Easter. It means the Smelling of the Breeze. A very evocative title, I always thought. Your mother and I spent it together once."

It was so like Anna to choose that day of all the days we had spent together. I remembered it perfectly clearly. I could smell the freshness of the air and Anna's perfume; I could see the jacaranda trees shedding their blue tears as we walked through the park, and hear myself, increasingly bloody and maudlin, as we had sat at Shepheard's.

"She told me that she'd been in love with you."

"Ah." I attempted a smile, but it must have been a very ropey affair, my mouth twisting sharply as I struggled for control. "She's a kind woman. The truth is, I was hopelessly in love with her. You couldn't have met Anna Kézdy and not fallen in love with her."

"I asked her what had happened between you two. She said she didn't really know. Just that you had left North Africa and drifted apart. I know it's none of my business, but I was curious and it seemed so strange that she hadn't mentioned your name, and she is my mother after all. I grew up with her joking about her old beaux." She looked me straight in the eye, and I had to look away. "She never joked about you."

It took all I had left in me to reply calmly, "I'm rather glad about that. Not that I would have objected to bringing a smile to her lips . . . After the squadron went to Italy, it became increasingly difficult to meet."

"But you did? Meet? Outside Cairo?"

"When we could, yes. From '44, we met several times in Italy, and once or twice back in Cairo. It was tricky to arrange leave at the same time. Your mother was needed at her work, and

I had the devil of a job to get away from the squadron. I do remember a time when she joined us at the base at Tortorella, just walked into the CO's office, and came to the mess. I felt very privileged then, the envy of all around. You cannot imagine how beautiful she was."

"Oh, yes, I can."

"It wasn't simply her physical beauty – she was so alive, so spirited, she exhaled *joie de vivre*. I remember her so very well."

"How sad that you didn't keep in touch."

"Our lives travelled different paths. It was unavoidable. But that makes me no less delighted to hear that she is so well – and happy?" I hoped to keep the question out of my tone, but Elena heard it.

"She and Dad are very happy. They always have been. They're what you might call a perfect couple. They'd love to see you if you ever come to London."

"Not much to take me back there now." I couldn't countenance seeing Anna again. "You gave her my greetings?"

"Of course." Elena stood up heavily, leaning against the table. "If I may, I'd really like to come back and hear about the days in Cairo – not for the book. If you don't mind, I'll head back to the hotel now. I feel terribly tired most of the time. Don't know why. I thought pregnancy was meant to leave you blooming but what do I know?" She smiled a smile so full of sweetness and doubt that I wished for an excuse to look after her. I waved from the porch as she headed down the lane.

Over the next few days I did not make any attempt to contact her. Quite the contrary, I restricted my visits to the village. I wanted her to come to see me of her own accord, not at my suggestion or by accidental encounter. I was surprised when Madame Guillot telephoned me one evening, about two days later, and asked me to come to the hotel. She told me that Madame Turcan was ill, and she didn't know whom else to call.

When I arrived, I felt somewhat embarrassed to be shown to Elena's room. I am of a generation – and an age – that is uncomfortable in the bedroom of a lady outside one's immediate family. She was lying in bed with the sheets pulled up to her neck; her face was the colour of parchment and beaded with sweat. I asked her if she wanted me to call a doctor but she shook her head and told me that there was nothing that anyone could do. She was losing the baby. She was visibly terrified. She gagged again and again, and sweat dripped down her forehead.

I hurried downstairs to call the clinic and found Duhaze still there. Sebastien Duhaze was the doctor who had cared for Chantal in the final months of her life. I hadn't seen him since, other than to pass in the street. Madame Guillot commanded the situation, while I sat in the salon feeling as useless as I have ever felt. When Duhaze arrived, I did not accompany him to the room, but could hear Elena's distressed shouting and Madame Guillot's remon-

strations. A short while later, Duhaze came down
carrying Elena in his arms, Madame following
behind with his bag. He was taking her to the hospital in Cahors. Elena's eyes were wild with fear.
When I asked her if there was anyone to call, any
way of reaching David, whether I should call her
parents, she shook her head, stretched out a hand
and asked me to come with her. I am ashamed to
say that not only did I avoid meeting her eyes, I also
ignored her request. It was the doctor who persuaded
me. I sat next to her in his car and held her hand. She
was weeping piteously.

In the waiting room, I sat still and thought about
Anna, and Chantal, all those years ago. I could not
escape the sound of Elena's sobbing and the desti-
tute look in her eyes. I did not have the courage to
call her mother. Duhaze appeared and told me
briefly that Elena would be fine and that, as far as
they could tell, miscarriage had been averted. The
baby was alive for the time being, but the next
twenty-four hours were unpredictable. He spoke to
me in a tone of disapproval, and I wondered with
horror if he suspected me of being the father.
Foolishly, I told him that the baby's father was in
Bosnia. Foolishly indeed, because once he had gone,
I knew he could never have even dreamt that I was
involved; it had been a moment of idiocy on my
part. Worse, I suspected myself of perverted vanity.
He had looked at me strangely, and rather coldly,
and I wondered how much Chantal had confided in
him, in those final weeks. I asked him if anything

could be done to help Elena, and I remember his answer: "It will be as God chooses. It is not in my hands, or yours. She'll rest for a day or two and then we will see what He has decided." He had replied with almost exactly the same words to a similar question I had asked ten years previously.

Anna and I had often laughed about the laps of the gods. There were times during the war when I was as passionate in my unbelief as any evangelist is in their faith. There were times, believing, when I knew that God had abandoned me, and times when I wilfully and happily abandoned Him. Now, I am not a man of faith and I would not give God credit for my blessings any more than I would attribute my sufferings to his account. I claim both for myself alone. I was, none the less, willing to pray for Elena and her baby, if that was what was required.

"May I see her?" I asked Duhaze.

"If you wish."

"Is there anything I should do – anything I shouldn't say?"

"No. I have told her she must rest and be calm, because that is all we doctors can ever say in this situation. There is no medical evidence that indicates rest does any good in these cases. I have no idea why some babies are born. Perhaps it is better for her, for the time being, that she believes the baby will be all right. In the end, it won't make any difference what she believes, or what you and I wish. Goodnight, Monsieur Hamilton."

I held Elena's hand. "The doctor says that you're

going to be fine, mother and babe. Right as rain."

She smiled wanly. "I hope so. I can't tell you how much I –" Tears began to spill, and she wiped them away. "I'm so sorry, Theodore. I'm awfully embarrassed about dragging you into this. My brother's in Paris, but he's about to go off to Hong Kong. I can't reach David. I don't want my parents to know – not now. Either everything will be fine or it will be too late by the time they get here."

"I quite agree."

She closed her eyes, and I looked at the dark lashes fanning out against the hollows beneath her eyes.

"Elena? Shall I leave you to sleep?"

"Please don't go, Theodore. Just stay and talk to me."

"Of course."

I started. "You'll be all right, my dear. All shall be well. You simply mustn't worry. You must try to sleep . . ." She was breathing easily but I didn't know if she was sleeping or not, or if they had given her anything to help her. Holding her hand, I slipped into reminiscence. "Did I tell you about the first operation Bob and Bert and Sam and I flew together? Chips, our wireless operator, had a wretched case of gippy tummy so we had another chap on board. I can see the leading aircraft leaving the head of the line and turning into the wind, and remember running my finger around the neck of my battle-dress and finding it dripping with sweat. I spoke to Bob down the intercom and asked him if he'd brought his boomerang, and he bellowed back, 'Not bloody likely, skipper! I nailed it over my bed. That's what's going to bring us home safe and sound. I'm going to write all me ops down on it, all thirty of the sodding bastards.' I sat in the cockpit of –" I was on the point of saying M for Mother, and hastily amended "– T for Tommy, feeling wave after wave of nausea coming up from the pit of my stomach, wondering if there was a chance of saying, 'Don't think I'll be going up tonight, after all, if it's all the same to you, old chaps. Tomorrow perhaps,' and wondering if they all felt as pig awful as I did. Then we were up in that empty sky, above a wisp of cloud, and I could see the moonlight making patterns on the water, like a filtered searchlight. When we came over the target, I dropped the nose of the plane and slackened the engines. The cockpit was flooded with an eerie blue light – great columns of real search-lights. The only people alive on the earth were the four men in the kite with me. I was damned edgy. I asked Bob if he trusted me, and his brassy voice came ringing through the intercom, 'Like my dear old Mum, skipper.'"

Elena did not respond, and I tried to withdraw my hand, but her grip on it tightened. I could see veins as thin as hairs on her eyelids. "I had a feeling of sheer elation after that first run. Back in the mess, we were reliving the flight, minute by minute, slapping each other on the back, and thinking ourselves fine fellows, when one of the older pilots came in and said that two of the crews were lost – Bingham's, and a chap I hadn't even met. I asked if Bingham had been a good pilot, and he gave me a peculiar look. 'Good pilot?' he said. 'He'd flown five ops. No such thing as skill at that stage – it's one hundred per cent down to luck. When you've done ten to twenty, then maybe skill comes into it – but not a lot. It's still ninety per cent luck, with a touch of skill to tip the odds in your favour. Or not. That's the way it goes, lad. That's just the way it goes.'" I was lost in thought, Bingham's face before my eyes.

"Tell me about your wife, and your first baby." Elena's voice was slurred.

"Well." I drew a deep breath. "Babies are always wonderful things, of course. Charming creatures, particularly when one doesn't have to do the business of bringing them on to the earth oneself. Chantal . . . Chantal . . ."

Elena opened her eyes. They were a shocking green against her pale skin, sharp as a traffic light. I looked for a hundred accusations in those green eyes. Women have so many complaints to lay against their men, childbirth not the least of them. That their suffering is greater, that their responsibility is greater, that their love and loyalty are greater. I have taken these accusations and the resultant guilt on my shoulders without complaint; I believe they are justified.

"She had the baby?"

The doctor had been prepared to tell Elena the truth, but I was not so confident. "Absolutely," I replied. "We had a daughter, and then a son."

"Tell me about Cairo . . ." she murmured.

"Righty-oh." I felt a great relief. "I arrived in 1941. The desert war was hotting up, and I arrived in spanking new uniform, waving the flag and ready to take on all comers. It was a most extraordinary place to be for a young man – shockingly glamorous and exotic, full of terrifyingly beautiful women, who had their pick of the combined Allied Forces . . ."

"Including my mother?"

"She hadn't arrived then. But when she did she wiped out all the others. She was very beautiful . . . I can vouch for that."

"Did you fall in love with her at first sight?"

I saw Anna as I had that first evening across the terrace at Shepheard's, as clearly as if it had been that very morning. Love at first sight? The hackneyed little phrase belittled what I had felt. Again I felt pressure on my hand.

"Did you?" she repeated.

"Everyone fell in love with your mother as soon as they looked at her. She had a gift for giving people a sense of confidence, and putting them at ease. She had that about her. You could take one look at her and forget all about the war and be filled with hope. Even if you had been drained of life the moment before. She had a healing property. I don't know if I fell in love with her then – I was certainly struck dumb. It took me quite some time to pluck up the courage to speak to her. I came to love her the more the better I knew her. But that's the way things should be – it would be dreadfully sad if we saw the best in people on first meeting, wouldn't it?"

She had fallen asleep with a smile on her lips.

I sat with her for a time watching her sleeping, and returned to the waiting room when the nurse came in to take her pulse. I stayed there all night. I felt such an old fool. There was nothing I could do to help her: I was too decrepit to be of any practical use and too distant to be of any real comfort. I did nothing but sit and think. I had nowhere else to go and no other demands on my limitless time.

Time is an even trickier old bugger than Fate. After years of willing time to pass, and years of regretting it passing so quickly, I felt no differently at seventy-five than I had fifty years earlier. It's an ill-mannered joke to play on a fellow, to etch upon his face all the markings of wisdom and leave his heart untouched by it. Some of my old chums lament their infirmity: just as they finally master the rules of the game, they find themselves retired from the field. Anna's determination to live for the present is a viable philosophy for life, to my mind, but the older I get, the more tempted I am to live in the past. Hospitals are excellent places for putting things in perspective: one can watch all manner of life come and go, and feel less absorbed in the trivialities of one's own personal fate. That night, an old man was brought in and pronounced dead on arrival. I felt neither envy nor pity.

In the morning, before returning home, I visited

Elena. She had colour back in her cheeks, and had had a promising report from the doctor.

"Is there anything you need? Books? Some fruit, perhaps?"

"I need a French dictionary. Or an interpreter."

"If I can serve . . ."

"No, I'm fine. The doctor says I can probably go back to the hotel tomorrow, provided Madame Guillot will have me."

"She'd like nothing better than having someone to mother." I didn't want to impose, but I wanted to give some more tangible form of assistance. "Elena, if you would be my guest until David returns, I would be more than delighted. I don't wish to intrude on your privacy, but perhaps you might be more comfortable . . ." I expected her to decline, but she smiled radiantly.

"I was hoping you'd say that. I can't think of anything nicer."

"In that case, I will collect you in the morning, all being well."

As I was leaving, Elena called my name.

"When I woke this morning, I felt certain that everything was going to be all right – my baby, David, everything. And I just wondered – you know how you said all the crews had talismans to ward off the gremlins? You said Bert had four. I was thinking that David has one, and perhaps I should have one, and I wondered – what was yours?"

"Oh, mine was very unoriginal. I had a little blue amulet. One saw them all over Egypt, even on the horses. They were believed to ward off the evil eye."

"Do you still have it?"

"Somewhere about the place."

"I'd love to see it."

"Then you shall, my dear. When you are well, I will endeavour to unearth it."

I did not tell her that my amulet was distinct from those touted by the scarab sellers and sported by the gharrie ponies of Cairo. Mine had been set in a locket, and was entwined in a circle of hair the colour of pure gold. Nor did I tell her that I held it clenched in my hand even as she asked the question.

CHAPTER THIRTEEN

It took nearly losing the baby to make me believe in it. Up until then, I had felt ambushed. The first sight of blood on the inside of my thighs was the first time that I genuinely wanted the baby. Before that, it had all been talk, and mainly to do with me and David, not the baby at all. I had spent the day in my room feeling alternately queasy and aching, convinced that I'd picked up some flu bug or food poisoning in Paris, and vaguely wondering what I could take that wouldn't hurt the baby. I went to bed in the afternoon, back and hips splitting with pain, and dozed off. When I woke I thought the stickiness between my legs was sweat. In the bright light of the bathroom I saw the blood and was instantaneously wiped out with grief. It might have begun with an ambush but the baby had battered away persistently at my defences, laid siege and worn me down as inexorably as water does a stone. When I saw the blood I longed for a baby more than anything. The second I saw the blood, all I wanted to know was whether I'd lost my little boy or my little girl. For about five hours, even when Theodore was with me, and regardless of what the doctor said, I knew I'd lost the baby, and lost David as well.

From the moment I left hospital, I had a new centre of gravity. I willed the baby to grow; I talked to it firmly, all the time. I didn't want it to have a chance to doze off and give up. I wanted to see my belly swell beneath my eyes, overnight, as proof of the baby's vigour. The word that I clung to was 'viable'. It was a word that had never had any real meaning for me before – I can't remember ever using it, and even now, in my mind, it refers only to a foetus, not to a baby. Two kinds of pregnancies, two kinds of foetuses – viable or non-viable. Viable. Capable of living, physically fitted to live, a stage of development as to permit continued existence, 'under normal conditions'. That was how the French doctor had defined it, in his precise English. Odd that a baby could be viable and inviolable, or non-viable and violated. I brought David's bag, including the pregnancy book, with me from the hotel, and I lay next to the pool in the borrowed black swimsuit turning the pages absent-mindedly and lecturing my baby in my head, encouraging, coaching, forbidding it to let us down.

Theodore crossed the terrace and put down a cup on the table next to me. "Herbal tea. No caffeine, and none of the demon drink. Doctor's orders."

"Did he really say that?"

"No, of course not. This is a civilized country. Doctors wisely advise expectant mothers to drink a decent amount of decent red wine. I'll dig out some burgundy tonight." He poured me a cup of tea, and handed me a newspaper, a copy of the previous day's *Times*. "Thought you might like to know what was going on at home."

"Thanks." I left it lying folded on my lap. "It's good of you to let me stay here, but I won't be able to if I feel I'm in your way. You mustn't change your routine for me, or anything."

"I won't. I'm going to paint a little, and then I'm lunching with friends a few miles away. They have insisted that I join them for a round of golf – a game I find tedious in the best of circumstances. I won't be back until early evening. Giselle will be here all day if you need anything. She'll get you some lunch. Ask her to bring it out here if you don't want to go inside."

"I can fix myself something. I really don't feel at all hungry."

"Nonsense. You're eating for two, don't forget. And watch out for the sun – mad dogs and English women, you know . . . You'll find some straw hats in the *pigeonnier* – if you do stay out, keep your head covered. Have a rest, and take things easily. Goodbye."

I opened *The Times* lazily. The front page carried a photograph of a street in Sarajevo, with a child's body flung across the rubble of a building. I didn't need to look at the credit to know that it wasn't David's. It wasn't his style. I skimmed the accompanying article, not taking in very much, wondering where David was while I lay by the pool. I didn't ever want to tell him about the past two days, not if everything was all right. I wondered how becoming a father would change him, if at all. I couldn't see him taking a desk job, and I didn't want him to. I couldn't imagine what he would become if he spent his time trailing round the party conferences and doing portraits of newly appointed heads of waterboards.

His obligation to put his life on the line wasn't just an unavoidable drawback of his job. Early on in our relationship, I had accused him of some deep psychological imbalance, of being drawn to danger because he felt guilty that he had survived when his godfather had not. He'd considered the theory far more carefully than I expected him to, but dismissed it. He said survival anywhere was a fluke. Perhaps, like Heff, David just wanted to be part of a group whose entry ticket was sharing the experience – maybe it was all a quest for some kind of connection. But David wasn't like Heff: David was far more of a loner, both at work and at play. He's always had a fear of not being told the truth, won't believe anything till he's been an eye-witness. He has an insatiable curiosity about every key event that has occurred in his own lifetime. For a man like David, not going was like not being invited to the big party of the year. There were times when I had seen him weighing up an assignment in Russia against one in an African state in the grip of civil war. I'd seen him in an agony of indecision, macabre in his cool analysis of which would be the more significant 'in the end'. Africa often lost the battle. In the case of Bosnia, 'not going' might mean missing the millennium party.

I could sit and read about the war in Bosnia for hours. I could mug up on the issues and learn about all the hereditary disputes between the Serbs, the Croats and the Muslims, but the bottom line was that it didn't affect my life. However poignant the images that people like David sent back, and however horrific the condition of people's lives, they were a million miles away from Notting Hill Gate and Sloane Square, let alone Sainte Cécile. While David might consider this *the* big event of the nineties, the one that would doubtless claim most column inches in the *Book of the Decade*, published in 2001 by *The Economist*, or *Time*, people back home didn't really give a shit, and I had to lump myself in with them. While I looked at *The Times*, my thoughts wandered aimlessly between the baby, David, Theodore, myself, my parents, the book, what I would have for lunch, whether I had the energy to attempt the crossword, the name of the creeper that crawled up the back of Theodore's house, why I hadn't remembered to ask the doctor if it was all right for me to swim . . . I *hate* to confess this. I hate to admit to such paralysis of empathy, but

I did not look at that photograph and think of the grief of that child's mother, and his friends, his family and neighbours. Maybe if I had gone with David, if I had been a witness myself, it might have reached me, and perhaps that was precisely why David went, to prove to himself that he was above addiction to self-interest. Maybe my humanity could be purchased by a cheque to Save the Children, but David had to pay a higher price for the same peace of mind. Maybe it was just a bad photograph. At that time, I didn't care why he went so long as he came back and loved our baby.

After lunch, I pottered around the drawing room. Theodore had returned the photograph of my mother to a low table there. It *was* a beautiful picture. She was sitting at a table, outside some-where, and it must have been windy – her hair was blowing about and she had one hand raised to hold it back off her face, and she was half laughing, half embarrassed. Although it was recognizably my mother, her expression was unfamiliar to me. Maybe it was just that she was so young. I had never seen her with hair that long, and there was something about her face that was dated – eyebrows strongly defined and thinly arched, lips heavily painted, high cheekbones. Of course her cheekbones hadn't changed, but the face I knew was softer and plumper. This woman was young, and sharp-edged, and nothing to do with my mother. Of course there were strong physical similarities, but I did not feel connected to that woman. I wondered if I would even like her if I met her. I wondered if this was the same woman my father had met and fallen in love with, or someone entirely different who belonged exclusively to Theodore Hamilton, preserved in that frame for half a century. Photographs are real things, not images or impressions, the way a painting might be an impression of a person or a landscape. A photograph was the thing itself, as real as a death mask or a thumb-print lifted off an individual. Photographs captured that split second in time and froze it. They were incontestable evidence. Unless you thought about how they could be taken from 359 different angles . . .

I slept most of the afternoon. I was woken by the sound of torrential rain thundering against the roof of the house and splashing in through the open windows onto the tiled floor. I rose to close the shutters. The sky was so dark that I thought it was late, but it was only six o'clock. I could hear Theodore talking to Giselle in the kitchen, and went to join them. The summer storm had rescued Theodore from his golf. He was standing at the stove, preparing a soufflé for supper. I liked seeing him cook: it reminded me of my father.

"How impressive."

"Wait until you taste it before you reach any rash conclusions. Giselle has a low opinion of my culinary endeavours." He winked at the girl, who grinned back at him. I watched him as he moved around the kitchen, chatting to her. My French wasn't up to following much of their conversation, but they were clearly at home in each other's company. Giselle got her coat, and Theodore tossed her a set of car keys as she said goodnight. "Giselle cycles here – quite some distance – but I don't want her out in weather like this."

"You sound protective."

"Good Lord! Don't let her hear you say that – she's the one who looks after *me*. She's a very independent young lady, as you all seem to be these days."

"Wasn't my mother independent?"

"Your mother?" He paused while he considered the question, wooden spoon in the air. "She was ferociously independent. Couldn't stand being mollycoddled. She was quite a tough character, your mother. Delightful and entrancing, but a free spirit. She didn't appreciate being told what to do. It was a jolly good thing she wasn't in the forces herself – she would never have taken orders kindly."

"Did you?"

"Of course. It's far more pleasant to take instruction from others than to act oneself. In squadron life, one happily took orders until one was elbowed into giving them."

"If you had flown mission after mission, and were dog tired, fed up and scared to death, what made you get back in the plane and go out again, night after night? Why didn't you just tell your CO to go fu- to hell?"

"Discipline!" He laughed. "That was the job.

Once operational, one knew the ropes and instinct took over – one didn't need to ask questions. You knew what was expected, and simply wanted to do the job as well as humanly possible. We were raised in the aftermath of the first war, in the belief that one must expect some hardship in life. Perhaps as parents we did our children a disservice by teaching them to expect complete gratification." He tasted the mixture on the hob, and reached for the salt. "I sound like a frightful old puritan, don't I? One is so determined that one's children's lives should be better than one's own that perhaps we shielded them too much from an acceptance, an expectation, of adversity. You claimed the other day that you had no great causes, no great moral dilemmas. We knew that a certain amount of adversity, not necessarily deserved, would be encountered in each of our lives, and that in some sense it was to be welcomed."

He poured a glass of wine for each of us, and started to fix a salad, refusing my offers of help.

"I understand the sense of having to – oh, pay your dues. Sometimes I have a presentiment of doom." I took a sip of wine, and felt Theodore watching me. "Like when I was in hospital. I thought I'd lost the baby because I didn't deserve to have everything go according to some perfect plan. It's all come pretty easily to me, I haven't had to struggle enough, so one day, something I really want and have taken for granted, will just – vanish, slip between my fingers. There's got to be some payback down the road – some Bad Thing will happen. Like a miscarriage."

"Which didn't happen."

"No – but it might have. Maybe it was a warning. There are other things that might, well, go wrong . . . David might be hurt."

"I'm sure he won't be."

"How do you know?"

He sat down opposite me. "All right, Elena. I don't know. Perhaps he will be hurt, or has been. Perhaps he will, heaven forbid, be killed. But if he is, it will be a result of *his* choices and *his* life, not because you did well at school or had a surfeit of Christmas presents. It would be an odd sort of God who taught you a lesson by extinguishing David's flame, wouldn't it?"

"You're the one who talked about adversity being undeserved."

"Oh, it can strike randomly but, in general, we make our own beds. By all means worry about the suffering you cause, but it isn't worth worrying about suffering you can't help."

Sitting there in that dimly lit kitchen with the storm raging around us, I didn't have the heart to ask him to account for the bombing of Italian and German cities. They must have been grateful for bombing in flights, so that they didn't know which of them was responsible for a direct hit on a civilian target. As in a firing squad, each man was allowed the possibility that his bullet was blank. I allowed myself the question: "Is there anything that happened during the war that you feel personally responsible for?"

"Of course."

"Such as?"

"Such things as I have no wish to recount to you." He said this perfectly calmly, and with a smile in his eyes. "Shall we eat?"

"It looks wonderful. Tell me about your family, Theodore." My memory of what he had told me that night in hospital was hazy.

"I've told you about my wife. She died ten years ago."

"How did she die?"

I have to confess to an awful thing. I don't think I'm alone in this – I hope to God I'm not – but I sometimes have a feeling of controlled excitement in the anticipation of hearing other people's tragedies, particularly if I don't know the person very well. It isn't that the knowledge makes me smug about my lot in life – far from it. It gives me a presentiment of disaster about to fall on my own head. It's like the sickening curiosity as to what's in the dawn ambulance going in the opposite direction from you, blue light flashing in the misty morning. I sometimes get an electric, quirky little buzz of curiosity when I'm waiting to hear. That must be why the tabloids and the telly are full of crisis re-enactments.

"She had cancer. The doctor you met, Duhaze, was one of a team who looked after her in the last few months."

"It must have been awful for you."

"It was worse for her. Don't believe people when

they say that it is hardest for the partner left behind. Chantal was not resigned to dying, she was in a great deal of pain, much of the time, and she was very frightened, but she fought for a long time. That was how we met Giselle – she moved in to help nurse my wife. Giselle was barely out of her childhood when she first came here. She was a comfort to Chantal. My wife always loved children and young people. Giselle made her laugh, even in the last few weeks, when nobody else could."

Theodore's voice was level, almost bland; he did not show any sign of emotion, but I wanted to say something other than "How dreadful" so I said nothing.

"It was difficult for the children. Liliane came as often as she could from Paris. During Chantal's illness, she spent all her free time here. She was not then married. She married – oh, some three or four years later. I wish Chantal had been there. It would have made her very happy."

"And your son?"

"My son Michel is a doctor. He works for a charity, Médecins sans Frontières."

"I've heard of them – wonderful stuff."

"Indeed. Unfortunately, we see him very rarely. He has spent most of the last few years in various African countries."

"You must be proud of him."

"He is doing what he wants to do, and I am glad of that."

"Is he married?"

"Not as far as I know. He wasn't the last time we spoke. Do you like the soufflé?"

"It's great."

"Now, it's your turn. Tell me about *your* family."

I thought how to describe them properly. There wasn't that much to say – no skeletons in the cupboard, no tragedies, no great dramas. We were just a happy, normal family.

"My father spent a lot of his life in Africa, and then joined the IMF and was all over the place. My mother stopped work when they married and travelled with him."

"That must have suited her. She loved seeing the world. I rather thought she'd stay in the diplomatic service."

"Well, I suppose she wanted children, or Dad's job prevented her from doing it, whatever."

"Do you have brothers and sisters?"

"One brother. Charlie. He drives my father mad because he's nearly thirty and he won't settle down. He told Dad last Christmas that he was thinking of starting all over again and going to medical school because it would take him at least another eight years to qualify. He only does it to annoy, as Dad says."

"Is he married?"

I laughed at the idea of Charlie being married. "He doesn't like making commitments – not to women, houses, countries, jobs. I can't imagine Charlie ever proposing to anyone if it meant more than a few weeks' duration. He likes to keep his options open."

"How does your mother feel about that?"

"Oh, Ma's just besotted. He's her baby, and can do no wrong. She thinks it's good that he's fancy free . . . Plenty of time to settle down, don't rush into anything, make the most of each day, blah, blah, blah."

"I can imagine her saying that. And you're not married?"

"No. David and I have been together for a couple of years. That's it."

"Do you plan to marry?"

I stabbed unsuccessfully at a stray bit of lettuce. It wasn't a plan I could make unilaterally. "I think not. Being married wouldn't make any difference. When David's not working, he's with me. When he is working, he's God knows where, and God knows when he's coming back. What would be the point in being married?"

"For the child, perhaps?"

"Why should it make any difference to the child? David will always be its father, just as much as I'm its mother. If we rush off to the altar just before it makes its appearance, how does that help the baby? Does it prove we wanted to spend our lives together? Does it prove its father loved its mother? It just looks like tidying up the paperwork. Like an afterthought. How does that help any of us?"

I hadn't discussed the subject with my own parents, and had avoided the issue with David, yet found myself talking about marriage openly to Theodore Hamilton.

"You may be right. There are all sorts of reasons for getting married, and children may not be the best ones. And, of course, you are not under any sort of social pressure to marry these days . . ."

"Maybe not social pressure but we may be heading for a degree of parental pressure!" I rolled my eyes. "Ma hasn't said anything yet, but I'm just waiting for some comment about her not wanting her first grandchild to be a bastard."

Theodore didn't smile. He sat opposite me with an expression of such gravity that I felt unnerved. "I always found your mother very broad-minded."

"Ah, but is she *now*?" I carried on, trying to make a joke of it. "Maybe she was fifty years ago but people change, you know. Maybe aged twenty-five in Cairo, gadding about as a girl-around-town, she was broad-minded. God, for all I know she even smoked! But that doesn't mean that in the establishment role of mother she has to be broad-minded. That doesn't follow at all. She's always been relatively broad-minded as far as my friends are concerned, and even Charlie, but when it comes to me . . ." I shook my head, and wagged my finger in my father's style.

Theodore still didn't smile. "Have you given her a chance? Have you talked to your mother about marrying David?"

"I'm no fool. The important thing with my mother is not to give her a chance – give her an arm, and she might have your leg off . . ." I stopped short because Theodore looked at me so strangely. "What

331

was she like? I looked at the photo you have, but I just can't see her. I can't imagine she was ever that young. What kind of woman was she? Was she a good girl? Was she wild? Funny? Serious? *Did* she smoke?"

"Certainly she did. We all did."

"I knew it!" I said, with satisfaction. "The number of times she told me it was an absolutely *disgusting* habit. The *battles* we had over it when I was young, the *flak* she still gives my father . . . Just wait till I get home. It's all coming out of the woodwork now."

Theodore was running his thumbnail up and down a groove in the wooden table, studying it with intense concentration as if it were the only thing in the room. "Your mother . . ." he began. "Anna was the kindest, the warmest, the gentlest and the most broad-minded woman I have ever met."

"That's why everyone fell in love with her?"

"No. Young men rarely put gentleness and kindness at the top of their wish list, more's the pity. Men fell in love with Anna because she was beautiful and enormous fun. You couldn't get her out of your mind, even if you were inclined to try. Men gravitated to her like bears to wild honey – women, too, she attracted everyone. You couldn't have designed a better antidote to the war if she had been blended in a chemical laboratory."

"You were really in love with her, weren't you?"

"I would have done anything for her."

"But not propose marriage?"

He looked up at me, his eyes tired and old, and at

that moment, at the kitchen table, he looked every year of his age.

"I asked your mother to marry me so many times and in so many places and in so many ways, I lost count."

"And she said no?"

He resumed his examination of the table. "We were apart a great deal, and it was . . ."

"She refused your proposal?"

"Not always, no. I wore her down, in the end."

"I don't understand. You were engaged?"

He closed his eyes and shook his head suddenly. "Yes, she did finally agree to marry me. We considered ourselves engaged."

"She had a *ring*?" I cried out.

He shook his head again. "No, I didn't give her a ring. I couldn't afford one."

"So you weren't actually engaged?" I said stupidly. "Not really?"

"We were very much engaged. We planned to marry as soon as the war ended. That's precisely why it was all so terrible, you understand."

"No – I don't understand. What was terrible?"

"That I loved her so much." He rose to his feet: I half expected him to stagger, but he was steady. "You'll have to excuse me, Elena. I have no right . . . None at all. You must excuse me," he repeated, as he walked to the kitchen door. "I am tired. I must lie down. Please don't touch anything. Giselle, in the morning." He waved an arm vaguely. "I'm not making any sense. Too tired . . . Perhaps it was the golf. I'm far too old for this sort of nonsense. Sheer foolishness at my age."

Even though he'd said not to, I slowly cleaned up the kitchen, too restless to go to bed. I couldn't stop repeating to myself that she had been engaged to him, that at one point in her life she had been prepared to marry somebody other than my father. My mother had often told me that she hadn't ever consciously wanted to marry, and then she had met my father, had fallen in love on the spot, and had known she would spend the rest of her life with him. Marriage had been inevitable. I remember her advising me never to marry until I couldn't help myself. Yet there it was. She had promised to marry Theodore Hamilton and she had broken his heart. I felt hot tears spilling from my eyes, but for whom they were I can't say. While I was putting away the glasses I dropped one and it broke on the kitchen floor. I bent to pick up the pieces and cut myself deeply on the heel of one hand. I watched the blood well up and sucked my hand, standing in Theodore Hamilton's kitchen with the rain beating down on the terrace.

CHAPTER FOURTEEN

I persuaded Giselle to stop work and join me on the terrace for coffee while I ate breakfast. Theodore was already out. It was a glorious day, as if the storm had never happened. Those meteorologically inclined might say it was thanks to the storm. The air was crystal clear, the sun already hot at half past nine. Giselle had squeezed oranges for me, and I felt very spoilt.

"Theodore, he says you are having a baby."

I glanced down at my tummy and nodded, with a smile. "That's right. In November."

"You are happy? To have a baby?"

"Oh, yes, very." Conversations in foreign languages – and I must say Giselle's English was far better than my French – promote simplicity. Had we chatted in French, I would have been saying, "I have a dog. Do you like dogs?" whether I had one or not. In my O level French oral I said my father was a teacher, to avoid struggling with 'development finance'. Luckily for me, Giselle didn't object to speaking English.

"Giselle, Theodore told me that you are really a nurse. You looked after Madame Hamilton?"

"I am not a real nurse. I helped the family when she was sick. When Chantal was very bad, she didn't want Theodore to look after her. She was – embarrassed."

"Embarrassed?"

"Yes. When you are very sick, you do not want the people you love to find you horrible. It was easier for her to have me look after her. I liked her. I did not know her before she was sick. I didn't have to lie to her like him."

"You mean, Theodore lied?"

"She wanted him to. He knew that. When she asked him if she was still beautiful, he would say yes. When she asked me, I could tell her the truth. Maybe that was better for her."

"You told her she was ugly?"

Giselle shrugged. "No, I told her she looked sick, and very thin."

"Theodore must have been devastated when she died."

"Devastated?"

"Grief-stricken. Very upset. Sad."

"Why? He was glad. Everyone was glad. She had been so sick and so unhappy, it was time she died."

I wondered if Giselle would sound more sympathetic if we were speaking French, but I doubted it.

"And the children? Liliane and – Michel?"

"Liliane was sad, and happy too. She loved her mother. Michel – I don't know. Michel is – how do you say it? – a sheet."

"A shit. Why?"

"He didn't come to see her. He was too busy. He is a doctor, but he didn't want to help her. It is easier helping people you don't know and don't care about to die."

"Chantal wanted to die?"

"In the end, yes. She wanted – too much medicine?" She raised her eyebrows questioningly.

"An overdose? She wanted to take an overdose?"

The expressive Gallic shrug again. Whether because she didn't understand the word, or wasn't prepared to confirm my guess, I didn't know. Her shrug said so much, but I wasn't confident I understood it. "God. How absolutely bloody."

Giselle stood up and began to clear the table. "No, there was no blood. One day she was very ill. She went to hospital, came home, and twelve hours later she was dead. That is all. Now, I must go back to work. Liliane and her Philippe may be here this weekend. I must prepare a room."

"Don't bother about lunch for me. I'm going into town so I'll get something at the café."

"OK."

It was market day. I wandered about, looking at the abundance of fruit and vegetables at the various stalls, cheese, honey, panniers of bread and flowers. There were even a couple of Sloane Rangers selling

fairy cakes. I hardly need add that they didn't appear
to be doing much business, demand for English fairy
cakes being limited, if not non-existent, in small
French market towns. Not that they cared. I stopped
at the basket stall next to theirs, and listened to them
talking about how drunk Rupert had been the night
before, and whether George was going to get his leg
over or not. Around noon, I sat down outside the
Méridien, half hoping I would bump into Theodore.

"Madame?" There was a light tap on my shoulder, and I turned to see Madame Guillot. She shook
my hand warmly, and I invited her to join me. She
had a huge bag over one arm, and refused, obviously
in the middle of her shopping, but once she had
convinced herself that I was completely fine, she
reported that Monsieur Turcan had phoned a few
nights before, which thrilled me. I knew how much
effort it had taken to call. My heart sank to my boots
when she said she'd told him I'd been taken to hospital, and had given him the number in Cahors.

After a sandwich, I asked at the bar for directions
to the local clinic, and walked there. I was lucky
enough to find Dr Duhaze getting out of his car just
as I arrived. It took him a moment or two to regis-
ter who I was.

"Miss Stewart." He shook my hand formally.
"You are feeling well? No more complications?"

"No, I feel perfectly well, thanks. I came to thank
you for everything you did."

"No need. You are lucky to find me. I have only
two afternoons a week here. And I am lucky to find

you. Someone called the hospital for you. It was a man, the nurse said. She didn't know where you had gone, she told him only that you had left. We cannot discuss patients with strangers, you understand."

"Of course. I know who it was."

"Good. Then I will say goodbye. You will call me if you have any bleeding." It was a command rather than an invitation, but I didn't mind. As far as I am concerned doctors are one of the few male breeds who can always assume the dominant position.

"Doctor, I wanted to ask you about the Hamiltons – Chantal Hamilton? The wife of my friend Theodore?"

"Yes, I know who she was." He looked at me sternly. "As I explained, we are not permitted to discuss patients."

"Even if they're dead?"

"Even so."

"But Theodore isn't your patient. I'm worried about him."

He sighed impatiently and began to take bags and files out of his car. I touched his arm.

"Miss Stewart, you should be thinking about yourself and your baby, not people who have nothing to do with you. If you will permit, I have a great deal of work to do."

"He's an old man, Doctor. He must have been very depressed by his wife's death. Couldn't you spare a moment?"

"After ten years? If Monsieur Hamilton wants to come to me for medical advice, he knows where to find me. I doubt that he will."

"Why do you say that?

He removed my hand from his arm. "He is not my patient. He has his reasons. Often, a husband and wife prefer to keep different doctors. They are not the same person. His wife may have shared confidences with me that he would not wish to remember. Now, I must insist, good day."

He leapt up the steps to the clinic, and I was left on the street mouthing, "Thank you – goodbye," into the air behind him.

I have an active imagination – always have had – but when I was pregnant it erupted into independent life, nourished by the dreaded hormones. All sorts of possibilities occurred to me as I walked slowly back through the village and out the other side, to the road to Le Bosc. The plot that took most tangible shape in my mind was this: my mother had spurned the noble bomber pilot because she had fallen in love with someone else. After all, if she had hidden one great passion from me, why not several? On the rebound, Theodore had met and married Chantal. She had never really loved him, and he had known it and was unable to comfort her even at the end. She didn't want him to touch her. The son, Michel, had taken his father's side in male solidarity and had been unable to forgive his mother as she lay dying. Perhaps Chantal had had an affair, and the daughter could understand and empathize with her mother, but husband and son could not. The doctor knew all, and had fallen into the semi-medical, semi-pastoral role that doctors often do, however poorly trained for the latter function.

This all made some sort of logical sense to me as I walked up the hill past fields of yellowing corn. I could hear the exchanges between father and son clearly in my head, Theodore being honourable and noble, asking his son to forgive and forget and love his mother, and Michel the idealist refusing to do so. I scripted the conversation between Chantal and the stiff young doctor, too, Chantal swearing him to secrecy, professing her refusal to give up on hope when she hadn't had her share of joy, and finally giving up on life. And Giselle's comments dovetailed in – of course, Chantal would take no comfort from Theodore's protestations of her beauty, if he had always looked on her through rose-tinted glasses and loved her despite her infidelities. His cloying devotion would drive her half mad. The cast of characters had the makings of a nineteenth-century novel: wronged but all-forgiving husband, bitter and faithless wife, their children dividing neatly down the middle in their allegiance, and all-knowing yet powerless physician. Some things didn't quite tally: with the finishing post so clearly in your sights, surely love and the rest of the crap just didn't matter . . . And there was the odd sub-plot of my mother's photograph. Perhaps, in a dreadful way, my mother was to blame for the whole thing, for Theodore's second-time-around broken heart and Chantal's unfulfilled life, even her son's disaffection.

Even if my mother had wreaked such havoc in

the Hamiltons' lives, I couldn't condemn her. I couldn't cast Ma in the role of heartless beauty. Even with the evidence of the photograph, I could barely believe in my mother's independent existence before I had arrived on the scene. I thought of my own past *amours*. I had never had any doubt that Nick and I would have been unhappy together, however much we loved each other. And Peter *had* proposed – and what if in some mental and emotional blackout I had said yes, and then reneged on my promise? My imagination galloped. Say I had realized my mistake on our wedding day, and stood him up at the altar. Peter would have gone apeshit with humiliation. I saw him cancelling the honeymoon (after checking if his travel insurance – which, knowing Peter, he most definitely would have arranged – would cover a bridal bolt) and turning up at the office, screwing up a few of his investments, then turning to drink and falling ludicrously in love with an assistant on the investment desk. She wouldn't love him but she'd marry him, and they would live unhappily ever after, until one day ten years later gin-soaked Peter would buy an Uzi sub-machine-gun, and mow down twenty innocent people on the residential streets of Wandsworth. Would it be my fault for saying yes when I should have said no? I saw Peter in the dock, his lawyer pleading long-term insanity, myself being called as a character witness and, in my guilt, saying that he'd always been a nice, well-meaning boy, staring into his lunatic eyes . . .

This wasn't as good a plot as the first. It lacked the

romantic backdrop of the war, and none of the characters was sufficiently noble or empathetic – certainly not Peter. I smiled to myself as I turned up Theodore's drive. Peter was probably even now engaged to some nice Sloane – the image of one of the two girls in the market – and the closest he would ever get to court would be the misappropriation of a pension fund, or the failure to perform some due diligence routine. Peter hadn't even been that upset when I turned down his proposal – he'd said something along the lines of "Fair enough, but I'm sure you'll realize it's a sensible idea if you sleep on it."

Theodore's old Citroën was back in the garage but the house was empty. I went to bed, and was deep in some pleasant dream when I heard regular, persistent banging, and Theodore calling my name. "Elena? Elena? Are you awake? There's a telephone call for you."

I got out of bed clumsily, fell over my own feet in the process, and flung open the door.

"Is it David?"

"No, it's a man, but I'm afraid I didn't catch the name."

I cantered down the corridor in bare feet, and picked up the phone in the drawing room.

"Hello?"

"Elena! It's Heff. What the hell have you been doing?"

"Sleeping. What is it, Heff? I thought we weren't going to talk till next week."

"Yeah, well. Listen, honey, Turk called last night.

Kind of *middle* of the fuckin' night."

"Oh, God. I should have guessed. He called the hotel and the hospital . . ."

"Bullseye. Hospital. He got through to us and went crazy. Said the hospital wouldn't tell him shit. He made me swear I'd find you. What he said was, he'd bust my fuckin' ass if I didn't."

"Did he leave a contact number? Is there any way I can call him back?"

"Like shit, yeah, you think he left a *mobile* number? Jeez, Elena, where do you think he is? Fuckin' Biarritz? Where the fuck are you, anyways?"

I didn't reply, and Heff's tone softened. "Listen, baby, what were you doin' in hospital?"

"Nothing. It was stupid. I'm fine," I insisted.

"Fine? Don't fuckin' give me some run-around, girl –"

"I'm *fuckin' A,* all right Heff? Does that satisfy you, fuckhead?" I shouted, more to hammer the point home than in genuine emotion, and in the corner of my eye saw Theodore standing in the kitchen doorway. He immediately walked away.

"Sounds good to me. But I promised the Turk, if I had any doubts I'd hightail it down to your neck of the woods, right?"

"For Christ's sake, Heff, this isn't necessary. I'm fine, honestly, I have friends here and I'm perfectly capable of looking after myself . . ."

"I don't give shit about that. I promised Turk I'd get there. Besides, you're having a *baby.*"

"Yes, I'm aware of that." I was shuffling about.

My bare feet were cold on the tiles and I had an ominous feeling that Heff was about to announce his imminent arrival.

"A *baby*, and you don't know shit about takin' care of yourself. So Mish and I'll see you 'bout six or seven o'clock tonight. All you have to do, hon, is fix us up a room somewhere, y'hear me?"

"Loud and clear, Heff," I said resignedly.

"Where do we head for?"

I found Theodore out on the terrace. "I'm sorry about that."

"No need to be."

"I'm sorry about his calling here and bothering you. And everything."

"No need, my dear."

"They're friends of David's," I explained. "David spoke to them last night, and he's clearly got the wrong end of the stick and bullied them into coming down. They're arriving tonight. I'll get my things, and move back to the hotel."

"Your friends are welcome here."

"Oh, you wouldn't say that if you'd met them."

"I would be delighted."

"I know you would, but they're a strange couple, and it might be best if I see them alone, and if your daughter's coming this weekend anyway . . ."

"Elena . . ."

"I know. Really. I'll see you in a couple of days, OK?"

On impulse, I leant forward and kissed him.

*   *   *

345

Heff and Mishi crashed into the hotel in the early evening. They might as well have parachuted in through a hole in the roof for the immediate pandemonium they caused in that little backwater. They were small, slight people, but they seemed to have been drawn on scale and a half compared to everybody else in Sainte Cécile. Unlike David, Heff was quite happy to let Madame Guillot haul his bags upstairs. He looped one arm through mine, the other through Mishi's and headed for the tiny bar.

"OK, Elle. You've got the mike. Why didn't you tell us in Paris you were having a baby?"

"I don't know."

"I just don't believe you're cookin' one. Way to go, Turk. Fuckin' *dog*." He coated the word with approval. "Did he know before?"

"Of course he knew," I said haughtily. "Maybe we thought it was a private matter."

"Yeah, well. Me an' Turk never had any secrets."

"Lucky you. I wish I could say the same."

"Elena," Mishi took my hand in hers, "David was truly upset when he spoke to us. He was distraught about you and the baby. The hospital only told him that you had been checked out."

"I'm *fine*. How many times do I have to say it?"

She pressed my hand. "And the baby?"

"The baby's fine too. I just . . ." Had I been alone with Mishi, I probably would have given her a blow-by-blow account, but I didn't want to discuss breakthrough bleeding in front of Heff. In this, I now believe that I did Heff an injustice. ". . . know it's fine," I finished lamely.

"Thank God," Mishi murmured.

"Praise be! Now, ladies, where are we going for dinner?"

Heff ruled out eating in the hotel. "No way. If I've been dragged to the fuckin' country under false pretences then I want *serious* regional cooking. I want high-calibre chefing. I want Michelin fuckin' stars . . ." He pulled the red book from his back pocket and flipped through. "An' it just so happens there's a place a way down the road. We'll bill it to the Turk."

"Oh, Heff, I don't know that I feel up to it. I haven't got a car or anything, and I've been going to bed really early . . ."

Heff was already ordering a taxi.

Forty-five minutes later we arrived at a very elegant restaurant in a small village in the back of beyond. The maître d' sniffed when he saw us on his doorstep. We looked a motley crew, Heff in dirty chinos, with tartan shirt-tails hanging out, Mishi in jeans, and me in shorts held together with string and one of David's shirts, but it was a Wednesday night and they welcomed any business. Their tolerance was well rewarded. Heff went to town, insisting that we all had the seven-course *menu gastronomique*. He chose it because it meant you didn't have to make any more choices – you did it all in one go. He said it was just like deciding to get married: it removed the necessity for having to choose who you'd call up each night, who you'd eat with, who you'd try to get in the sack, and who you'd end up shagging. Bang. One decision, and sling the menu back.

The *sommelier* chorused the maître d's disapproval when Heff waved aside the wine list, and asked for a bottle of each of the house wines. "A white and a red?" he asked, his eyebrows disappearing into his hairline, and a nostril flaring in synchronization with a curling lip.

"What, buddy? You telling me you've got *green* on special offer? Yeah, a white and a red, and if you've got a rosé, we'll have one of those too." Heff shook out his cigarette packet, and offered it to me and Mishi. An ashtray materialized as if by magic on the table, and Heff grunted and lit up. There was an orchestrated flurry as our glasses were removed, replaced and carefully repositioned. Heff waved away the waiters.

"These guys. I'd give them a fuckin' tip *now* if they'd just leave us the hell alone."

It got worse. When the first course arrived, we were surrounded by waiters poised to remove the great silver domes that covered our plates. We carried on talking, and one cleared his throat. Heff still carried on talking, and all three coughed simultaneously. Heff spread his hands wide in mock bewilderment. "What's the beef, guys? If you've all got some contagious throat disease, we'd be real grateful if you'd back the hell off from our plates, you hear what I'm saying? You know – you could be spreading *germs*."

He received a baleful stare, and then the greyest of the three intoned: "La mousse d'artichaut et de fromage de chèvre, sur un lit d'herbes fines." They lifted the covers off our plates with flawless timing to reveal little pyramids of pale beige mush swimming in pools of bright green liquid.

"Fuck me. It looks like puppy puke on a bed of toxic waste." Heff let out a low whistle. The waiters were at last satisfied, and vanished as if they had been beamed up by Scotty.

I picked up my fork and plunged it into the small offering. "How was David? Did he say when he was coming back?"

Heff opened his mouth, and Mishi interjected hurriedly, "He's fine. He's tired and all, and it's kind of crazy there, but he's just fine. He was strung out about you, on top of everything else."

I saw them exchange a meaningful look. "On top of what else?"

"Nothing, Elena. It's a tough ride down there, y'know? We warned him. He knew what was going down. It's kind of rough – not so much coming back as getting out."

"But he's all right?"

Mishi nodded quickly, and bent her head to her plate. Heff wiped his with a hunk of bread then shoved it half-way across the table, nearly knocking over the candle, and coughed. That cough seemed to bring everything up from way down inside him – I don't mean phlegm or garbage in his lungs, it sounded like he was bringing up stuff from his groin.

"David got hit."

While I stared at him, he lit another cigarette. Got hit. My head wouldn't function. Got hit. What did it mean? Punched? Shot? If he'd been shot, he couldn't have been on the phone.

"Ain't no matter, Elle. The problem wasn't getting shot – I mean, it isn't like the Turk hasn't been shot at before, an' he'll get shot at again an' all, but this time he got hit."

"He got hit?" By this stage, I must have sounded truly stupid. That's how I felt. Stupid and cold.

"Yeah. He didn't go into detail, but I'll bet it was on the airport road. It's a fuckin' turkey shoot. That's the problem with fuckin' Sarajevo – the only way to get your sweet ass out is that one fuckin' road. You ain't got no choice." He dragged deeply on his cigarette before correcting himself. "Like, sure, you've always got a choice – you can hole up in some cellar like a rat, and hope they'll all have gone to play somewhere else by the time you find the guts to creep out, *or* you can do the fuckin' turkey run."

"How do you mean he got shot?"

"He just got shot. Bam. In the leg. Sounded like a drilling job. It ain't a personal thing, Elle, they weren't trying to waste him, not personally. Some journalists get whacked, but this sounds like it was crossfire. There's a couple of goons with guns and folk scrambling around on the deck, and shots get loosed."

Mishi tried to take my hand, but I snatched it away from her.

"Elena, he's all right. He said it was clean. He was lucky. He always *is*. He's been taken care of, there are doctors there . . . He really is OK. Look. Heff wouldn't be here if Turk was hurt bad. He'd go to him."

"Like I wouldn't? Well, that's a relief." If I had been given the choice then to reverse time, and not be sitting in that restaurant, and not be pregnant, and not to have had anything at all to do with David Turcan, ever, I swear to God I would have taken it. I was cold with anger.

"Elena, some guys treat a hit like that like they've been awarded a medal. He'll probably *get* a fuckin' medal, or some honorary award at least. He'll pin it on the wall, and when the kid grows up, he can use it as a dart-board. Turk was more fucked up about you an' what was going on here than he was about himself. If it was his leg, then shit, he's got two of them! That's why we've got two of just about everything, so we've got a spare. Well, not quite everything, I guess you're meant to keep a pretty close eye on your *dick*, but everything else, know what I mean? You've gotta understand, sugar-pie, it's the name of the game."

"Which game is that, Heff?"

"The Wheel of Fortune. Shit, I dunno – Russian Roulette. It's not a question of whether you win or lose, it's how you play the game. Yes, siree! Or maybe it's more like poker," he was relaxing into his stride now, running easy and loose-limbed, "seven-card stud, one-eyed jacks wild. Mexican Sweat. It's all in the face. And all deep down in your heart." He patted his breast pocket, where he always carried a little notebook and pen. The huge grin on his face made my hand itch.

"Not Happy Families, then? Not Family Fortunes?"

Heff whistled through his teeth. "*Shee*-it, Elena, don't you go turning all mean and nasty on me, girl!"

The men arrived again with their domed platters, and I sat with gritted teeth as they repeated, with even greater solemnity, the unveiling ceremony. I had lost my appetite, and we were only on the second course.

"Did David say when he was coming back?" I repeated.

"Hun, he's not in a position to give an ETA. He'll get out as and when he's good and ready. When he said ten days to two weeks, I thought that was optimistic."

He'd said a week to ten days to me. "And there's no contact number?"

"I'd be real surprised if there's more than one phone there – Reuters'll have a satellite phone but you won't get through. The Sarajevo Holiday Inn ain't the Dallas Hilton, you understand me?"

I pointed my knife at his chest, poking it just below his notebook. "Heff, if you don't wipe that patronizing smile off your face right now, stop treating me like a child, stop cracking pathetic jokes, and actually give me some answers, then I swear to God I am going to plunge this blade straight in the middle of your ribcage, open it up wide, and rip your fucking heart out with my bare hands. You understand *me*?"

The waiters were flocking around, fretting like a cluster of disgruntled chickens. Mishi was quiet, her black eyes turning from me to Heff. Heff took my hand gently, and I dropped the knife on the table. He spoke in a quiet tone that I had never heard him use before. "I'm real sorry, sweet-pea. I wish there was something I could do to stop you feeling scared, but there ain't. Turk isn't hurt bad – I promise you that. But he's not sounding like himself. He said all kinds of crazy things about you and the baby, and what to do if he didn't come back. The only thing that made sense was that he wanted us to come here and make sure you were OK. I told him to get his ass back here and look after you himself, and he said he probably couldn't get out for a while." Mishi was shaking her head sadly from side to side, a small frown furrowing her brow. "Mish and I talked about it all the way down, and we agreed not to tell you about his getting shot up. But I reckon it's best if you know. There's only one thing you can do –"

"What? Go to Sarajevo and drag him out kicking and screaming?"

"No, sweetness. There ain't no way you'd get in there and be any use, and it'd be a sure fire way to kill him. Only thing you can do is get the agency to get him a message you're OK. Then tell yourself he's coming back, sit tight and bite down hard."

I don't think any of us ate much of that two-star dinner. I know that it put me off serious restaurants for life. I also know that I drank a lot – far more than I would ever be willing to admit to disapproving teetotal pregnant girlfriends, community midwives or the likes of Miriam Hilton's ladies, but I didn't give a damn. I was listening to snatches of voices in my memory, mainly David's, or at least his was the loudest and strongest, insisting that he was going to be fine, that he'd be back, that he knew it in his bones or he wouldn't go. Behind him, I heard Theodore saying that the price I paid wouldn't be at David's cost. Strangely, there was a third voice. I heard Claire Babington telling me that sometimes bargains were a mistake – sometimes when you promised anything for your man's safe return, the trade was booby-trapped: you got him back, but no longer quite what you expected.

We went back to the hotel and I went straight to bed. There were no more messages. Again, I dreamt of home, except that it wasn't home. I dreamt that my parents and I were in a strange metal building, some-thing like an aircraft hangar. In the dream, I kept telling everyone that everything would be all right, but I couldn't work out what was wrong. It was there, the danger, and the threat, but I just couldn't pin it down, and no one would tell me anything. All I knew was that my father was weeping, and I had never seen him cry in my life, and the sound was so strange that I kept on rushing over to him and slap-ping him on the back as if he was choking, although I knew he wasn't. He was sobbing. I woke in the dark, and the pillow and my cheeks were wet.

The nose of the heavy plane lurched 45 degrees as

they dive-bombed into their descent. The airfield was being shelled, and the pilot refused to lower the landing gear until the last minute, in case a crack shot liked the look of his tyres. The fleet of military transport planes used for the UN airlift were known to the press corps as Maybe Airlines – Maybe you get there; Maybe you don't.

"Where's your jacket?" the pilot reminded him.

Flak jackets did not seem to make much difference to a safe landing. The pilot himself sported a plated jacket, gloves, goggles, a schute, an oxygen mask and a helmet. David reached between his feet and put on his jacket. He was always sensible about protection; before leaving England he had invested in a new 305 overvest, not a top weight one but a decent middle-range job. The salesman had agreed that his old one had 'seen a little too much life', which was a nice way of putting it.

David crouched low and ran for the control tower. His fitness and speed were an advantage in the job, but his bulk was something of a handicap. You don't overlook a man who's six foot three however low he crouches. It was only sixteen hours since he had left Elena sitting in the Marais. At each stage of the journey, Marais to de Gaulle, Paris to Zagreb, Zagreb to Sarajevo, he had felt increasingly fit and alert; he loved the climbing in and out of planes, scenting the difference in the air on each landing. The airport

*cowered like a little animal between the Bosnian
and Serb front lines; the smell here was of cordite.
The control tower had the appearance of a five-
year-old's Lego model after a major tantrum.
David found two men sitting inside, trying to
land the planes, and simultaneously finish a card
game. Above their heads was a sign that read
"You don't have to be crazy to work here, but it
helps". It reminded him of a clapped out New
Jersey gas station. He took a photograph of it,
chatted for a moment and went to find a lift into
the city. A body was propped stiffly against one
wall of the airfield hangar. A woman's brightly
coloured scarf had been draped decorously over
the head but, other than that, nobody had paid it
much attention. It might have been there for
days, waiting for transport, like the rest of them.
David lifted a corner of the scarf and looked
dispassionately at what remained of the man's
head. He did not photograph it.*

*There were photographers who would have
snapped the corpse as it lay, and others who might
have adjusted the position of the limbs, redraped
the scarf to reveal what was only half a face,
moved back the arm to expose the hole in the side.
David had never been squeamish about death or
mutilation, but he did not believe in tampering
with a body. He did not think of his settings as
war zones or combat zones, or pits of atrocity,
he thought of them as survival zones, for himself
as well as for the people he was there to photo-*

graph, and his interest was primarily in how people survived rather than the manner of their death.

Every sight and sound carried a lesson. You had to remember everything you'd ever learnt along the road about staying alive, and you had to learn from the locals, pick up the new tricks peculiar to each place. A veteran of Vietnam was not a veteran in Zaïre, or in Sarajevo. He was a beginner, and he had a lot to learn in a very short time. Some lessons travelled from one place to another: as soon as you set foot in your hotel room, you taped up the windows, if the room still had windows. You went to sleep with a torch strapped to your hand. You put your boots next to the bed, or else you slept in them. You knew how to make a basin of water last all day. When you passed through check points, you made sure you handed over the correct press pass – accidentally offering the wrong one could be a suicidal error. You did not travel in cars with people you didn't know, not even fellow journalists; every companion had to be reliable – at the least, predictable. You made sure that your agency and your blood type was written clearly on the outside of your vest or jacket. Above all, you moved fast, but not too fast, not so fast that you lost your concentration.

David shared a lift into Sarajevo with the corpse in a Red Cross truck; the driver dropped him at the Holiday Inn before going on to the morgue. Once in Sarajevo, the final stages of the chameleon process on which he relied were completed. He knew most of the hotel residents, and he knew the questions to ask. The Holiday Inn stood square on Sniper Alley; the southern façade of the building faced the Serbs and was uninhabitable. The north side was comparatively safe, but fully occupied. David took a third-floor room on the west side and got out his masking tape. Then he visited the Reuters office on the fifth floor, checked out the phone rates, chatted with old friends over lunch at the long communal tables, hassled to find an interpreter, and then went out to work. The only thing that surprised him was that his thoughts kept returning to Elena.

Some three days after his arrival, David broke one of his rules and called her. He felt an overwhelming hunger to hear the catch in her voice when she heard his, to hear her scold him for his selfishness in waking her up . . . That evening, from his room, he had watched a heavily pregnant woman run across Sniper Alley, with one arm dragging a little girl, pushing the child in front, then behind, shoving her against the wall, changing the girl's position all the time, and her other thin, braceleted arm held protectively across her stomach. He had gone straight to Butch on the fifth floor and bargained for the phone. When he spoke to Madame Guillot, he started making deals; when he spoke to the nurse at the hospital in Cahors, he decided that if there was a God, he'd have nothing to do with him. By then, all deals were off. He could not think, and would not sit and try to think. He wanted to keep moving, to get on the plane, get off the plane, change the film, caption the negatives, get on the plane, get on the plane . . .

The next morning, he was shot trying to keep moving. By then, he knew that there were no deals to be had. Twenty-four hours later, he was sitting in the small apartment of a Muslim leader, taking pictures. The man was so certain of his imminent death that he gave David his own typed obituary, and asked him to get it to the London Times. David tucked it into a pocket of his vest, thinking, "Ah, sure . . . like the Times is going to run the obituary of some thirty-year-old no-name Bosnian?" He knew he would rather be dead than be a Muslim living there, that he would rather die a hundred times over. He wished that there wasn't a soul on earth that he cared for, or who cared for him, not even a dog. He did not concern himself with the question of his own death; that did not seem a legitimate use of his time. Nor was he unduly concerned with how Elena and the baby would manage without him; they would go with the flow, adjust to circumstance as everyone had to. He simply could not confront how he might feel without them. That evening, he explored a looted house of a

Muslim family, turning over the detritus of family life with the toe of his boot, things that had been abandoned, considered unessential – photographs, a small doll, a leather purse ... That night, David returned to the Holiday Inn and went to bed with a red-haired AP reporter called Micky. They had slept together four years before, in another place, their love-making charged by the sound of gunfire and shelling. Micky's climax was erotically escalated by seeing his blood on the coarse bed sheets.

There was a rule in the press corps, a rule that everyone knew: the scariest time of all is when you stop feeling frightened. David used to say that to the new kids over a beer, just to let them feel OK about crapping themselves, but it had never really meant anything to him. He never had been scared before, not even when he had been shot. Then he found himself taking pictures of women, beautiful women with their heads held high, and he felt frightened by them. They had a feminine, secretive seriousness, and he knew that, as he tracked their paths, he was quite lost in the deeply intricate maze in which they moved swiftly and easily. He was shocked with love, the love he felt for women and children, and overwhelmed by their dignity. David made it his mission to live his life as close to theirs as he could. He queued for bread with them, even though food was not scarce at the hotel; he ran when they ran, and travelled with them, and talked to them all the time. Sometimes he did not wear his flak jacket, fearful that it would put too great a distance between them. Also, he was superstitious: he'd already been hit once, and he wasn't going to get shot again, not out in the street. As ever, he had a finicky passion for perfection in his frames, but he was willing to wait for the perfect moment – determined to stay there until he got it.

Fear lent him energy. He negotiated the loan of a BBC Land Rover to follow up a story he'd heard on the outskirts of town, on condition of taking a reporter and translator with him. He knew the route out of the hotel's underground garage, heading straight into the Serbian snipers with their sights trained on the exit. He crawled the car up the first stage of the ramp, then gunned the engine and heaved the wheel wildly left as shots rang out. He got the pictures he wanted, and they headed back on the road through no man's land, down the mountain into the city at dusk. David had been well briefed on that road. It was the target of both Serb and Bosnian snipers, some armed with anti-aircraft guns, some with anti-tank artillery that did not respect the BBC's investment in bullet-proof Plexiglas. The only thing to do was to drive at great speed, to drive so fast that they couldn't set their sights on you, even if you were worse than fish in a bucket – a white truck against a scorched mountainside. The only thing was to drive fast, but not so fast that you went out of control. Two *bullets came through the windscreen, one of which hit the reporter in the arm. Another bullet came through the side window. The road was mined on either side. David had been warned about the curve, the particular corner where guys had piled off the road straight into a minefield. The reporter wanted to throw himself out of the car and take his chance on the road, where he would at least have had the satisfaction of knowing he was dead. David knew how he felt. David thought about Elena, and about his child and prayed they were both alive. He shifted the car into first gear, and slammed his foot on the accelerator as he drove into the bend.*

CHAPTER FIFTEEN

When the telephone rang, I threw myself across the bed to answer it in the hope that it was David. It was my mother.

"Oh, *Ma*!" I burst into tears. "Mother, I can't tell you how good it is to hear your voice."

"What in heaven's name is going on, Elena?" The voice was tense and impatient, but it was hers and, second to David's, it was the one I most wanted to hear.

"It's just been awful. David's been shot, and I don't know where the hell he is or when he's coming back . . . *If* he's coming back." I was sniffing so much I had to wipe my nose on my sleeve. Good thing Ma wasn't there to see me do it.

"I'm on my way up."

"What?" I sat up in bed.

"I'm in the lobby, Elena."

Two minutes later, my mother burst into the room and took me into her arms. As she held me against her, I felt all that warm, spongy softness and breathed in the powdery scent of her, and wanted only to be held there for ever as I sobbed.

She became uncharacteristically brisk. She plumped up the pillows behind me, smoothed the sheets, pulled up the blanket, and ordered breakfast in such abysmally awful French that I couldn't help smiling through my tears. Then she drew up a chair and sat down next to the bed. "Now. First things first. What do you mean David's been shot?"

"Steve Heffner told me yesterday. He said David was all right. He'd spoken to him."

"And so have we. He can't be dead. Now. Why were you in hospital?"

"I started bleeding one night. I panicked – it wasn't very much, but it didn't stop. I thought I was having a miscarriage. The hotel called a doctor and he took me to hospital. They did a scan the next day and everything was fine so they let me go. It was stupid. *I* was stupid because I was frightened."

"But you didn't think to call me?"

"Oh, Ma, don't be like that. It was the middle of the night – what could you have done? I was in good hands, there was no point calling you."

"Not even when you got out of hospital?"

"No. By then I knew everything was OK, that I'd overreacted."

"You hadn't. At least you had the sense to call a doctor. If not me."

"I didn't want to worry you when there wasn't any need, and if I *had* called you, the first thing you would have done is overreact yourself, and flown over here in an almighty panic for nothing." My mother stood up and walked to the window to draw the curtains. When she turned round, I could see how pale and drawn she looked. She looked years older than when I had last seen her. "Which is exactly what you *have* done. So I was right not to call."

"I don't care if you were right or not, Elena. Did it cross your mind how your father and I would feel hearing that you were in hospital somewhere in France, alone, and not knowing what was wrong?"

"Who told you?" I asked quietly. "Theodore Hamilton?"

"Theodore?" She was nonplussed by the suggestion. "No, David. David called up in a terrible state. He didn't mention that he'd been shot. He said you'd been in some hospital in Cahors, they wouldn't tell him why, and you'd disappeared. Then the line went dead. I was certain you'd been in a car crash. Certain of it. Can you imagine how we felt? Can you even *begin* to imagine? Did it cross your mind just once? I do wish you would think of other people occasionally, Elena." Her eyes flashed.

I rolled over in bed, turning my back on her in a sulk.

"I can't win, can I, Mother? If I'd told you what had happened, you would have got in a flap, and since I didn't, you're in even more of one. It isn't my fault that David called you."

"Yes, it is. He was absolutely right to call, poor

man. If you had acted a little more responsibly, if you had stayed home and taken care of yourself as I begged you to do, none of this would have happened. How do you think David feels? I have been out of my mind with worry for twenty-four hours, not to mention your poor father. Did you think of him? He still doesn't know you are all right – that I'm all right, even. We had to find a flight to Toulouse, and your father was insisting on coming but I wouldn't let him because I knew he wouldn't be able to cope if anything was seriously wrong with you. This has been a nightmare, from beginning to end. We had no way of reaching you, no way of contacting David, Charlie's left Paris and, just like you, hasn't the courtesy to let us know where he is."

"If you're *so* concerned about Daddy's feelings, then why not call him, tell him that everything's fine and stop lecturing me as if I were five years old?"

"Because I don't know that everything *is* fine," my mother snapped. "I'm still waiting to hear what you've got to say –"

"For myself?" I finished for her. "Mother, I am not a child. I am thirty-one. I am old enough to make my own decisions. When I heard you on the phone, I felt so *happy* that you were here, and now you crash in and start telling me off as if I'd left the back door open for burglars when I'd promised to lock up or something. I wish you hadn't come. God. I wish Daddy *had* – he'd never react like this. Why won't you accept that this is *my* life and support me and stop telling me what I'm doing wrong? I mean, fuck, Mother, how do you think I feel right now?"

"There's no need to use such foul language –"

"Oh fuck, fuck, *FUCK*!"

There was a knock at the door. I buried my head in the pillow. The Guillots' daughter must have heard me cursing but backed into the room without a glance at me or my mother, placed a tray on the dressing table and slipped out. Across the tray lay a large bouquet of flowers. My mother picked them up.

"Oh, Christ, Ma, you *didn't* phone him, did you? You didn't tell him you were coming? Just so he'd send you flowers?"

She stood in the middle of the room, staring at the bouquet she held and didn't reply. She blinked quickly several times before she laid the flowers on the bed and went back to the window. There was a card from Theodore: *Elena – Hope these brighten your room, and that you will come to say goodbye before you and David leave Sainte Cécile. Theodore.*

I should have apologized to my mother right away but I wasn't big enough, and while it dawned on me that I was in the wrong, there was still a slim chance she could be persuaded to share the honour with me. "Are you going to see him now that you're here? You might as well. I bet that's why you really came."

My mother turned to face me, and now there were tears running slowly down her cheeks. "I don't understand how you can be so cruel. One day, Elena, one day you might just understand a little bit, but right now . . ." She caught her breath, and as I threw back the covers with overwhelming remorse, she was already at my bedside and we embraced, both talking at once.

"—I'm so sorry, Mummy, so sorry, it's been so terrible."

"—I know, darling, but it's all all right now, it's fine, I'm here, sweetheart."

"—I didn't mean to be horrid, I've been so frightened. I love you more than anything, I couldn't want to hurt you."

"—I know. Hush now, darling girl, you're always my baby, nothing's ever going to change that, and there's nothing on earth that matters so long as you are all right. Nothing at all."

After much nose-blowing, we shared breakfast, and my mother listened to me about David and what Heff had said. "The main thing is that you know he wasn't badly hurt."

"I don't trust him. He wouldn't say if he was. What did he tell you?"

"Nothing. We barely gave him a chance to speak, and he's not the most forthcoming of men."

"You can say that again."

"Elena, has the baby changed anything between you and David? You're still all right together, aren't you?"

"It hasn't changed much at all. I thought that fatherhood might make him feel differently about himself, but I don't think he's even thought about it."

"David's never been a man to wear his heart on his sleeve, has he, sweetheart? And having a baby can't *change* a man, darling, it just brings out whatever's already there. Your father was always a sweet man – My God, *Ben*! I must call right away. He'll be worried sick."

I spoke to my father briefly. Hearing the relief in his voice made me want to cry all over again, but just as his voice caught, he cleared his throat scratchily and said, "Now, you two girls look after each other. Not too much gallivanting around, either of you, and, Elena dear, do *try* to keep your mother out of the shops. She's armed to the teeth with credit cards and highly dangerous . . ." He spoke to my mother for longer, and although I couldn't hear what he was saying, I watched her eyes smiling, and when she hung up they were sparkling again.

"Silly old fool," she said, with enormous tenderness.

"What did he say?"

"He told me to take you out and put some flesh on your bones, and to buy each of us a present on his behalf, and then to hurry home, because . . ."

"Because?"

"Oh, because he pretends he's lonely without me. Silly old fool."

"I'm so jealous. I honestly don't think David's ever missed me."

"Nonsense."

"He certainly wouldn't admit it. Daddy's always telling you how much he loves you."

369

"There aren't any perfect men, darling, or women. All you can do is hold out for the big things. Maybe David isn't sentimental but he brings far more important things to the table, and he's the right man for you. You've known him long enough to hear what he isn't saying." She patted my cheek. "You're just too stubborn to listen. And as for Daddy, he isn't always so affectionate. You should have been there the last time he saw my Amex bill."

"David never murmurs sweet nothings in my ear . . ." I said unfairly.

"I would say that David went to enormous lengths to make sure you were all right and being looked after, given where he is right now. That has to count for a lot more than sweet nothings. David loves you passionately."

"Then why doesn't he say so?"

"Maybe he will. But actions –"

"– speak louder than words." I smiled back at her.

My mother took a compact and lipstick out of her handbag and began to do her lips, pulling them down hard over her teeth in a grimace. When I was a little girl, I was fascinated by the ritual. I thought it a gesture uniquely her own. If I spotted other women doing it on television or in real life, I believed they were copying her.

"Darling, why don't you have a bath, and then we can go shopping and obey your father?"

Over the sound of the water, I gave her the bad news that Sainte Cécile didn't really have anything in the way of shops, not that she would consider tempting.

"There must be something!" she called.

"Nothing bar a baker."

"Let's at least *look*. You might have missed something."

When I came out of the bathroom, she was in front of the mirror, leaning close to it and studying her face.

"Ma, seriously, don't you want to go and see Theodore? He'd love to see you."

She patted her hair into place. "No, darling, it wouldn't be sensible. Besides," she smoothed an eyebrow, "I'm too vain."

I left a note for Heff and Mishi, who had a large 'Do Not Disturb' sign stuck on their door at midday, and, once I'd convinced Ma that there wasn't a shop within ten miles, chose a secluded table in the hotel restaurant. I wanted to be alone with her, and didn't feel up to Heff's unique brand of bonhomie. My mother was girlish during lunch. Monsieur Guillot flirted with her outrageously, although she must have had ten or twenty years on him and told him so. He persuaded her to have a kir royale, and brought us a bottle of wine on the house. I swam in and out of the feeling that I was having lunch with my mother and having lunch with a friend my own age. In the mother–daughter stretches, our conversation kept returning to David, then veering away from him, like a dieting woman opening and shutting the fridge door.

"What if he doesn't get out of Sarajevo, Mother?"

I would say in each lull.

"He will," she'd reply simply. "He will, when he can and when he's finished his work. You just have to believe a little harder, Elena."

"What if he's hurt badly?"

"He's not. You'd know if he was. Have faith. Just think positively, and try not to worry so much. Don't dwell on it."

"What if he doesn't really love me? What if he doesn't want to be with me?"

"I know that he does. Loving his work doesn't mean that he doesn't love you. I am certain he does. But if he doesn't," she finished pragmatically, "then you're just going to have to deal with that."

It was more comforting to steer clear of David, and talk about men in general.

"When you were young, how did you know if you really liked a man?"

"How does any woman ever know? Instinct. I'm not *prehistoric*, you know, darling, although I look it. Courtship hasn't changed all that much."

"I don't mean that. I mean, were there specific features you looked for in your perfect man? Like eyes? Or," I lowered my voice, "I don't know, their *bottoms* or something?"

She laughed. "I don't remember ever rating a man on his rear end, no. I guess the eyes were always important. And the voice. However much I loved the American boys, and however close I felt to them, it was an English accent that made me fall hook, line and sinker. In the most crowded bar in Cairo, you'd hear these beautiful voices carrying across the room. And there's something about the way an Englishman says 'darling' – whenever your father says it, it still sends shivers over my skin."

"I like the American 'darlin'' far more than the old stiff upper lip 'dahling'."

The two of us practised the different accents for a few minutes, correcting each other's intonation.

"That's because I made the mistake of bringing you up in England. If you'd grown up in the States, you'd feel the same way I do."

"What else?"

"Let me think . . . I always liked big men – tall men with broad chests, who made me feel little. I don't like those skinny, scrawny little boys – whipper-snappers, Daddy calls them. Daddy, Theodore, David, they're all big men, something to get your arms around. Men in uniform. Intelligent, educated men. Men like your father, to be honest. He was always my dream man. Still is, when he's behaving himself."

"But how did you know if they'd be . . ." However intimate I felt with my mother, I couldn't quite bring myself to say 'good in bed'. It wasn't that I felt shy, and it wasn't as if she didn't know. She was clearly a woman who had attracted a lot of men in her time (in her *time*? If she'd had hers, when would I have mine – or, God, had I had it already?) but I still couldn't say it.

"You mean sex? You don't have to go to bed with a man to know if you're going to be sexually compatible. I did my courting in gentler, easier days, when we weren't expected to sleep with a man as soon as we met him. That doesn't mean you didn't have a pretty good idea. Mother Nature was just as active then as she is now. And there are other ways . . ."

"Kissing?"

"That helps, certainly, but I wasn't thinking of that. I was thinking of dancing." Her eyes were all soft and dreamy, and she had such a soppy smile on her face that I couldn't help grinning at her. "Don't be so fresh! I was a good dancer in my day – a very good one, if I say so myself."

"Sure, Mother, but *ballroom dancing* is hardly the most erotic of activities, you have to admit. All that moon, spoon, June, sentimental rubbish."

"What have you got against sentiment, Elena? And you're entirely wrong about it not being erotic. Dancing, real dancing is – what do you call it? – sex on legs, literally. You've missed out on all that. The music you dance to now –"

"Mother, I don't *go* dancing any longer. I'm too old for it. I haven't been clubbing since I was twenty-five. David and I have never been dancing. He'd faint if I suggested it."

"You don't know what you're missing. Imagine a slow fox-trot, and if you're good, and your partner knows how to hold you and move you, you have perfect body line, not a fraction of light between your bodies. I remember a naval officer one night in Ankara who danced like a pro – it was a dream, dancing with him." Her hands and arms were raised, as if holding a partner, and then dropped back to her lap. "The only problem was he couldn't maintain a conversation so we had to keep dancing all night, but, oh, to dance like that! You could lose yourself. It didn't really matter who you were with, you could pretend you were in anyone's arms. Half the men on the dance floor were probably pretending they were with somebody else, and the other half were falling in love with someone they shouldn't. It's a powerful drug, dancing like that. You're never too old for it, it's still there in the bloodstream." She closed her eyes, and hummed a little. When she opened them again there was a wicked glint in them. "And it tells you everything you might want to know about the man. So tell me, darling, explain to your old mother. If you don't go dancing, how do *you* measure up your suitors?"

I think I may have blushed a little, but I just replied, "All sorts of little things. The way he looks at you. What happens to his voice when he speaks to you. The way he touches you. Snogging is a big clue."

"Darling, at least call it kissing. Snogging is such an ugly word. It belittles it so."

She was quite right, of course. When it was any good, I never thought of it as snogging. Snogging *did* have a great ring to it: "He's a really good snogger." I remember the dorm after school dances, when Bec and I and the other girls would discuss who we had or hadn't got off with. Snogging could be used with different implications, from the forced confessional, "All right, yes, he wasn't much cop, but I snogged him anyway – only once, honest!" which would meet with a wave of giggles, and cries of "You didn't! You *couldn't*!" all the way through to the thrilling, secretive, delicious, "God, we snogged for ages and *ages* . . ." At the same time that Bec initiated the ten-foot, five-foot test, we devised a kissing version of Snakes and Ladders, except that we called it Snakes and Lappers. Landing on either square catapulted the unwitting male player back to the starting block or, in extreme cases, off the board. As single girls, Bec and I would get home from a date, give the one-word summation 'Snake' or 'Lapper', and no more needed to be said. Ten years later, we still use it sometimes. If we're watching a movie or speculating about a man walking down the street, we'll look at each other knowingly, and say, "Bet he's a real Snake."

Snakes are immediately assertive, with rigid pointy little tongues that dart between your teeth, prod around urgently and leave little to the imagination about sexual technique. Lappers, on the other hand, are less irritating but somehow comic, with great spit-splashing tongues that drool all over your face, spraying slobber everywhere, like an over-eager Labrador who can't keep his blundering front paws out of the water bowl when he drinks. Personally, I could stomach the Lappers for longer than the Snakes, but Bec disagreed. She wanted to carry one of those oral Hoovers that dentists use for sucking

up excess fluid. Although I must have snogged –
kissed – a good fifty men and boys, I've only gone to
bed with four and they were all good kissers. Of
course, brilliant kissing technique *can* be deceptive.
Perhaps some men have been taught how to kiss by
a patient female instructor, just like anyone can learn
how to dance a few steps, but when you move from
a sober waltz into the tango, they fall to pieces.

I didn't share this crude analysis with my mother,
but I had a comfortable sense that she knew it and
agreed intuitively, even if she might have expressed
it differently. There was a deeply companionable
atmosphere between us during lunch.

"Mummy? Tell me about Theodore Hamilton."

"Elena, my dearest darling. What more can I tell
you?"

I wanted to say, Well, for starters you can tell me
why you didn't marry him, but it seemed a little
blunt. "Did you leave Theodore for Daddy?"

"No." Her tone changed again. "I hadn't seen
Theodore for three or four years by the time I met
Ben."

"You said that you had been in love and just
drifted apart. Theodore told me you were engaged.
What happened?"

My mother leant back in her chair, holding her
wine-glass up to her lips and gazing at me over the
rim. "It's such a long walk down Memory Lane,
darling."

"Is it an unhappy one?"

"Not entirely. Like most memories, there's a

mixture of good and bad. We had a lot of fun in those days."

"So you keep saying."

"It's hard to explain. I suppose I was in my early twenties; I was twenty-five or -six when the war ended. But I wasn't the same twenty-five that you were. In many ways, we behaved like teenagers. These days you grow up so much faster than we did then, particularly you girls. Going out to Cairo was my first real job, my first time away from home. I was like you going to university. It was the same for the boys – most of them were very young. Learning to grow up while fighting a war was quite different from what you young people do now. Men like Theodore had to mature very fast. They carried enormous responsibility, and they had to deal with situations that are now unthinkable. When I met him he was only a year or two older than me, but he seemed like a man in his thirties. We weren't emotionally mature even so – well, not about love and commitment." She put her glass back on the table, and sighed. "You can't believe how handsome he was. So tall and elegant. He looked like a movie star, to my mind. Heads turned when he came into the room – male as much as female. But it was more than looks. Much more."

"So what went wrong?"

"When the war ended, which was supposedly what we'd all been longing for, everything that we had come to see as familiar changed. We'd spent over two years scheming where to meet each other, how to slip away from a party to have an hour alone, always talking about 'next time' . . . Once the war was over, there were all sorts of other considerations – home, families, civilian work. That was when Theodore and I stopped seeing each other."

"You broke off the engagement?"

"Technically, I suppose I did. Marriage was a frightening thought. I had only been to England once and knew nothing about his life. My experience of England was the two weeks before we boarded the ship to Cairo. We'd come out on a troop ship from the States, about twenty of us State Department girls and God knows how many GIs. It was such a funny journey – I wish I could paint the scene for you . . ."

"Try."

"We were pretty dizzy-headed, we girls, setting off on our great adventure. That's when I met Millie Barclay, boarding the ship in our smart city suits, carrying combat helmets and teetering about in high heels, with GIs shouting, 'Hey, you! Blondie! Third from the left – how about a date tonight?' You can't imagine the attention. Anyone in a skirt had her pick of twenty dates a night and, of course, it went to our heads. We had great laughs, but it was all very innocent, and we said our goodbyes. My most poignant farewell was to my parents. In the States, you know, families put a star in their window for their boys fighting abroad. My daddy put a star in the window for *his* soldier overseas . . . Well. When we landed in England, we were taken to an American replacement depot, I can't recall where –

Limehurst? Lidgefield? We all crowded into the back of a huge lorry with a red flag hanging from the rear, and drove through pitch dark. I remember Millie relieving herself in her helmet . . ." She wiped a tear from her eye. "At the Army base we had to march, still in our high heels, you understand, with the soldiers. I can still see the face of the drill sergeant trying not to laugh. You know the story of sharing showers? I must have told you *that*."

"You've never told me any of this, Mummy. I don't know anything about you in those days."

"While we were at the base in barracks, we had shower drill. Girls' showers were from seven till seven thirty, then the boys came in. They always arrived early – they'd put the clocks forward to catch us in the washroom – and there would be a screaming panic as we clutched our towels and robes and ran. One girl – Lord, what *was* her name? She was a riot – said we should wrap a towel around our heads and run so no one would recognize us. None of us had the nerve."

"Then to Egypt?"

"That was quite a different journey. It was a British troop ship. We were used to the American boys whistling and hooting and calling, then we boarded the British ship and none of them looked at us for three days. One of the Brits told me later that they *felt* just the same as the American boys but they were too shy to say so. We always had to wear our Mae Wests – we had many practice drills, and one real action stations when a submarine was spotted going through the Med. We had to rush and pack emergency necessities – toilet paper, medicine, valuables." She smiled at the memory. "The first thing I grabbed was a collection of silk underwear my girlfriends in DC had given me as a farewell present. It was the only thing I couldn't stand to lose. The journey took a few weeks so we got to know each other pretty well, and everyone was in love with someone – at least temporarily. There were all sorts of shipboard romances but I landed in Egypt with my heart intact." She patted my hand and smiled. "You remind me of myself, sometimes."

"Then Cairo?"

"Yes. We split up in Alexandria. Some girls went to Ankara, some to Palestine, Millie and I to the American Mission in Cairo. And threw ourselves into work and play in equal proportion."

"And you met Theodore."

"About six months after I arrived there, yes."

"And you were in love with him until the war ended?"

"Yes, I suppose I was."

"What I can't understand, Ma, is why you didn't marry him. You really loved him, and he loved you . . ."

"He told me so, many times."

"He's told me too. The war was ending . . . I don't understand what could have separated you. You're not naturally cautious. Why would moving to England scare you? You were perfectly prepared to move with Daddy."

"You're right, I never *have* been cautious – quite the opposite. I wish I'd had a little more sense sometimes. I suppose the bottom line was that Theodore and I didn't know each other very well at all. Our love affair was conducted so much through snatched meetings and letters and cables – maybe it wasn't part of real life. Maybe we were both too frightened of the reality of it."

I put my hands palm down on the table. "Just let me get this straight. Did you break it off, or did he?"

"I don't think that matters, does it?"

"For God's sake, Mother, it matters enormously! It certainly mattered to him."

"Then you'll just have to ask him, won't you? I can't speak for him."

"You don't want to talk about it."

"No, I don't want to talk about it."

"But you parted with no hard feelings?"

"No hard feelings," she repeated.

She turned her face away from me. I could see the far side of her profile reflected back in the mirror behind her, the skin slack under her jaw but the still lovely line of her cheekbone, not so very much altered, really, from the photograph that Theodore kept. I wished David had been there to capture the expression on her face. I would have liked to have kept it.

"Are you sure you don't want to see him, Ma? We could drop by for coffee. Just for old times' sake?"

"Old times' sake? No, I wouldn't feel right about

that. Theo and I had our time, and it was a happy one, all in all. We wouldn't have anything to say to each other after nearly fifty years. Can you imagine meeting one of *your* old boyfriends in fifty years' time? Peter – or Nick?"

"I guess I wouldn't want to see them. But I'd be curious what had happened to them, what they'd done with their lives."

"Darling, that's the beauty of this. *You* can tell me what Theodore has done with his life!"

"I guess."

"So?"

"We haven't talked much. He practised as a lawyer. They had two kids, a daughter called Liliane, who is married, and a son called Michel, who is a doctor and works with Médicins Sans Frontières. The wife –"

"Chantal."

"Yes, she died of cancer ten years ago. It sounded grim."

"Poor woman."

"And now Theodore lives alone in a lovely house in this very village – twenty minutes' walk away, Ma. He paints weird paintings and he's interested in photography and sees his family at weekends."

"That sounds good. I'm happy for him. I bet his children aren't as wonderful as mine."

"Just a *touch* of bias creeping in there, Mother. And he gardens and swims and looks fit."

"He always did."

"And he keeps a photograph of you on a table in

his drawing room."

My mother folded her napkin very precisely, and asked Monsieur Guillot for the bill. "This is on your father, baby girl. And talking of your father, I should get back to him tonight."

"You're not going to stay?"

"If you need me, of course I will. I wouldn't ever leave you if you needed me, but I don't like leaving Daddy alone, either. He can't be trusted to look after himself. Nor can you, for that matter."

"Do you love him, Ma? Really?" It slipped out very casually, as if I'd asked her to pass me the bread.

My mother looked astonished. "Who? Daddy? Do I love Ben? After forty years? What do you think, Elena?"

"I just don't know. I don't know how to tell."

"I love him with my whole heart. Every ounce of it. Now, that doesn't mean he doesn't drive me up the wall, but he's a prince among men. Not to mention the fact that he's the man who gave me you and Charlie."

"Go on home, Mother. I'm fine, the baby's fine, and I have Heff and Mishi staying for the next couple of days, and then, well, maybe soon David will be back."

She squeezed my hand. "Just believe that, dearest girl. Trust me. I know it for a certainty."

"You're amazing, Mother. Really. You're wasted on motherhood and marriage. You could have been anything. President, even."

"Oh, darling girl; I could have been more than

that. I could have been the President's wife!"

I wasn't quite sure if she was making a feminist statement, or stating the truth. It was perfectly possible that she'd once been courted by a presidential candidate. I wouldn't put anything past her.

We went out to the airport. In the taxi she asked me not to mention to Theodore that she had been there, and I agreed, a little reluctantly. Having felt that I was in danger of betraying my father by the simple fact of knowing about my mother and Theodore, I now feared betraying Theodore, who had been so kind to me. I reasoned that my mother just didn't want to hurt him again. It was instinctive and convenient to take my mother's side. If I ever had cold feet about marriage, I hoped I would have the courage to face up to it. My mother is all about facing up to things. I hated saying goodbye to her, worse than ever that time. I'd glimpsed a part of her that I hadn't seen before, and I had the awful feeling that it was too late to get to know her properly. I stood in the viewing room until I saw her plane take off for London, and then hired a car. Much as I hated driving, I wanted to be able to move about freely, and not be dependent on anyone. As I drove back to Sainte Cécile, it struck me that my mother had known Chantal Hamilton's name, and I had never mentioned it to her.

Tortorella

Squadron Leader T. R. Hamilton
37th Squadron
DAF, CME
Italy
12 February 1944

My beloved Anna,

I wish that I had never moaned about the heat in Africa. It is so bloody cold here, fires impossible in tents, and sunshine a dim memory. I sleep on the floor, my bed being blankets below and above, with trench coat on top, and my inner flying suit for pyjamas, which renders me a poor imitation of a plucked chicken. Not an image destined to arouse admiration in a female breast, and certainly not that of the only female I am interested in. Talking of females, the only ones we glimpse are Italian peasants who come through the lines collecting laundry and selling eggs for cigarettes. It is the worst racket I have yet seen – ten smokes per egg, which represents a profit of about 400 per cent. Time goes damnably slowly. My personal day begins at 4.30, and ends promptly at 4.32 when I've checked the mail and found no word from you. For the first few weeks, I held you blameless, as mail deliveries were nil for unmentionable reasons, but now the flow is back, and you remain silent. I have tried like all hell to blame the postal systems, but it's well beyond that now.

Dearest, damned woman, I am wretched with worry, and on my knees to you, quite literally if you would have it that way. If you know in your lovely little head that there is no room in your heart for one Squadron Leader T. R. Hamilton, then for God's sake, woman, write and tell me so! I am old enough to hear if the even fondly dreamt-of 'we' has gone away, leaving behind the realistic 'you' and 'me', and you owe me at least the chance to fade out of your life gracefully, while I am still somewhat whole – if not whole in heart, because I will never be that again. If you have shot me down, set me free of this eternal, infernal waiting. Can it be that for all those times, all those wishes and dreams and promises, our romance has gone 'phut' just like that, with no word, no farewell? There have been times in the past year when I have believed that it is only loving you that has kept me alive, and now I can hardly begin to cope with the not knowing if you love me still. I am torturing myself to discover what I have done wrong in this bloody battle against time and human nature to cause you to shoot me down. I have relived every moment we have spent together over and over – Alex, the felucca ride, the Continental, Sham el Nessim, the Kit Kat, Tunis, Shepheard's, where it all began and where it may have ended just as abruptly, and I search my mind for what I said or failed to say to you. You told me no promises, and now I fear that I made too few – what promises can I give you, golden girl? Not even my life to carry on loving you through. Have I promised you too little, or promised you too much? Put me straight, woman, tell me what gives, and my final promise will be that I will take it like a man, with no wetting of the eyes.

And that promise is as frail as all the others, and I am digging myself into a trench of self-pity and morose heartache. These glum moods are not helped by the fact that my friend and fellow flight leader Jimmy Stafford-Clark was hit last night. I saw the searchlights probe and group and pin him down. I knew the guns were on him, but he peeled off before I saw the ack-ack, and I heard him say on the radio, "I'm hit – my engine's packing up – see you at home, lads!" And we had the straight run into target. When we arrived back at base, no one had seen or heard news of the crew. All day I have been unable to sleep, and after my habitual check of the mail rack, it struck me that it should have been me and not Jimmy last night, because without you I have nothing to live for, and he had a wife and babe back home.

It seems a lifetime ago since I saw you, and several since I held you in my arms, and the question that gnaws away at my heart is why? Why, Anna? If there is someone else, for God's sake, tell me so, and I won't blame you, I swear it.

C'est la guerre, we keep telling ourselves, and there's no grace in saying, "We'll make it, we'll pull through, we'll get by," when all over the world there are types just like us who aren't getting by, and won't. I am as browned off as I can remember, and it would take so little to have me back up in the heavens, knowing that I'm the luckiest devil on earth. If you haven't decided to shoot me down already, you will when you receive this drivel, and know me for the self-pitying beast I am. I don't know if the beast is in me, or upon me, crushing my chest with great hairy paws at my throat. I may be the beast myself. Take pity, gentle lady. You have warned me against planning our future, but if our futures are to take their separate paths, dear God let me know it, and so be shot of this blasted doubt once and for all.

Enough. Something has calmed, the fury passed over like a storm, in no small part thanks to the Groupie's decision to step up the rum rations, which are supposedly medicinal but help the spirit more than the body. The weather is the bloodiest thing of all. We should be on double sorties, but we're holed up in the wind and the rain like rats and unable to exploit the advantage of air superiority, having taken so damn long to establish it. The desert seems a haven of both peace and blessed activity. Here we have the worst of both worlds – constant readiness, land activity intense, so no leave, yet no flying due to

389

the cursed, damned, bloody weather. In England I treasured the changeability of the elements – even the drizzle had a charm of its own. Now I could quite thankfully agree never to see another raindrop for what remains of my life.

Last week we had a visit from some Lib flyers, two of your compatriots, one of the boys from a Southern state – Georgia, as I remember. An interesting fellow, and a gentleman. As we chatted, I couldn't take my eyes off his cigarettes – same brand as yours – and each time he put one out I found myself looking pathetically for the traces of lipstick and imagining that you were there in his place. The photograph you gave me and your letters (letters of last year, at the risk of returning to a jaded and unpleasant theme) lie under what passes for my pillow, and your amulet hangs always around my neck, reminding me of the pure gold of your hair. And if you were with me now, I would be torn between the wish to tear that hair straight off· your head in frustration, and the longing to kiss and stroke each and every cherished and priceless strand . . . To think that you parted with so many to encase that little stone, and to think what I would give to have the whole head of them in hand's reach . . .

Dear God, there's enough love in this letter to make any blighter not in love sick to the stomach. Hate, too. Yes, truly, my beloved, don't toss your head like that and flash those torch eyes at me. I'm a poor stray who, having been taken in by a kind mistress, becomes slavishly devoted, only to find himself thrown back on the street without so much as a word of explanation. What can such a mutt do, except haunt his benefactress's back door and howl to the moon in his distress? Better never to have taken the dog in and given him a taste of security and love only to snatch it away as he grows accustomed to his basket beside the bedroom fire. Dogs have loving eyes and devoted hearts, but they have teeth that bite and hearts that break, too. And if we were together again at our table at Shepheard's, you would say, "But men are not dogs, men are noble creatures and rise above the instincts of mere beasts," to which I would reply, "There's not so great a difference between a man and a dog – certainly not this man – and if you treat a man like a dog, and train him to guard and to fight, you must expect him to behave accordingly," and you would respond, "Then I don't choose to have such a dog in my bedroom. Its place is in the kennel, with the rest of the pack." I would have no answer to that, while fervently wishing it wasn't so.

Still no word of Jimmy, and now we must face the worst. I would give anything (not quite anything, you know what I wouldn't give) to see the boy stroll into the mess and demand a drink. Perhaps today both my dreams will come true – a loving letter from you and the sight of Jimmy in his accustomed place at the bar. If those two *things happen, then I shall be happier than the aforementioned dog could ever be. Until then, I will battle on, dreaming, wishing, praying, fearing, yes, but loving too, all of them with my whole heart, which belongs only to you, always, whether you want it or not, wretched, heartless and adored woman.*

Theodore

It was to be another ten days before Anna's letters caught up with Theodore, and two months before they saw each other again. They had been apart for nearly six months. In the spring, Anna sent word that she could get passage to Italy and would reach Tortorella by train mid-morning. Theodore waited impatiently at the railway station. One train had pulled in but Anna had not been on it. As the second and last train of the day arrived, and she did not appear, he stamped out his cigarette and returned by jeep to the airfield, riddled with bitter frustration. Since the Allied assaults on Monte Cassino, air operations had been incessant and he had barely had time to think of Anna, but once he knew she was coming, he had thought of nothing else. As he pulled in through the makeshift gates of the airfield, Jimmy Stafford-Clark flagged him down. Theodore let the motor idle.

"I was loitering around for a shufti at your American catch, Hamilton. Where've you hidden her? Couldn't take the risk of letting her lay eyes on me, hmm?"

Jimmy's plane had had a hole the size of a man blown in the fuselage, but he'd managed to land the scrap heap in a ditch only sixty miles short of Tortorella. When he had strolled nonchalantly into the mess after being missing for thirty-six hours, Theodore had cracked open a bottle of 1934 champagne that he had been keeping for victory. The friendship between the two men had been cemented further: Jimmy and Bob were the only men in the squadron in whom Theodore confided his feelings and fears about Anna.

He helped himself to Jimmy's cigarette and took a long drag before climbing out of the Jeep and tossing the keys to one of the drivers. Draping his arm around Jimmy's shoulders, he feinted a punch at the other man's head. "Didn't show up."

"Maybe she met a better-looking fellow on the train. Wouldn't be difficult."

"Maybe she couldn't face meeting you, Jimmy, even for the chance of seeing me."

"Or she's sick to the back teeth of your binding on. I told you not to write moaning letters. The only way to handle a filly, Theo, is with a firm but tender hand on the reins. Listen to your Uncle Jimmy."

"Bollocks."

"Shame you were out, Ham. You missed an amusing sight half an hour ago."

"What was that? One of the Eyeties pulling a

fast one?"

"Better than that. A flash Yank pulled in, full colonel, escorting an entrancing little thing in high heels and silk stockings. Feathers dragged her into his office and shut the door." Jimmy pulled a comb from his breast pocket and passed it to Theodore. "You might want to give yourself a wash and brush up before she sees you. I'd say she's worth the effort."

Theodore's slow stride broke into a run.

"Enter. If you dare."

Group Captain Feathershawe was sitting on the edge of his desk, leaning forward to light Anna's cigarette, as Theodore entered the small office. "Ah, Hamilton. This poor young lady has been trailing around the countryside for an hour or so trying to track you down. Not very gallant of you to keep her waiting, old chap."

Theodore stood uncomfortably in the middle of the room, longing to sweep Anna into his arms, but inhibited by the amused eye of his commanding officer. "Logistical confusion, sir. I was waiting at the station."

"I'm sorry, Theo. I had a change of plans. When my plane landed, I was offered a lift to Tortorella, so I took it."

"Lucky break for me, eh, Hamilton?" The Groupie winked. "Otherwise you might have squirrelled the lovely lady out of sight, and I'd never have had a chance to meet her. As it is, I've

had time to persuade her to join me for lunch."

Anna smiled up at the older man, and Theodore condemned him to eternal damnation.

"You're invited too, old man, if you tidy yourself up a bit. We'll pop over to the American Club so the lady feels at home. Better grub, too. Now, if you two will excuse me for a moment, I'll sort out a driver and meet you outside in – ten minutes sharp?"

Theodore lifted her off the floor, burying his face in her neck and breathing in deeply.

"My God, Anna, six months – six months of not seeing you, and I have to share you with that old bastard –"

"He's a sweetie, Theo. I couldn't very well refuse."

"You could. You could have told him to mind his own business. My God, to have you in my arms again. Let me look at you."

They gazed at each other in silence.

"You are lovely, Anna. Even more beautiful than you are in my dreams. How long do we have?"

"Four days – maybe even five. Depending on flights back. I have to check the bulletin board in the American officers' hotel for a trip home."

"Right. Then lunch with the Groupie, and high-tail it out of here for Naples. I can't wait to be alone with you. If Feathershawe drags out lunch, I might just have to shoot him."

"You threatened that once before."

"Different CO. This time, I won't be held responsible for my actions. I can plead temporary insanity."

"Why temporary?" She stopped his lips with her hand. "Don't be unkind. He means well."

"He most certainly does not. He's just pulling rank to annoy me, because he knows I can't tell him to go to hell. He knows perfectly well how I've been waiting and scheming to be alone with you."

"One more hour or so . . ."

Theodore groaned. "One more hour – intolerable. I can put up with so much, darling, but to sit at a table with the old man between us, to be so close to you and not able to touch you and feel your body –"

"Ham-il-ton!" There was a roar from outside the room.

"Let him wait." Theodore kissed her again slowly.

"Hamilton, what in the blazes are you doing in there?"

Theodore slipped his arm through Anna's. "Your carriage awaits, milady."

For the next year, Anna and Theodore were only to meet like this, in sudden spurts, at the convenience of the Royal Air Force and the United States Government. The Allies entered Rome in June 1944, but the offensive on the Italian north continued relentlessly into 1945.

There were times when Anna arrived in Italy, only to find Theodore unable to join her. At other times, Theodore had leave but Anna was needed in Cairo. Even with the supportive co-operation of Group Captain Feathershawe and Minister Arthur McClure, it was increasingly difficult for them to be together. Theodore could not travel outside Italy, and Anna's request to be transferred there was turned down by Washington, much to Mac's relief. Despite the obstacles to the union, Anna and Theodore were content. They were confident of victory, even if it was a moveable feast, and confident of their future. They saw in the New Year together in Sorrento, certain that in twelve months' time they would not be separated again. They would be married by then.

CHAPTER SIXTEEN

It took four days after my mother left to persuade Heff and Mishi to go back to Paris. I knew they were genuinely reluctant to abandon their posts as guard dogs until David was back: Heff feared having his ass busted and he was enjoying himself too much to leave. On such a city boy, and a New York City boy at that, a few days in a sleepy little village had the same effect as a trip to Disneyworld on a five-year-old who's never left the Outer Hebrides. He drank in everything through eyes wide with wonder. Everything from fields of corn to the slow service in the café provoked the same low whistle, and the exclamation "*Jeeez . . .*" One afternoon he stopped the car to make sure that Mishi and I fully appreciated the miracle of three brown cows in a field. Even so, after four days, rural over-indulgence had taken its toll and it wasn't too difficult to pop them back on the train. All I had to do was promise to phone between noon and one every day. No earlier, as they wouldn't be awake, and no later, as Heff wouldn't vouch for being sober. If I didn't call, they threatened to be on the first train heading south. I was fond of them both but it was a relief to be on my own. The only person I wanted to be with was David.

I spent ten days entirely alone. I had growing sympathy with the frustration that Theodore had expressed, the tediousness of having nothing to do but wait for the scramble. I was waiting for my baby, who was not going to hurry up on my account, and for David, who just might. I'd heard nothing from him. The agency confirmed that he had been shot, but assured me he was all right and promised to get a message to him that I was, too. They also told me to get hold of *Life* magazine and the *Sunday Times* if I wanted to see what he'd been up to. This was not as easy as it sounded. Sainte Cécile had one newsagent, whose only English papers were the *Daily Mail* and *USA Today*. I alerted my parents to scan the mags, and checked with Theodore that he could get hold of the *Sunday Times*. It was good having something practical to deal with.

Every morning I had breakfast at the Méridien, and then worked on the book in the hotel sitting room, writing up my notes on the portable PC, correcting, editing and learning more about ailerons and ammunition and astro fixes than I ever wanted to. Every lunch-time I dined at the hotel, occasionally with Theodore, who was patient enough to answer a million questions and correct my errors.

Every afternoon I had a long nap and then made an excursion somewhere in the countryside. I toyed with the idea that David and I should move to Lot-et-Garonne after the baby was born. It wouldn't make any difference to David's work, as it was easy to get to Paris, and from Paris the wide world was in easy reach.

It may sound strange, given that David was injured and in Bosnia, but I was happy during those meandering drives. When I was a little girl my grandmother used to ask me several times a day how I was and each time I would reply, 'I'm very well, thank you Grandma," and she would ask, "But are you well *in yourself*?' Somewhere between my mother arriving out of the blue and disappearing again, I had accepted that there was nothing to do about David and the baby except love them. I couldn't stop David being hurt or even being killed. If I were to miscarry, I couldn't prevent that either and it wouldn't be my fault. The night that Theodore Hamilton had taken me into hospital, the only thought in my head had been that I was losing the baby because she knew I didn't really want her, not in my heart of hearts. Somewhere between learning of the babe's uninvited arrival and its threatened departure, I had fallen in love, and felt very well *in myself*. Not that I faced motherhood with an entirely light heart. I had seen myself teetering on the edge of the chief-cook-and-bottle-washer role in a very literal sense, and I couldn't rely on David in the role of deputy-cook-and-bottle-washer. And there was that nagging time-bomb factor: the baby's birth, walking, talking, reading, dating, working would trigger the count-down to my labour, backache, middle-aged spread, menopause, grey hair and osteoporosis.

Four months pregnant, I didn't care any longer. I wanted to hold that baby so much it hurt. My arms ached with emptiness. When the doctor told me that, as far as he could tell, everything was going to be all right, and he showed me the little feet and tiny curling toes on the screen, and I heard that heart race, tapping frantically away with all it had to give, the only thing I wanted was to keep it as safe as it could be for the rest of its life, and have David there to see it and hear it too. The minute David got to Sainte Cécile, I'd bully the dour Dr Duhaze into another scan to introduce the baby to its father. I couldn't wait until we got back to England.

I drove aimlessly down those winding lanes, in brilliantly brittle yellow sunshine. I even stopped to look at a couple of houses, weighing them up as family homes, oblivious of whether their owners had any intention of selling them. I began to have second thoughts about swimming pools. They were all very well but they would have to be enclosed, and in such a way that little hands couldn't pry open the gates or little bodies squeeze beneath railings. Maybe we'd wait for a pool until the child could swim. And just how *did* you child-proof a house? What about all these stone terraces and their death-risk drops? Lot-et-Garonne began to look like a bad idea. And what about the dog that I had fantasized as such an essential part of our cosy family unit – companionship for David and a playmate for the baby? What if, out of the blue, the dog turned vicious? Cats were out – too many tales of treacherous felines sleeping on top of the baby with smug-faced murderous intent. In the hospital, I had been given another chance to care for my child, and I was not going to put a foot wrong.

One Sunday afternoon I drove to Cahors to ferret out a copy of *Life* and buy all the English papers. I sat in a café for two hours turning pages. Images of Sarajevo were everywhere. David had eight pages in *Life*, and three spreads in the *Times* mag, plus the cover photo. It is no easier to describe a photograph than it is to describe a painting like the *Birth of Venus*. You *have* to see them, and look at them for a long time. Once you start describing it, the story is diminished. Words only trigger the visual memory: just as you might say, "You know – it's the Botticelli woman with the small tits on the scallop shell," and not mention the ease and intimacy with which the hands of the angels blowing her to shore are entwined, or the way a single rose has caught on the cloak, so in the work of photojournalists, words only work as a caption. 'Muslim Wedding, Sarajevo' will conjure up the picture of the best man, eyes alert and skewing over his shoulder, the bandolier of the AK 47 slung casually across his chest. In David's photographs of the besieged people of Sarajevo, it was the details that spoke. The silvery glint of an elegant buckle on the woman's shoe as she ran across Sniper Alley. The eyebrows carefully darkened with pencil. The cigarette the soldier held loosely in his hand, burnt through the filter to his fingers. The bored expression of the old man resting by a corpse. They did not need words. I knew that David would be proud of this work, and that he would be acclaimed for it. These were some of the photographs that would remain as testimony, the definitive moments of that time and place. Worth being shot for? They had to be.

The following evening I took the magazines to Theodore's. He was in the garden, starting up a barbecue when I pulled into the drive.

"Elena! How lovely to see you again, and looking so *well*! You're positively blooming, my dear."

"Thank you. It's about time. Like the desert, after rain." I walked up the stone steps and he kissed me.

"Have you heard from David?"

"Indirectly. I haven't spoken to him, but he managed to get through to Heff in Paris and I spoke to the agency. The good news is that he's fine, the bad news is he was shot."

"Yes, I know. I wasn't sure that you did." Theodore wiped his hands carefully. "There was a piece about it in yesterday's *Times*."

"God – I got today's papers, but I only looked at the photographs. What did it say?"

"I left it out for you. I wasn't sure whether you

knew or not. Rather sparse on detail, I'm afraid. It's over there on the table. On the front page."

I studied the photograph of a family, the children huddling against their mother's skirt. You only knew how many dark little heads were nestling among the folds of the black cloth by counting the pairs of eyes. The woman stared blankly through the camera. In the second paragraph of the accompanying article it said that David Turcan, the photographer who had taken the front-page photo, had been caught in crossfire moments after taking that picture but was 'expected to make a full recovery'.

My hands were trembling, making the paper jerk up and down. I had thought I was all right about it, until I saw the words 'a full recovery' in black and white. "Were you ever injured, Theodore?"

"Mercifully not. I had two or three prangs on landing, bashed a shoulder about a bit. One night I had a small section of the instrument panel lodged in my face, but I got off very lightly compared to most. I have very few battle scars."

"I can't imagine what it's like to live in fear of your life."

"It wasn't like that, Elena. I'm sure it isn't for David, either. No one can do the work in a state of permanent fear. There's precious little of your 'red section, bandit on your tail' stuff. There *were* moments of sheer terror but they only lasted a matter of three or four minutes before you felt yourself out of it, or knew you weren't. Chaps who couldn't step away from their fear had to get out of the war. They couldn't last. A good flier has to be well balanced. There are difficult decisions to make, and you might have to select an unpleasant option and persuade your body to carry it out. One's life depended on cool heads – your own, and those around you, who could jeopardize your survival as much as their own. Has David been shot before?"

"I don't think so – certainly not while I've known him. I don't know that he'd even tell me. I know he's seen friends killed. He once had to bring back the body of a friend."

"What a wretched job." Theodore was nursing the barbecue, spreading and rebuilding the coals around the flame.

"Did you talk to my mother about the bad times, when you were frightened?"

"Only very briefly. There was nothing to gain by it. It was better to exorcize the demons with those who shared them. If you've got away by the skin of your teeth, you don't want to revisit the scene of the crime. Besides, I was never in the mood to talk about dicey ops when I was with Anna."

"Maybe she would have been less frightened if she had known the truth."

"There is a great difference between the experience your mother and I shared and the situation in which you and David find yourselves. In our case, everyone was in the same boat. I fear for you that is a far lonelier experience." He looked at me through the smoke with a sad smile. "Would you like a swim before dinner? I have some things to do in the kitchen."

"You don't have to disappear, you know, Theodore. We're old friends now." I slipped my arm lightly around his waist. "You know what? I'm beginning to feel proud of being pregnant. I even catch myself wishing I looked more pregnant than I do."

He looked faintly embarrassed by my admission, but also pleased. By the time I stepped into the swimming pool, however, he had retreated into the kitchen, whether from tact or from culinary necessity, I do not know. He took the photographs with him. I paddled around in the shallow end for a while before I began to swim lengths, and thought of the baby swimming around inside me. I swam underwater.

As I surfaced at one end, I was shocked to find Theodore's face looming down at me. He was kneeling at the edge of the pool and holding a towel. "David's on the phone, Elena." He pulled me out, and I ran into the house without another word.

"David?"

"Elle – are you all right? *Elle?*" I couldn't make my mouth work; I don't think I breathed. The sound of his voice gave me some sort of muscular freeze. I heard him say my name four times before I could even answer in a gasp of breath, "I'm here."

"Are you OK?"

"I'm just fine. What about you?"

"The baby?"

"Absolutely fine."

"Thank God for that. *Jee*sus Christ, Elle. You have no idea."

"I do, darling, I do. Are you –?"

"I'm all right. I'm coming back."

"When?"

"About two or three hours. Better say three."

"*What?* I couldn't hear you properly."

"I'm in Paris. I've got a flight to Toulouse in twenty minutes. I'll get a car and come on to you as soon as I land." He was shouting, and now I recognized the background noise as an airport Tannoy. I leant against the wall, dripping wet, and slid down to the floor.

"David, I can't believe it. You're in Paris *now*?"

"Yep. I have to go. They're calling the flight."

"*David* –"

There was no reply.

I pulled the towel around my shoulders and walked shakily back to the terrace where Theodore waited with an expression of apprehension.

"He's coming back." For a few minutes, those were the only words I could say. I was still trying to get the water out of my ears, shaking my head like a dog with a flea in its ear. "He's in Paris now. He's on his way home."

"Thank God. I'm delighted for you, for you both."

"How long will it take me to get to Toulouse?" It was only two weeks since I'd taken my mother there. I knew it would take about an hour but I wanted somebody else to take the decision, every decision. I began to look for the car keys, emptying my bag on the terrace. "He gets in in two hours."

Theodore looked at his watch. "You should set off in forty-five minutes."

"What if he *is* hurt badly? Maybe that's why he's come back – something's gone wrong. Maybe I should just take him straight to the hospital. I ought to call Heff. Or the agency. I should book a flight straight to London. D'you think there's a flight to London this late? I don't know what to do . . ." I felt my eyes well up with tears. Theodore draped a robe around my shoulders and gave me a gentle shove.

"Get yourself dressed, and dry your hair. Then come and sit down for half an hour and have a small drink to settle you before you collect him. I doubt very much he'll need a doctor. If he's in Paris, he's not in bad shape. You are the only person he will want to see."

I took my time getting ready, to steady the pounding in my chest. By the time I rejoined him, Theodore had opened a bottle of champagne. I eyed the bottle warily. "I can only have one glass."

"I daresay I shall be able to manage the remainder. A glass is enough for a toast" He raised his. "To you, David, and your baby, and many years of happiness to come."

"Thank you." There was something that I wanted to tell him, but I felt shy and ended up being rather incoherent. "You know, all the time David's been away, and since I went into hospital and thought I was going to lose the baby – and, Theodore, I have never thanked you properly for everything you did that night, and for being there, and staying there."

"I did absolutely nothing," but he inclined his head.

"I am grateful, really, I can't tell you what a difference you made. Ever since then, I've been telling myself that if David can just get home, just comes back in one piece, then I'd never be angry with him again. I'll never not trust him or resent him or play stupid games ever again. I'll count myself very, very lucky to have him. And now, I've been so absolutely certain of what I would say to him, and so sure that after all the nonsense that's gone on the past few months, all I want to do is tell him that I want to be with him . . ."

"He's a lucky man, Elena. Very lucky to come home to the woman he loves."

"What if he doesn't want to be with me? David's been alone all his life. Maybe it's too late for him to change. It won't be easy for him having me around and a baby in tow. The last thing I want, ever, is for him to feel that he has to stick by me, or marry me or something, just because I'm pregnant. I couldn't stand it if I felt he was doing it out of duty, or – oh, God! – pity. Dad teases my mother about that. He says he picked her up and dusted her off because he felt so sorry for her being left on the shelf."

"Anna never struck me as the sort of woman to inspire pity. Nor do you."

"He only says it to annoy her. Which it

normally does."

Theodore didn't smile. He picked up the bottle, but I clamped my hand over my glass, and he refilled his own and looked at me steadily. "There are few thoughts quite as absurd as that of Anna Kézdy being left on the shelf. You have asked me several times to tell you why it was that your mother and I didn't marry."

I held up my hand to stop him. "Don't say another word. I should never have asked you. You should have told me to mind my own business. Please forget all about it."

"*That* is something I can never do, even if I wanted to. I would like to tell you about it. It might even help you a little. If you are willing to listen."

Oh, God, Theodore, I thought, not now, oh, God, oh, God, I don't care *now*. I twisted nervously on my chair, twirling the stem of the glass between my fingers and avoiding his eyes. "Theodore, I don't know that I *am* willing to listen," I said finally. "You've been a good friend to me, and I'm incredibly glad that we met, but I don't want to know anything horrid about my mother. I'm sorry if she broke your heart. I'm sorry things didn't work out the way you planned, and I'm sorry you feel sad about it, and I'm sure she still does, in a way, but I just don't want to know. It won't change anything. Why drag out old skeletons when it can't change anything? And I can't – I have to go, you see, it's not a good time –"

"*Anna.*" He spoke the word sharply, and it took

me a moment to realize that he used it as an address. He covered his eyes with one hand. "Excuse me. *Elena.* You should listen to me for your own sake, not for mine. It is a story that needs telling. It could have happened to anyone – I'm sure that it did, to many others during the war. I am not trying to tell you –"

I covered my ears childishly, angry with him for not respecting my refusal. There we were, he refusing to hear and me refusing to listen. He took my hands gently and pulled them down into my lap. "Your mother didn't do anything wrong or 'horrid'. The error was mine. The responsibility has always been mine. Didn't you know that?"

"I don't understand."

"That is exactly what your mother said when I ended our engagement." He smiled crookedly. "You cannot imagine how closely you resemble her right now. You are the living image of her."

"She's not dead," I said sharply, and then slowly, "*you* broke off the engagement?"

"Yes, I did."

"But she *just* told me that *she* broke it off. Why? Why did you stop loving her?"

"I never stopped loving her. It was all quite simple, although at the time I thought it was the nastiest snarled-up mess I could ever have got myself entangled in."

His bony hands were on his knees, three fingers drumming restlessly, and he was looking over my shoulder across the empty countryside. His face was sad enough to break your heart with one look. I knew that if I didn't listen then, I might never have another chance to hear his story, but my heart was thumping against my ribs and I was thinking about my own story and wanting to get on with it.

"Theodore, I'm so sorry."

"Mmm?" He glanced at me abstractedly, and then looked at his watch. "Good Lord, Elena, you should be getting your skates on! You don't want to keep the chap waiting, do you?"

I kissed him quickly and picked up my bag. As I ran past the barbecue on the way to the car, I saw two lumps on the grill burnt to a blackness indistinguishable from the charcoal.

I arrived at the airport in plenty of time to meet the last arrival from Paris. There were few other people waiting: a woman with two small children who raced up and down the smooth halls of the terminal, skidding and colliding into chairs without the mother turning her head; a driver, cigarette glued to his bottom lip, a cardboard sign hanging loosely from one hand, ready to be hoisted when anyone in a suit came through the automatic doors; two Australian girls with backpacks the size of container lorries. I pressed my nose to the glass wall, but couldn't see David anywhere. Eventually the trickle of arriving passengers swelled into a steady flow, then dispersed back to a trickle. The Australians left the lounge, arms draped around the waist of another heavily burdened girl, the chauffeur found his businessman, the children their father. When David arrived I was dripping with sweat. Minutes before I turned round I could feel his eyes on the nape of my neck. He was walking towards me across the hall, just the same, cameras slung around his neck and over his shoulder, and swinging a bag in his free hand. He was dishevelled and he was limping heavily, but he looked perfect.

I began to cry as soon as my arms went round his neck, and he kissed the top of my head. We stood still.

"Hey, sweet."

"David, oh, *God,* I've missed you so much."

He touched my face, and then my stomach. "Me too. Let's get out of here, OK?"

"Do you have any bags?"

"Nope. Just what I'm standing in. Let's go pick up a car."

"I've already got one outside."

"*You* driving, Elle? I've just come through hell and back, got a bullet through my leg, and you want me to trust my remaining limbs to your driving?"

"I've changed. A lot. I'm a really good driver now."

"Yeah, I'll believe that when I see it. Hope you haven't changed too much, sweetheart." He bent down to pick up his bags and winced.

"Let me carry them, David."

"I'll manage. I'm not a cripple." I let him alone.

David didn't speak again until we were on the outskirts of Toulouse. I was so preoccupied with having him there in the car with me that I took the wrong turn from the airport and ended up in the middle of the city. David sat next to me with his leg held out stiffly and his eyes closed. I sneaked glances at him. He was very pale, and the dark shadow of stubble, added to the unnatural glow of the street lights, made his face ghostly. I hoped he was asleep. I adopted my usual method of urban navigation, which is to shove the map under my backside and keep turning down the busiest streets in the hope of finding a sign that will point me in the right direction. I have more faith in signposts than in my map-reading. At times, this technique has obliged me to go from Notting Hill Gate to Putney via Barnes, as the only sign to Putney I can count on is just off Barnes High Street. I have even been known to go to Holborn via Islington. I ambled around Toulouse contentedly until I spotted a blue sign for Montauban-Cahors, which had to be vaguely north so vaguely in the right direction. David slept on as I fumbled around the streets like a drunk. Now that he was home, I was in no hurry to be anywhere. I wanted the three of us to be safely contained in that metal box for ever. From Montauban, I had a feeling I had to bear left, and kept my eyes peeled for a familiar-looking road. Fat chance. Convinced that I'd overshot the road, I took one left turn, then the next, and ended up on a broad, congested street.

I took advantage of a red light to pull out the map and began searching for Sainte Cécile. There was a furious honking of horns, and shouting, and I looked up to see that the light had changed. Before I could react, David had stretched across me and switched off the engine in one fluid movement. He opened the passenger door and stepped out of the car. I followed him in the rear-view mirror as he limped back to the car behind us, and leant in at the window. I could see the driver shouting and gesticulating, pumping a loosely clenched fist in the international symbol for wanker. The next thing I knew David was reaching into the car and lifting the man half-way through his window, shaking him. My palms were sweating on the steering wheel. David threw the man roughly back in his seat as the light turned red again. Horns were still squealing all the way down the line. David wiped his hands on his jeans and limped back to the second car in the line. I saw the driver hold up both hands in submission and wind up his window. David shrugged, and loped unevenly back to our car. He leant across and started the engine.

"OK, Elle, wait for the next lights, and move on slowly. You've got all the time in the world."

I drove straight ahead for about ten minutes, then pulled the car over to the side of the road and switched it off before turning in my seat to look at him. "What was that all about, David?"

"What was what about?" He honestly didn't know what I was referring to.

"Back there. The guy in the car."

"That? Shit, Elle, it was time the fuckhead learnt some manners. He could see you were looking at a map. If the dumb shit knows how to read, he knows it's a hire car. Even if he can't read, he can see you're female. He knows you're a stranger. There's no call for that kind of behaviour, not in a civilized society. I don't like it, that's all."

"What did you say to him?"

"Nothing. I was polite."

"I can't believe you did that."

"No big shit. Don't make a song and dance about it."

"It's road rage, David."

"Road rage?" He howled with laughter. "That isn't rage, Elle darling. That isn't rage. Nowhere close. Now, d'you mind if we get on back to the hotel? My leg's kind of stiff sitting here." He picked up the map and gave me directions to the village.

"Are you sure you're all right, David?"

"Never been better."

When we arrived at the Lion d'Or, David didn't want to eat. Monsieur Guillot made me a sandwich, and David drank whisky as I ate it.

"Are you going to tell me about Sarajevo, David?"

"Sure, sweetheart, sure, in time. I just want to know first how you ended up in hospital."

I held his hand and told him simply how I'd felt. "The great thing was the scan. David – I *saw* the baby. I saw it quite clearly. Hands, feet – I could even see a face. And I heard the heart beating, so incredibly strongly, it was ferocious. It's a real little fighter, David, this baby. The doctor said everything would be fine. That was it."

"It isn't meant to happen, Elle."

"What isn't?"

"Bleeding. It's a bad sign. It's not meant to happen, not after twelve weeks. You ought to be prepared for bad news."

"David, I'm so sorry you were worried. But *trust* me, everything's all right, I just know it. I feel well, and it's really starting to grow. Feel it. No one will recognize me by the time we get home."

He didn't touch my stomach, just repeated quietly, "It isn't meant to happen, Elle." I did not want to interpret this. He might have been referring to the bleeding, but he might just as well have been talking about the baby, or us. He ordered another drink, and I persevered.

"If you like, we'll go to the clinic tomorrow. You can see for yourself." He nodded vacantly. "David, what happened? How did you get shot? Are you really all right?"

"Sure I am, baby." He emptied his glass in one swallow. "'Drink never touched his lips.'" He chuckled.

"What?"

"Something your old pilot said to me when we were talking. He was telling me about a friend of his, and he said, 'Drink never touched his lips – it just went down without touching the sides.' If it's OK with you, my darling, I intend to get absolutely rat-arsed."

"Be my guest. But tell me how you got shot."

He took a long drag on his cigarette and pointed the burning end at me, eyes narrowed through the smoke. "You *could* say I got shot because of you." He was grinning, but there was something menacing in the gesture.

"How do you mean?"

"Aw, I don't mean it, baby. I got shot because I didn't have my wits about me. Everything was OK, it's an unbelievable mess there, but I did some good work. You seen any of it?"

"Yes. Yesterday's *Times* had the picture of a woman and four children."

"I thought that one'd sell. Women and babies – good copy. Not as good as domestic animals but second best. Have you seen *Life*?"

"Yep. It's fantastic. And the *Sunday Times*."

"How much?"

"Uhh – God. Six pages in the mag, plus the cover, and three spreads plus four pages in *Life*."

"Good."

"So what happened?"

"*What happened* was that I had an impulse to phone you, just for the pleasure of hearing your pretty voice. One of the Reuters team is an old friend, and I gave him some spiel about it being life or death, and finally persuaded him to let me use the phone, at about fifty bucks a minute. By the time I'd spoken to the hospital, I was convinced that you had had a miss-ca-ridge." He enunciated carefully, tapping his cigarette hard on the ashtray with each syllable. "Butch – he's the Reuters guy – let me stay

on. I called your folks, I called the hotel again, I tried
Theodore, I called the agency. Thought about calling
the police. I got in a fight with a Trib print type over
the fuckin' phone line. I got drunk with some jerk
from AP, went out the next day and took some
pictures, and I made a *mistake*. That's all. The kind
of mistake that a farm kid fresh off the Georgia
Greyhound wouldn't have made. I ran across a
corner of the street to get to a building when I should
have stayed put. I was fucking stupid. For a second,
I wasn't thinking. I ran and I got shot. That's it, Elle,
nothing complicated."

"Who shot you?"

David blinked at me and snapped his fingers.
"Shit me. I couldn't bet my life on it, but it may
have been one of the guys I'd photographed a couple
of days before. I should have stopped to ask. We
could've exchanged names and addresses – sent each
other Christmas cards for the next ten years. Now,
why didn't I think of that?"

I began to weep again, and David looked up at
the bar. Monsieur Guillot put a bottle of whisky on
the table.

"You're a gent. Will you join me in a drink?" he
asked him in English. Monsieur Guillot shook his
head and said goodnight. We heard his footsteps
overhead.

"How's your leg?" I asked, wiping the tears away
with the back of my hand.

"Oh, fine. Didn't even stop me running. A bullet
doesn't feel like you think it's going to feel. A sharp

shock and a dull ache, like someone's dropped a ton of bricks on your leg. I thought I'd pissed myself at first, then I realized it was blood. The bullet went straight in and out the other side. Didn't even splinter the bone. It looks real neat, like I just stuck a long nail through my leg. I'll show you later. There was a Lebanese doctor at the hospital who cleaned it up. Funny, I've been in Beirut some six times or more and never met a Leb doctor."

"Does it hurt now?"

"No. Let's quit it, Elle." Just for a moment, his grey eyes looked soft and steady. Then he jerked his head and shouted, "Hey! Can we get any service around here?" I pushed the bottle towards him. "Hell. I forgot it was self-catering. Aren't you going to keep me company, kitten?"

David had never called me 'kitten' before. Nobody had.

"Sure? Why not?" I replied, and got myself a glass from behind the bar.

David became simultaneously eloquent and incoherent, if that's possible. He talked vividly, but the images slammed into each other with random force, like bumper cars. He kept on talking about people in car crashes but I couldn't make any sense of it. If I asked him exactly who had crashed, he shook his head and said I wasn't listening. At about three in the morning, I helped him up the stairs and he fell across the bed. I got his T-shirt off somehow, and spent about ten minutes inching off his filthy jeans. Just below the groin, on his right leg, a bandage was wound around the thigh, nearly down to the knee, back up and across one buttock, then round his waist. There was a small dark bloodstain on the front and back. My stomach heaved when I saw it. David was just about unconscious but still talking. I crawled up the bed from the bottom so as not to disturb him. When I was on the edge of sleep myself, he suddenly flung his arm across my face, nearly knocking me out with the force of it. His watch must have bashed my lip against my teeth, and I tasted blood in my mouth. I wanted to go and look at it in the bathroom, but David groaned, and put both his arms around me, and I heard him say fiercely, "Don't leave me, Elle, don't leave me alone." I lay awake for I don't know how long, with David crushing my chest, his grip fierce.

I woke up at some point that night. It must have been approaching dawn because I could see David's face. He was sitting on the window ledge, cigarette between his lips, and holding negatives up to the faint light, looking at them intently. I closed my eyes, pretended to be asleep and lay as still as I could.

421

CHAPTER SEVENTEEN

The morning after Elena had gone to the airport David Turcan arrived at Le Bosc. I was not surprised that he had come. He was professional. He shook my hand. "Good to see you again. Is this too early? I would have called first, but I didn't want to wake Elena up to get your number."

"Not at all, old chap. Come inside."

He stood on the doorstep, squinting up at the sun.

"I'm just here to do the shoot, Theodore. Looking at the light, we should probably stay outside."

"Wherever you think best, but come in for coffee first. I need one before I'm ready to have my picture taken." He was like an edgy stallion being coaxed into a box. After several shies, he came inside with a shrug and dropped his paraphernalia in the hall. I was uncertain whether to raise the matter of his injury or wait to see if he would bring it up.

"I have enjoyed spending time with Elena while you've been away, David. She's a lovely young woman."

"Yep. She told me last night what you've done for her. Thanks."

"Believe me, I have done nothing at all." He shrugged in response: it was an involuntary gesture, almost contemptuous. "How was your trip?"

"OK."

"How do you take your coffee?"

"Black." He laughed abruptly. "Funny, isn't it? We grow up with this great sense of black and white, believing that, in the end, good is going to tip the scales."

"You think it doesn't?"

"I don't think shit. I just take the pictures. People have to make up their own minds."

"I've often wondered quite how much the photographer controls what we think, simply by what he selects to photograph." I put two mugs on the table.

He drained his coffee in one swallow, and I nudged the jug towards him. "Don't give us so much credit. We're busting our balls for an image that says it all. Bang. You take thirty-six exposures, and maybe, if you're real lucky, five are good. You can hope there's some subtlety in it, that it's more than bare bones, but you'll be lucky to get a good composition. You can't fake it, and you can't plan it – it's either there or it ain't."

I felt quite at ease with him, perhaps even more so than with Elena.

"I found the Sarajevo photographs very moving. Have you seen them yet?" He shook his head, and I put the two magazines and the picture from *The Times* on the table. "Would you like a swim before we do the photographs? We don't have to do them today, unless you're in a hurry."

"Maybe I'll swim – sounds good. A drink sounds better. Hair of the dog. Have you got a Scotch?"

It was slightly after nine in the morning. I decided to give him a drink, in the hope that if he drank enough he would pass out and sleep. I put a bottle of whisky on the kitchen table, and David poured a large slug into the dregs of his coffee. He opened *Life* magazine, looked at it briefly and nodded at a picture of three bodies. "I must have taken thousands of pictures of dead people. See this guy? He looks like a child asleep, cheeks all puffed out and downy. The guy next to him looks like wax, like he never breathed at all. There are ones where you don't believe that it *ever* could have been a human body. The pieces don't fit, like a jigsaw the dog's chewed a bit. I didn't do much of this type of thing in Sarajevo – this was the only one I liked."

"You sound as if you may have had enough of this line of work, David."

"Death's never bothered me. It's only one part of the process. This time I was more interested in what was happening after. There's was a spirit there, the people want to show the Serbs they're not giving up."

"What about that swim, old man? Get in the water, and put it all behind you."

"You think it washes off?"

"No, but I think you could forget about it for a while. Memories come back."

"Elena has a theory that only good memories stay."

"I think I know where she got that theory. Anna was insistent that we should only have happy memories."

David looked at me cynically. "But you don't buy it?"

"I don't believe that I do. Not now. It seems to me that the nasty trick of memory is that it is the good ones that tend to fade. The older I get, the sadder happy memories become. One knows one cannot recapture or relive the emotion that accompanied them. The original joy is lost for ever. Unfortunately, when the lights go out, less happy memories seem to regain their immediacy."

"D'you have nightmares, Theodore?"

"No. Only certain moments that I . . ."

"Want to black out?"

"Never quite that. I'm attached to my ghosts, good and bad. How is your leg?"

"Fine." He lit a cigarette and dragged deeply, and I saw that thousand-yard stare in his eyes, the leaden look as his eyes turned inward.

"You were extremely lucky."

David tipped his chair back off its front legs and

grinned at me. "You know better than that. I was pig stupid, that's the truth of it. I've been doing this long enough to know better. No matter how cool and experienced you think you are, you can fuck it up in a split second if you ever lose your concentration. You know what I mean?"

"We called it finger trouble. Taking your mind off the controls for a second."

"Exactly. Finger trouble." David picked up the *Sunday Times*, and began to look through his work.

I decided to leave him in peace. "I'll be out by the pool."

I had been swimming for the better part of an hour before David reappeared. He limped out onto the terrace, and I had stepped out of the pool and rubbed myself dry before he spoke. I tossed him a pair of trunks. When he stripped off I saw that his wound, as he had said, was very neat.

"When you took Elena to hospital, did you happen to speak to the doctor about the baby?"

"No. As I wasn't a relative, they wouldn't speak to me. Elena told me that they'd given her the all clear. She certainly seems much better, and happier."

"How did you feel when your wife was pregnant the first time?"

This was a natural question for him to ask, but it was a difficult one for me to answer. I made a balls-up of it. "Initially, when she told me, I was simply stunned. I remember feeling completely knocked for six." David nodded. He was listening intently. "I am ashamed to say that when it sank home, I did not feel in any way elated. I did not think of a child at all, not then, only about myself. I had a great sense of injustice, resentful of the responsibility that life was thrusting upon me. I was twenty-seven. Many fellows that age are fathers, and no doubt fine ones, but I had spent five years in rather unnatural circumstances and I was not prepared for it. Eventually, I did have a sense of wonder, that my own child was in the making. It is a miraculous thing. And *being* a father is an even more miraculous one."

"I guess you decided you'd done something right. Elle said you have two children."

Perhaps it was the effort of dissembling to Elena, or perhaps it was simply that I felt I was speaking to a man of my own heart, but I decided to be honest with David. His rationality may have rubbed off on me. "I should explain that my wife was unable to have children. She suffered a miscarriage the first time, and subsequently the doctors advised against it. She continued to try but it was not to be. I did not explain this to Elena, for reasons you will understand. We adopted our children, raised them happily and loved them dearly, but Chantal felt that she had failed in the one great endeavour of her life. It was nonsense, of course, but I could not convince her. For a time, I wondered what it might have been to see my own children grow up, but I had no regrets. She felt she had robbed me of some essential experience. She had not. When she was dying, my greatest wish was that she should know that."

"Did she?"

"I cannot be certain of that. She was not always lucid, and when she was, it was more important for her to talk than to listen to me. I believe she understood. When you have spent your life with a woman, the details don't matter very much. I was happy with my life. I am confident that she knew that."

"It must have been real tough on you taking Elle to hospital. I need to thank you for looking after her."

"Not at all, old man."

"Elle is obsessed with the idea that you did her mother wrong – or she did you wrong or something like that. I can't always work out what's going on in her head. I don't see why it matters so much to her, what happened fifty years ago. I can't see that what happened ten days ago matters very much."

"I imagine that it matters to her because she's going to be a mother herself. That tends to focus the mind acutely."

As I was talking to him, I saw Elena's car pull up in the driveway.

"Theodore, good morning." Elena's tone was breezy but she looked pale. "Hello, darling. You should have woken me up before you left." As she drew near she looked at David's leg, and I saw her falter and take a deep breath. David stood up. She went straight to him and kissed his cheek.

"It's OK, sweetheart. Go ahead and look. Nothing gory."

She knelt down and examined both the back and

front of his leg minutely, like a pathologist. "Maybe the doctor should take a look at it? What d'you think? It would make sense before we go home." Elena glanced quickly at me, and then back to him. "David, didn't you want to see Monpazier? I thought we could go for lunch. You could take some pictures. We'll just wander around – be on holiday."

"Elle, sweetheart. You don't have to talk soothingly to me like I'm a half-wit. The bullet went through my leg, not my head." Her hand fluttered at his thigh and he batted it away. "I'm not hungry, and the last thing I want to do is sit in a car." The next moment he embraced her as if he would never let go, and I decided it was time for my exit.

"You're welcome to stay and join me for lunch. Giselle has the day off but I'll willingly knock up a salad."

Ten minutes later Elena stepped into the kitchen. "He's not himself."

"He seems all right, my dear. Nothing for you to worry about. He's bound to be tired, and however much he trivializes his injury, it must have taken a lot out of him to carry on working after it."

"He's not himself," she repeated. "He was so odd last night, I thought he was crazy. I don't know him. I don't know who he is at all." She was tugging at her hair, twisting it round and round her hand.

"He's been perfectly reasonable this morning."

"I haven't seen him like this. Not angry. He always takes time to come down, but I've never seen him like this."

"Just give him more time."

"I should call the doctor." She was chewing a finger and not listening to me. "No – I'll call the agency. They'll know someone to sort it out. They must have someone he can see in Paris."

"Elena? Why not let him be for a day or so? I'm not pretending to be a professional, nor do I wish to interfere, but I do believe that the only thing he needs is some peace."

"Theodore, you're sweet, and I know I've relied on you, but really, David can talk to *me*. He always has. We've always been able to talk to each other."

Elena had often struck me as contradictory. She ricocheted between the pragmatic and the quixotic, seemingly uncertain as to where she felt most at home. I had only known the couple for a brief month, but I very much doubted whether their relationship was founded on verbal communication.

"My dear girl, you know best. If I can make a hesitant suggestion, I would say that you are perhaps the last person that David might want to talk to. When you intend to spend your life with a woman, you do not necessarily want them to share your bleaker moments. He may feel protective of himself, or may want to protect you. He has absolutely no reason to protect me, both because he believes that I have seen worse, and because he feels, quite rightly, that he can do me no harm."

"Surely all David needs to believe is that he's fine, the baby's fine, and that I love him, no matter what?"

I patted her arm. "I am sure you're right, my dear. You talk to him, or don't talk, if he doesn't want to. Perhaps it isn't necessary."

Elena couldn't sit still until she had jousted with the enemy, or what she imagined was the enemy, head on. She flung open the doors and went out as bravely as if she were carrying a crusader's banner. Some twenty minutes later she was back, her car keys in her hand and her head downcast.

"He doesn't want to talk to me. I've missed him so miserably . . . I thought so long as he got home . . . He doesn't want to be with me . . ." Her voice trailed away and she looked no more than ten years old. She reminded me vividly of Liliane at that age, when her best friend had ditched her for another schoolgirl. Liliane had sat in that very kitchen with her head on the table, saying she would never have another friend, her life was over and she wanted to die. It had been difficult not to smile at her fears, but they had been all too real to her.

"David is in a thousand pieces, Elena. Even if he seems to be composed, he needs time to bring them back into shape. He needs to reorganize his world."

"And me out of it?"

"Not at all," I tried to soothe her, "quite the opposite. It is you and the baby that he needs to make space for."

"What do I do?" she wailed piteously. "I can't walk away from him. I need him too."

"Let me spend some time with him, and I will call you at the hotel, as soon as I can. It will be all right, Elena, in the end. I promise you that."

I could see she didn't trust my assurances, but she got into her car and drove away. I left David until he came to me. I waited in the drawing room, from where I could see him lying on the terrace in the sun. I held Anna's photograph on my lap, and prayed that I would at last be able to do her some small service, make some atonement. Great God, at my advanced age simply to feel useful in any capacity would be reward enough.

"Wing Commander? Do you feel up to those shots now?"

"Certainly, David. I am at your disposal."

"I've had a wander around. I'd like to take some under the vines, on the lower terrace, and try some in the *pigeonnier*. We may come back in here."

"I'm in your hands." I glanced down. "Would you prefer me to look more respectable?"

"No. You look good to me. It's not about clothes, after all."

"What is it about, exactly, David?"

He was rifling through the pockets in his vest and busy with his cameras. He wasn't really listening to me. "Oh, this stuff's just about selling books. Men who had a turbulent experience and survived it. It's like Sarajevo. The indomitable human spirit. How does that sound to you?"

"That might be true if there was a reason why one of us had survived rather than another, but it was a random selection, I'm afraid. Nothing indomitable about any of us old relics."

David nodded me towards a chair that he had positioned under the vines. I feared I would look like an ageing vintner. "Random is good. If we knew whether we were going to survive or not, would any of us bother with it? You'd have to be insane."

"Only part of us is sane and reasonable. When I was flying, I used to picture myself, years on, sitting before a roaring fire, next to a certain grey-haired lady, and contentedly stroking the golden retriever at my feet. Perhaps even sitting on a vine-covered terrace. Would you rather I didn't talk?" David shook his head. "At some point, I came to the realization that part of me was on the very edge of madness. Some part of me consciously and willingly elected trouble, perhaps preferred it. The absolute catastrophe – utter devastation. One can feel irresistibly drawn to disaster."

"You don't really think it's random at all." David lowered his camera for a moment.

"On the contrary. If it wasn't random, we would be entirely mad rather than partly so."

He watched me through the lens. "Did you ever try to kill yourself? When you were flying?"

"Good God, no. Nothing so straightforward. I took unnecessary risks, that's all, and only towards the end. One could convince oneself that there were no risks at all – if one was meant to go for burton, that would be it. It was more a question of being too tired to take precautions, too tired to think properly. Finger trouble." The camera clicked and clicked, but after the first few minutes I found it easy

to ignore. "I was not at heart a reckless man –
certainly not when it came to flying and not when
I had a crew in the kite. Sanity is inclined to resur-
face when you take responsibility for others."

"Could you look towards the house for a
moment – a little higher?"

"It must be a different business for you, David.
Not having anyone to answer to, or be responsible
for."

"I like working alone."

"Do *you* have nightmares?"

"Nope." He moved much closer to me, snapping
infrequently – it certainly wasn't the click-click-click
of the paparazzi to which television has accustomed
us. He looked at me often, as if considering whether
I was quite up to scratch. David Turcan felt far closer
to the civilians of Sarajevo than he did to old buffers
posing for a glossy book.

"That disappoints me. I had comforted myself
with the notion that everyone has nightmares."

"You said you didn't."

"I lied. Perhaps they are not quite conventional
nightmares – having to catch a train and finding
oneself stuck in quicksand. I am mercifully free of
such nocturnal disturbance. But I have recurrent
images that I cannot escape. Mainly of Italy. For a
time, well after the war, I considered living there –
my wife was keen to return. I found myself unable
to come to terms with the place even on short holidays. It was as if certain things had happened there,
when in fact they hadn't. I never truly escaped them,

only found a way to hold them at bay. Does that make sense to you?"

David Turcan shook his head, laid the camera down and spoke abruptly. "You can stop now. I don't like this at all. I'm not happy with it. I can't control it."

"I beg your pardon?"

"The shadow. The shadow's wrong and I can't lose it. We'll have to move, I'm afraid."

He limped ahead of me, down towards the *pigeon-nier*. I felt myself a very old man, and utterly spent.

David shifted with the change of scene. He became almost loquacious.

"That's more like it. You don't look so – stuffed. Shit, I hate taking pictures like this, straight portraits, I really do. You have to worry about how you've posed them, and what the writer's going to say. Too many people involved. D'you know the story about the filming of an execution in some South American hell-hole? You haven't heard it?"

He put his camera down on the grass, picked up another one and loaded it, then returned to his original choice as he continued.

"The sound crew arrived first, found the condemned man blindfolded and back against the wall, and the militia obligingly waited for the camera crew to turn up. The prisoner – can't remember what he'd done, deserted, insulted the general or the general's wife – was getting fretful so they went ahead and blew him away. When the camera crew arrives, they find the guy slumped on the ground, covered with blood, and the firing squad getting ready to go on parade." While David talked, he would pause occasionally, drag on a cigarette, look at me and then click again. "So the director listens to the sound tape, knows it won't make good telly, hands out a wad or two of tenners, and gets the guys to re-enact it. They shove a ramrod up the dead guy's back, pack the bullet holes with cloth, dress him up in a clean white shirt – probably the *director's* shirt – and shot him all over again." He smiled tightly, and switched cameras. "It was still crap footage, because when the guy fell, he keeled straight over. He didn't crumple, he went down like a tree because of the stick tied to his back. Anyone could see it was a fix. He didn't even twitch. How many guys get to die twice over, hmm? That's good – that's nice."

"Not a sight you could forget in a hurry."

"No. Well, it was one of the ones I missed." He chuckled to himself.

"David, have you ever considered that you might be suffering from post-traumatic stress?" I stared into the lens of the camera, David's finger resting on a button. For several seconds, neither of us moved. Then he took a snap and lowered the camera. He looked disappointed.

"I never thought a man like you would use a tired old phrase like that. Post-traumatic stress. Yes, I've thought about it, talked about it. What else do you think correspondents do on a rainy day? We all *talk* about it. Personally, I think it's a load of shit. Guys didn't like the sound of nervous breakdown. *Crise des nerfs* is a little nicer, but it still has that old tag that you've lost your bottle, right? Journalists don't like that. If you lose your nerve, you lose your livelihood. So, instead, everyone has post-traumatic stress, and either they know about it or they don't."

"And where do you stand?"

As if I had asked the question literally, he rubbed his thigh and eased himself down onto the grass. "I don't. I don't think there's anything wrong with me, but if there is, I don't think it's to do with stress or trauma or that shit. If stress was going to get to me, it would have happened a long time ago. It's to do with Elle being pregnant." He lit a cigarette, and I watched the smoke slip surreptitiously from his lips.

"How do you feel about it?"

"I feel . . . I feel . . . Amazed. Like she's the first woman in the world ever to get pregnant, like it's the first baby ever to be born. I don't believe it. I'd like to see it for myself. When I first knew, I spent a weekend at my studio looking through all the pictures I'd ever taken of babies. I couldn't get it through my head that I was going to feel what all those folk had felt. I don't think Elle took it on board much either, but over a couple of months she's settled into the whole thing. She talks about it the whole time. I don't feel part of it."

I opened my mouth to speak, but he held up his hand and continued. "Don't think I'm not happy about it – I am. But I don't feel relevant, and I don't feel much changed." He stretched out flat on the grass, addressing the pure blue sky. "Excepting that in Sarajevo, I felt scared. I never was scared before. Not even in Vietnam. I never felt scared, because it never seemed to matter much either way. It didn't matter fuck if I lived or died, so long as I got the perfect frame. In Sarajevo, everything shifted."

"Because you had two people who were waiting for you – two people who were dependent on you and your survival?"

He grinned, and rolled over onto his stomach, wincing as he did so. "No. Because I felt dependent on *them*. Before, I didn't care squat that something could happen to me. I'd walked straight into it with my eyes open. I'd chosen that way to go. I've been doing it for twenty years. It didn't strike me like a bolt from the blue that I could get hurt. It was the thought that something could happen to *them*."

"When did you learn that Elena was in hospital?"

"The third night? The fourth? I don't remember when. I wanted to check up on her, make sure she was OK. I couldn't stop thinking about her. The old woman at the hotel told me she'd been taken· to hospital and I thought she was dead, for a minute or so. Then I knew that, at the very least, the baby was dead. Part of me's still sure of it."

"When did you get shot?"

"Later. For a while there, I was as mad as hell. I didn't want the shit and all the bloody effort of dealing with it. I couldn't be arsed. I just wanted the absolute end. Cat-a-clys-mic carnage. And I didn't get it."

"And you went back to work?"

"What else can you do? I got patched up in a couple of hours, and then I went back to the Holiday Inn, which was filling up with the press pack. Some are guys you'd happily die for, and some of them are war whores."

"And then?"

"I just got on with the job. That's the stuff you've seen. That's when I began to feel really intimate with those people and started taking good stuff. That's also when I knew I wouldn't give up the work. I'd been telling myself I was too old, I'd made my mark, I had different responsibilities. I was kidding myself. It isn't that kind of a decision. I'm never going to hear the news or open a paper and not feel that I have to be there. Not yet, at least. It's an addiction."

"It's a mission. David. You need to talk to Elena."

"About the baby?"

"About it all."

"Sure, but first, I need a drink."

I went inside to get him one.

Naples

Theodore stood on the doorstep of the house at 18, Via Giuseppe Cotronei, in a once gracious but now shambolic quarter of Naples. Most quarters of Naples had become poor. He held a small bunch of daisies that he had bought impulsively from the flower-seller on the corner. He had been so struck by the sight of flowers for sale. They reminded him of the blooms Anna wore in her hair.

He had already met Signora Molesini three times, once in a social club for United States officers to which he had been invited with Group Captain Feathershawe, once in a corridor of the building requisitioned as 205 Group HQ, and once by chance in a goldsmith's shop, when he had been struggling to find a gift for Anna. Signora Molesini had helped him to select a small brooch in the shape of a winged horse and invited him to her flat for a home-cooked meal. This was the evening they had arranged for dinner, and Theodore was not altogether sure that he wouldn't prefer to be back at the mess bar. Group Captain Feathershawe had encouraged him to go in the name of fostering harmonious relations with the Italian civilian population. He checked the scrap of paper on which she had written her address, but there was no apartment number. He stepped back from the building. Looking upwards, he spotted her leaning out of a window watching him.

"Come up. It's the third floor." She closed the window.

The hall of the narrow house was dark, but not dark enough to hide the shabbiness and atmosphere of decay. The stale odour of food and ancient grease hung about the central staircase. As Theodore walked slowly up the steps, doors opened and faces peeped out at him suspiciously.

A small, black-eyed child was playing on the landing of the third floor. Despite his friendly smile, she burst into wailing tears as he bent to pat her head. Another door opened and Signora Molesini appeared, spoke a few words to the child and stepped back to let Theodore pass. "This house is full of children. You have to be careful not to tread on them. We are infested with them as other houses are infested with rats and mice. Frankly, I prefer the children. Children, widows and rats, those are the epidemics of Naples." She accepted the flowers with a small smile, and put them in a jug on the only table in the room. "Would you like some wine? No whisky, I am afraid."

"I would prefer wine, thank you."

"Then take your jacket off."

She waited, arms outstretched, as Theodore unbuttoned his dress jacket, and hung it carefully on a hook behind the door, stroking it as she did so, touching the wings on the lapel.

"Make yourself at home." She gestured to the sofa. "It's not very comfortable," she shrugged, "but I'm not going to apologize. I'm sure you've seen worse places."

Theodore nodded, and sat down as she handed him a glass of wine. She was wearing a black skirt and a cream blouse, and her dark hair was pulled back severely off her face. Theodore couldn't tell how old she was. Her face was unlined, but he saw strands of grey in her hair. He supposed she was in her thirties.

"If you'll excuse me for a moment, I'll just finish dinner."

"Is there something I can do to help?"

"No. I enjoy cooking, and I don't often have the chance to cook a meal for someone. If you like," she suggested hesitantly, "you can come into the kitchen and talk to me while I finish. It isn't a long walk." She pointed to a beaded curtain that separated the living area from a little kitchenette, and Theodore followed her through, bending his head beneath the low lintel.

"It's very good of you to entertain me, Signora Molesini."

"Chantal, please. I may be old, but I'm not that old. Call me Chantal. I like to entertain. I like the company. Everyone needs company occasionally, even those who have grown used to being alone."

"It is still good of you. One can grow tired of dining in the mess, despite the company."

"Do you miss home cooking? It's Theodore, isn't it? Are you married, Theodore?"

"No . . . I am not."

"You say that as if you're not absolutely certain."

"I'm not married."

"But you have a girl back home?"

"I have a girl, yes."

"That's good. Every soldier should have a girl to think about. Would you open this for me

please?" She passed him a tin and a knife. As she did so, Theodore noticed a wedding band and heavy signet ring on her hand. "Not much, I'm afraid, but what we have is from the Americans, and we have to be grateful for it."

"American rations are better than what we're used to, I assure you."

"Don't worry. I'm not going to give you 'bully beef'. Stefano – my husband – always told me that he knew he was fighting on the right side because they ate so well. Even in the desert, even when the campaign was going badly, they still had large dishes of pasta, fresh meat. He used to write to me and say that we were bound to win the war as our rations were so much better than yours. POWs would look at their food in disbelief. Italians care greatly about food. Perhaps even more than the French." When Theodore had first met her, the Group Captain had told him that she was French, but had lived in Italy for many years. Feathers had taken quite a shine to her.

"Do you live here alone, Chantal?"

"There's hardly room for more than one. Until Stefano died, I lived with his parents. They have a large estate, out in the country. They are an old Neapolitan family. At one time, they owned a bank but no longer. Now they have only the estate, but it is a good one. When we learnt that Stefano was dead, I moved here. I couldn't bear the sound of his mother weeping all day. She was so hopeful that he would still come home.

Even now, she keeps his room ready and has the servant leave food on the kitchen table every night, just in case he walks in hungry. He has been dead for nearly three years, but Mamma still puts food on the table for her hungry boy. That is touching, no?" She gave him a sideways glance as she worked at the single gas ring. *"Sometimes I think she is a little mad. They think I am mad, of course, to prefer these rooms to their home, but I had to get away from the family. All those tears. Italians are good at crying – better at that, too, than the French."* She shivered. *"Could you let me have a cigarette?"*

"Of course." He shook out a couple. *"Three years isn't so very long. You must miss your husband very much."* She took the cigarette but declined a light and put it on the table.

"Yes. He shouldn't have died. We had a notice, giving him some award for bravery. Post– after he was dead? How do you say that?"

"Posthumously?"

"Yes, that is it." She didn't attempt to repeat the word. *"They told us he had been very brave, that he had taken on six British planes single-handed and brought down four before he was hit himself. Perhaps it was even your squadron? I don't think so – that would be too great a coincidence. Not that it matters. A year ago I met a pilot from the same* squadriglia. *He told me Stefano had been shot down by Italian guns, not by an English plane. I was angry when I heard*

that. Now, I think it is a good thing. It is good to have a little – irony, no? And maybe it would comfort Stefano that it took an Italian to defeat him . . ." She stretched both arms over her head suddenly and pulled a comb out of her hair, letting it tumble down her back. For the first time Thoedore saw that she must have been a pretty girl. Her face was too long, too thin for his taste, and her skin had a sallow tinge, but as her hair fell around her face it softened. "We can go back into the other room, now. It will be only twenty minutes, then we can eat. Pasta, and then chicken."

"I brought a tin of peaches."

"Tinned peaches! You spoil me! Cigarettes and fruit." Theodore detected the note of sarcasm, and felt faintly humiliated. He wasn't to know if she was supplied with fruit from the family estate. Her smile seemed genuine. "Thank you. Now I have told you my story, come and tell me yours, Squadron Leader."

Chantal sat at the table while Theodore resumed his place on the sofa. He felt too large for the little room, self-consciously shifting his legs around so that they didn't take up all the floor space. "You're a pilot? Like Stefano." She inhaled deeply on the cigarette, closing her eyes as she did so.

"What did your husband fly?"

She nodded. "A CR42, when he was in North Africa. I don't know what else."

"A fighter, then. I fly Wellington bombers."
He waited for her to comment on the devastation British bombers had wrought on Naples, but she only raised a shoulder.

"I don't have much interest in the machines."

"I don't suppose you would, signora."

"Chantal." She reminded him. "How long have you been in Italy, Theodore?"

"Since Christmas 1943. What about you?"

"Oh, my invasion was ten years before yours! I came here as a young girl. I was just twenty. I wanted to study painting restoration and this was the place to be. I studied under a master in Florence. My parents opposed my coming. They felt I was too young, and it would be improper for an unmarried woman to be alone in a foreign country. I didn't care about that. They weren't much happier when I met Stefano and married him. It made me a respectable married woman, but he was a foreigner. At least he was Catholic – that was some small compensation." Again he heard the bitterness in her voice.

"Have you managed to keep up your interest in art?"

She laughed shortly. "No. It is a pity, because there is now a great need for restoration. I could have made a very decent living... Stefano didn't want me to work. He considered that improper. His people are very traditional. Until the war. Now everyone is allowed to work. Stefano joined the Reggia Aeronautica not long after we were married. He was only twenty-three when his unit was sent to Spain to fight for the Fascists. He went to Libya almost immediately after, in 1940. I never saw him again. I was asked to do some translation work for the 'war effort'. I speak French and Italian, of course, and some German. My English, as you can see, is not very good, but it was good enough for them."

"It sounds very good to me."

"It has improved greatly in the past year. There has been more need for English speakers than French or German so I had to learn. Now I work for the Allies."

As she spoke, she wound her hair round and round her hand, braiding it over one shoulder, letting it fall loose and rebraiding it. He found it disturbing, watching her play with her hair.

"You must have had a difficult few years."

She smiled properly for the first time since his arrival in her home. "It is kind of you to say so but I don't agree. Others have had a much harder time. I haven't been bombed. I haven't had children to lose. And my family – Stefano's family – haven't lost all their money. Not yet, at least. In Italy now, everything comes down to money. That wasn't true before the war, but now it is the most important thing. For many, a few lire means the difference between living and dying. This may not look much to you, but I am far better off than many. I am rich, in many ways. And I have been able to work, and it helps to *keep busy."*

"Why didn't you return to France?"

"To what?" Her lip curled with scorn. "Occupied France? I haven't spoken to my own family for years. I was married to the enemy. Everyone in France is in the Resistance, although it is a nice question what they have all been resisting. My brother is dead. My husband is dead. My parents may be dead, although I doubt it. Why should I go home? This is my home."

"I'm very sorry for all your loss."

"Don't, please, say that! You didn't cause it. This is my chance to greet the conquering hero. The victory is yours. It doesn't matter if I am French or Italian – I don't care any longer. We are all of us conquered peoples, perhaps even you English."

"I don't see it like that."

This amused her. "No, I imagine you wouldn't. Tell me about your girl. I'm sure she's pretty."

"She's more than that . . . She's American."

"And Americans are more than pretty?"

Theodore laughed. "No, some of them are downright ugly – most of the men, that is. But Anna is very beautiful."

"Blonde?"

"Yes, she is."

"I thought so. And how did a nice English gentleman pilot meet a Yankee girl?"

"I met her in Egypt. She works there."

"Ah. So she makes her war effort, too."

"Yes."

"I wish you well. You and your American girl." She raised her glass in a toast to him.

"Thank you. The wine is very good. Far better than –" he had nearly said Benito's Blood, as they referred to the cheap Chianti pilfered from the Eyeties, but he caught himself in time "– we have in the officers' mess."

"It is from my parents-in-law's estate. It is my . . . widow's pension? Come. Sit down. Let me feed you."

Chantal Molesini took pride in her cooking, and presented what was a meagre meal with flair. As they talked, Theodore lost a little of his discomfort and began to enjoy her company. She encouraged him to talk about Anna, and after some urging, he indulged himself.

She listened attentively. "She sounds very special, your Anna. You must take care of her. A woman like that will have her pick of men. You will have children?"

"We hope to."

"I am very fond of children. Many of the children living in this house are orphans. I like to look after them."

Theodore did not presume to ask why she had none of her own. As the evening wore on, and Chantal opened a second bottle of wine, she also relaxed and laughed easily at his stories of squadron life. He told her how he and the mess officer had been the victims of the seemingly

449

innocent but canny Italian peasants who worked the land around the airfield. "Mamma and Papa see us coming down the lane, and send the children off to hide the fattest pig or calf or goose in some far-off hut. Then they swear till they're blue in the face that they have nothing left that the Jerries didn't take. They declare their family is starving, with black eyes wide and their stomachs bulging over their belts, before inviting us inside for a bottle or two of wine. You have to admire them – they end up with pockets stuffed with money and cigarettes, and we walk off with a couple of half-starved chickens they wouldn't consider putting in their own pot."

"Yes, in Italy now it is good to work the land. We feel that what the Germans didn't take on the way out, the *Inglesi* have stolen on their march through. You should listen to my father-in-law."

"I'd like to meet him."

She laughed, a rich, throaty sound. "I am afraid he would not say the same about you, Squadron Leader."

She invited him to come to dinner again, when he could. In exchange, he asked her if she would like to go to the opera with him one evening. It was a relief to have female company, even if it was not the female of his choice, and pleasant to talk of things other than flying. He bought tickets for a performance of Rigoletto and wired Anna, but she couldn't get away: there was civilian unrest in Cairo and Mac didn't want her to leave her desk. Theo was disappointed not to show her Naples: the blossom was out that March, apricot, cherry and hawthorn fluttering prettily against the bombed backdrop.

Three weeks later, Chantal met him in front of the San Carlo Opera House. Her hair was pinned up, her grey suit clean but badly worn, and she wore no makeup. He couldn't help but think uncharitably what a poor deputy she made for Anna. During the performance, in the cool darkness of the auditorium, he was moved to see her cheeks wet with tears. After the opera, they walked through the streets of Naples, stopping at a bar for coffee before he escorted her to Via Giuseppe Cotronei. She asked him to come in and stay for a glass of wine.

Theodore looked at his watch, and felt her fingers close loosely around his wrist. "Don't look at the time. Time passes too quickly. Keep me company for a little longer, please, Squadron Leader. I feel lonely tonight. Stefano and I used to go to the opera whenever we could – in Rome, in Milan, in Verona. Most to San Carlo. This is the first time I have been since . . ."

She handed him her key, and he opened the door and followed her up the stairs. Once in the apartment, she passed him a bottle of wine and two glasses, and left the room. He stood at the window, looking out on the dark street. When she came back, she had removed her suit jacket, undone the top button of her blouse and her hair was loosened again. She joined him at the window, pointing out her neighbours across the way.

"That is the home of Signora Bertolini. Do you see her there, in the window? The fat woman. She has seven children and no husband. He died in the first year of the war. Next door is Signora Giocorda. Her husband came home but he is a cripple and has only one eye. She thinks it is not so big a price to pay. They live in four rooms with their two children, and his brother and his brother's family. He is a very amusing man. Beneath them is Signora Fiammetta with her two daughters. They have a small dressmaking business." She brushed her skirt. "They made this. They are not very good, I am afraid, but they work very hard, and we all have to make a living, however we can. Do you see the light on – there," she leant far out of the window, pointing to a house on the corner of the street, "next door to the bombed house? That is the room of Sofia Maschini. She is twenty-four. She has the face of the Madonna. She was a student when I moved here, and now she is a whore."

Theodore moved to close the window, but her hand stopped him. "Leave it open please. I can't breathe tonight. Besides, I like to hear my neighbours about their business." She undid another button of her shirt, and poured out the wine.

Theodore offered her a cigarette, although he felt a sudden impatience to leave. "Can you feel the heat rise up from the streets? And the smell. What do you smell, Theodore?"

He had to press himself against her to lean out of the window. He inhaled deeply, but he was only conscious of her standing next to him and being with Anna at the Smelling of the Breeze.

"I don't know. Garlic. Garbage. Dogs?"

"You can smell people's lives." She breathed in. It made her shoulders lift and rub against his. "Poverty. Love. Men and women close together. Shame. Hope. Passion. You can smell all of them, if you try."

Theodore felt his skin prickle, and a cold sweat ran down the back of his shirt. He could feel her eyes on him and stared fixedly at the house opposite, watching Signora Bertolini as if he needed to commit it to memory. Chantal was so close to him that he felt the steady pressure of her hip against his thigh. As she twisted her body to face his, her breast brushed against his sleeve and her hand covered his on the window ledge.

"Chantal, I'm afraid this isn't a sensible idea. I ought to be getting back." He addressed the night sky, lifting his face to the stars.

"Why? Because I am a poor widow in a foreign country? Because, perhaps, my husband shot down your friends? Or, perhaps, your friends tried to shoot down my husband? Would it matter, if any of them were true? Perhaps you *think I work for the Gestapo?"*

"No. Simply because I love someone else."

*"And this beautiful American Anna of yours
– she will never forgive you, you suppose, for
finding a little companionship when she is far
away?"*

"I don't know."

*"This loving girl, who wants to be your wife,
she would want you to be lonely, when she can't
be with you?"*

"I don't know."

*He stared resolutely out of the window, hand-
some face straight ahead, while her lips brushed
against his throat and her low voice murmured
against his ear, "You are a good man, Theodore.
I know that. You fear you will betray her. You
will not. In this place, in this war, infidelity
means nothing at all. Nothing. It is an empty
word. It doesn't translate into any of the
languages we use now. This is nothing to do with
her. This is not the future, not 'back home', not
one day, not even tomorrow. In the morning,
you will be with your squadron. One day soon,
you will go home, with your lovely Anna,
and you will have children and great happiness together. You will be a loyal and loving
husband. You won't remember me and you
won't remember tonight, and it can do nothing
to hurt you." He could feel her mouth moving
softly against his throat, and his own pulse
beating against her cool lips. "If we go to bed, it*

doesn't have to be me – you can pretend that it is her you hold in your arms. If you close your eyes, you can imagine she is with you. I don't mind. If only you will stay, I will be anyone."

He turned and took her into his arms, his lips joining hers. He kissed her partly with pity, but partly with something not far from revulsion that she should be prepared to humiliate herself to such a degree. He wondered how many men had unknowingly stood in place of her lost Italian fighter. How tightly did she have to close her eyes to imagine Stefano beneath the skin of Americans or Poles or British? Her hands slipped beneath his jacket to unbutton his shirt. As her fingers trailed over his chest, they closed on the locket around his neck, and tugged teasingly on the chain. He took hold of her wrists and pushed her gently but firmly away from him.

"Chantal. You are a lovely, desirable woman, but I can't do this. It goes against everything that I believe in. I can't be such a cad and I can't bring Stefano back for you. No one can." He kissed her cheek. "You may be right about Anna. She probably would understand, somehow. And yes, I feel lonely, as lonely and as chilled as you, and I can think of no better cure than making love to someone. But tomorrow morning will come, and what would we have? Nothing. Only guilt, and my thinking of her. I would be lying if I said that I didn't want to take you to bed . . ." She pressed herself against him, her lips looking for his, but he

455

groaned and twisted his head away. As she heard the sound she stepped back from him suddenly, her arms folded tightly across his chest.

"Go now. If you won't stay with me tonight, please leave right away." There was an imploring note in her voice and Theodore felt sickened. He reached out for her but she shook her head. "Please don't touch me. If you knew how long I have waited for a man to touch me, how long since I wanted one to touch me, even for one night, you wouldn't do it and then change your mind. I don't ask you to bring Stefano back. I am not like his mother – I don't keep my bed warm for him. Now go, and don't come back." She wound her long hair into a twist, and looped one end through the dark coil, knotting it together. "Good luck, Squadron Leader. Avanti."

Theodore buttoned his jacket and walked out of the door. As he went down the three flights of stairs in the gloom he cursed himself for a fool. If anyone had told him at Oxford that an attractive French woman would one day as good as beg him to make love to her, and that he would decline the invitation, he would have laughed out loud. And yet, here he was, politely declining for the sake of Anna, who had not the faintest notion where he was or who he was with, and who was probably at this very moment dancing in some other man's arms. There should never be any regrets, as she said. Once outside the building, Theodore's pace slowed, and he looked up at the third floor. He removed his jacket. The air was steamy with the day's heat. Chantal had turned off the light, but he could see the dark shadow of her body framed in the window. He turned and walked slowly down the street.

As he was about to turn the corner, a voice called softly, "Hey, soldier!" He turned on his heel and saw a beautiful girl leaning in a doorway and beckoning him with the gentle brown eyes of a doe. She had a bruise across one cheek. He understood why Chantal had said she had the Madonna's face. He shook his head with a smile and saluted her as she smiled back at him. After a moment of looking at her, he turned back to number 18. The front door of the house was still ajar. He walked slowly up the stairs, past the playing children. He felt angry that no one had bothered to put them to bed. He pushed open the door of the apartment. Chantal was sitting hunched on the floor next to the open window. The cheap fabric of her skirt had ridden up around her hips. Theodore threw his jacket on the sofa, picked her up in his arms and carried her into what he correctly assumed was the bedroom.

CHAPTER EIGHTEEN

I arrived early to meet Theodore. I had come back from Monpazier mid-afternoon, and got a message to meet him in the square at six, but I was waiting on a bench before five thirty.

Even now, I can't think of Monpazier with any pleasure, despite it being a lovely little town. I had spent the day there so miserably, wondering what was going on at Le Bosc, that even now I feel forlorn if I hear the name. The town has been contaminated for me. It is just like hearing the words Banja Luka, Sarajevo, Mostar, Gorazde. They are all tainted, for millions of people, and will be for God knows how long. Whole cities, towns, countries become synonymous with barbarism. What will it be like in 2005 for the poor kid who grows up perfectly happily in Enniskillen or Gorazde, with normal memories of childhood, to find older generations flinching in distaste when they mention the place of their birth? Even Christian names can become irreparably sullied. When I was a student, I had three Yugoslav friends, Milan, Dusan and Slobodan. In 1982 I had no idea – and I still don't – whether they were Serb, Croat, Bosnian, Muslim or anything else. Now, from listening to David and reading the papers, even those 'Christian' names are enough to make my stomach heave. Poor, innocent names.

I had expected David to be with Theodore, but the old man came alone, strolling across the square. He sat down and rather than inviting me back to his house, had the nerve to ask me to stay away for another couple of hours. "I have asked Dr Duhaze to come over this evening. I want him to check David's leg. Have no fear, David is sound in mind and body, and I must say, I think he has the physical and emotional resilience of an ox. Your husband –"

"He's not my husband yet," I pointed out pedantically, and stupidly, but I simply wanted to play some role in the conversation. Theodore sighed, and closed his eyes momentarily.

"As you know better than anyone, David has spent twenty years in war zones, on and off. Twenty years of intense pressure. Four times as long as I, and seeing far worse. I don't know how he's done it. I'm curious to know certain things about David, and I thought you would be able to help."

"Theodore, I don't want to be rude but I can look after him myself. All I have to do is call a couple of people, talk to his agency and I can get everything he needs, and take him wherever he can be properly looked after." I did not want to say the phrase post-traumatic stress syndrome. Theodore wouldn't have a clue what I was talking about.

"I hope you do that, but I do not believe that David is suffering from post-traumatic shock, and neither does he."

"He can't not want to see me."

Theodore looked at me with infinite tenderness. "Of course he wants to. Elena, many men of my own generation never talked to their wives and their children about their experiences. Even now they cannot. You and David have a future together – you will have all the time in the world to talk. Don't press him until he chooses to talk to you."

"What do you want to know about David?"

"David told me that he never knew his parents."

"They were killed in a car crash when he was twelve."

"I see. Who brought him up?"

"He went to boarding school. He spent holidays with his grandparents, somewhere in the south. When he was eighteen, he went to Vietnam with his godfather who was a photographer, and Mitch was killed by a terrorist bomb."

"And since then?"

I shook my head. "Well, his grandparents died. He's just been working ever since. No, that's not true. He got married. He's always told me it wasn't really anything – they barely saw each other for two years and then they divorced amicably. He's been divorced for well over ten years."

"And no one else?" I stared at him. 'Until you?"

"I don't know." I whispered. "I don't think so, but I don't know. Maybe I don't know him at all."

Theodore stood up and was his reassuring, soothing old self. "Nonsense. You know him better than anyone else, and it is you and your baby he has come home to. Believe me, Elena, it is only the love of you that has kept him sound. I know the feeling. I felt the same way about your mother."

I looked up at him, not knowing what to say, and then I felt a surge of indignation well up within me. After months of dithering, years of playing the defensive and sitting on the fence, I would rather have been damned to hell than let David Turcan go. "I'm coming with you," I said loudly. "I don't care if I sit in the car or hide in the garden. I don't care if he hits me or hates me or whatever the hell he does, but I'm bloody well not going to sit here and bow out gracefully. I don't give a damn if he wants to see me or not. I *need* him. I'm sorry if you don't agree, and you may be right, but I have to find out for myself. If I slink away and cower in the hotel, I'll never *know*. I love David, whether he loves me or not, I love him and I love this baby, and that's all there is to it."

"You are so very like your mother, Elena. It gives me joy simply to look at you."

I was taken aback by his words. "I've never felt that I took after her. I never felt that I was nearly as pretty, or as popular, or as strong. Your talking about her confirmed that."

"If you had that impression, you were mistaken.

You're the spitting image of her. Just as ferocious, as bonny, as impetuous, and perhaps even a little more difficult to manage, although I could never have imagined such a thing possible before meeting you." His eyes twinkled. "Your father and David are courageous men. Lion-hearted. You have to be, to take on a lioness." He winked at me. "Now, my dear, if you insist on coming with me, we must get a move on to be back before the doctor arrives."

Theodore had been cagey, but he hadn't warned me that David was absolutely smashed. I'd never seen him as drunk as he was that night. From the doorstep, we could hear him singing. This was not the manifestation of post-traumatic shock that I had prepared myself for; I had expected David to be raging like a wild beast and throwing furniture around the room. He was closer to blissfully arse-holed. The tune was familiar – 'Clementine'.

Theodore winced as he opened the front door. "Elena, I take full responsibility. We had a bit of a sing-song this afternoon – I never thought he'd remember it." He put a finger to his lips as we crept down the hall. We stood outside the drawing room listening to David singing to bust a gut.

"Take-off from the Western Desert
Sixty, Fuka, or O nine,
Same old aircraft, same old aircrew,
Same old target, same old time.

"Seventy Squadron, Seventy Squadron,

Though we say it with a sigh,
We must do this bloody mail run
Every night until we die.

"Navigator! Have you lost us?
Come up here and take a look,
Someone's shot our starboard wing off!
We're alright, chaps, that's Tobruk!

Seventy Squadron, Seventy Squadron,
Though we say it with a sigh,
We must do this bloody mail run
Every night until we die.

Oh to be in Piccadilly,
Selling matches by the score,
Then we would not have to do that
Bloody – mail – run – any more . . .

Seventy – "Oh, fuck!"

As David began the refrain again, Theodore pushed open the door. "Theodore, I can't remember the first sodding verse – Elle!" He staggered to his feet and limped over to wrap me in a bear hug. He kissed me so intimately that I had no doubt he was soused beyond any possible recollection of sobriety. That one had to be described as a serious throat-investigator snog. "Elle," he murmured, "Elle, my darling, darling . . ." I would have been perfectly happy to stand there supporting him for a month. I'd never realized quite how good being drunk could be. His head reared up from my shoulder. "Theodore, how does the first verse go? I've driven myself mad trying to think of the first fucking verse."

Theodore began the line,

> *'Down to Flights each ruddy morning'*

and David joined in, waving his arms to the tune,

> *'Sitting waiting for a clue*
> *Same old notice on the flight board,*
> *Max'mum effort – guess where to?'*

As they launched into the chorus in unison, it struck me that Theodore Hamilton was drunk too. I heard the song twice through. I can still sing it, and I do – I find myself humming it in the car, waiting in traffic, and I sing it to the baby. The words flow as easily as if I had been in the Western Desert myself. That old man and David caroused like long-lost buddies. I was the only person to notice the serious face of Dr Duhaze, gazing upon us as if he had stepped into an asylum. He walked into the room, and said abruptly to Theodore, "Which of the three of you is my patient tonight?"

Theodore jerked his thumb at David, who promptly collapsed into an armchair. "You'll have to remove your trousers," Theodore said severely, and David actually giggled.

I went to help. David was co-operative: it took

only a minute to pull off his jeans, but I thought I'd pass out when I saw spots of fresh blood on the bandage. Dr Duhaze knelt next to him. He put on his glasses, and looked at us as if to ask if we would leave the room, but neither Theodore nor I budged. When he did unwrap the bandage, I sat down suddenly on a chair. The crimson stain had led to me to expect a seeping, pustulating mess of raw flesh. David's leg looked no different from this morning.

"It's good. Two to three weeks old? Perfectly clean. I don't often come across bullet wounds in Cahors. I've never seen one so fortunately positioned. There is still a little swelling," he prodded around at David's thigh, "and more bruising than I would like to see." He took off his glasses. "I presume you have had physiotherapy since your accident?"

David lifted his good leg in the air and crowed. "Physiotherapy? Fuck me, no, Doc. Oddly enough, it wasn't that easy tracking down a decent physio in Sarajevo. I got some fucking good drugs, though."

"Which doubtless enabled you to use the leg before it was advisable." Duhaze was utterly humourless. "Your leg is essentially intact. There is no infection. It was well looked after." He glanced at me. "It is not common for a bullet to hit skin and muscle at *this* point, without hitting an artery or becoming embedded in bone." His fingers probed gently and lovingly around the greenish-grey bruise. "There is, naturally, some muscle damage, and if you want to recover full use of it, I would advise you to stay off the leg for a few weeks. Make sure you have a course of physiotherapy. You should have done that from the start. I will clean the wound, rebandage it, and give you a precautionary injection of antibiotics. Then all you need is rest."

I watched the doctor take a wad of bandage out of his bag and drench it in liquid. David was rambling on to Theodore. I flinched as Dr Duhaze pressed the pad against David's open wound, but the doctor smiled grimly and shook his head at me. "He won't feel it. I don't think he'd feel it if I rammed a hypodermic up his arse." He then proceeded to ram a hypodermic into David's buttock, and David began to sing, wildly off key, to the tune of 'Over the Rainbow'.

> *'Somewhere, over Benghazi, way down low,*
> *There's a Wimp on one engine*
> *Chased by a one-one-oh.*
> *Somewhere over Benghazi, Heinkels fly,*
> *They fly over Benghazi*
> *Why then oh why must I?'*

The doctor packed up his bag, and passed me a prescription. I followed him to the front door as Theodore joined David in song. They both had terrible voices.

"He's feeling no pain." I wanted to make Duhaze smile, just once.

"He shouldn't drink when he is taking the antibiotics. He certainly shouldn't drive."

"OK." I doubted the wisdom of going back into that room and telling David it would be advisable to refrain from alcohol.

The doctor paused on the doorstep. "This is a strange house, this House of the Englishman. It is curious that I should have treated three people associated with this house. And all so lucky."

"How do you mean, lucky?"

"You were very fortunate to keep your baby, Miss Stewart, at that stage in the pregnancy. Your friend is lucky to have been shot in the manner in which he was shot. An inch or two to the right, and he might have lost that leg."

"An inch or two to the *left*, and he wouldn't have been shot at all."

"You can look at it like that. Monsieur Hamilton – well, he is a fortunate man, too. To come through the war and to be in good health. Considering . . ."

I raised an eyebrow at him.

"His age. And Madame Hamilton was very lucky to die when she did."

"I'm sorry?" I wanted him to repeat what he had said.

"Why be sorry, when you are the beneficiary of good fortune? Be glad."

"Doctor, I know you don't like me, for some reason – no, I can guess why. You think I'm always wasting your time."

"Not at all. It is as much a doctor's job to relieve the mind as the body. After all, that is where most physical malaise starts. If my patients are worried, I

467

prefer them to call me."

"In that case, could you see your way to my bringing David in tomorrow and letting him listen to the baby's heart?"

"Of course. I will be at the clinic only from one until two. You can come then. Otherwise, you will have to come to Cahors. Don't let him drive. Goodnight, Miss Stewart."

I didn't get a smile out of him.

When I returned to the drawing room, the mood had altered completely. David had stopped singing. He had his leg stretched out and was talking into the middle of the empty room, as if no one was there. Theodore was sitting on the far side in the dark. I leant against the wall listening to David.

"What d'you think, Wing Commander? Elle's young – she's still so young. I had a nineteen-year-old translator working with me in Sarajevo, a Muslim kid, who was twenty years older than her." Theodore's eyes met mine across the room. "She told me stories about fathers forced to rape their own teenage daughters to save their lives – their daughters' lives, not their own. About a woman who'd been given the choice of biting her nineteen-year-old son's balls off with her own teeth, or seeing him disembowelled. The *choice*. I sat there thinking about Elle and me having a baby and raising a kid, and all the time a woman begged me to take one of her kids out with me. She said it didn't matter if she never saw it again, she just wanted it out of there.

Maybe years after the event people will say that the barrage of photographs and news footage and acres of print made some difference, wore down the West just like barrage bombing wore down the Axis. But at the time they do nothing. You tell everyone, the West will not allow this to happen. What else can you say? But it doesn't stop. Maybe if you find the one picture – one image, one moment, one face amongst all that . . ." He was rhythmically rubbing his thigh, up and down, up and down. I focused on his hands moving over his leg. "The only thing that stops are the reporters. It is the correspondents who get fed up and decide they can't take it any longer. I have to believe that it will make a difference, however long it takes, that there'll be a record, proof that this happened, and we all sat back and let it happen. If I'd got that image . . ."

I had tears running down my cheeks; I could taste the salt of them. Theodore stepped forward in his chair, and put an arm around David's shoulders. "My friend, you will."

Theodore held David against his chest for a moment, and then stood up and left the room.

I took his place.

"David, darling."

"Elle?" David looked confused. "Sweetheart, I didn't know you were here."

"I just came in. I was saying goodnight to the doctor. Are you OK?"

"Just fine . . . Tired. Like I could sleep for a week."

"Maybe you should."

"Back here with you, I don't want to waste time sleeping."

I rubbed my cheek against his rough one, sitting awkwardly on the arm of his chair and trying to avoid brushing his leg. "Do you want to go home, David? Shall we just go back to London?"

"Whenever you like, darling. At the moment, I'm not sure that I have the energy to get into bed."

I tried to get closer. I wanted every inch of me to be touching him. The room was quite dark. Theodore had left a small table light on across the room, and the door was ajar so that some light streaked in from the hall, but all I could see was the outline of David's face as he continued in a low voice, "If we are going to be together, you need to know some things. I'm tired of living different lives, and I'm tired of worrying I may not live up to the hero that you want me to be."

"I don't want you to be a hero."

"Yes, you do, sweetheart, even if you don't know it yourself. You've always wanted to love a hero. That's why you love all these pilots."

"No, David, it's not true."

As he stroked my hair, I thought reluctantly of something a Dutch friend of mine had said to me once. I had been talking about how alike the English and the Dutch were, and she'd disagreed. She said that for all the similarities, they were fundamentally different, because the Dutch were realists at heart, and the English were romantics. I laughed when I heard that. The English must have the worst reputation in the world for being tight-arsed, unemotional, cold-blooded masters of repression. Romantic was not the word that leapt to mind. Defending herself, she gave examples of 'English' romanticism, the striving for the perfect life, in domestic miniature – slippers warming on the Aga and scones in the oven, home-made jam bubbling on the hob; the village green and the sound of leather on willow – and the big picture, lives spent for a cause, freedom or justice or truth, the national addiction to honour, 'I could not love thee dear so much, lov'd I not honour more'; patriotism and all the associated nostalgic mumbo-jumbo of Elgar, Churchill, and 'I Vow To Thee My Country' . . .

David was right. I *did* want all of them to be heroes, and the more obsolescent heroism became, the more I thirsted for it.

"I don't want to sit at your funeral and have two thousand people tell me how noble and heroic you were, getting blown to pieces trying to save somebody else's child. I want you to do whatever it is that you want to do. But I want you to be alive and with me more than any of the rest of it. I want you to love our baby *more* than all the millions of babies in the world."

"I do, sweet. Elle, I don't walk around weeping over every baby and every dead teenage soldier. I just do my job, and I know how, and I know I'm good, and that's all I'm confident about. But I'm not certain what you want, or what's going to happen to us, and I think we should talk about it."

"I don't. I know everything's going to be all right.
You need to get well and take some time off." I
slipped down to the floor and squatted between his
legs so that I could see his face. "I only care about
you. I've spent two years telling myself that I'm OK,
that I love you but I'll get by perfectly well when
you leave, and now I won't any more. If you move
away from me, I won't survive it. Everything about
you, everything that you are, good and bad, makes
me ache. So long as the baby is all right, and you are
all right, then I want to carry on just as we are.
That's all."

In my passion to persuade him, I must have leant
my full weight on his thigh, and David's face went
into a spasm of pain. "Oh, God – oh, God, I'm sorry,
sorry, sorry."

"It's OK, sweetheart. But I don't go along with
that." Oh, God, no. However brave I felt, I braced
myself for the blow that he didn't love me or he
didn't want the baby, or that he was going straight
back to Bosnia tomorrow. Any of those three, and
all my reasoned resolutions would be blown apart.
His hand rested on my head. "I don't want to carry
on as we are. I want to spend the rest of my life with
you, and if you don't believe that," he placed one
large hand against my right temple and cheekbone,
and the other on the left, and he pressed his hands
together, "I may just have to break your silly head
open."

"How on earth can you possibly think that I see

472

you as some sort of romantic hero model when you behave like this? Sometimes I think you do this deliberately just to spoil my fun and stop indulging my sacrificial fantasies. I mean, honestly, David . . ." I felt his hands press more firmly.

"Elena . . ." he said threateningly.

"All right then. Fine. If you insist. If it makes you feel better . . ."

"Elena . . ."

I tipped my head up to look straight at him, and felt my bottom lip tremble as he kissed me and I spoke through the kiss. "Yes, I believe it. Thank God. Thank *God* you want me." As his mouth covered mine, I had to stop, but when his lips moved across to my cheek, I carried on talking. "There are conditions, however. You have to see a physiotherapist when we get home." All the time he was kissing me. "You can't ever make me any promises and then not keep them. I'm quite happy if you never make any at all. I don't think I want to make any myself, come to think of it. But you can't ever forget my birthday or the baby's birthday, no matter where you are."

"Jesus Christ, Elle, can't you ever keep your mouth shut?" He kissed me insistently. Which was exactly what I had intended. I was taken aback when he wrenched his head away, with his eyes shut tight. "*Elle* . . ."

"I was only trying to make you laugh, David, I couldn't give a fuck about birthdays, honestly, I hate them."

"Get your elbow out of the hole in my leg – like *now*."

We didn't talk about love again. I think he was too drunk to remember we ever had. When I got him to bed, and we lay in each other's arms, David kept murmuring about driving down a road, watching out for a dangerous bend. He knew every twist of that road in detail. I didn't know where it was. I am not, as I have said, an aficionado of anything to do with driving, but I got the gist of what David was saying: the technique was to enter the bend at high speed, and shift rapidly down gear seconds before the sharpest point, keeping the foot flat on the accelerator. The goal was to take the curve at seventy-five miles an hour in first gear. I lay there thinking about the dangerous bends David and I had yet to navigate.

Rome

"How do you feel about being a lawyer's wife?"

They were in the bar of the Hotel D'Inghilterra, which had been requisitioned, appropriately, as a British officers' hotel. It was late May, two weeks after VE Day. Anna had expected to find scenes of jubilant rejoicing, but there was a subdued atmosphere, a listlessness among the representatives of the various Allied forces gathered in the hotel bar. She considered his question for a moment, then wrinkled her nose with distaste.

"It would be OK, I guess, if I have to. I'm not sure how I'll feel about you out of uniform."

"I had the distinct impression you rather liked me out of uniform . . ."

"Squadron Leader! How risqué!" Anna batted her eyelids at him. "I've been picturing myself as a flier's wife. I like your wings, you know."

"And you don't want to marry a fallen angel, golden girl?"

Anna caressed him. She had seen the shadow cross his face and wouldn't have her jest taken to heart. "Don't look so serious, darling. You'll always be my angel, however far you fall."

"I would stay with the RAF, if you wanted me to."

Anna shook her head and looked around the bar. She leant across and whispered, "What is the matter with everyone? My God, isn't this what we've been praying for? Here, of all places, they should be on cloud nine."

"It takes a little while to come down from the clouds, dearest. Not everyone has your talent for optimism. For a start, some of these boys aren't going to be going home for quite a while. For others, it's too much of a shock to handle. None of us knows quite what we're going home to, after all. Two weeks ago, I was sitting with some of the chaps in a field that a few weeks before had been a Luftwaffe stronghold. We were feeling

*bloody sorry for ourselves, listening to the cele-
brations courtesy of the BBC. 'Hostilities in
Europe cease at midnight tonight . . . God save
the King!' After Winston had stopped spouting,
one of our gunners, a lad who's spent the war on
a short cut to suicide, poured out the rum. None
of the rest of us could find any words, but Gregor
raised his mug in the air and said, 'Huh, out of
a job again!' I don't think I'll ever forget the look
on his face."*

"How did you feel?"

*"I thought about you. How much I wanted
to be holding you as I heard the news. Wondering
if now, at last, we can begin to plan for the
future. Thinking of the friends who hadn't made
it that far. Sam and Tommy – all of them.
Imagining how their families felt as they heard
Churchill announce that it was all over."*

"Oh, darling! I wish I could help – understand. I think I do a little."

*"There is no one on earth with as big and
generous a heart as yours, Anna. There are so
many men, women, too, who have lost the ability
to believe in goodness and kindness and happy
endings . . . I'm not sure that life's worth living,
if that happens to you."*

"But it hasn't happened to us, Theo. We're
here, and whole, and we have a future."

"Yes, golden girl, you're right. When will you
marry me?" Theodore held her hand and brought
it to his lips.

"Whenever you like. I want you to meet my parents. I want to go home, if it's the last time I call it home."

"And I want that more than anything. Your parents won't think much of me, will they? Carting off their beloved daughter to foreign climes. And I have no job. How will your father feel about that?"

"I don't think he'll object to having a lawyer in the family. Don't know how he'll feel about an Englishman . . ."

"How do you feel?"

"Happy."

"You are the loveliest thing on this earth. I could kiss you till hell freezes over. I want to be able to tell our children about tonight. When we're old, I'll tell our sons that however fortunate they may be, they will never win the prize the gods gave me."

"Don't you ever tell them that! Besides, what if we have daughters?"

"I'll ring every bell in town I can lay hands on. So long as they look like you. I can have ten or twenty of them and not tire of looking at that face."

"You won't feel that when I'm old and grey."

"You never will be, not to me. You will be always be just as you are at this minute. One day, we'll have a mantel full of photographs of sweet babes, and I will look at them and think of you, and how you look tonight."

"All these months of not daring to speak of the future, and now you're seeing photographs of babies?"

"That's the only comfort Cupid gives us, darling; the certainty of future bliss. Why else would we put up with the flak he hurls at us? If you knew how often I've gazed at that mantelpiece, you'd laugh at me for a sentimental fool."

"How soon will you be demobilized?"

"There, we're still in the laps of the gods. I've had a word with the Groupie, put in my request for as early a date as he can manage. He wants me to stay on. Lots of bumpf about promotion and golden futures. To be honest, my darling, there is a financial case for staying on, with a wife to support. But I believe I would prefer to take my chance in Civvy Street. If you agree."

"Just you try and say something I don't agree with, Squadron Leader."

"If I say you're a fool for getting involved with an ass like me?"

"I'll go along with that."

"That I'm a useless, god-forsaken wretch not worthy of kissing the hem of your skirt?"

"If you insist on putting it that way."

"That a woman like you shouldn't be committing herself to a chap with no sure future, no job, no prospects?"

"You have a point, I'm forced to admit."

"That you are the most beautiful creature on earth?"

"You were doing fine, but you've gone too far."

"And if I invite you to accompany me to a quiet room so that I can kiss you until your lips are purple, and you faint from lack of breath?"

"You've always promised me the Purple Heart, and it's about time you delivered. There's just one thing, Theodore."

"What is that, light of my life?"

"You also promised we'd go to the embassy Victory Dance. That's the reason I'm here at all."

"Lord in high heaven. What wrong did I ever commit to end up with a woman who puts work before love?"

"I just like to combine the two, when I can. And I'm in the mood to dance, even if no one else is. Shall we go?"

"What about that quiet room?"

"It will wait, Theodore. If there's one thing you and I have learnt how to do, it's wait."

When they arrived the party was in full swing. Theodore was simultaneously proud and irritated by the number of officers and diplomats who claimed Anna for a dance. To say that she was the life and soul of the party was inaccurate; there were many who competed for the title, but to Theodore's troubled mind she was the essence of victory. She was all he had fought for and all that had kept him alive, yet having not only a gentlemanly but a generous nature, he was prepared to share her for a few hours more. As he leant against a wall in the ballroom, watching her dance with a heavily beribboned brigadier, Anna's boss approached him.

"Squadron Leader?" Arthur McClure extended his hand. "I wanted to offer you my warmest congratulations, Theo."

"Thanks, Mac. Very sporting of you."

"Have you and Anna decided where the ceremony will be?"

Theodore smiled as Anna passed near. "No . . . We haven't got that far. Between you and me, I couldn't care less. I'd marry her on the spot, if she'd agree. If she wants to do the deed at home, then I'm more than happy to go to America. I'd go to Timbuktu if she fancied it."

"Just so long as I can play a role, friend. I'll be your best man, if you like, or give her away, if she'll let me. Anna's a bit of a favourite around here. Don't know what I would have done without her, to tell you the truth."

"I second that."

"You haven't had an easy time of it, you and Anna. I'm damn glad I found Elisabeth before the war started, and didn't have to make sacrifices you've had to make."

"It never felt like sacrifice, Mac. I consider myself a very lucky man."

"I wonder if you know just how lucky?" Mac looked at him quizzically, and slapped him on the back. "Well, fella, the victory is yours, and all the spoils of battle. I'll shake you by the hand, and tell you that if you ever hurt a hair of that angel's head, then allies though we be, the whole US military will be gunning for you."

"Are you threatening me, Minister?"

"Darn right I am, Squadron Leader. That," he jerked his thumb at Anna as she passed in the arms of a British staff officer, "is the flower of American womanhood. I love her like a daughter. I'd be damn proud if she was my daughter. We Yanks don't like handing a prize like that to the other side, but there's been no reasoning with her. She wants you, and nothing but. Always has, since that damned night at the Kit Kat. I knew it then, from the look in her eye. You should be thanking your lucky stars."

"I am, believe me."

"I know you are, buddy. Just so long as you know how much that little girl loves you, and what a helluva big heart she has. You know what, Theo?" Theodore shook his head. "Much as it pains me to say this to a non-American, I think you deserve her. I wish you all the blessings that God can bestow."

"Thanks again, Mac. I'll bear your offer in mind – about being my best man. I think that might please us both, very much."

It was a time when men couldn't quite embrace, but they pumped hands and slapped each other's back. As Mac drifted off, Theodore lit a cigarette, and admired his fiancée's perfor-

mance. He did not feel jealousy, only pride. At long last, Anna and love were within his grasp. He had held his hopes at arm's length for so long, had so often feared that her heart might slip away from him, and now he held it in his fist as he watched her dance. He speculated how little time he'd get with the bride at his own wedding, and grinned.

"Could you spare me one of those?" The voice startled him.

"Chantal, I didn't expect to see you here." She looked elegant, in a neat black dress, her dark hair coiled on top of her head.

She leant against the wall next to him. "Didn't you? I told you I did some work for the Americans. Perhaps they thought there wouldn't be enough women around. Could I have a cigarette?"

"Of course." He lit it for her. He hoped she wouldn't suggest they dance. "I didn't know you were in Rome."

"I didn't know that you were. Aren't you dancing?"

Theodore patted his thigh. "I'm sitting out tonight. Gammy leg."

"What a shame. I haven't seen you since before the victory."

"It's been busy. Office work, really, bureaucracy, and we're still flying."

"You don't have to make excuses. That's your girl, isn't it? There. La bionda." She waved her

cigarette in Anna's direction. The music had stopped, and Anna was standing in a group of three Americans. As Chantal pointed at her, Anna turned round and smiled at them. "You were right. She is beautiful. Quite lovely. Would you introduce me?"

"That's not a sensible idea, Chantal."

"You don't think I would do anything to hurt you, do you, Theodore? Or do you think we would have nothing to say to one another?"

Whatever Theodore thought, it was too late. Anna was weaving her way through the crowd to him, just as she had two years before. His heart raced.

"Darling, I didn't mean to abandon you," she was breathless. "I had no idea how many old friends would be here. Hello. I am Anna Kézdy. And you are . . . ?"

"Anna, may I introduce Signora Molesini? Miss Anna Kézdy."

"Chantal, please."

"I'm happy to meet you, Chantal."

"As I am to meet you. You dance very well. You look like a professional."

"Thanks. I've had practice, that's all. Are you enjoying the party, Chantal? You're French, aren't you? I don't have much of an ear for accents – there are so many nationalities here, I'm getting confused!"

"You're right. I am French, originally."

"Come join us for supper soon. Please. We're

forming a party of eight and would be delighted to have you at our table."

"That is very generous of you, Miss Kézdy."

"Call me Anna. This is no night for formalities, is it, Theo? Tonight of all nights?"

"Then thank you, Anna, but I am afraid I cannot stay for supper. I have to return to Naples early tomorrow. I should leave now."

"What a shame! Never mind. I'm sure our paths will cross again." Anna's hand was held out to Chantal Molesini, but her eyes were already on Theodore's.

"Perhaps – you never know. Squadron Leader, you will come to say goodbye before you leave Italy? I would like to see you before you go."

"Of course. Goodnight, Signora. And a safe journey home." Theodore kept his eyes locked on Anna, and his hand at her elbow.

"You will come to see me? Before you leave?"

"Yes, yes."

"We should talk."

"Yes." Theodore finally turned to her with ill-concealed annoyance. 'I will come to pay my respects, signora. I give you my word." Chantal walked away from them and straight up the stairs.

"Who was that, Theo? It didn't sound like you like her much."

"She's an interpreter, the widow of an Italian shot down in the desert. It makes me uncomfortable talking to her, that's all."

"What did she want to talk about?"

"I don't know, some nonsense. Probably looking for a job." The band struck up the haunting opening bars of 'Sentimental Journey'. "Dance with me, Anna? Now it's all over."

Theodore did not go to see Chantal Molesini. He gave Naples a wide berth. He sent her no word of explanation, and felt he owed her none.

Early one evening, eight days after the embassy dance, Theodore sat in Feathershawe's office, discussing his future over a whisky. The Group Captain's aide tapped on the door. "Excuse me, sir. There's a lady outside to see the Squadron Leader." Theodore stood up.

"Anna? What a pleasant surprise! Good Lord, Hamilton, you do keep your cards close to your chest. Brought her along to twist my arm, did you? Very devious." Feathershawe patted the side of his nose with a finger. "Don't keep her hanging around, old chap! Show her in!"

"I'm sorry, sir, the lady was very specific. She said she wanted to see Squadron Leader Hamilton, and only Squadron Leader Hamilton."

"That doesn't sound like Anna." Feathershawe cocked his head. "Hamilton!" he barked, as Theodore strode to the door. "Not so fast. That'll do, Beecher." The aide closed the door behind him.

Theodore turned to face his group captain reluctantly, his mouth in a tight line. "I suspect it's Signora Molesini, sir. She mentioned she might visit the base the last time we met."

"And she wants to see you and only you, hmm? Very devious. Do you want to sit yourself down and tell me what's going on, you silly fool?" Theodore lowered his eyes. The older man grunted. "I have a damn good idea what this is about. I can't entirely blame you. You're not the first chap to find his will-power sliding when he's not sure he'll get his allotted share of . . . Well, Hamilton, you'd best see her in here. I'll make myself scarce. I expect you to come and find me in my quarters when the lady's gone."

Theodore spoke to Chantal for an hour and was back in front of the Groupie before dinner. He spent two hours arguing with Feathershawe and left with a pass for indefinite leave, and permission to transport a Mosquito to Cairo the following morning. He sent Anna a signal.

She met him at Almaza, as beautiful as he had ever seen her. She leant against him in the rear seat of Mac's open car, her hands wrapped close around his upper arm, her flushed cheek against his shoulder. "Mac's away. When he heard you'd managed to scheme a trip to Cairo, he said the least you deserved was a car and driver. We can go out to the Pyramids, or as far as Luxor, if you like. We could get the train. Millie went last week. *Did I tell you she's going to marry an Egyptian? Oh, Theo. I can't tell you how I felt when I got your wire. It's only a few weeks since Rome – I never dreamt you'd get leave so soon. How did you pull it off? Is Feathers still in one piece? There's a catch, isn't there? You've got to work all the time – you're being transferred to London or something – out with it! Give me the bad news, I can take it.*"

Theodore sat stiffly and silently.

"*Theo? What's happened?*"

"*Nothing, darling. I'm just tired.*"

"*You're not sick, are you? Theo, I know something's happened. You've lost someone, haven't you? Not Jimmy? Dear God, not Bob?*"

"*No. It's not that, I promise you, darling.*"

"*Where do you want to go? Shepheard's?*"

"*As you like, Anna.*"

She leant forward and spoke to the driver, then continued talking. "*I booked a room at the Continental. I said we might meet Millie and her fiancé for a drink, but if you're not in the mood, we don't have to – we don't have to do anything at all you don't feel like, so long as we're together. It's all over now, isn't it, darling? All over, the wishing, and wanting and praying . . .*"

He pulled her tightly against him, closed his eyes and wondered if there was any more wishing he could do. He wanted to get out of the car and be alone somewhere with her, and there wasn't anywhere in the whole of Cairo where they could be alone. When they arrived at Shepheard's, and the manager came out to greet him and kissed Anna's hand, Theodore felt the crowds close in around him, and found the noise and heat oppressive. Only half the terrace tables were occupied.

"God damn this city," he said suddenly. "It's impossible to find any peace and quiet."

Anna looked at him with eyes wide in surprise. "Theo, Cairo's dead. It's as quiet as the grave. Italy must be crashingly dull if you find this too much. It sounds to me like you've been working too hard. Let's have champagne, darling. It's back in the cellars at last, and 1934 at that. Let's celebrate!"

"Anna, we have to talk – I have to tell you –"

"Shush, darling. Not now. Let me just look at you. Let me sit back and look at your face and pinch myself until I'm certain that you're really here."

Theodore looked at those emerald eyes and full red lips, and the auburn gold of her hair, and watched his dreams dissolve. In the background, the music played on and the low chatter of voices filled his head. He had come to say goodbye, but when he looked at her, he doubted he would have the courage to see it through. Even then, he wondered if there wasn't a way out of it all – if he could escape Chantal, deny that anything had ever happened, if he could run so fast and so far that he would never be caught, and Anna need never know anything. He looked at her and wished that he had been shot down rather than arrive at this point.

"Something is wrong. You're hiding something from me." She leant across the table and took his hand. "Darling, do you remember Sham el Nessim?"

"How could I ever forget it?"

"You have the same expression on your face – it's making me nervous."

"I'm sorry, golden girl. I've felt so lonely the past few weeks, and I don't seem able to pull myself out of it."

"Then you listen to me. The war is over. We're all going home and everything's going to be fine. I want you to meet my family – but if you don't want to, that's fine, too. It may just break my daddy's heart, but if you want to get married first, and then go home and meet the crew, that's fine by me. Whatever you want. I want you to be happy, and happy you will be!"

"Anna, could we go to your apartment? I want to get away from these people. I have to be alone with you."

"Not in my apartment you won't be . . . We've got three girls staying with us and Millie's getting ready for a party. She's had a party every night this week – I haven't had a glimpse of the silver dress – Guess what? She said she'd give it to me as an engagement present, just as I was saying I'd do the same for her – I think I'll treat myself to a new dress – She's dying to see you, darling,

we planned on a joint celebration. The barman
at the Turf sold me three cases of champagne on
the cheap, Cairo's awash with the stuff. We'll go
over there now if you want. I'll need to change,
but you can sit on the edge of the bath and talk
to me while I get ready . . . Oh, Theo. I've never
let myself believe until now. And here we are!
Let's drink to it." She raised her glass, and
touched his lightly.

Theodore stood up and walked into the hotel.
A few minutes later, he came back and took her
by the arm. "Come on. We're going upstairs."

"Darling, can't you wait a little bit longer?
Till after the party?" He pulled her along at such
a pace she complained she'd fall off her heels. He
took a key out of his pocket and opened the door
of a suite. Anna's eyes shone even more brightly.
"Theodore – how romantic."

"Anna, sit down."

"What?"

"Just sit down, dearest. I need to talk to you."
Anna sat on a small stool in front of an ornate
dressing table. Theodore paced the room until
there was a tap at the door.

The suffragi brought in a tray of drinks – the
champagne they had left on the table, a bottle of
single malt whisky and a single red flower. He
bowed low. "With the manager's compliments.
The whisky – he only has ten bottles – is a gift to
Squadron Leader Hamilton. The flower is for
Miss Kézdy. He says he misses seeing a flower in

her hair." He withdrew with the sound of his slippers slapping against the marble floor.

"How sweet of him," Anna said quietly. Her eyes were tracking Theodore's restless pacing.

"Yes. Very decent."

"Pass me my glass."

Theodore did so, but in front of her fell to his knees and laid his head in her lap. Her hand hovered above his head, before gently stroking his fair hair. "Anna," he groaned. "Anna, I don't know how to say what I have to say . . ."

She spoke so quietly that he had to lift his head off her knee to hear her. "I know what you want to say, Theo, and I don't want to hear it. Not now. Tomorrow you can tell me everything, but now, I don't want to know."

"Anna, you don't understand. I have to talk to you. I have to tell you –"

"No, you don't. I don't want to hear bad news. I want to celebrate the end of our war, whatever it is that you have to tell me. Don't rob me of this, Theo. If you love me at all, do as I ask, please."

The temptation to pretend that things were otherwise was too great. He wanted to slip into blissful oblivion, even at the cost of a worse awakening in the morning. Still kneeling at her feet, Theodore embraced her. "Anna Kézdy. Listen to me carefully." She stiffened against him. "No, my golden girl, I am not about to make confession. Let's have tonight, as we are, as you say. I love you, Anna. I love you with all my heart. I always will. You are my life. Always."

Anna slid down from her seat until she was facing him on her knees, trembling in his arms. Theodore began to weep, the sobs racking his chest, and Anna held him, as she had before, at Sham el Nessim. And as she had then, she unbuttoned his jacket and shirt, and laid them on the stool, and gently led him to the bed. For a long time, Theodore lay crying in her arms. She knew that he was mourning someone but not who it was, and she held him as his body shuddered against hers. Slowly, he calmed under her touch, and although he tried to hold himself away, and although his eyes remained full of sadness, passion overwhelmed them and he lost himself in her. For some time after Anna lay awake. She had no doubt that he loved her, but something about him had changed, and it frightened her. She woke often to search his face and smooth the heavy frown that scarred his young brow.

At dawn, she slipped out of bed and stood naked at the window, relishing the sensation of the slight breeze against her bare skin. The streets were silent. The city was beginning to resettle itself into peacetime, no longer beset by the bustle and noise of troops. Anna wondered what her mother would say if she could see her there, and thought how shocked she would be by the knowledge that her daughter had a lover. She believed that her parents would love Theodore as she did.

She had been raised to be a good girl. She had expected celibacy before marriage, and fidelity after it, and to raise a family of good girls and good boys, and the war had changed everything and nothing. The war had given her a ticket to freedom and allowed her to fall in love, and falling in love had caused her to do things and think things she hadn't expected. Now that the war was over, she would not go home to her family. She would go to England and become part of Theodore's family and would raise one of their own. She wondered how much she would tell her daughters of the lessons she had learnt during the war. She returned to bed, and fell asleep on Theodore's chest.

When she woke, he was dressing. She watched him through half-closed eyes, admiring the smooth muscularity of him and relishing the secrecy of her observation. He knotted his tie carefully and combed his thick hair. He started when she murmured his name. She stretched out her naked arms.

"Darling . . . Good morning."

"Anna . . ." He sat beside her on the bed, and tentatively touched her hair.

"I feel like a newly fallen woman all over again . . . It's rather delicious."

He turned away, and put his head in his hands. "Anna, please get dressed." His voice was tense. She rose quickly and shyly, feeling

Theodore's eyes on her back, and began to dress. Once she had slipped on her skirt, and was rolling on her stockings, Theodore began to speak.

"What I tell you will make you hate me. Even more so, now."

"So, tell me." She stretched out her leg, carefully smoothing the stocking so as not to snag it.

"I met a woman in Naples."

"Oh, yes?" She sounded as if he had told her that his WingCo had a new posting. "I thought so."

"Anna – Lord God!' His jaw clenched, a muscle twitching. "Come here, Anna. Please."

"In a moment. Let me finish."

"Anna, we had an affair."

"I know."

"I felt – she's a very sad woman – she's French –"

Anna stared at him. "It was that woman, wasn't it? That strange woman at the embassy dance – the one who wouldn't let you go. Jesus, Theodore, you even introduced me to her! How could you?"

"She's the widow of a pilot who bought it in '41."

"I don't care to hear about her or her husband. It doesn't make any difference to me, does it? Not where she's from, or when he got the chop." She spoke with brutal lightness.

He lit a cigarette, and as Anna held out her hand, passed it to her. "No, I suppose it doesn't. It made a difference to me."

She looked up at him quickly, holding the cigarette an inch from her lips. "Then I was wrong, it does matter. Tell me about her."

"I saw her several times. I wasn't attracted to her. I pitied her. She was so alone."

"I see."

"I wish you could. I wish I could myself." He dragged his hands through his hair. "It was nothing. I went to her home for dinner . . . I took her to the opera."

"In Rome?"

"No, in Naples. Does that matter, Anna? Does it matter where we bloody went?"

"No, I don't suppose it does." She was putting on her shoes, turning her feet this way and that, checking her seams with great concentration.

"I escorted her home –"

"How gentlemanly."

"Stop it, Anna. There's nothing you can say that makes it worse for me than it already is."

"I'm sorry. Do go on." Anna took a lipstick out of her bag and, although she was sitting in front of a large mirror, a small compact, and began to paint her lips carefully. Theodore could see her hands shaking. She made an exasperated noise as she wiped her lips with a handkerchief and began again.

"I went to bed with her, Anna. That night, and afterwards."

"Thank you for telling me. Are you going to

tell me precisely how many times?" She pulled her skirt down as she stood up, and cleared her throat with a small nervous sound.

"Four. Anna. The thing is that she's pregnant."

"Oh. I see." She blinked slowly several times, feathery lashes batting against her cheeks. "No, I'm not so sure that I do."

"She's going to have a baby. My baby." Anna stared at him uncomprehendingly. "I had decided to break it off. From the very first night, I regretted it. It was a mistake. I didn't love her – I don't – I tried my damnedest to avoid her. When I was with her, all I could see was you. I told her it couldn't happen again. I couldn't do anything –"

"Except make love to her?"

"No! Each time I saw her, I went to tell her it had to stop. She wouldn't accept it – she wouldn't listen. She knew about you. She said you would understand, that it didn't mean anything. She said that when the war was over, we would go our separate ways in time. She said you'd be glad for me."

"She said what?" Anna's question hung in the room.

"In the beginning. That it was only a night's comfort. Oh, God. I can't lay the blame on her. I swear to God I didn't want to sleep with her, not then, but once it happened . . ." He sat down heavily on the bed, running his hand repeatedly *through his fair hair, unable to look at her.*

"And now she's going to have a baby?" He hung his head. "And you really believe that you are the father?"

He nodded. "She's not what you think, Anna. She's a decent woman."

"What on earth makes you think that?"

"Anna. Oh, God in heaven –"

"She might be sleeping with ten different men for all you know. Maybe she just fixed on you as the most gullible. Perhaps the others are already married, or smarter than you are. She saw a good-looking, unattached English flier, and thought, That'll do, that'll be the way to change sides . . . If we hadn't won the war she'd be looking for a handsome young Luftwaffe officer."

"Anna, don't."

"Don't what?" She stumbled as she stood, and grimaced with pain as her hand went to her ankle. Theodore moved to her side. "Don't touch me!" she snapped at him, and sat down again, rubbing her ankle. "I can't believe what a poor innocent fool you are, Theo. You're no more than a schoolboy, under that uniform."

"Anna, I believe her. She's not a loose woman. It was a mistake. It was my mistake. It happened. I have to face it. I have to be honest with you."

"This morning, but not last night?"

"Anna –"

"Oh, don't bother to defend yourself. So you tried to tell me. Fine."

She swivelled round to face the mirror. She swept a comb through her hair and picked up a black velvet bow to hold it back. Theodore watched her silently. "She has to take responsibility. That's what women have to do, after all. I'm sorry for her, really, but it's up to her now. There are things she can do, if she's not willing to have a baby."

"Anna, she's a Catholic. She can't."

Anna stopped, one arm arched over her head as she patted the bow into place, the other frozen as if reaching for her cigarette. She looked at him in the mirror. "So am I, Theodore. So am I," she said quietly.

"If I leave her – if I do a runner – I'm not worth having – can't you see that?"

"You can give her money. For the child."

"I won't be worth anything at all if that's what I do."

"You're not worth a red cent now."

Theodore flinched. "If I had never told you, if I had just lived with it myself, it might have been possible. I don't know. I think it would have driven me insane. I cannot be an honourable man and walk out on her. Can I?" He spread his hands wide, in a gesture of inquiry.

Anna stood up and steadied herself against the edge of the table. She picked up the bottle of whisky that had been untouched the night before, poured a shot into her dirty champagne glass and drank it with a grimace. "Would you pass me *my jacket?"*

He handed it across to her, and she put it on.

"Anna, it's blazing hot outside."

"If it's all the same to you, I'd rather not go about Cairo in my blouse. Don't look so blue, Theodore. We always agreed there would be no tears, no regrets, and no recriminations. I'm going to keep my side of the bargain. I'm going to work now. I don't suppose we'll meet again." *She picked up her purse. "Before I go, I want you to know something. I want you to know that I did love you – that I do love you – as much as I can ever love a man. And I am going to say goodbye, but I wonder how you would feel, what you would consider the 'honourable' thing, were I to find myself in the same position as your French whore?"* *As she stepped past him, her fingers briefly touched the wings on his jacket and then he heard the door close behind her.*

Theodore moved to the window. For all the hurt he had felt in the past four years, all the fear, all the grieving for the friends he had lost, and those he had left behind, he had never had such a pain in his heart as he did then. From the window he watched Anna walk down the steps, her head held a fraction too high. He watched her pass the figure of the old Arab who habitually stood near the terrace of Shepheard's, just far enough away to avoid being moved on by the doormen. He could hear the vendor's plaintive, piercing cry: "Cigarettes! Chocolate!

OBEs!" and his eyes followed her until she was lost among the people going about their regular morning business.

It ended as it began, on the terrace at Shepheard's.

CHAPTER NINETEEN

I wanted to see my parents – that was what made me go home. Otherwise, I would have quite happily scrapped the publisher's deadline and spent the summer vegetating on Theodore's terrace. David was happy in either place; his sole motivation seemed to be to accommodate me. Much as Theodore tried to nudge him in the direction of the *bastides* during our last week, David wouldn't take any photographs except of me and Theodore, and he took us endlessly. I have virtual mountains of photographs of myself from that week, the last of me pre-baby. The photographs of Theodore are precious: there are enough to devote a book to him alone. I even suggested it to David – a kind of 'portrait of an old man' thing.

It was hard leaving the sanctuary of Sainte Cécile, where I had felt cosseted from the realities that had to be faced, but my memories of that final week are tooth-tinglingly sweet. David's stunned expression

when he heard the baby's heart. The doctor's sudden
broad smile. My laughter, and how it made the baby
jump. And always Theodore's gentle courtesy and
care. I will never forget him. But all week, I missed
my parents, and I knew that my wilful state of paralysis was drawing to its close. I booked tickets home
for the Friday, and arranged to have dinner with
Theodore on the Thursday night. When it came to
six o'clock, David stalled.

"You go, Elle. I'll join you later."

"What are you talking about?"

"You go have dinner with him, Elle, and I'll come
in a while. I promise."

I went to Theodore's on my own. I had the
feeling I could be doing that a lot in the future.
Theodore kissed me on the doorstep, as did Giselle.
We headed for the terrace. His home had become as
familiar to me as my own. "You've been so good to
us, Theodore. I honestly don't know what I would
have done without you. I don't like saying
goodbye."

"Then don't say it. I count on you and David
coming back to introduce me to your child. I will
hold you to that."

He had the sweetest face. I know how silly that
sounds. If I describe him – a tall old man with a
stoop, lean-featured, deeply wrinkled, with creases
that shaped and draped his skull, eyes bleary, hands
with the occasional tremble, hair thick and lush and
yellowish white – even then, you could never see
what I saw. But if you look at David's photographs

of him, you can see everything, all his experience and all his hope and trust. The wrinkles only emphasized the elegance and dignity of his face. He was the second kindest man I have ever met, and I absolutely hated saying goodbye.

"Theodore, we're going home tomorrow. We have to finish this book. Talking of which, I brought my trusty tape recorder again. Can I do one last session on the RAF? For old times' sake?"

"I'm prepared to ignore the dratted machine, but I don't know that I have any more to say."

"Try. For me. If you had to sum it all up, once and for all, what would you say?" I pushed the on button. I didn't want this for the book. I wanted a record of his voice.

"Thirty years ago I stopped thinking about it as an experience of war. I never dreamt anyone would come asking questions. It shocks me how fresh the memories are, and how pleasurable it has been to speak of them." He spoke slowly, pausing often, and considering each sentence with care. "They were probably the happiest years I ever spent. Naturally, there were heavy costs – grief for the loss of friends, alarm for one's own life, boredom, and depression too – but to have that companionship, to enjoy good health, be physically fit, and take responsibility for a well-defined job . . . Those are enormous compensations when one is young. I also remember having the deepest respect for the enemy. They were talented airmen and, by and large, honourable men, I am certain of that. There was a comradeship in enduring the same danger."

"So what was it really about? For you personally."

"It was the most vivid part of my life. A thrilling way to come of age. Many of the types like myself had never before left England, and were thrown into the Middle East – leaves in Tunis, Tripoli, Cairo, of course. There was an air of exotic adventure. And one felt useful. The victory on the North African front was an enormous morale-boost to the Allies – at least, so we told ourselves. And I loved flying, from the first time to the last. Entering the blue, the release from the pull of the earth, gave me the feeling of being almost, if not, quite immortal."

As we ate, I let the tape run, and Theodore talked easily. I thought about excising everyone else from the book. Theodore took the plates inside and came back with another bottle of wine.

"Theodore, if my obstetrician knew how much I've had to drink in the past month, I would be struck off his books and held up as an object of ignominy. I'll be the talk of antenatal classes from Islington to Chiswick."

"What did Dr Duhaze say?"

"He said red wine never did man, woman or child any harm in his experience, so long as it was decent quality."

"Thank God for men like Dr Duhaze. Let's drink a toast to him. If anyone ever questions you, say you acted on medical advice. Here's to the noble doctor."

"Why is it that he doesn't like you?"

"I don't think he doesn't like me, my dear, but he suspects me."

"Of what?"

"Oh, of killing my wife, I suppose." Theodore sipped his wine, and closed his eyes, savouring the taste. "And he's quite right to do so. I did kill her, technically." As I stared at him, he went to check the pool filters, but came back quite unconcerned.

"She was in great pain at the end. I had promised myself long before that I would never allow anyone to suffer such pain, let alone someone I loved, and I had promised her that if there was any way I could stop it, I would. Duhaze was a willing if covert accomplice. We have never talked about it, and I trust you to destroy the evidence your blasted machine makes, unless you fancy seeing us on a murder charge. Chantal was on heavy doses of a pain-killer – basically morphine – but in the end it wasn't enough, and I couldn't stand to watch her. Duhaze had been zealous in telling me which drugs could be fatal. I listened to him and acted on it. I robbed him of his patient. And time of its course."

"He must understand how you felt – and that Chantal would have wanted it."

"Elena, it wasn't quite as simple as that. It never is. Can you imagine either of your parents or your brother – Charlie, is it? – or David, or a child of yours, and see yourself as the agent of their death? Even if they were in a state of extreme pain?"

"No, but I *can't* imagine any of them in that position, and what's more, I do my damnedest not to. I don't know if I'd be able to say goodbye."

"You're quite right to feel that. I believe that Dr Duhaze felt as you do. As a Catholic, he could not officially countenance it, and as a doctor, he could not permit a layman's intervention in the course of disease. Most of all, he did not accept the purity of my motive. "

"He must have seen that you did it for her."

"Elena. I have wanted to tell you this story a number of times. It is a story that concerns your mother, and that is why I want you to hear it, but it has a bearing on Chantal and Duhaze. I didn't kill my wife because I loved your mother. I killed Chantal because I loved her, and for no other reason. Not to spare myself, not even to spare Liliane. But for Dr Duhaze, your mother was a factor. Not that he knows that Anna is *your* mother. I wonder what he would think if he did?"

He smiled as he refilled our glasses. Then at last he told me the story that I had been hungering to hear, and had persuaded myself I shouldn't know. This is what he says on the tape.

"I have said that I loved your mother more than life itself, and that is true. I have only to look at her photograph to feel twenty-six years old and sick with love again. I recover the feeling merely by looking at you. Anna had a magic about her. Wildly sophisticated and worldly to my eyes, yet she had an innocence. It is easier for me to appreciate her qualities now than it was then. Then, the thought of her drove me near mad, I wanted her so much. And no, my dear, before you blush, I don't mean just physically. That, too, of course – passion played its role. Yet it was not only that. I saw her as my hope for the future. One looked for symbols, and Anna was mine. She was my perfect amulet. And I betrayed it."

I wished with all my heart that I could have seen her as she was then, just for a moment. In my mind, I could see her bustling about, on those flat feet, and telling me off without putting real effort into it, and lying on her bed with her glasses on top of her head and papers spread all around her. I could see her at Christmas, and walking the dogs, and hailing taxis in the rain, and persuading complete strangers to do all sorts of extraordinary things for her, and I could see her old and exhausted as when she had arrived in Sainte Cécile a few weeks previously, but I couldn't see her in 1943, in Cairo.

"How?"

"In the spring of 1945, the 37th was still stationed in Italy. The Group Captain, a good man called Feathershawe, introduced me to the widow of an Italian pilot, Chantal Molesini. She was French, but had lived in Italy for some ten years. When we first met, we kept each other company, quite innocently. When I went to Naples, and couldn't see your mother, I took her out or had a meal at her house. One night, we went to bed. I knew I would regret it before it happened, and I did, but that did not stop the affair immediately. Neither of us intended anything to come of it. Chantal told me she was pregnant a few weeks after VE Day. Your mother and I were planning our wedding. To my shame, I toyed with the notion of abandoning her. It was not entirely concern for Chantal that prevented me from taking that route: it was the thought of your mother, and my remaining vestiges of self-respect. You cannot elect happiness, after all, but you can choose whether or not you listen to your conscience. I told Anna the truth and married Chantal. I tell you this now, because I do not want you to think for a moment that your mother has ever done anything wrong in her life. She has not. Not to my knowledge."

"But you loved her?"

"My God, I loved her so much I could not contain it."

"Why couldn't you just tell that to Chantal?" Theodore looked at me strangely. "It wasn't the done thing then?" I suggested limply.

"It isn't the done thing now. I may be old-fashioned, but I still believe people should take responsibility for their actions, however foolishly they are committed."

"Surely she could have had an abortion?"

"She wouldn't consider it. She never pretended it was a question of religious devotion. She simply wanted the child."

"You could have given her money – anything. Supported them . . ." I couldn't help thinking of David.

Theodore shook his head. "Even beyond the

social disgrace, Chantal was the French widow of an enemy airman. I had no confidence in how the occupying forces might treat her. Her husband's people were a respected, upstanding Catholic family. How might they have treated her, and everyone else she knew in Naples, when they found she was expecting a child three years after her husband's death? Had I abandoned Chantal and married your mother, I would have been a cad, and worse, I would have known myself to be one. Your mother deserved better than that. And I am sure she found it."

"What did my mother say? What did she do?"

Theodore slumped back in his chair as if I had struck him. For the first time he seemed frail.

"She was generous, as was her nature. I told Feathershawe the truth, in order to get special leave. He tore a strip off me, then told me to fly myself to Cairo and not come back. He was fond of me. I told Anna quite simply what had happened, but it was not an easy task, telling her goodbye. I never saw her again, after that night. I have never stopped loving her, I want you to know that, but also that I came to love my wife very much."

He reached for his glass on the little table, but his hand was shaking so much that he knocked it over the edge. It smashed on the stone flagging. As I bent to pick up the pieces, he continued abruptly, "Being in love may not be the best precursor to marriage. Romance depends on desire and expectation; perhaps all romances end at marriage. Chantal loved me from the first, or so she said, but it took me years to learn to love her. I wish that it hadn't. I wish she had believed on the day she died that I had loved her as much the first time we met as I did that day."

I wondered how many days my mother had wept, after Theodore had told her it was over, and if Theodore was the one-and-only great love of her life. I wondered how I would feel, if David had told me the day he'd got back that he'd slept with some woman and that she was pregnant, and that he had to stand by her. I wouldn't care what kind of a shit it made him, I'd expect him to dump her, whether I was pregnant or not. I thought how my mother, since I'd told her that I'd met Theodore Hamilton, had never said one word against him, never even given the impression that he had been at fault. She had even encouraged me to think she'd been responsible. I thought of a young woman preparing for her wedding day, and learning that the man she adored and had waited for was walking away. All that romance, all that love and hoping, came down to nothing but a bleak description of accidental pregnancy. As I sat silently, listening, the floodlights came on around the pool, and Theodore started talking again.

"When Chantal was dying, she became very upset about your mother. I know that she spoke to Dr Duhaze about it. She felt she had robbed me and, more, robbed Anna. They met once, you know. Chantal was in great distress over it. I did everything I could to reassure her, but she insisted that I found out what had happened to Anna Kézdy . . . I was reluctant. All I knew was that Anna had married an Englishman called Ben Stewart. I dreaded what I might learn. In the final week of her life, I lied to Chantal. I claimed to have contacted the US State Department, and learnt that Anna had married a diplomat in January 1946, and that they were living in Singapore." He spoke with a clipped voice. 'That Anna and her American husband had four children. That Anna was happy. That I probably hadn't crossed her mind since 1945. The last might have been true. That night, Chantal wanted to drink champagne. She couldn't drink at all – she was fed by a tube. She wanted Liliane to be there, and I got a bottle of champagne – I remember it was warm, stupidly I had none chilled – and Liliane and I sat with her, and I held a glass of champagne to her lips. She *choked* on it. We didn't speak of Anna again. Liliane and I finished the champagne that night. Three days later, Chantal asked me to stop it all. I remember how she put it." The pool lights glinted on the snail-like trace of tears down his weathered face. "She said, 'Let me fly once, Theo. Help me to *fly* once.' I killed her that night."

My face was wet with tears. "You didn't kill her."

"I know that. Not everyone agrees."

"You mean the doctor? Fuck him."

"Oh, he didn't mind about the overdose. He simply hears her saying that I never loved her, never wanted to marry her, only did so because she was pregnant, that she ruined my life, and the life of a

511

beautiful American girl – that's what he hears when he looks at me."

"Do your children know why you and Chantal married? Liliane was the baby? I mean, that pregnancy? Did you tell her?"

"I told Liliane everything that night. But no, Elena, she wasn't the baby. Chantal and I married on my return from Cairo. I immediately rejoined the squadron, although Feathershawe offered me emergency demobilization. Six weeks later, when I was at the airbase, hating her, Chantal miscarried."

"Oh, *God*." I hadn't meant to speak.

"That's precisely what I thought. I was on the point of calling your mother and saying we could marry as if nothing had happened. Except that it was too late. We couldn't go back. Chantal had six miscarriages in all. One every year. Those were the years when I grew to love her. Eight years after we married, we adopted Liliane. Two years later, we adopted Michel. He must be your age now."

"How awful for you. How awful for *her*. I'm so sorry. How . . ." I wasn't avoiding a word, I just didn't know what to say, just as I'd felt when he'd first told me that his wife had died of cancer. What can you say? What can anyone say? What do you do but weep, and pray like all hell that nothing like that ever happens to you?

"You thought how ironic, didn't you, Elena?"

"No, I didn't."

"I did. The first time, and the second time, if I'm honest. I felt God was mocking me. Chantal was in a US military hospital in Naples when she first miscarried. I received a signal at the base. I didn't go to her, didn't even request permission for three days. I sat tight, trying not to think. The second time we were in London. I took her to hospital and walked out on her. I walked around King's Cross, and thought, How ironic. How *ironic* to say goodbye to Anna Kézdy for this. I may not have abandoned Chantal, but I was still an out-and-out cad."

"But it *did* work out all right. It had a happy ending, didn't it? For you, and my mother, and Chantal, and your children. Ma asked me if you had children – she *wanted* you to have been happy and have children. My mother spoke so highly of you when she was here. She still thinks you are a wonderful man."

"She was in Sainte Cécile?"

I was hesitant to confirm it – I'd promised my mother, but not all promises are meant to be kept. "After I came out of hospital. Just for a day. You should have heard how she talked about you – so warmly. If she ever blamed you, she certainly doesn't now. She wanted to come and see you, honestly, but she didn't have time."

Theo played with the leaves of the vine that trailed along the terrace. "It is easy to tell someone that you love them or that you forgive them. It is easy to say all manner of things." He paused for a while and I waited. "I believe you should watch what people do, and judge them on that. Perhaps Anna forgave me, but she did not want to see me."

513

"Only because she's too vain. She wants you to remember her as a beautiful young woman, not an old bag."

"There has barely been a day since you arrived in Sainte Cécile when I haven't thought of her as a beautiful woman. Can she imagine that, at my age and decrepitude, I expect her to be young? Seventy-five years must sit easily on those shoulders."

"She wouldn't thank you for that. She's only seventy-three."

He gave his great barking laugh. "A slip of a girl!" He smiled at me with his old spirit. "Do an old man a favour, Elena, when you get home. Tell her it would be a great honour for me to escort her to dinner, if she would be my guest. It would be a joy. Give her my number, and persuade her to use it. There are so many things I would like to tell her."

"You want me to arrange a blind date? A dinner date? Dancing?" I asked mischievously.

"You do me an injustice, but it is worth it to be teased by a pretty girl again."

"And what about my poor old father?"

"I would be honoured to meet him as well. Please tell him so. Now, if I am not mistaken, David is about to join us."

Theodore's eyes were keener than mine. I followed his gaze, and saw a dark shadow moving up the drive. I ran towards him, regretting that I'd taken the car and made him limp all the way from the hotel.

"Shush, darling. Have you had a good time? I

wanted you and your pilot to have some time alone. "

"*My* pilot?"

"Yes, sweetheart, *your* pilot."

I don't know that I would have described the evening with Theodore Hamilton as a good time, but when David appeared out of the dark, I was walking on air with elation. We strolled back to the pool arm in arm, David swinging a bottle of champagne in his free hand.

"Theodore, excuse my late arrival. I'm bearing gifts."

Theodore staggered slightly as he rose to shake David's hand, and I put my arm out instinctively. "I'm all right, my dear. I'll just go and get some appropriate glasses."

I went instead. When I came back, they were both laughing loud. There was something between them that always made me feel as if I had walked in unannounced. David poured the fizz, then made me sit on his lap. I sat lopsided on his good leg.

"I'd like to propose a toast: to old friends, and absent ones, and journeys and homecomings. To three-legged horses, and the ones that get away. To the desert, and to Sarajevo. To the 37th Squadron, to wild young women, and wild old men –"

"*David!*" I elbowed him in the ribs, but he only laughed.

"And to *you*, Wing Commander."

I wanted to jump to my feet and salute Theo, make some gesture, however silly, but I didn't have the nerve. We raised our glasses to him, and there was a pause as Theodore looked at us. Then he stood up, shoulders flung back, back straight, chin up. "Unaccustomed as I have become to making speeches, the evening calls for something, ah, formal." He cleared his throat, hummed a bar of Lili Marlene and sang at the top of his voice,

> *"There's a certain Squadron, way up in the blue,*
> *We don't need no orders, we know what to do.*
> *We bomb Benghazi every night –*
> *And when we don't, we all get tight.*
> *We're going to bomb Ben-ghazi, we're going there*
> *tonight.*
>
> *Wing Commander Simpson leads us on our way*
> *Leads us when we're working, leads us when we*
> *play,*
> *Give him a ladle when he's tight,*
> *And eight five-hundred-pounders the following*
> *night,*
> *He's going to bomb Ben-ghazi, he's going there*
> *tonight."*

Would anyone have believed that in the midsummer of 1992, the three of us sat around a pool in Lot-et-Garonne singing songs about bombing cities? To all right-minded liberals, it would have been a disgrace, if not unconscionable. It wasn't either. It was a privilege to be with him.

London

Although dusk had fallen, they did not turn on the lights. They sat in the gloom side by side, on the sofa, holding hands. They had been talking there most of the afternoon, almost without moving. Everything had been said over and over, each taking opposing sides. When one changed their mind, the other courteously took up the abandoned position. After a silence, he raised her hand to his lips, and kissed it lingeringly. "My dearest girl, enough. You must go. You know it as well as I."

"I can't." Anna's eyes were red with tears, but they were wide and steady when she looked at him. "It's too late. I can't. There's no point."

"You must. For your own sake, darling, and for mine."

Anna stood up and walked to the open window, lifting back the curtain and staring into the street, dappled with lights. She automatically began to deadhead the red geraniums in the window box, scattering the brown petals into the still air and watching them drift to the street below. When she had finished the job, she moved aimlessly around the drawing room, plumping a cushion, moving an ornament, lingering over a photograph.

"David's left his cigarettes. Do you know, I

517

think I might just smoke one."

"Go on – you can afford to live dangerously. Shall I fix us a drink to go with it?"

"Why not?" She lit the cigarette carefully, holding it stiffly between unpractised fingers. "Elena looked well, didn't she?"

Ben dropped ice into two glasses, and splashed on Angostura. "She certainly did. Positively blooming."

"She's lucky. I never looked that good when I was expecting her."

"Are you begging for compliments, my darling?"

"No, Ben, I'm just stating a fact. She's taller than me, and thinner. She carries it better. I do so hope that they're going to be happy." She accepted the proffered glass, and returned to the sofa.

"Of course they are. It's high time you stopped worrying about them. They're both adult, they're well on their way, and she's earned our confidence."

"Even so, she can behave like a big kid. I wish she wouldn't go gallivanting all over the world. I wish they would both just settle down here. It's not as if David can't work here."

"Anna, old girl, they're all right."

"When David was shot in the leg only a month ago? How can you want that sort of a life for your daughter? Or your grandchild? Who knows what might happen next time he's on the road?"

"Quite. Who knows indeed? 'Who would be glad, then let him be; of tomorrow there is no certainty.'" Ben took off his glasses and pinched the bridge of his nose. "It's not for me to choose her life, and sadly, dear heart, it's not for you either, however much you wish it otherwise and however good a job you might make of it."

"Oh, Ben, she's much smarter than I was at her age – than I am now. I'd feel a little bit happier if they were married at least."

"Would you really? I had quite the opposite feeling. I think the last thing they need to feel is that they're doing what is expected of them. Let them bide their time, and wait for the baby. A baby will sort them out, you wait and see. Ours did the trick for us."

"I sorted you out, Ben, not the children." She smiled at him.

"You're right as ever, my love . . . They seemed very excited about the baby. That must please you at least?"

"Of course it does. I just don't want her to be hurt. Isn't it natural for a mother to want the best, to protect her child from hurt or harm, however old she is?"

"Yes, my dear. Of course it is. And Elena will be just the same with her child, and her child will resent it just as Elena has, and so on down the line. And by then we will be happily in our graves and well beyond the range of interference.

That's how it should be."

"Oh, Ben."

He laid his hand gently on her knee, and his wife gave him a long, sideways look. "I'll give you precisely twenty minutes to take your hand off my leg . . ." They laughed together at the old joke. She had said it to him the night they first met.

"Anna, sweetheart, will you ever stop worrying about your babies?"

"No. It's my greatest indulgence and my only vice and you should have the civility to let me get on with it."

His eyes twinkled at her beneath his heavy brows as he raised his shoulders in resignation. "All right, my love, you know best."

"I hate the way you say that. I can always tell when you think I'm in the wrong. You only say it to annoy."

"It is my greatest indulgence and my only vice . . ."

"You silly old fool." Anna patted his cheek.

"Elena was very surprised that I knew all about your old pilot."

"Wasn't she?" Anna smiled as she remembered the look on her daughter's face when Ben had calmly recounted the tale of her romance in Cairo. "She's always leapt to conclusions, ever since she was a little girl."

"Takes after her mother . . ."

"She wasn't amused by your saying that if

men only knew how devious women are, they would run a mile from them."

"She showed a lamentable lack of humour on that one. David, on the other hand, saw the joke. Now, about this old boyfriend, Anna."

"Ben, I've said my piece. I'm not going to France and that is that. You're not going to bully me on this one." Anna's jaw set in an indomitable line, and Ben's eyebrows arched clear above the rim of his glasses.

"Perhaps you could give me an example, just one, Anna, of when I have ever attempted, let alone succeeded in persuading you to do anything against your will? If anything even faintly resembling bullying has occurred in this household, I consider myself to be the victim rather than the perpetrator. I have long been a martyr to the monstrous regiment of women."

"Oh, stop it."

"All right, I will. Let me say one thing more on the subject, and then I will hold my peace. Were I in Theodore Hamilton's shoes, it would mean a great deal to me to see you before I . . . met my Maker. He sounds a very decent chap, from all that Elena has told us, and from what you yourself have told me about him over the years. We should be grateful for his care of our daughter. What reason can there be not to share good memories with an old friend?"

"Would you have said that if he had turned up twenty years ago? Thirty years ago?"

"Yes, my dear. I can say, old hand on old heart, that I would. I have nothing to fear from him, now or then. I owe him a debt of considerable gratitude, after all. His downfall was to my great benefit."

"You wouldn't feel just the tiniest bit jealous? Just a touch – apprehensive?"

"No, my dear old girl, not the tiniest bit." Anna frowned, and Ben corrected himself hurriedly, "Unless, of course, you would prefer me to feel jealous, in which case I might be able to work myself up into a dramatic rage or two. I could always bludgeon the blighter about the head with my walking stick, challenge him to a duel of canes."

"Ben, you're not taking this seriously at all."

The grin faded from his face, and his expression turned grave. "Quite the contrary, my dearest. I take your well-being more seriously than anything else in life. I firmly believe that, whatever your doubts, you would greatly enjoy talking to Theodore about the time that you spent together. That is a gift that I cannot give you."

"I wouldn't feel the same way, Ben. I wouldn't be one bit happy about you swanning off to see some old flame from the days before we met."

"Then I shall endeavour to keep mum should the situation arise."

"Ben!"

"All right, my dear, all right. Look at me, Anna." He tipped her chin so that her face was towards him. "What do you see?"

"An old fool," she snapped, before saying gently, "the man I love. A dear, honourable, good, sweet man."

"Ah, my dear, you'll break my poor old heart." His eyes filled with tears suddenly, and he did not attempt to hide his emotion. "Anna, I have not always been a good man, but I have always put you first, and I do not have a jealous bone in my body. I would feel happier if you went to see your Theodore. If I had doubts, I would certainly tell you of them. I'm an honest fellow: I would not have rejoiced had you set out to find him thirty years ago, perhaps not even ten years ago. However, at this stage in our lives, you and I know each other too well to be fearful, and Elena has brought him to our doorstep. This is for you to decide, but do not let worry about my feelings enter into your decision. You have more than my blessing."

Anna leant forward and kissed his head. "Of course, even if I did go, he'd never recognize me," she said firmly. "Not after forty-five years. He'd think me monstrously fat."

"Just filled out nicely, as my old tailor used to say."

"And I don't have anything to wear – no, really, Ben, before you say anything, I don't. No, I can't see that there's any point in this at all, unless you were to come with me. Or perhaps we could invite Theodore over here for a drink one evening."

Her husband shook his head with a smile.
"Have you listened to the tapes that Elena left?"

"No, not yet."

"In that case, I believe I'll retire to bed and
leave you to it."

"The tape won't change how I feel, no matter
what he says."

"You sleep on it. See how you feel in the
morning, old girl."

Anna Stewart sighed. "You see? It's just as I
said. You're nothing but a terrible old bully."
She followed her husband to bed a little later. She
did not listen to Elena's tape.

Anna Stewart, née Kézdy, refused to be met at the
airport that September day. They had met and
parted at so many, from Almaza and Payne
Field, to Pomigliano and Marchianese. She could
not add Toulouse. As the taxi pulled into
Theodore's drive, she saw him waiting for her,
sitting on a low stone wall, hands on his knees.
She got out on the far side of the car, keeping a
distance between them as long as she was able.
Theodore paid the driver, then held out his hands
to her. "Dear Anna. How good of you to come,
and how well you look!"

"Hello, Theodore." She was tongue-tied with
shyness, and clutched her handbag to her chest
with both hands to keep them occupied.

"You don't have any baggage?"

"No, I left it at the hotel. Where Elena stayed."

"Excellent. Would you like to sit outside, or is it too warm? We could go in if you would prefer, if you would be more comfortable . . ."

"I don't mind." She looked at him directly for the first time. "Oh, Theo. This is very strange. Do you remember . . . ?"

He tucked her hand into the crook of his elbow, patted it twice and led her to the terrace. "I remember, Anna. I remember it all."

For some time, they talked as old friends catching up on the news, asking each other about their children and boasting gently of their progeny's achievements. Anna rather inflated Charlie's academic triumphs, as Theodore did Liliane's. This was perfectly natural, and they were tolerant of each other's parental pride. They talked at length about Elena and David. Theodore wanted to know everything about Anna's career after the war. Anna asked him about his practice, and whether he had qualified at the Bar. They were looking for markers, just as Theodore used to ask his Bert to get an astral fix to plot an accurate course for the homeward journey. Slowly, the conversation moved in ever-decreasing circles towards Cairo. They began to talk of old friends in common. Anna told him that Millie had seven grandchildren, and had moved with her husband to Florida. She told him of the memorial service in DC following Arthur McClure's death ten years previously, and how many of the old Cairo hands had turned up out of the blue, some frail, some hale, and how good it had been to see them again.

"What about M for Mother, Theo?"

"Of her original crew, only Bob, Bert and myself were with the squadron in the final days. After the war Bob went back to take over his people's sheep station in Queensland. He's still there but handed over the reins to his son some time ago."

"And Bert?"

"Bert and I corresponded for years. He stayed with the RAF until he retired, to somewhere in Dorset, I believe. I last wrote to him five years ago, and Bert's daughter replied to let me know that he had passed away, quietly, in his bed. She wrote that he'd always been very proud of the fact that of all the crews that had served in the desert since 1941, ours must have been one of the few to have three out of five members survive into old age. He was a good chap."

"Yes, he was. I remember him well."

"I'd forgotten that you ever met him, Anna."

"I never did. I knew him through you, and your letters."

"I must have written a great deal of rubbish to you in those days."

She didn't reply. She didn't yet want to tell him that she had all his letters still, and having kept them untouched for some forty years, had read them several times through before coming to

France. They were in her suitcase at the hotel.

"Whatever happened to Drongie Broek?"

"Drongie Broek?" Theodore was momentarily puzzled. "He bought it, Anna, shot down at the tail end of the war. I never saw him after we moved to Italy."

"What a pity. I don't know if I ever admitted this to you, Theo, but when I first arrived in Cairo, before we met, I couldn't understand why people kept saying, 'He bought it.' I used to sit there thinking, Bought what, for God's sake? We'd be at the Continental or Shepheard's with a group of boys, and one of them would say, 'Where's Rick?' and I'd look around, not sure who Rick was, and another one would say, 'Gone for a burton.' I thought it was a quaint British expression for needing the men's room . . ."

Theodore laughed delightedly. "No, you never told me that."

"I was a complete greenhorn."

"Not by the time I met you."

"No. Well, we all had to grow up pretty fast. It took me a week to learn the language, and two or three months to learn how to react to it. By the time I met you, I'd started worrying that I wasn't caring any longer."

"Nonsense. You never stopped caring. I always knew that."

"You know what I mean. Accepting that's the way it was, and not thinking, Why him? He had family, he was too young . . ."

"Are your memories so sad?"

She gave him a long look, raising her chin in the defiant gesture that he knew well. After all, he had seen it recently. "You know me, Theodore. I don't believe in talking about bad memories. Not when there are so many happy ones."

"Anna . . . I have a memory that I would like to talk about. When we said goodbye."

"Don't, Theo." She bit her lower lip and shook her head vehemently. "There's nothing to say that we didn't say then, and now it all seems too silly. I should never have been so angry with you."

"I want you to understand why it happened."

"I understand that it happened, and I can even think that it was a good thing. I understand why you had to stay with Chantal, and I'm glad that you did. Elena told me how much you loved her. It was what I would have expected of you. You don't owe me explanations, Theodore. I came to see you out of friendship."

"Anna —"

"No, really, I'm quite certain of this. Oh, sure, I was cut up with the shock of it at first, but I recovered. You had so much to cope with. We were so young. Blaming you would be like scolding you for breaking a vase when you were ten years old. And when I met Ben, I knew it had all been for the best. How often did those wartime romances stand up to real life, after all? I might have made you very unhappy, and you and Chantal had a good life together."

"Anna –"

"Let's not talk about it, Theo." She laid her cool hand against his cheek for the briefest of moments. "Now, would you show me around your villa? Elena told me it was her dream house, and I can see why she –"

"Anna!" Theodore's shout silenced her. He ran his hands through his hair in frustration, and then smiled. "One of the things I loved about you, one of the many, was that you had a great talent for listening. That sounds bloody selfish of me, doesn't it? None the less, it was true, and I cannot believe you've entirely lost the gift. Could I speak for a moment?"

If they had been observed at that time, two elderly people sitting on a stone terrace in the afternoon sun, it would have been hard to decide if they were husband and wife or brother and sister, but a stranger would have settled on one or the other. There was an ease in the way they interrupted each other, a naturalness in the rhythm of their bodies leaning in towards the other then moving apart. Anna, for all her fears, felt no discomfort in his company. She liked the way he looked, and she recognized the young Theo looking through the old man's eyes, and heard a young man's vigour, when she had dreaded a querulous note. He held her hands in his, making it impossible for her to resist.

"Oh, if you insist, Theodore. Just remember you can't pull rank and tell me when to shut up.

Your stripes never cut any ice with me."

"Good of you to point it out. You always knew how to put me in my place, golden girl." At the old nickname, Anna's heart stepped out of beat for a moment, and then steadied.

"I said that I wanted to explain why it happened, not how. You know that I had an affair with Chantal, and that she became pregnant. You know why I felt I had to stand by her."

"Yes, I do." Anna's reply rang with determined conviction.

"You may not be so certain why I felt the need to become involved with another woman, when I was so hopelessly in love with you."

Anna's mouth moved rapidly to check the lump that she felt in her throat. She wanted to tell him that the only explanation that had made any sense to her was that he had not, after all, loved her, certainly not hopelessly.

"I was, you know, Anna. Quite lost in love. Perhaps . . ." He cleared his throat. "Let me begin at the beginning. When I arrived in Cairo, I could barely dress myself. By the time I met you, I was an old desert sweat. But in matters of the heart, and dealing with the fairer sex, my experience was limited to buying tea and buns for Waafs who thought the flicks wizard and the war beastly. Very charming they were, too, and that's what I thought women were about. Wizard young girls on cycles, who would blossom into English ladies and English matrons. When I saw you, across the terrace . . . you cannot imagine what I saw. It was like a man colour-blind from birth waking up one day to see cerulean and azure in what had been a uniformly grey sky. It changed everything for me, how I felt about women, about myself, the desert, the war, everything. So many of the chaps I knew wanted to fall in love, would have married any girl who'd have them just to tick it off the list and give them something to come back for, a homing device. Not I. I thought you were wonderfully wise to say, let's live for the moment, and after all, that's all we had. Wonderfully wise, and wonderfully reckless, it seemed to me."

"I'll settle for reckless. Stupid might be closer."

"Do you butt in when your husband is talking?"

"Never."

"Good. It could drive a man mad."

"You said I was reckless . . ."

"The thought of you, and the uncertainty of you, kept me fighting fit. It was enough until we went to Italy. I could not have wished for more. I was even glad we had to be apart, because it made the coming together so much sweeter. But once in Tortorella, it became impossible for me to live on that alone. I plagued myself – and you, I know – with needing to be sure, wanting a commitment. You seemed so far away. It was intolerable that we weren't even on the same continent any longer. When I met Chantal, I was nothing but brassed off with the whole war, and the country and being apart from you. She was as different from you as the wizard Waafs. She was as unfamiliar to me as you were, but not in a desirable way, more in the sense that a foreign language spoken in a crowded room passes clear over your head. One doesn't even hear it, after a moment. If you have studied the language a little, familiar words ring out resonant and clear, but an utterly foreign tongue is meaningless. She was much older, sadder, scarred. And absolutely removed from any vision I had of myself, let alone of that indefinite 'we' that filled my thoughts. That's what Chantal was to me then. I pitied her all right, but I didn't love her. To be quite honest, I don't believe I even liked her."

Anna's plump cheeks were damp with tears; she did not want to hear this, and yet his voice was irresistible. She wanted to joke and laugh and talk of the good times, not to be reminded of how sharply her heart had fractured.

Theodore's eyes were dry and his look gentle. He continued to talk in a steady, level voice. "In that time and place, infidelity didn't seem to have any meaning for me. It was no more than an unconscious act. An itch, to put it crudely, like pulling up a blanket in your sleep. Certainly, I was dry with loneliness, but her arms cured that no more than an evening in the mess – rather less than an evening in the mess. No, it was meaningless. *After the first time, I was filled with remorse, but life continued. It did not reduce my yearning for you, it accentuated it. I wrote lovingly with sincerity, if also with guilt. Three times I went to see her to break it off, and three times failed, perhaps because failure was the easier course. It was only a matter of hanging on until the war was over, and that end was well within my sights. When Chantal told me that she was expecting a baby, and insisted on keeping it, I had all manner of evil thoughts. I willed her to lose the baby, and my wish was granted, albeit too late.*"

"Oh, my God, Theo. Poor woman."

"*I longed for a chance to fly, but our work was over. We only had the odd delivery to the Yugoslav partisans – nothing that might have cost me my neck, and spared me having to tell you, and the wretched shame of it all. What wouldn't I have given for the sight of a Messerschmidt 110! I would have happily sawn off my leg for the chance to reverse time by a month or two. That was when I realized that my personal test was not in flying and facing death, after all. You were my test, and I had failed it, for all my high-falutin' thoughts of honour. My only hope of redemption was to do the decent thing. It was the only thing left.*" He put a finger against her cheek to stop a tear's slow path. "*No tears, dear girl. Not for me. We always said, no tears, no regrets.*" He handed her a handkerchief.

533

"I wish you'd told me all this at Shepheard's."

"Would it have made any difference?"

"Not one goddamn jot."

"If you make a major cock-up, you can't start making excuses and blaming the weather, or the rigger, or the radio transmission. You have take it on the chin. Besides, I had no excuses. A frank confession was better than a full one, even at the price of your hatred."

"I never hated you . . . I just didn't understand."

"Perhaps I should have tried to explain. I couldn't run the risk of your showing me a way out."

"I know. I don't think I would have, though. I thought I'd brought it on myself."

"How could you have thought that?"

Anna blew her nose and sighed heavily. "I'd promised God that if he let you survive, if you finished the war all right, then I'd give you up."

"Darling Anna."

"My God, Theo. How long ago it was. We were different people then. I was soppy to the nth degree."

"You're still as lovely, Anna. Just the same. Still golden."

"And you, my old friend, still have the gift of the gab."

Theodore took her to the airport the next morning, for old times' sake. When he came to collect her at the Lion d'Or, Anna gave him the package of his letters.

Theodore was shocked to see them. He refused to accept them. "They were written to you, Anna. They belong to you. I'm only surprised that you didn't burn them."

"I thought about it, believe me, but I just couldn't do it. I'm glad I didn't – they brought back my youth. We're old enough to wallow in the past from time to time. Read them, Theo. Remember the good times. We had so many." She pressed the package into his hands. "Yesterday was another one. I won't forget it."

At the boarding gate, Anna held out her hand hesitantly, and laughed when Theodore flung his arms wide. "Don't forget you've promised to come and stay with us in London. Ben's itching to meet you."

"And I him. I shall come, I promise you that. Anna, one last thing – would you give this to Elena for me?"

"What is it?"

"Something she wanted, and I don't need any more. A memento. I won't tell you what it is, but neither she nor I will know if you open it on the plane, will we? Goodbye, golden girl. God bless you."

Anna was irritated to find herself crying again as she buckled her seatbelt. A sign of age, she scolded herself, all those useless tears. As the plane climbed *into the skies, she opened the little package and found the locket encasing the blue amulet that had kept Theodore safe from harm.*

CHAPTER TWENTY

We did the last ten interviews over the next couple of months, all in England. David took the snaps, had sporadic physiotherapy, very grumpily, and tried his best not to look pained when Bec talked about nipple sprays. Graham liked the interviews, but he worshipped David. He began angling to get David to do another book, and suggested us doing a series of interviews with families in Bosnia. I rejected it at once. For one thing, all I wanted to think about was the baby; for another, I didn't see how I was going to work in Bosnia carting a baby with me. I could have found a way round it, but I was dead against treading on David's turf.

Five weeks before the due date, I'd finished the book, finished my sessions in Islington with Miriam Hilton, and had nothing to do but lounge around on my mother's sofa, talking about life in Cairo, and wallowing in the tub. The bathroom became more than ever my favourite place. In the water, I could see the baby beneath my skin. My stomach was as taut as a drum, stretched as thin as the skin on a eyelid, and bizarrely covered with a complex tracery of fat and thin veins. I never tired of the fascination of watching those extraordinary shapes jutting out of me at odd angles: the baby had at least twelve elbows. In bed, flat on my back, I'd see a small hard football rolling beneath the surface tension, and shout for David. We'd argue about whether it was a buttock, a shoulder, or an immensely large foot. It was heaven, but it was also purgatory: the baby's feet were virtually in my throat, and its head must have been wedged stubbornly on top of a nerve deep in my groin that I had never known existed, but wasn't ever going to forget. The pain went past my left knee. Breathing became a luxury, and walking a torture.

Heff and Mishi came to London, about four weeks before the EDD – all my chronology circled around the specific 'expected delivery date' of 16 November. Heff was trying to persuade David to set up an agency with him. David was reluctant, and I was amazed that Heff was keen, until Mishi told me that she too was pregnant. She had a serious case of morning sickness which lasted from five a.m. to midnight. I felt like an old hand. Heff started arranging meetings with other freelance photographers, while David stalled. One evening, David came home from dinner with them and asked me how I'd feel if he went back to Bosnia for a week. "I'd be back well before thirty-eight weeks."

"Are you sure?"

"If I go now, I'd get back the thirtieth of October at the latest. I promise you that. I'm not going into Sarajevo. I'm going to Banja Luka with Mishi. She says she needs to do something to stop her puking. I won't have a problem getting out – if that was the case I wouldn't go."

I was surprised that Mishi was going, more that Heff let her. She'd been so sick, but I knew how she felt – not at all ready for the world to stop. David had barely left my side since we'd come back from France. To be quite honest, I didn't want him hanging around. It was quite possible that the baby wouldn't make its appearance until the end of November, and the idea of David kicking his heels until then wasn't a pretty one. The knowledge of his support was what mattered. New man or not, his opinion on electric or manual breast pumps was something I could live without.

"So long as you guarantee you can go and not get killed and come back by the first, then go. If you fuck up, I'll kill you. I mean it. I will personally kill you if your butt isn't on that sofa on the first of November. But you can go with my blessing. You'd better take good care of Mishi, or I'm not the only one you'll have to deal with. Oh, David, you realize this means you'll miss Fathers' Night?"

David blanched. "It had crossed my mind . . ."

"That's the real reason you're going, isn't it? I'll reschedule. If I have to go through it, then you do it.

I dread it worse than labour."

That time, I did go to the airport with him. My father drove the four of us there. At the check-in, I fastened Theodore's amulet round David's neck. He insisted that I left then, but Heff wouldn't come back to London with us: he wanted to hang around until the last minute. He called me late that night, and I saw him every other day for a meal or a cup of tea. He was like a dog left out in the cold.

On 28 October, I had a sudden and compelling craving for turös palascinta, the Hungarian sweet pancakes that my mother used to make when Charlie and I were little. I hadn't tasted them for at least fifteen years. When I called home, in the hope of twisting my mother's arm to reach for the blender, there was no answer, but I persuaded Bec and Michael to come with me and waddled between them to the Gay Hussar, where I indulged mightily. I went to bed early, sated and vast. I woke up at 3 a.m. and staggered towards the loo. The baby was bouncing on my bladder. Barely had I put feet to floor when something extraordinary happened. I looked down. My feet stood in a puddle of water about four feet in diameter. I shook with terror till my teeth chattered. When I inched a tiny step, there was another Niagaran gush. All I could think was that I damn well wasn't going to have the baby until the sixteenth. I made it back to the phone, puddling and dribbling all over the bedroom floor, and spoke to a midwife at the hospital, who told me to have a shower and come in during the next hour. I couldn't believe that David wasn't there. I toyed with telling her I could make it in three days' time, but not in an hour . . . Then I called my mother. My father picked up the phone sleepily.

"Elena, your mother's in Suffolk. Ever since she met Theodore, she's been hunting down old chums."

"Oh, no!"

"It's all right, my dear, this one's a lady."

"Daddy, I'm having the baby."

"Dear God, Elena. Shall I come and pick you up?"

"No. I'm fine. *Fine*. I'm not having it yet. I'll call you later. Don't tell Mum anything."

I called Bec, and got her answering machine. Not surprising at three in the morning. Then I called Heff. No one in the world can imagine what it is to be looking childbirth in the face, and having to call Steve Heffner. He picked up the phone on the first ring. "Mish?"

"Heff, it's me," I whispered. If I spoke normally, water seeped out of me.

"Hey, babe."

"Heff, can you get hold of David – quickly?"

"How quickly?" His voice was slurred, which could have been because I'd woken him up, but it was quite possible he hadn't yet gone to bed.

"Very quickly, Heff. My waters have broken."

"What, Elle? Burst pipes? Yeah, I can reach him, but it'd be a darn sight easier getting you a plumber . . ."

"I'm having the baby. I'm going to St Mary's now."

"Holy shit – fucking *Jees*-us H. Christ. *That* kind of water. OK. I'm with you, Elle. I'll pull some clothes on and meet you there. St Mary's. St Mary's. St Mary's is where?"

I had a horrible vision of Heff as my birthing partner, felt immensely calm, and spoke very slowly. "Paddington, Heff. David knows. Don't get dressed. Just do what you can to get him."

By the time I reached the hospital, I was having contractions, but they were not the incapacitating agony I'd imagined. Three hours later, they were worse than that. A midwife asked me if I had considered an epidural, and I nearly ripped her arm off.

"I'll call the consultant. There's plenty of time." For what? I wanted to scream – for me to die? "By the way, there's a man outside going crazy. Says he has to see you. I can't let him in, you understand."

"Is it my father?"

"He doesn't look like anyone's father."

"I don't care if it's God Almighty unless he's carrying major pain relief."

I had absolutely no intention of being brave, trying to breathe through the pain, imagining it at the bottom of the bed, or any of that crap. I was badly shocked by how much it hurt, and bitterly resentful that no one had warned me. I was scared witless, and I wanted top-drawer drugs. I'd thought I'd be too frightened to have the epidural, but, oh, boy, that fear didn't come close to the one of not having it. As the midwife left to call the man with the magic, not running as quickly as she should have, I heard shouting in the corridor. I couldn't help smiling in the tiny space between contractions, when I heard Heff shout, "I'm the fucking father, for fuck's fucking sake!" They wouldn't forget *him* in a hurry. A minute later, he barged into the room, dragging a hefty midwife behind him.

"It's easier getting in to see Yeltsin than you, I'm telling –" He stopped dead, open-mouthed.

I was wearing one of David's shirts, but even vaguely covered, I wasn't a pretty sight, and Heff hadn't been to Fathers' Night either. "Did you get David?" I gasped. He stood frozen at the end of the bed.

"I left a message. Three."

"Good. Get out." I could feel the electric ripple heralding the surge of a contraction.

"Elle, David asked me – if anything happened –"

"Get out!" I covered my face with my hands and yelped.

"Oh, Elle . . ." When I opened my eyes, Heff was still stuck there, the muscles in his face flinching.

"Heff, I do not want you here. Unless you want to help them stick an eight-inch needle in my spine, would you get the fuck out?"

He shook off the midwife, pulled something out of his pocket and looked at it. "Turk asked me to give you this. If anything happened. He gave it me at the airport." He leant over me and very gently put Theodore's amulet around my neck as I groaned again. "I'll be downstairs, Elle. I'll be waiting. I'll stay here if you want."

"You won't be doing anything of the kind, young man . . ." Two midwives bustled in with a saint in a suit and a trolley. Heff backed out, holding up one hand in farewell. It crossed my mind that he knew I was going to die.

Putting in the epidural was a piece of cake, and five minutes later everything changed so dramatically that I hoped they'd leave it in there for the rest of my life. Much as I know the arguments against them, and much as I respect each woman's right to have a baby in whatever way she chooses, I have to state categorically that the epidural is one of the top ten discoveries in the history of mankind. Maybe number one. If I ever had to choose my desert island discs, I'd have a lot of trouble on the music front but my luxury would be an epidural, with someone trained to put it in. No woman who has experienced the perfect joy it brings could ever settle for a piano or a lifetime's supply of champagne. Once the cold stuff had trickled into some secret part of my back and down one of my legs, I was a new woman. I even watched television. OK, so maybe labour slowed down, but who's to know? It gave me time to think about the baby, which I hadn't since leaving home. There's a great sense of accomplishment in childbirth, a sense of taking the test, and my pass grade was due to the epidural and a midwife called Mary who stayed beside me. I drifted in and out of sleep. Mary seemed to know a lot about me. She sat rubbing my hand, and chatting about David, and I chatted back, and time slipped away . . .

There was never a point where I hit transition and started running down the corridor. What happened was that sometime mid-morning, a consultant examined me. Mary and a midwife called Eileen came back wearing plastic painting overalls, which made me a little suspicious. I think I asked for more drugs, but I didn't get them, and then it was the literal scramble for dispersal. I don't remember much about the final stage. I remember laughing with the two women, and I remember it hurting like almighty hell, and thinking my ribs would shatter with the effort of getting the baby out. I remember hearing a strangled yell, that shocked pitiful cry for help. All I can see clearly is Mary handing me a slithery little scrap, saying, "Here's your daughter, Elena." I took one look at her slaty unfocused eyes and couldn't stop crying. Then somebody else was there, trying to take the baby away, and bells started ringing somewhere way down the corridor, and everything went black, and I don't remember anything at all.

After a few minutes I opened my eyes. My mother and father were sitting next to my bed. I was in a different room. I didn't know if I had had the baby, or if it had been a dream and I was still pregnant.

"Mummy? What are you doing here? What's the matter?"

"Oh, Elena, my darling little girl . . ."

I clutched my stomach. It felt flabby and detached from me. I sat up suddenly and my head spun. "Where's the baby? Where's my baby?"

My mother pushed a button above my head. "She's fine, sweetheart. She's beautiful, and utterly perfect. They took her to the nursery. Just to give you time to rest."

"I want to see her – where is she?" I tried to swing my legs over the edge of the bed, but they wouldn't move. "Mother, what is going on? Why are you here? Daddy? Where's my baby?" I could hear the shrillness in my own voice.

"Darling, it's all right. Hush now. Daddy and I have seen her, and she's a joy. They'll bring her to you now. We've only been worried about you."

"What's wrong with me? Am I paralysed?"

"Nothing, dear girl."

"You had a haemorrhage after she was born. You're fine and she's fine. You've both been sleeping."

"What do you mean, I had a haemorrhage?"

Ma's face crumpled. "You lost so much blood – oh darling! You could have died." I couldn't believe that. I felt quite normal, except that I had a drip in my arm, felt as if I was floating five feet off the bed, couldn't move my legs and had no body.

"Where's David?"

"On his way. Heff's downstairs in the waiting room. He's been there all night. Would you like to see him?"

"I want to see my baby!" As I said it, a woman came in the door holding a blanket.

"Here she is, Elena, here's your little girl. Good as gold, and twice as pretty."

When I held her in my arms, everything in the room vanished. Even my parents. She was very tiny, and she glared at me ferociously. She had a straight sweep of reddish hair and bright blue eyes, and perfectly arched miniature eyebrows pulled into an intense frown. She looked mightily displeased at my appearance. Her eyes travelled my face centimetre by centimetre. She bristled at me, mouth in a perfect *moue*, brows pulled down, face tilted up in her meticulous examination of mine. She had one hand tucked under her tiny chin, showing off five pearly nails like droplets of water. The other arm was wrapped tight beneath the swaddling. She didn't blink, just stared and stared intently.

"Elena," my father's voice was cracking, "does my granddaughter have a name?"

"She should, shouldn't she? What do you think, little bird? Gabriella? Delilah? Tabitha? That was your shortlist." I craned to read the little pink band on her wrist: Baby Stewart. 29.10.93. 10.34 a.m. 7 lb 6 oz. "Baby Stewart. *That*'s what I call a rotten name." I looked up at my parents. "What do you think?"

"Precious." My mother was crying.

"Precious Stewart is even worse." She let out a yell like a sick cat.

"She's hungry, and I don't blame her. It's four in

the afternoon, Elena. High time she was fed." The midwife began to plump up cushions around me, but not before my father shot to his feet.

"Sweetheart, we'll leave you both in peace and be back later."

I nodded, but I only had eyes for Lily. That's what we'd call her, if David agreed. That's what she looked like. Arrogant, stunning, stroppy for all her tininess. I wanted to hold her in my arms for as long as I had breath. All the time, she fixed me with that unconvinced stare, but after I had fed her, her lashes fluttered and she smiled at me.

"Did you see that? She smiled."

The midwife peered over my shoulder. "Wind."

"You've got no soul, Eileen, that's your problem."

Lily closed one eye slowly and winked at me. Wind, my foot. As she slept in the crook of my arm, love washed through me as if I were blotting paper. I couldn't soak up enough, I had no limit to what I could absorb of her. I was enslaved. Enraptured. We dozed together.

I woke up to find Lily in a plastic cot next to my bed, and Heff sitting on the edge of a chair, peering nervously at her.

"Hi, Heff. Is David here yet?" I said drowsily.

"Hi, gorgeous. I've been watching you two for about ten minutes. They wouldn't let me up till now."

"They wouldn't believe you're the dad?"

"No such luck. I was threatened with the cops. I've been in the waiting room since five a.m." The clock beside the bed said ten p.m.

"You're sweet, Heff. Really sweet."

"I wanted to be here. I looked at the baby a couple of times in the nursery. She's so . . . so . . . *clean*."

"I think they wash them, Heff. They don't come out like that."

"I want one just the same."

"Yours might look a little different."

"Yeah, but I want one just that size and shape. Can she open her eyes yet?"

"They're not puppies!" We were whispering to each other.

Then Heff grabbed a yellow plastic bag from between his feet. "I brought a bottle of champagne – two, in case Turk made it back – glasses, OK, plastic, but . . . I meant to get flowers. D'you want some?"

"The whole bottle. Don't let the midwives hear." Heff clamped his hand over the cork and eased it out silently.

"To you and your baby."

"To you and yours."

"I had to stay, Elle. So I could tell Turk what the two of you looked like. He'll kill himself for missing that."

"Not his fault. I told him to go."

"You're not angry with him?"

"No. I just miss him."

"Here's to the Turk. Father of the baby."

"Father of the baby," I echoed.

"And to the mother of the baby."

"Mother of the baby."

"And here's to the baby."

"To the baby." I was giggling now, pain free, in a state of euphoria that had everything to do with Lily and a little to do with the drugs.

"Here's to me! The surrogate father!"

"The surrogate father – but just watch who you say that to."

"And here's to the amazing black midwife with the gorgeous boobs. May she deliver my own infant."

"I thought Mishi would have the baby in Paris?"

"You're saying the woman can't travel?"

"The amazing black midwife with the gorgeous boobs."

"And here's to three-legged horses . . ."

"The One That Got Away . . ." As I waved my glass, Lily yelped. Heff and I both froze. On her second yelp, I looked at him, and he looked back at me.

"Pick her up."

"I can't."

"Why not?"

"What if I drop her?"

"Heff. Do you want to be her godfather?"

"Her godfather? Like holy fuck I do!"

"So pick her up and pass her to me. See you tomorrow."

I fed Lily again, and fell asleep. I was woken by her mewing in my arms. Her eyes were closed. The room was dim, lit only by the faint glow of the night-light and emergency bell next to my bed. David was sitting beside me. It was four a.m.

"Darling . . ." I whispered.

He knelt next to the bed. He put his arms around me, between the drip and over Lily, and lay half on the bed and half on the floor, eyes on our girl. "Do you like her?"

"I don't know. I can't see her . . ."

"I want to call her Lily."

David eased her from my arms without waking her and held her against his chest. He pressed his lips to the top of her head. "Hello there, Lily." Her eyes flashed open and she treated him to her myopic stare. "Welcome, sweetheart." He looked at me in complete astonishment. "She's incredible, Elle. I never imagined anything like this."

"Did you bring your camera?" David winced. "Don't tell me that you of all people didn't bring even *one* camera? Don't say it!" I began to laugh.

"Mishi took them. I came from the airport, and she took the cab on home with all my kit. I didn't think – I just didn't think –"

"Look at her. Have you ever seen anything more perfect in your entire life?"

We gazed adoringly. I wondered what she thought when she looked at us. She had such a mature expression for such a little face. Right from the outset she seemed to know far more than we did about life. David lay down on the narrow bed next to me, with Lily lying along his chest, as we talked in whispers.

"I'm so sorry I wasn't here, Elle. I shouldn't have gone."

"It's all right, darling. It's fine."

"I didn't want you to be alone."

"It was OK. I had lots of help. My parents. Not forgetting Heff. Lily most of all. And I had Theo's locket. I meant *you* to wear it."

"Tough. Oh, sweet . . . I can't believe what you've done. I wanted to be here."

"Oh, you were . . . Ask Mary. At least after the epidural. Before that, I'm almost glad you weren't."

"Did you swear blue at the doctor? Behave real bad?"

"Horribly." Lily opened her eyes and strained to lift her head. It lurched in agreement.

"That's my girl! And what a result!"

David held her up in the air, her face ten inches from his own. "Who do you think she looks like?"

"I thought she had a look of my father, but Ma says she's the spitting image of you. What do you think?"

"I can't see myself at all, thank God. You – there's something about the chin, and something about the stare that makes me scared she sees straight through me."

"I want to give her the world, David." I couldn't even give her what she'd already given me. He kissed my head and Lily gripped his finger, wrapping him instantly around hers. David was enthralled. "Can I take her for a walk?"

"Don't be too long. I'll miss you both . . ."

David eased himself carefully off the bed, holding Lily, wrapped tight in a cloth and still clutching his finger. His face shone. I watched them leave my room, listening to David murmuring to her.

CHAPTER TWENTY-ONE

The next few weeks were a lesson in beguilement. Lily seduced us with her every action. I was obsessed with the smell of her velvet head, its soft hollows and the heat it generated. The urgency of her waking cry stopped my heart and soaked my shirt. Her contented hiccups as she fed made me grin inanely, and David's face wore an expression of intense satisfaction whenever he made her burp. Even dog-tired, when we were standing up at the kitchen counter fast asleep, her smallest sound would make us spring to attention. Comatose in bed with Lily between our heads, the small spew of milk into my hair would make me smile and coo at her, just for being there. Yes, I know all mothers – and fathers – think their babies are in a class apart, but Lily actually was. For eight weeks she beguiled us, so that in the ninth, when we were walking on our knees and wanting some faint hope of freedom, it was too late for the spell to be broken. We were lost for ever. Lily was one hundred per cent David's daughter. At ten weeks, she had an enormous presence. She could silence a room with a glance, and bring the world to her feet with the smallest sound. Her smile dissolved the walls around you. It had taken two days of being back in the flat with her to know ourselves for what we were – her humble and obedient servants. She colonized my parents and Uncle Charlie about a week later, and then set her sights on conquering the rest of the world.

Lily was just on three months when David went to the corner shop to buy nappies – we never seemed to have enough in the house. He was gone for an hour, which was odd, because we had perfected the run down to eight minutes. I could do it in seven, door to door. I hoped Lily would hold out, but she had an unpredictable . . . temperament. David came back in the nick of time with a smug look on his face. "Hi, my best girl, and my second best girl . . ."

"Are you going to tell us which way round that goes?"

"Do you think I'm a complete idiot?"

"I don't," I nodded at Lily, "but *she* does." Lily was lying on her back on the carpet, trying to get a film cartridge into her mouth. David pulled an envelope out of his jacket pocket and waved it under my nose.

"This is for you."

"What is it? A contract from Geoffrey?"

"Better."

"There isn't anything better than a contract from Geoffrey, unless it's a letter from the building society waiving the rest of the mortgage payments."

He dropped the envelope on my lap. "Go ahead, open it. It's for you and Lily. But it's really for you." Inside were three plane tickets to Cairo. I stared at them stupidly. "You've said often enough you wanted to go see for yourself. You said you wanted to give Lily the world, didn't you? The Pyramids are a good place to start."

"I'm not sure we'll have a holiday with Lily around."

"You underestimate me. Look at the third ticket – it's for our guide and doting nanny."

One ticket was in my mother's name. "David, it would be amazing – but have you asked her?"

"Do you think I'm a complete idiot?" he said again. "Of course I have. I wouldn't take a step like that without clearing it with Anna. I asked Ben too, but he declined."

"When do we go?"

"Next week. For a week. I'm going to have to get back to work after that, Elle. But first I want you to have your dreams come true. And Lily can start her world domination."

"D'you think she'll remember it?"

"No. But you will."

I kept warning myself that Cairo wasn't going to be the way my mother and Theo had described it. I wasn't going to understand my mother, because she was no longer the woman she'd been then. Besides, she'd resigned the maternal role in favour of being Lily's grandmother. I knew Shepheard's had burnt to the ground in 1952. I knew the Continental was gone, too. I knew time had moved on, and that was as it should be, and there was no point in glancing hopefully over my shoulder for ghosts that weren't there. I knew that it was stupid that David's work was trying to get wars stopped, and there I was hankering after a war long gone, and one, for me, at least, cloaked in a heavy veil of nostalgia. David and I had been blissfully happy since we had come back from France, but neither of us had dared to risk the apple cart by talking about our future. If David was set for a return to normal life post-Cairo, then I was determined to make the most of that week.

So I didn't count on a big, slush-soaked sentimental trip, but I was still disappointed. Cairo was bleak, modern and dirty. Even before we saw the city the hassle started. There was a positive army of official, semi-official and unofficial guides waiting to pounce as we came through immigration. David handled everything, waving a press card that he later showed me was years out of date and entitled him to press access in Zaïre. Some pathetic little childish thing in me wanted to find a horse-drawn gharrie, and go clip-clopping down the street in a flurry of falling jacaranda petals. Instead the four of us climbed into a beat-up taxi and shunted down the motorway in heavy traffic. My mother's eyes danced as we approached the centre.

David had booked rooms at the Mena House. It was a good hotel, and a nice old building, full of neo-Islamic twiddles, and my mother remembered it well, but there was nothing there for me. There were no *suffragis* in soft-slapping slippers, only smartly uniformed bellboys. No Allied officers in dress uniform, just tourist parties spilling from coaches in sweaty shorts and grumbling about being ripped off. No jangle of twenty different languages, only English and American. No Gabardine Swine, no Long Range Desert Group, no Desert Rats, no RAF types, no beautiful American girls in silk stockings and red lipstick, no orchestra playing, no sunset, no class, no beauty, no romance. Just me, my mother and David with Lily on his lap, sitting in the lobby bar waiting for something, anything to happen. When a waiter asked us what we would like to drink, David ordered a beer, and I asked what cocktails they had – just for old times' sake. Sentimental or what?

"Cocktails, madam? A gin tonic? A Harvey Wallbanger?" he suggested in a bored voice.

"No, no, no. What would you have ordered, Ma? A Gimlet? What about a Gin Sling?"

"That was the Far East, darling. Let's have Suffering Bastards. Those were for the Desert Rats."

He bowed, but looked doubtful. "I will speak to the barman."

"Elle, don't expect too much." David stroked my hair. "The war's over, sweetheart. You can't bring it back, even if you wanted to."

"I know. I know. I just wanted to pretend, just for a moment."

My mother smiled first at David, then at me, and took Lily, bouncing her on her knee. "Did you know, little Lily, that the King of Greece escaped here in 1941, and lived here, quite openly, with his English mistress, before it became a hotel? It was one of the favourite topics at dinners. We Yanks were shocked. Do you remember when I brought you and Charlie to Cairo, Elena?"

"Vaguely."

"We were on our way to join Daddy in the Ivory Coast. You can't have been more than eight, so Charlie was six. I took you to the Pyramids then. You loved the camel rides."

"It must have been strange for you, Ma. Seeing all the old haunts."

"I thought it would be, but they were gone. During the revolution against the British, they were all burnt down. Madame Badia's, the Turf, Shepheard's, everything went. Cicurel's, even the Auberge des Pyramides. I didn't mind a bit, to be honest. I came to show you and Charlie the sights."

The waiter came back and put two glasses on the table. "Gin tonic," he announced. I wanted to sit beneath a positive waterfall of nostalgia and be drenched in it, and all I got was the faint fizz of a bottle of Schweppes.

"Bottoms up." David raised his beer.

"Here's mud in your eye," my mother replied, winking at him. I scowled.

"Do you think there's a risk Lily will be quite as silly as you are, Elena?" David said. We all looked at her reaching for the olives.

"Do you think there's a risk you might get a smack in the face?" I felt quite left out: I was the only one still looking for something.

"David, have you had any thoughts about work? Over the long term." I gave my mother a dirty look when she said this. She ignored it. She and David had become much closer since Lily's birth.

David swirled his beer around in his glass. "Heff's talked about setting up an agency with him."

"Photographic?"

"No, Ma, a *dating* agency. What d'you think?"

"I don't know, David. I can't see you sitting in an office telling young men where to go. Or young women. What would happen to the Turk?"

"Turks grow up, just like everyone else. I told him I'd think about it."

"No harm in that."

I paid no attention to them, but I couldn't see David sitting behind a desk either. You'd have had to hobble him to the chair leg to keep him off a plane.

We spent the week in Egypt being tourists. I didn't find a single thing that let me think of my mother's youth, not that she was bothered. The Americans had a fully fledged embassy in a new building, the Kasr el Nil barracks had become a glitzy hotel, the hospital at Heliopolis was gone, the building where she had taught English with Millie was a motorway. We *did* go to Groppi's, but it was shabby and not as I'd imagined. We 'did' the museums, and we did the Pyramids and the Sphinx, and yes, they are amazing, but that wasn't why I'd wanted to come. I only wanted to see them sandbagged. We took a felucca ride on the Nile, but had to get off the boat by eight o'clock. I had no sense of drifting under the moon, no sense of the great Nile – let alone the lady of the Nile. I looked for my mother everywhere, at the Cataract Hotel in Aswan, in the streets of the Bab al-Bahr quarter, in the desert. David and I left Lily and Ma at the hotel for a day and went as far as Mersah Matruh in Rommel's footsteps. I wanted to go deep into the desert, to the forward landing grounds where Theodore had lived. The taxi driver looked at me as if I was insane, and shook his head. We went to Ismailia, but I couldn't imagine the Officers' Training Camp. We saw the Bitter Lake, but it was ugly and meant nothing to me. My mother was baby-sitting for us, but Anna wasn't there – she wasn't anywhere. She had gone long ago, with Shepheard's and everyone and everything else.

On our last day in Cairo, David went off to take some photographs, taking Ma with him, and I wandered around the Mouski with Lily in the sling. I had grown sadder each day of the trip. I didn't even want to buy anything in the bazaar, and that's a sign of major depression for me. When we got back to the Mena House, David was waiting in our room and in high spirits. He told me to change into something smart because Ma was going to have room service with Lily and he was taking me dancing. My jaw must have hit the floor. I didn't feel up to it, but Ma insisted. Then I said we should all go, but she refused, and said she hadn't seen Lily all day and she'd be far happier alone with the baby. I felt rather the same way.

Outside the hotel, David took my arm, and we walked for what seemed like miles before he dipped into an alley, and led me to a dark doorway. We stepped into a little room, with soft lighting. David nodded to the lady at the front desk, and held back another curtain. It was a nightclub, of sorts. There was a man at a piano, and a quartet, and seven or eight couples sitting at small tables around the room. The pianist stood up as we came in, and shook David warmly by the hand, as if they were old friends. He showed us to a table just on the edge of a tiny dance floor, and a few moments later a bottle of champagne appeared. The pianist sat down with us and accepted a glass. He was a young man, whose teeth flashed bright in his dark face when he smiled.

"You're Elena? It's great to meet you." He spoke with a strong American accent.

"It's good to meet you too. You're from the States?"

"No, from Cairo, but I played in New Orleans for a while. Best time of my life. You all have a good time, and I'll see you later." He winked at David, picked up his glass and went back to the piano.

"David, what's going on?"

"Nothing, sweetheart. I just felt that we hadn't found the right sort of place for you. Your mother spoke to a few people at the US Embassy, and heard about this place. I checked it out this afternoon."

The pianist began playing a jazz piece as we talked.

"I feel like I've dragged you here for nothing, haven't I? We shouldn't have come. Aren't you angry with me?"

"No, darling. I dragged *you* here, remember? How could I possibly be angry with you?"

"Because it was all such a pipe-dream. It hasn't worked. I thought I'd be able to feel what she felt. That I'd understand everything."

"You can't ever do that, Elle, however hard you try. Anna had her life. You'll only know as much as she's prepared to tell you, and as much as she wants to remember." The pianist began to sing in a soft, sweet voice, and several couples stood up. "Elle, will you dance with me?"

"I'll be seeing you, in all the old familiar places,
That this heart of mine embraces,
All day through.
In that small café,
The park across the way
The children's carousel, the chestnut trees and
wishing-well . . .

563

I'll be seeing you in every lovely summer's day,
In everything that's light and gay,
I'll always think of you that way,
I'll find you in the morning sun, and when the night is blue,
I'll be looking at the moon, but I'll be seeing you . . ."

My mother would have cringed if she had seen how badly we shuffled around the dance floor, but I wasn't thinking of her any longer. Cairo became *our* place, and somehow the songs became ours, too. I leant against David's chest through all those sentimental ballads, feeling his lips against my hair and his arms around my back, and I thought, If I can remember this for the rest of my life, this moment, this contentment, then I will take whatever comes with a light heart. I didn't want the music to stop, I didn't want to open my eyes and see anything except David's face. Everyone was dancing, everyone was lost in the mood of the music, the great, lone, nostalgic lament of the trumpet . . .

When we sat down, David took my hand. "Elle, I'm not going to ask you to marry me."

"Oh."

"I'm not going to."

"Fine. There was quite a romantic build-up there, for a moment or so. I'm not saying that I was expecting you'd propose, it never crossed my mind." Thank God that that story about lies falling as frogs from the princess's lips was only a fairy tale. "I'm perfectly happy with things as they are. Marriage doesn't mean that much, anyway. It's just a bit strange to go to all this trouble to tell me that you're *not* going to marry me. We could have had an early night – as much as Lily will ever let us. I mean, if what you wanted to do was dance, we could have found someone in London to play this kind of music. I could have bought a tape, for God's sake."

"True."

"It's nice, anyway. Being alone, and having champagne, and the music . . . He's good, isn't he? He has a nice voice. And it's a nice place." Under pressure, I can do banal like nobody else. "All my life I've made fun of Ma for liking this music. Maybe she was right all the time, or maybe I'm just getting old. You should have brought her; she would have loved it." I looked around the room vacantly, humming along. "I'd marry anyone who proposed to this kind of music."

"Anyone?"

"Near about."

"I'm not asking." He grinned at me evilly.

"You've made that perfectly clear. I'm not stupid. Could you stop drumming it in? Jesus wept."

David rested both elbows on the table and leant close to me. "I'm not asking, Elle, I'm telling you, you have to marry me. I'm fed up with your goddamn talk."

And the band struck up.

Waiting for the train to come in
Waiting for my man to come home
I've counted every minute of each livelong day
Been so melancholy since he went away
I've shed a million teardrops or more
Waiting for the one I adore
I'm waiting in the depot by the railroad track –
Looking for the choo-choo train that brings him
back
I'm waiting for my life to begin
Waiting for the train to come in . . .

The next morning, David left me in a café on a square opposite a garden. Temporarily, I mean. I don't know the name of the square. I wish I did, so that I could go back there. We'd wandered around, and he wanted to take more pictures of my mother and Lily so I sat down to wait for them.

It wasn't the most beautiful of street corners. The traffic was heavy, and there were cars and trams everywhere. Petrol fumes were visible, hazy and blue in the heat. I asked for a coffee. It came thick as tar; the first sip made me shiver. I thought about David. David had had no road-to-Damascus experience – he hadn't suddenly become as soft as butter. I knew well that he was as driven as ever. But he had taken a decision when he didn't like taking them. And done something for me, purely for me, to give me the kind of memory that he knew I wanted to have. And even if the memory of how I felt that night

fades, even if when I'm fifty, or sixty, or seventy or more, I can't remember the feeling of celestial lightness, I will always remember that he did that for me. He'd even bought me a gold band. I held out my hand a foot from my face, and waggled my fingers like any and every new bride in her first private moment. Then something happened that may be hard to believe. I have told myself many times that it didn't happen, and I know that the mind is a powerful thing, and that I was susceptible. But this I did not imagine. It happened.

The waiter asked me a question. As I raised my head, I saw behind him, across the square, a young woman standing on the far corner. I can describe where she stood exactly. She was waving at me. I turned around to see if there was someone behind me, but the other tables were empty. I looked back, and she nodded encouragingly, and beckoned me. She knew me, and I knew that I ought to recognize her. I dimly heard the waiter say something. She was wearing a red coat and her hair was golden; it bounced in loose waves around her face. I sat staring at her, and green eyes looked back at me, smiling and laughing. She held her hair back from her face with one hand, and jumped back from the pavement as a tram passed. I remember thinking that she had great legs, and noticing the strappy high heels she was wearing, without a thought that she looked out of place.

I stood up, grabbed my bag, and began to run across the road. I could hear her voice. She was

waving, and I think she cried, "Darling," but the noise from the traffic was terrible, and I was too far away to make it out. I kept my eyes on her. She was so pretty, and so full of joy, and she raised her hand in a sort of salute. I stretched one arm out towards her as I ran. A tram was coming slowly towards us; it would pass right in front of me. I saw her open her mouth to speak, and then I saw her look away, at someone else, someone at the end of the street, and heard her call out, "Darling!" again, quite distinctly. When the tram had passed, I was standing in the middle of the road, and she was gone. I tried to cross the road, but there were people around me, the waiter from the café, waving a scrap of paper and shouting, a policeman, and another man, holding my arms back. I tried to shake them off, I could feel that she was close, that she'd stepped just a little way down the street, or round the next corner. I knew she was still there, and that she wanted me to find her – she wanted to tell me something. I fought against the men, trying to pull myself free before she disappeared for ever. As I reached the pavement, I tripped and fell heavily, scraping my bare knee, and I screamed.

"What the fuck is going on? Let her go!" It was David, with Lily in his arms, moving in like the wrath of God.

"David, I have to go – I have to go and find my mother!" He grabbed my arm with his free hand.

"She ran off without paying the bill."

"She ran straight into the traffic – crazy lady –

straight in front of a tram –"

"Here, take the money, take whatever the fuck you want – no, calm down, I'll take care of her, I'm her husband, yes, yes, very sorry, fine, now go away, please."

"*David!*" I heard my own scream. "Let me *go*. I have to say goodbye to my mother."

David let go of my arm and I ran down the street to the corner. She was gone. Just gone. I felt so tremendously sad. "She must have got on the tram."

"Who, darling?"

"My mother."

"Sweetheart, I've just left her at the hotel. She's packing. I left her ten minutes ago. We came to pick you up."

"Oh, David, I *saw* her. I'm not crazy. Not my mother – Anna. When she *was* Anna. I *saw* her. She was standing right here. Right here. Right *here*." I stamped my foot. "You don't believe me. You think I'm crazy."

"No, Elle, I don't think you're crazy. I believe you. I guess Anna's still here, somewhere, and I guess you had to find her."

"Did you see her?"

"No, darling, I didn't. But she wasn't looking for me."

On the way to the airport, I looked down every street, searched every face trying to see her again, just for a moment, just to say goodbye, but she wouldn't come. It may sound silly to say that I said

goodbye to her then, in the airport bus. My mother was sitting next to me, holding my hand loosely in hers, and chatting to David as he bounced our daughter on his knee. I said goodbye to a part of her in Cairo that night. Not goodbye to my mother, but goodbye to Anna, whom I had glimpsed so briefly. I wished David had seen her; and my father, and Theodore. That everyone could have seen how lovely and happy she was.